SHATTERED BLUE

BOOK ONE OF THE LIGHT TRILOGY

LAUREN BIRD HOROWITZ

SHATTERED BLUE

BOOK ONE OF THE LIGHT TRILOGY

SKYSCAPE

SKYSCAPE

Text copyright © 2015 by Lauren Horowitz

Published by Skyscape, New York

www.apub.com

Amazon, the Amazon logo, and Skyscape are trademarks of Amazon.com, Inc., or its affiliates.

ISBN-13: 9781503949973
ISBN-10: 1503949974

Cover photograph by Conrado/Shutterstock
Cover design by Elaine Damasco
Printed in the United States of America

for
Leslie
who shines the Light

. . . and Ninj, who wagged with every word.

PART I: NOA

YOUR SISTER IS DEAD. They were the first words Noa thought every morning, the moment she opened her eyes. Her dreams had become smudges: long stretches of gray or blue, humming faintly against her eyelids. Sleep anesthetized her. It was a relief in that way.

But the moment Noa woke up, the moment she opened her eyes, the words hit her again: hard and sharp, discrete and precise—Isla is dead.

If Noa had been a different kind of girl, those words might have crushed her, curled her in under dark lines and letters. But every morning, Noa woke to their sting in her cheeks, their buzz in her teeth—and got up anyway.

Getting up was different now. Three months ago, when Isla had been alive, she and Noa would wake up together in their room at Harlow Academy, California's answer to elite East Coast boarding schools, in the wilds outside Monterey. Noa and Isla's dorm room was only a blip in Harlow's creeping expanse—but it had been theirs. Fifteen-year-old Noa and seventeen-year-old Isla: their hideout.

But that was Before. Before winter break. Before they'd gone to that cabin, that ruin. Before The Accident. Now the new term at Harlow was underway—Noa's essential-to-the-future junior year—and there was no hideout. No theirs. Now Noa was part of that strange outsider group called 'Commuters,' day students who, for various reasons, had to live at home. Reasons like 'family healing.' Apparently, close proximity to one another, sadness bound in on sadness, was supposed to help—though how exactly was never explained.

Because after losing Isla, Noa's parents couldn't bear distance—from Noa, from home, from one another. Of course, Hannah and Christopher Sullivan had ostensibly let Noa decide—*it's up to you*, their mouths said, words intended to be true—but Noa had seen the real words on their faces: *You cannot go.* Noa's mother like the moon: pale and paler, the shadow of grief taking more and more light. She was sickle moon now, just a sliver. She'd be swallowed without Noa. The cycle would never renew.

So this morning, when she'd return to Harlow, Noa woke up at home. The words—*Your sister is dead.* A blink, then bare feet on the cool wooden floor.

In gray light, Noa tiptoed over the small girl burrowed into the sleeping bag. Her Other Sister—the Still-Alive Sister—three-year-old Sasha. Noa smiled at Sasha's small face, golden under its crown of dark-chocolate curls, and watched Sasha's eyelids flutter open. Almond eyes, dark and rich, fastened on Noa's pale gray ones. Her cheeks drew her mouth into round little *O*.

"Harl-oh?"

Noa smiled at Sasha's wonder, still possible after Isla's loss. She wished her parents could take comfort in it the way she did.

But Noa suspected all they felt when looking at Sasha now was a kind of relief—that Sasha, unlike Noa, did not look so like the one lost. Isla and Noa had stood fair and pale as twins, but Sasha was foundling-strange: dark tones, gold skin, rich, pillowed lips. When her parents saw Noa now, they saw Isla. A living mirage. Haunting them.

Now, at least, Noa would spend the day at school. So would Sasha. With Noa's father back at work—Christopher had returned to his law firm in Carmel two days after Isla's funeral—new arrangements had to be made. Their mother-the-moon was not a childcare option. So Harlow's headmaster had agreed to let Sasha join Harlow's kindergarten, part of the Harlow Youth Day School, despite her being too young.

Spitfire Sasha was thrilled, knowing nothing of Harlow's cold grandeur, its swallowing marble halls—not that the school, or anything else for that matter, could be a match for Noa's sister at full force. Sasha's uniform had arrived days earlier, pressed flat in tissue in two long rectangular boxes, and she'd insisted—in her trademark banshee yell—on wearing it continuously. But Noa saw her, when Sasha thought no one was watching, gently stroking the shield at the breast. Noa folded that moment like a secret, warm against her chest: her fiery sister, gentle and still. At night, when the quiet felt too cavernous (people not asleep, not awake), Noa would unfurl it, wrap it around her, let it fill the space.

"Harl-oh . . ." Sasha smiled.

Noa smiled back, pulled down a chocolate ringlet and nodded. "Harlow."

• • •

"THEY'RE STARING, AREN'T THEY."

Noa wasn't really asking a question. She was in a familiar Harlow hallway, in her familiar Harlow uniform, talking with Olivia Lee, her familiar Harlow best friend, but everything was different.

Everyone was looking at her.

It didn't help that Noa and Olivia were at her commuter's locker, something she'd never needed before, when she'd been herself, familiar. But she couldn't change books in her room because Isla Had Died. She was not like the others, because Isla Was Gone.

She was Different.

Olivia—tall and thin, with gorgeous dark eyes—craned her neck down the hall.

"They are staring, it's true." She ran a hand over her shining black hair. "I should have tried harder with my 'fro." Olivia's eyes twinkled. To the casual observer, Olivia Lee looked straitlaced and studious: uniform crisp and clean, posture perfect—but that was a facade. Underneath, the real Olivia, Noa's Olivia, was a secret hellion of snark and wit. The subterfuge was to appease her 'tiger parents,' who frequently called in for reports on their daughter's 'comportment.' Olivia made sure to paint the picture they expected . . . but only until the door to their dorm room closed.

"Oh crap, I hope they don't think you can't afford to board anymore," Olivia said vehemently. "The only thing worse than being Creepy Death Girl is being Poor Girl."

"Heaven forbid," Noa agreed dryly.

Olivia snapped her fingers. "'Heaven forbid!' That's a good one. I should write that down. Good swear-substitutes are so hard to find when speaking to the 'rents." She absently rubbed at the spot behind her ear, where, Noa knew, perfectly tinted concealer was covering one of six secret tattoos. That particular one was of a candle, in honor of Olivia's favorite band, Ours.

"Hey, Noa."

The sweet bell-like voice startled Noa and Olivia. Ansley Montgomery, Harlow's reigning deity of perfection, had spoken Noa's name. Ansley was someone who'd always be noticed; students parted around her naturally like waves, faces cresting upward in awe. She ran Harlow's only secret society (all female), the Beautiful Little Fools, and though she'd been in school with Noa and Olivia for years, she might as well have lived on Mount Olympus.

But now Ansley was taking Noa's hand, looking right in Noa's eyes. "I wanted to come to see how you were." Her voice was gentle and earnest, her eyes emerald green, her hands softer than any Noa had ever touched. "I'm here for you, if you need it, OK?" Noa breathed in lavender from Ansley's gleaming platinum hair. Ansley moved one hand to Olivia. "We're your family here."

Despite herself, Noa didn't want Ansley to let go of her. When she did, it was like losing the sun.

"I know that was about her, not me," Noa said after, "but . . ."

"That's why she's Ansley."

"And that's why I know there is something beyond reality in this world. She has to have some kind of magic in her blood."

Olivia shook her head ruefully. "You and your Spidey sense."

"It's not Spidey sense, for the millionth time."

Olivia rolled her eyes. "Fine, your obsession-with-fairy-tales sense. You read too many books, woman. You need to be forced into pre-pre-premed like me. *Wha-pash!* Crack the whip!"

Noa heard herself laugh. Olivia beamed, evidently just as surprised as Noa.

"You know," she said, more sincerely, "I'm glad you still believe in your magical fantasies, Nose."

"No snark?" Noa asked suspiciously.

Olivia sighed. "Well . . . maybe a little."

• • •

AS THE DAY WENT ON, Noa felt her classmates' eyes follow her everywhere. Students she barely knew greeted her like old friends, but without Ansley's grace. They spoke tinny words of comfort, wanting her grief to make them interesting.

Lunch was particularly hard. Noa had hers at a different time than Olivia and their other best friend, Miles, and suddenly, all the eager, comforting hands from the hallway melted away. It was one thing to become a part of Noa's story tangentially, but to actually sit with her, talk to her at lunch—that was different. Her classmates watched her over their trays at a safe distance, fascinated but wary.

Finally, Carly Ann Connelly asked in her whispery voice to sit with Noa. Noa nodded, never so grateful to see Carly Ann's freckled cheeks and frizzy orange-red hair. Carly Ann was an outsider, too. She boarded without a roommate—in a 'psycho single,' per Harlow slang—but Noa had always liked her. She was shy, yes, but sweet, and when Noa, Olivia, and Carly Ann had together learned they weren't tapped for the Beautiful Little Fools the previous year, Noa had been secretly grateful for Carly Ann's sincere expression of disappointment. Somehow, it made it more OK that she felt crushed, too.

As Carly Ann quietly ate her pasta salad, Noa watched the dense freckles on the back of her hand move up and down. She knew Carly Ann wouldn't start a conversation but just kind of be with her, and that was perfect; it was as much as Noa could handle.

But when Carly Ann finished eating and floated up out of her seat, with a whispery, apologetic "I'm so sorry, Noa. I have to go meet Dr. Chandler to go over my essay," Noa had the absurd feeling she might cry.

She was alone with the eyes again.

Without hesitating, Noa jumped from her seat and delivered her still-full tray to the conveyor belt that led to the kitchen, making a beeline toward the dorms—

—where she no longer had a room.

Crap.

There was nowhere to escape—except outside. Noa pushed open one of Harlow's heavy mahogany doors and winced when the crisp Salinas air stung her cheeks. As the door shut heavily behind her, she turned toward the forest of massive oaks outside the Boys' Annex and ran straight into Mr. Green, Harlow's sour, gnarled groundskeeper. Noa gulped breath so hard she choked as she instinctively backed away.

No one pricked Noa's 'Spidey sense' more than creepy Mr. Green.

Mr. Green didn't look the part of Harlow's distinguished faculty, and he was as mean as his crippled body was twisted. But he was incredibly gifted—the artist of Harlow's stunning wild-like grounds—so the administration bent backward to keep him happy. They even permitted his eyesore of a shack to stand in one distant corner. Mr. Green had no patience for students; as an unspoken rule, they did not wander his grounds. Noa immediately dropped her eyes and spun back inside.

Ironically, it was Noa's sister Isla, enfant terrible in the eyes of the faculty, who'd been the one student Mr. Green tolerated. Isla, who could never stay indoors, whom he'd find up trees or wandering in the dark. Mr. Green had always brought her back, but he'd never reported her. Isla once mentioned that sometimes they even talked. When Noa had asked about what, Isla had just smiled mysteriously, in that taunting my-special-secret way she had. It didn't surprise Noa that Mr. Green didn't seem to recognize the ghost of Isla's face in her own; she had the tingling sensation that he saw, quite clearly, how very different they were.

Without another destination, Noa went early to her AP History class in the Humanities Wing and slid into the last row.

She laughed a little: more like Isla by the day.

In the past, Noa had always been a zealous front-seater in Harlow's cult of grades and competition. Isla had never cared. Among a school of would-be nerds, she was an object of wonder: never fretted an A-, never stayed up late studying, never agonized over college. Teachers puzzled over her "lack of motivation"; boys found her inscrutable and captivating. It wasn't that Isla wasn't interested in things—she was. She drew, painted, made moccasins once, often sang—but not particularly well, nor was she motivated to improve.

She just didn't care, always smiling in that secretive way she had.

Sometimes Noa would look over her mountains of books at Isla, who'd be lying unencumbered on her bed, and want to ask not why, but how. *How can you live without everything touching you?*

But now she, Noa—the younger, neater sister, the more obedient, academic, diligent sister—was sitting in back, looking out the window, homework not done. And she really didn't care. Other details were more important. Details held the world together: brushing Sasha's hair before bed, making full plates for her mother that remained untouched. But school details, grade details, college details—those details were small now, far away.

At least Noa knew that in class she'd see Miles, who'd been away with the lacrosse team. Noa had been texting with him (illegally, of course, as Harlow strictly banned smartphones), and he'd sworn he'd be back in time.

Miles got to class late, clothes rumpled from the trip, sandy hair askew, and when he saw Noa, he broke into the huge grin she'd privately named his 'golden retriever grin.' He ignored Dr. Chandler's pointed gaze as he made his noisy way to the seat beside Noa's. Few Harlow boys would have gone straight to class without pausing to change and carefully muss their hair first, but Miles plopped down next to Noa, freckles out in full force, smelling faintly of airline peanuts.

As Dr. Chandler resumed his zealous Civil War lecture, Miles surreptitiously tossed a Now and Later toward Noa. She caught it on the fly and popped it in her mouth, and for a second, a split second of a second, she felt normal. Miles struggled with a Super Lemon wrapper, then with a huff sneakily de-pocketed his most illegal and prized possession—the many-tooled Swiss Army knife Noa had given him for his birthday (engraved with "M HB N"— the letters were expensive!). Miles slid open its tiny scissors to cut the wrapper. A moment later, his eyes watered in gleeful torture, and Noa fought the urge to laugh.

The second class was over, Miles scooped up both their books and linked his arm through Noa's as they walked out. His blazer was crushed in back—she hoped he didn't end up with a wardrobe citation for her sake.

"How was the tourney? You trip over your lacrosse stick?" she teased. He shook the sandy, uneven bangs out of his eyes and grinned.

"Couple of times," he conceded. "But the good news is we won. Not that I played many minutes, but hey, benchwarming counts. Especially when you're a teammate with an accessory." Miles pulled his asthma inhaler from his pocket and gave it a sardonic twirl.

"Asthma's not so bad for lacrosse . . . and running. . . ." Noa offered.

But Miles was distracted, agog at Noa's spectators. "It's been like this all day?"

"I'm morbidly popular. Huzzah."

Miles patted her back. "Don't worry, you'll head back to obscurity soon enough."

"It's nothing personal, Noa!" he added when she swatted him, holding up his hands. "But Alumni Week is soon, and even you can't pull focus from floats and dances and the epic class wars. JUNIOR PRIDE!"

As answering shouts of 'junior pride' rang out around them, Noa closed her eyes in relief. She'd forgotten Alumni Week was soon—Harlow-speak for Homecoming—and she couldn't have asked for a better distraction. The 'school spirit wars' between the classes culminated in a fierce float-off at half-time, and followed that night by the Alumni Ball—Harlow's Homecoming dance.

"Trust me, you'll go back to your usual unimportance," Miles assured her.

"You say the sweetest things to me."

"I do try." Miles suddenly seemed to get nervous, shuffling his feet. Noa felt a familiar sinking feeling. "Speaking of that . . . I was thinking, if you wanted to just make it easy . . . I mean, I know with everything—"

Noa held her breath. She adored Miles, but not romantically, no matter how much she wished she did.

"The ball, we could just—"

"I'm not going," she said quickly, unable to even let him finish, let alone meet his eyes. "With everything"—she gestured feebly at her onlookers—"and Isla and the floats, it was the one activity she actually seemed to like. . . ."

Miles nodded in understanding, making Noa feel worse. He smiled gamely.

"Let's find Olivia. I picked her up some contraband on the road!"

• • •

IT WAS ACTUALLY a relief at the end of the day when Noa realized that she would now 'commute' home, leave this place that had once been her sky, space, and all constellations. While Olivia showered, and Miles unpacked, Noa helped Sasha into the waiting Harlow shuttle, ready to speed them Somewhere Else.

In theory, Noa's father Christopher could have picked them up himself, like the other commuters' parents, but he didn't seem to want to leave work. And Noa, like most boarding-school teens, had never gotten her license. So Noa and Sasha had become the only passengers on the shuttle. Noa leaned back, took off her cross tie. Sasha snored beside her, sweating as she dreamed.

The Sullivan house, large and cold in its gated Monterey enclave, was dark when they arrived. Noa frowned. No lights meant no mother up and around. After carefully depositing Sasha in their shared bedroom, she went to find her.

Hannah Sullivan was sitting in the dark at her writing desk, a blank journal in her hands.

"Mom?" Noa asked tentatively.

Hannah started, turned. So pale and tired, and that moment—that infinitesimal flinch, seeing the imposter. No, Mom, not Isla. Noa.

Hannah rose and looked down at her robe, suddenly embarrassed. She smoothed her tangled hair, more gray now than blond, and smiled an awkward, piecemeal smile, constructed step-by-step.

"I've been writing," her mother said, closing the blankness of the journal. Noa nodded, as if this was still Before, when Hannah had been a travel writer. Traveler and scribe, even a blossoming photographer . . . a woman once so restless for adventure, now so reluctant to leave her room.

Her breakfast plate lay where Noa had left it, untouched.

"Mom . . ."

"Don't worry about me," Hannah said, waving her thin wrist. She walked to her unmade bed, began to straighten out the sheets even though the day had passed.

"I'll make you something else if you want. How about lentil soup?" Noa's mother had always loved lentil soup—all colors and all kinds, from continents near and far.

The doorbell rang.

"I'll get it, and then your soup," Noa said with a cheery smile.

Hannah stood up straighter, tightened her robe.

"I can get it," she protested, but Noa quickly slipped down the stairs.

It was Celia Robsen, their neighbor and the aunt of her classmate Jeremy, who once upon a time had been graced by a fling with Isla. Celia's housekeeper stood beside her, holding a covered casserole dish.

"Hi there, Noa. Is your mom—"

"She's in the bath just now," Noa replied politely. "Been writing all day."

Celia's eyebrows lifted. "That's wonderful, honey." Celia's housekeeper nudged her gently. "Jeremy mentioned you were back at school, so I had Malene make you all four-cheese truffle macaroni. Not the healthiest—"

Noa was no longer listening. "Thank you, Mrs. Robsen," she said quickly, taking the dish and nearly slamming the door in the woman's face.

"Noa? Who was it?" Hannah called from upstairs.

"Wrong house!"

Noa hurried to the kitchen and frantically began to scrape the macaroni into the garbage disposal. When half of the tray was gone, she ran the water, flipped the switch, and let it grind.

"Macaroni?"

Noa paused, took a moment to compose a smile before turning to Sasha, now sharp eyed and awake.

"Sasha my love!" Noa said brightly, using their mother's endearment, the one Hannah once had used for all of them, but now never, ever uttered. "How about some lentil soup? Rainbow lentil! Your favorite!"

Sasha screwed up her nose, narrowed her eyes. "Macaroni!"

Like all three-year-olds, Sasha was mercurial, but more vol-canic than most. Noa loved Sasha's special intensity—the joy in her laugh, the swell of her hope, the rush of her love—but not her explosions. Noa didn't love wiping matter from walls.

The front door opened, followed by the sound of their father's steps. Sasha's face brightened instantly. Sasha pounced on him, and Noa ground the rest of the macaroni into oblivion.

Christopher entered the kitchen moments later, Sasha in his arms as he flipped through the mail. His suit, as always, looked as neat as it had when he'd left.

"Got that lentil soup for dinner, Dad, just like you wanted," Noa said meaningfully.

"Yes," her father nodded slowly. "Can't wait. How 'bout it, Sash?"

Sasha squealed "LENTIL!" as if she'd never heard a more delicious suggestion in her life. She squirmed from his arms and twirled happily from the room.

Once Sasha was gone, Christopher and Noa stood awk-wardly. Noa reached for a clean coffee cup, began to wash it just for something to do.

"Your mom?" he asked cautiously.

Noa focused on the cup. "Says she's writing. But, Dad, Mrs. Robsen dropped off some macaroni and cheese—"

"She—"

"I ground it up," Noa assured him quickly.

"Ground what up?" Hannah asked as she walked in, still in her bathrobe but with evidence of having brushed her hair. Her eyes went to the tray on the counter, still crusted with bits of macaroni. Her face drained.

Noa grabbed the tray, began scrubbing it furiously in the sink. "We're having lentil soup. I already have some in the fridge—"

But Hannah had cowered back, wrapping her robe more tightly around her. "I need to lie down. Please, eat without me."

Christopher tried to take her arm, but she shrugged him off. He followed a millimeter behind her instead, braced to catch her fall.

Macaroni and cheese. Mrs. Robsen just *had* to bring that. Isla had been obsessed with macaroni and cheese, and their mother had fought her over every unhealthy bite. Hannah finally banned it—*I don't care if you starve!*—causing Isla to storm out in anger one dark night.

She never came back alive.

• • •

NOA BROUGHT SASHA'S lentil soup to their room, picnic-style. Sasha's eyes saw woods and sun, not their mother lying down, their father closed in his study. As Sasha spoke to something only she could see, Noa's eyes swept past the darkened windows, and for a moment, saw Isla—raising a hand, long blond hair falling wavy past her shoulders. Noa reached back, opened her mouth to speak across space and time—but it was only her own reflection. Her pale hand, with bitten nails; her tangled hair pulled back.

Noa sighed, chiding herself again. These 'ghost moments,' as she'd named them, had been happening from time to time. She could hear Olivia teasing her, not for believing Isla was actually still alive—that, Noa knew, would never be—but for thinking that Isla was in some spirit form, perhaps, reaching to connect.

In the moment Isla's ghost disappeared, Sasha began to sing a song of nonsense words in her clear and lilting voice.

• • •

"WHY THE SCOWL, NOSE?" Olivia asked later that week, leaning against Noa's locker.

"Got a notice to see the counselor."

Olivia made a squinchy face. "Ms. Jaycee? Gross. Ms. Rainbow Bright in heels."

Noa frowned. "Great. Make me less excited."

"You know, I bet her office is full of conflict-resolution posters and books about teenage grief." Olivia snapped her fingers. "You owe me Flamin' Hot Cheetos if there's a poster of a wave with the word 'Teamwork' on it." Noa glared, and Olivia grinned. "Just promise me, no nude yoga."

Noa leaned into her locker. "She asked me to meet during history. That means Dr. Chandler knows. Ugh, I must be an 'official faculty cause for concern.'"

Olivia laughed. "I would have thought they'd find me out before you!"

• • •

MS. JAYCEE'S DOOR was closed when Noa arrived. A sign on her door declared: ALONE WE CAN DO SO LITTLE! TOGETHER WE CAN DO SO MUCH! IN SESSION! Exclamation points, Noa sighed to herself, poor Helen Keller.

Noa hated when words were mishandled. Language was her special obsession—in secret, she was not just a reader, but a *writer*. Noa the poet, her most precious self, lived in stolen, hidden moments, when no one else could see. She'd started as a child, pretending to be sick in order to curl up with a journal, heart and pen beating fast. Poem after poem, story after story she'd tattoo across the pages: maps, landscapes, galaxies where none were there before. And when a journal filled, Noa would always hide it in the most unnavigable cavern she knew, that perfect war-torn ruin which kept any secret safe: Isla's closet. Once Noa started boarding at Harlow, her opportunities to write became more frequent—any night restless Isla sneaked away. . . .

Noa wasn't sure why her writing became a secret, or once it was, why she kept it so. She wasn't afraid of 'getting caught' exactly—it was more that writing felt intensely personal, almost primal. Something entirely, essentially hers, that she didn't want to share. Noa wasn't a writer the way her mother was a writer; Hannah wrote precisely, clearly, always for an audience. Noa's writing was messy, words bursting wetly from inside. Sometimes it was painful, bloody; sometimes not like words at all. But it was always true.

Now that Noa was back home, writing felt even more important. Sasha had migrated from her sleeping bag into Noa's bed, a hot tangle of arms and legs and hair around her, so every night, Noa waited for the little growl-like snores, then carefully pulled out her journal.

So as Noa waited to see Ms. Jaycee, staring at that cheerful, exclaiming sign—ALONE WE CAN DO SO LITTLE! TOGETHER WE CAN DO SO MUCH! IN SESSION!—she knew her relationship with the counselor was not going to be happy. Tired of waiting, she finally got up, brushed her uniform kilt straight, and approached the young receptionist.

"Ms. Archer—"

Ms. Archer held up a perfectly painted peachy fingernail—

That's when the boy walked in.

He was someone Noa had never seen before, and an eerie prickle ran down her spine. She instinctively took a step back, yet couldn't look away. The boy was towering, at least 6'4", and moved silently, like liquid. His skin was deep olive, as if from some far away, sun-baked place; his hair unkempt, tossed in downy almost-curls of mahoganies and browns. And thick, Noa thought suddenly, like duck feathers. Like rain would never soak through. In that moment, Noa had an odd compulsion to touch his curls, even as a strangeness spun inside her.

Embarrassed, Noa looked down, but then peeked back up— he was looking back. His eyes were not like her eyes, gray and flat, but spiraling amber, one horizon brighter than his hair. And they were watching her carefully, almost . . . warily.

"Callum Forsythe?" Ms. Archer broke in, just as the counselor, Ms. Jaycee opened her door.

"Noa! I'm ready for you!"

Noa turned reluctantly to Ms. Jaycee's blown-out sausage curls, her red heels to match her nails. A thirty-something living exclamation point. Noa sighed, moving toward her, but couldn't stop herself from looking back, just once—

The boy was gone.

• • •

"SIT ANYWHERE YOU LIKE!"

Olivia had been right: Ms. Jaycee's office was self-consciously 'informal,' screaming *Open up! Be at ease!* Noa walked right past the bright purple beanbag chairs toward the squashy, mustard-colored couch. She hesitated before perching on one of its arms, so she could at least look Ms. Jaycee in the eye. She didn't take off her blazer, or lean back, or indicate in any way that she wanted to stay long.

And there it was, the wave poster. She owed Olivia Cheetos.

"Noa, how are you?"

Noa executed a smile. "I'm doing well."

Ms. Jaycee nodded, as if she had expected this response. "It must be a difficult transition."

Noa shrugged. "I missed my friends."

"The thing is, Noa," Ms. Jaycee said confidingly, "some of your teachers are a smidge concerned. You're behind, and they say you're seeming a tad disengaged. It's of course to be expected, after losing Isla."

The spasm Noa always felt at Isla's name seized her stomach. It didn't matter if she was prepared for it or who was saying it or in what context—just hearing *Isla* in someone else's voice . . .

Ms. Jaycee waited patiently.

"I'm OK," Noa said finally, unable to bear the silence any longer, angry to hear her voice shake. A spark of satisfaction flashed through Ms. Jaycee's eyes. Noa searched desperately for the words that would set her free. "I'd like to go back to history now, since I have a lot of catching up? It's junior year, and I can't afford to get behind?" She hated that her words were coming out as questions, not statements, but prayed it didn't matter. She was playing the academics card, the only one she had.

Ms. Jaycee frowned. "OK, Noa. But I want you to know I am here to talk. I know you don't board here anymore, but I'll work around your schedule. I think it would be helpful. But I can't force you."

Noa tensed, ready to leap off the couch arm.

"But—" Ms. Jaycee warned, "if you don't choose to do counseling, I need to see movement on your end. Involvement in student activities and progress in your classes. Is that a deal?"

Noa shifted, wary of a trap. "Student activities . . . like what?"

"Well, how about the juniors' float? That might be a great way to alleviate adolescent social isolation!" Ms. Jaycee beamed, energized by her buzz words. "The theme this year is Literary Classics, and Dr. Keely says you're a real standout in English class."

Noa bit her lip. *The floats are Isla's thing.* But she nodded. Anything to get out of there.

• • •

NOA SANK INTO the chair Miles had saved for her in history, trying not to notice the stares as she came in late. Miles passed her his notes and Noa smiled: While some of his scrawl did in fact detail Chandler's lecture—*Battle of Fredericksburg 1862*—it quickly dissolved into jokes and cartoons he'd inserted for her benefit. He threw her a Now and Later with a wiggle of his eyebrows—a gesture purely Miles.

But a different boy was on Noa's mind: Callum Forsythe. That strange feeling prickled her skin again, like uneasiness and . . . anticipation.

What? Miles mouthed across the narrow aisle in between them, face cocked. Noa shook her head, blushing. Miles shrugged: *crazy girl.*

Noa felt a pang of guilt. She hadn't betrayed Miles. She hadn't even talked to Callum. She didn't even want to talk to Callum . . . did she?

Noa was so lost in thought that suddenly class was over and Dr. Chandler was catching her and Miles. Dry-erase dust was smudged all over his oxford shirt, his post-lecture brown hair everywhere. "Guys, I hate to do this, but you two have fallen below the Threshold of Concern."

Noa and Miles exchanged a guilty look. Harlow code for earning C-grades . . . or lower.

"I know there are special considerations," Dr. Chandler continued awkwardly, with a look toward Noa. "So I'm starting an extra-help salon, Monday afternoons."

Noa cleared her throat uncomfortably. "I have to pick Sasha up after school."

"Ms. Jaycee has agreed to watch her. It will be you two and one other student, OK?"

As soon as they were in the hall, Miles groaned.

"At least we'll be together," Noa linked her arm through his. When he brightened, she felt another pang, but didn't pull her arm away.

• • •

NOA DIDN'T SEE the boy again, *Callum*, until AP English. Noa still loved English—unlike her other classes—and Dr. Keely, who looked like a sweet, gray-haired librarian. She liked to imagine Dr. Keely living in rooms lined with first editions and rare manuscripts, words on cats on words. While Dr. Chandler loved to lecture and perform, Dr. Keely loved the words themselves. This comforted the secret poet in Noa: It meant any work, *her* work, was alive all on its own, living secrets shaped in ink.

Olivia dashed in at the last moment, sliding into her usual seat beside Noa, who raised an eyebrow at Olivia's mussed collar. Olivia rolled her eyes and fixed it. Harlow prized punctuality but notoriously gave no time to get between classes.

"I had a very entertaining weekend with your creative response papers," Dr. Keely began. "Some of you have . . . intriguing . . . hidden recesses." She looked pointedly at Jeremy Robsen, the class clown. As the class laughed, Noa bent to take out her anthology and felt the room suddenly become alert. She looked up.

Callum had just walked in.

Olivia stared, Jeremy looked suspicious, Ansley and her equally exquisite best friend, Leticia Fields, smiled mysteriously. Noa was relieved to see she wasn't the only one who seemed . . . intrigued . . . by Callum, but strangely, she also felt a sense of loss. He wasn't her secret anymore.

"Any open seat is fine," Dr. Keely told him.

Callum nodded and turned to face the class. The two open seats happened to be directly to Noa's left. When he saw her, he seemed to give a little start—*what did that mean?*—then he watched her warily as he moved to sit beside her. At the last moment, though, he seemed to change his mind; his face closed off, and he chose the far seat instead. He faced forward and did not turn her way again.

Noa felt a flush of disappointment but also, weirdly, anger.

Olivia tossed a note onto her lap. *How do you know him?!?*

Noa quickly wrote back: *I don't.*

Olivia rolled her eyes, clearly thinking Noa was holding out. Ansley and Leticia were staring at her.

Noa tried to focus on the lecture.

"Whitman connected the grass to democracy and America," Carly Ann was saying, frizzy hair trapped in an updo with a pen.

"But what about *Leaves of Grass* as a personal epic?" Dr. Keely prompted. "He called it 'Song of Myself' after all. OK, Callum?"

The class turned as one to Callum, who'd raised his hand. For some reason, Noa got that strange tingle again. It actually reminded her a little of how she felt when she saw Isla's ghost. *Stop it*, she chided herself.

"The poem is his effort to explain himself, decide who he is. He kept rewriting because he couldn't get it right. In the end, he decided he, and the grass, were 'untranslatable.'"

Noa felt, against her will, her heart beat faster. Callum knew poetry.

"Yet poetry still comes out triumphant in the end," Dr. Keely responded, "as being the best tool we have. Words are limited and the soul is limitless, but words approximate it best."

"So the poem ends with the 'yawp'?" Ansley asked, her eyes on Callum, a flirty half smile on her perfect lips.

"Exactly," Dr. Keely said, oblivious. "A word unlimited by a specific definition, but filled with emotion and with hope. The closest we can come to describing and translating our essential selves." Dr. Keely checked her watch. "Let's switch gears here to our other American today. Olivia, read Dickinson's first stanza?"

Olivia smiled her straight-A-student smile and began, clearly and evenly:

There's a certain slant of light,
On winter afternoons,
That oppresses, like the weight
Of cathedral tunes.

Noa closed her eyes; she loved Emily Dickinson. That chill . . . that otherness.

Jeremy raised his hand. "Why's she saying *light* oppresses? Isn't light good?"

Someone answered, and to her surprise, Noa realized it was she herself. "That's the whole idea. Light is supposed to be happy. But sometimes, in your 'winter' moments, that makes it worse. When everyone feels warmer, fuller, but you . . . That light kind of . . . suffocates you." Noa trailed off, looking down. Olivia caught her eye, nodded toward Callum. He was watching Noa intently, as if trying to understand something important.

For the rest of the class, Noa did her best to focus on the material, but her eyes kept creeping Callum's way. More than once, she caught him staring at her.

At the end of the period, Dr. Keely had saved time to share highlights from their creative response papers, which they'd been free to do in any form, in response to any classic work. Predictably, Jeremy immediately volunteered and read his hilarious (if semi-lewd) free-association essay inspired by *Lolita*. Then Ansley read her reimagined *Emma*, set in present-day Harlow (and now starring an Emma more like her). When no one else volunteered, Dr. Keely said she would read one piece anonymously, a poem inspired by J.M. Barrie's *Peter Pan*.

Noa swallowed hard. She hadn't even planned to turn her poem in; she'd written a safer response paper instead. But after she had written the poem (in the dark, with Sasha's legs wrapped up around her and her parents sleepless down the hall), she'd had one of those fleeting moments when she saw Isla's ghost. Isla had seemed to urge her to use the poem. Later, in panic after turning it in, Noa had reassured herself that only Dr. Keely would see it.

So much for that.

"The title is 'The Lost Girls,'" Dr. Keely said, and then began to read:

The Lost Girls

Nomad girls are Lost Ones too,
with leaves at foot and crown;
they too seek shelter in the trees,
drink Red and Gold and Brown.

their circlets made of steam and rain,
their lashes powdered ash,
they're firelight, they're fox's kill,
they're blood and sweat and scratch.

Lost Boys fly forever, and crow the rising sun.
they play all day in Neverland, their laughter
    mermaid-spun.
but Lost Girls live underground:
they steal from hole to hole.
They drink the shadows, wear the night,
and paint their cheeks with coal.

And when the wind turns colder,
they split a doe and climb inside.
still-warm sinew
    wraps their hands,
dead muscle soaks the light.

You'll never tell what's girl, what's beast,
once bloody fur's been trussed—
so think your happy thoughts, Lost Boy,
wish on your Fairy Dust.

When Dr. Keely finished, Noa could barely breathe.

"Comments, anyone?"

"We should totally do our junior float like that poem," Leticia piped up. "Like, inspired by *Peter Pan*."

Ansley jumped in excitedly. "We could be fairies with really delicate wings, and the guys could rig it up so we'd look like we were flying!" Ansley and Leticia's enthusiasm was like a lightning rod, pulling their classmates in as the block came to a close. Eager chatter carried everyone out the door. Even Callum was momentarily forgotten—except by Noa.

She turned to find him one last time, just as he was passing by her. He moved so smoothly she almost didn't notice the way he subtly lifted his arm as he passed, to ensure they would not touch.

But she did notice.

And she noticed when, as he brushed by Leticia's shoulder on his way out, their connection seemed electric, like it had given off an actual spark.

• • •

"OOF," NOA GRUNTED as she tried—and failed—to smoothly exit the shuttle that night with a sleeping Sasha in her arms. Even asleep, Sasha was a handful.

Sasha's teachers had noticed. Tall bespectacled Ms. Finlee and sweet squashy-plump Ms. Messing had just about given up hope that classroom routine would eventually calm Sasha's tides. If any routine was developing with Sasha, it was of explosive, swerving energy.

The solution came unexpectedly. To escape her classmates' endless staring, Noa began eating lunch in Sasha's classroom, and one afternoon, she told Sasha and another little girl a story she spun out of the air. For a whole hour, as the story wove its filaments around them, Sasha sat transfixed, then calmly napped, right on schedule. It was the first time Sasha had consented to nap at all, and the teachers' relief had been so evident Noa resolved to tell a story every lunch she could.

And the stories Noa told! Sometimes stories she made up, sometimes ones she remembered, sometimes pages from her favorite volumes brought from home. She'd begin at the top of the hour, and in a blink, they'd have traveled far and wide. Soon, the entire class was waiting when she arrived, seated quietly. Sasha's teachers never said that Noa's storytelling turned the tide, but Noa felt better all the same.

Now as Noa carried Sasha, she thought oddly of Callum. He was mercurial, too. Even in his physical details: hair and eyes not quite any color, somehow every color, brown and red and copper. Like Ghost-Isla in the glass—fluid, with the unstable edge of the unreal.

The cold doorknob, dark foyer, and frigid house snapped

Noa back to reality. There was something else, too. Was something . . . burning?

Noa quickly put Sasha in their room and dashed to the dark kitchen. A red light blinked through the blackness—a burner left on, beneath a pot of what once was soup.

Her mother had apparently gotten up and tried to cook. But the vegetable soup was now a charred pot of ash and smoke—with Hannah nowhere to be found. Noa grabbed a pot holder, flung the burning pot quickly to the sink. She turned on the cold water; steam hissed and filled the kitchen. She was trembling.

Noa's memories of this kitchen had always been filled with hearty smells and happy pots. Hannah Then, Hannah Before, was always cooking soup, juggling it and so much else with her special mother's magic. Noa had never even paused, running in and out and growing up, to notice cooking might take care and time. The soup, the merry pot, the smell of good things cooking right—these were *home*.

The soup pot hissed in the sink, ruined.

Noa looked at it, suddenly paralyzed: It was all too much.

She fell backward against the wall, let her body crumple down the familiar wallpaper to the floor. She coughed on the smoke; tears streamed down her cheeks fast and slick and silent.

Too much, too much for me.

Noa closed her eyes, and gave herself five minutes. Five minutes to cry and shake and shudder; to hate Isla for dying, her mom for fading, her dad for running away. Five minutes to give up, give in, scream out, a yawp of despair and pain and rage.

And then.

To come back.

Slowly, carefully, Noa stood. She took a napkin, wiped her face. She turned to the sink and scrubbed the pot. She forced her mind to think only the word *scrub*.

When she reached for more soap, she looked up. Isla was looking back through the kitchen window. Noa froze, but the face shimmered and became her own, so close in feature that she was left wondering, as she always did, if Isla had ever been there at all.

But as Noa turned back to the pot, something made her look up again. She looked back, and was startled to see not Isla, but, inexplicably, Callum. The way he had looked when they'd been eye-locked in the office, his gaze intense, his hair askew. She lifted her hand to reach out to him—when Sasha burst into the room, howling for her dinner.

• • •

"AND THAT'S THE BLOCK," Dr. Felton, Noa's precalc teacher announced, and the class scrambled to make a hasty exit.

As usual, Olivia was already waiting by the door, as if she had packed up and left ages earlier. Noa never knew how Olivia managed that, as she always seemed carefully attentive until dismissal.

"Noa, you're lagging," Olivia whined. "And you owe me some serious explain-o about that new guy. And we don't want to miss today's *delicious* Tahitian stir-fry."

Noa crinkled her nose in disgust automatically. In truth, Harlow's gourmet cafeteria was stellar, but that didn't stop students from complaining. "Don't you have drama now?" Noa asked.

"Canceled today. I think Dr. Bensemon has the *lady troubles*. Or some audition. Maybe a John. Who knows? What's important is that you have a dream come true: *moi* on your lunch period!"

"Oh, *that* dream."

"Hey, Noa." Noa and Olivia froze as Ansley Montgomery directly addressed them for the second time in their lives. Ansley's green eyes sparkled as they swept over Noa's face. Leticia and their third bestie, auburn-haired Mary Jane, eyed her with equally sharp attention.

Ansley placed a hand on Noa's, leaned in conspiratorially. "So tell me what the deal is with this Callum."

Noa darted a look at Olivia, who shrewdly pursed her lips. "I don't know," Noa mumbled.

"You know him, don't you?" Leticia demanded.

"Actually I've never even spoken to him before," Noa said truthfully.

"Leticia has a little crush," Ansley said with a pretty eye roll. "Apparently they had a moment. Hey, why don't you two sit with us today? We're headed to the caf."

Noa was stunned. She had *dreamed* of an invite like this—a sit-down with her class's most important Beautiful Little Fools, the girls who had inherited its reins from Isla—but the idea of talking about Callum with *them* . . . with *Leticia* . . . Noa looked at the gorgeous girl, whose dark, full eyes were narrowed sharply, and she remembered the spark she'd sworn she'd seen when Callum and Leticia had touched. Noa didn't want sit across from her like some childish little girl.

Not that I like him or anything. Noa didn't have time to like anyone, and besides, she didn't even know if she thought he was attractive or just . . . eerie.

"I actually can't. It has to do with the arrangements for my sister," Noa said quickly, hurrying down the hall and out the double doors before anyone could protest. She sent a silent apology back Olivia's way and hoped her bestie had ESP.

• • •

AS NOA TOOK HER PLACE in Sasha's classroom, her head was too full of burnt soup and phantom sparks to make a story up. She rooted through her bag and pulled out *Peter Pan*, the source material for her "Lost Girls" poem. It had worked its magic on Sasha many times before.

As the familiar words left her mouth, Noa felt her muscles and mind relax, weaving a world where kids didn't have to grow up if they didn't want to. Every so often, Noa would glance up from the words, mid-line, to see Sasha's eyes, rapt and shining. When Noa reached one of her favorite parts—how the island seemed to dim when Peter was not around—a particular shiver passed through the room.

She knew that shiver.

She looked up: Callum Forsythe had walked in.

Noa stumbled on her words, confused when Ms. Finlee nodded easily toward him in recognition. Why was Callum here? How did Ms. Finlee know him? Why, oh why, was he coming to sit with the kids? She saw the exact moment he noticed her. Genuine surprise washed over his face, but, her heart pounded, he didn't seem upset. In fact, he looked intrigued—the way he'd looked in the office, before his odd avoidance of her in English class.

Noa read absently as she watched Callum kneel quietly beside Sasha. He didn't sit right away—rather, he seemed to ask Sasha for permission first, in that special language of gesture and feeling most people forgot with adolescence. And surprisingly, Sasha allowed it. In fact, she and the other kids seemed almost unconsciously to scoot closer to him, snuggling up like kittens.

Noa looked back at the book, willing herself to focus on the story. She didn't look up again until the hour was over and Callum was rising to his feet. Noa was almost surprised to remember how tall he was; he had fit so easily with the kids. He looked at her, and she quickly stuffed *Peter Pan* into her messenger bag.

She didn't have room in her life to get on this roller coaster.

Noa was out the door and almost at the end of the hallway when he called after her.

"Wait up!"

She wasn't going to pause, but must have because suddenly he was beside her.

"I have to get to class—" she began.

"I do, too. Want to walk outside?" he asked. He moved his head subtly, making it impossible for her not to look him in the eyes. She barely managed not to gasp as the browns and changing golds hit her full force. Whatever else, she had to admit it: He was gorgeous.

She forced herself to turn around. "I can't."

Again he was somehow immediately in front of her. "It was your poem, wasn't it? 'Lost Girls'?"

Noa froze. He smiled easily.

"Come on, let's walk outside." He went out a side door and held it for her, though did not go so far as to offer his hand. Noa looked around for Mr. Green, not sure if she hoped he'd be there or not—but when she didn't see him, she had no choice but to go through.

Callum matched his gait to hers but didn't speak again. Noa's mind raced. How had he known the poem was hers? Should she try to deny it?

"There!" he said suddenly, interrupting her thoughts. He'd walked them into the grounds, was beckoning her eagerly. "You have to come here to see it best."

Noa hesitated, but his expression was so earnest she couldn't bring herself to refuse. He moved quickly, excited, and Noa had to trot a little to keep up. Finally he stopped, turned all the way around, and gave a little yelp of victory. "Here!" he said, directing Noa to spin.

When she did, she landed in full panoramic view of a particularly large, majestic California oak, still bare from the wintertime, stretching out across the harvest sky. She gasped.

Callum grinned. "Like a warrior, right? All the muscles and ripples in the branches?"

"You—you already found the tree grove? Didn't you just get here?"

"I'm not so used to being indoors. I've been exploring in the mornings. This one's my favorite."

Noa followed the tree's branches from its center to its tips; the sprays of skeletal muscles against the sky.

She watched Callum carefully. "What about Mr. Green?"

Callum waved a hand and laughed. "Mr. Green and I are friends."

Noa narrowed her eyes. "Really."

"Well, maybe *friend* is a stretch," Callum hedged, pulling nervously at a curl. "You're very precise."

"What were you doing in my sister's class?"

Callum rubbed the back of his neck, looked down. "I'm new so I'm supposed to get involved in things. I told them I like kids and they said I could visit, something about 'alleviate adolescent—'"

"—social anxiety,'" Noa smiled dryly. "Ms. Jaycee gets points for consistency."

Callum laughed, relaxing. "You too, huh? But you're not new."

"No." Noa paused, then decided to continue. "My older sister Isla died last year in an accident." She'd never said it out loud at Harlow before, hadn't even used Isla's name. It came out like glass: not cold or hard, but clear.

Callum's face didn't crumple in sympathy; he didn't offer some tinny 'I'm sorry.' He nodded once, and waited.

Noa swallowed. "My poem? It's not something I'm ready to share. Not even with my parents."

Callum nodded again. For some reason, she trusted him.

"I have to get back to class," she told him, realizing she was reluctant to go.

They walked back inside, and in the threshold Noa's shoe caught a crack in the marble. Callum instinctively reached out to catch her, and the instant they connected, the instant they touched for the first time, Noa swore she saw white fire—a spark shot from skin to skin and lit the room. It was intense and ecstatic and incredibly blinding. And then it was over, and he was standing over her, hands hovering, face swirling with confusion and something else—

Maybe fear.

"Are you OK?" he asked urgently, hands inches from her body.

Noa blinked, tried to clear her vision, put up a hand to have him help her up. He didn't, so she awkwardly got to her own feet instead. He stayed right beside her, looking for possible injury.

"What was that flash?"

"What flash?"

"That blinding light! Didn't you see it?"

"I saw you almost face-plant into the marble—"

"No—there was this flash, I know there was—and I saw something like it before, too—" Noa rubbed her neck, saw his expression. Her cheeks burned with embarrassment. "Maybe . . . I imagined it," she said uncertainly.

"Do you often . . . see things?" A smile tugged the corner of his mouth.

She couldn't help but smile back. "All right, all right, give a girl a break. I did almost kill myself just now."

He was instantly anxious again. "Are you sure you're OK? Let me take you to class—"

"I'm fine. Hallucinations aside."

"Please," he insisted.

Noa sighed, but let him walk beside her.

• • •

CALLUM OPENED THE CLASSROOM DOOR, and Noa slipped into the seat next to Miles, late again. His face was taut. Noa looked at him questioningly, and he shook his head. Noa drew a little cartoon on her notebook, like the ones Miles always drew for her: a stick-figure student asleep at his desk. *Notes or Notezzzzz?* she wrote, the z's coming out of the mouth.

Miles glanced at it, then looked toward the door where Callum was still visible through the small narrow window. For the rest of the class, Miles focused on Dr. Chandler as if no lecture could absorb him more.

• • •

"WELL, WHAT DO you expect from him? The boy has been in love with you for years, and suddenly Jolly Green's sneaking you late to class," Olivia said, wincing as her tattoo needle made its mark. She and Noa were in one of Harlow's 'psycho singles,' the one proudly occupied by Annabelle Leighton, who had enterprisingly made it into a contraband lair. You could purchase cigarettes or weed there, or rent the space for whatever you needed, which currently was Olivia's self-imposed tattoo job.

"Are you sure you don't want to wait for a professional, Liv?" Noa asked doubtfully, as Olivia's effort to draw a woven vine came out a messy smudge. "And if you tattoo your finger, how on earth will you hide it when you have recitals?" Olivia was, among other things, a concert-level pianist. She'd even given concerts on Cannery Row, which, of course, she'd deny to her deathbed.

"It's because of the piano that I need this one, and it can't wait until our next free city day. I can't bear all the practicing and perfect-ing without something to look at that reminds me of *me*. But don't worry, the needle I'm gonna use has UV ink. So as long as I don't go into black-light freak-fests with my parentals, I'm fine." Olivia grinned. "Besides, you're here now, and you've been there for every tattoo. It's good juju."

Noa raised an eyebrow. "I still say it's hypocritical for you to ride me about my 'Spidey sense' when you worship the almighty *juju*."

"*You* believe in mythical-fantasy-magical-fairytales. *I* believe in hedging my bets. Big difference. Now tell me my smudge looks amazing." Olivia thrust up her finger.

"Eh," Noa said.

Olivia rolled her eyes and started in with the tattoo needle and its invisible UV ink, cringing the whole way. "I hope there's no, like, major vessel or something in this finger, cause I'm flying blind. The YouTube how-to vid was kind of hard to see on Miles' burner cell. I need to find a way to get a contraband iPhone up in this joint before I move on to piercings." When Noa didn't respond in alarm, Olivia looked up gleefully. "Noa! You're totally thinking about him! You *were* hooking up before history!"

"*No* for the millionth time!" Noa protested. "We were just walking, and talking, it—it wasn't anything. And it ended weird." She stopped short of telling Olivia about the strange light she'd seen when Callum had caught her, and, she swore, when he and Leticia had touched. She knew Olivia would make fun of her 'Spidey sense' acting haywire.

Olivia snorted. "You liiiike him."

"I do not!" Noa cried, knowing her cheeks were burning. "Besides, this year I don't have time for boys, remember?"

"But he likes *poetry*, Noser. What if he can make you . . . *yawp*?" Olivia raised her eyebrows suggestively.

Noa threw a pillow at her, which Olivia easily ducked, grinning and singing. "*Noa likes a boy-y, Noa likes a boy-y . . .*" When she had finished her tattoo, she looked up at Noa, suddenly serious. "Come on, Nose. Break your rule, see where it goes."

Noa squirmed. "Why?"

"Because," Olivia said, "he looks at you the way Isla used to look at you."

"Like a loser little sister?"

"Like he can't wait to find out how you're gonna shine."

"Besides," Olivia added a moment later. "You can't let Leticia snake your hottie. I forbid it."

• • •

THAT NIGHT, THE SMELL of a cooking dinner hugged Noa as she opened the door—simmering beef, potatoes, a hit of nutmeg—and Noa almost cried in relief. She didn't even mind when it was not her mother, but her Aunt Sarah coming through the passway with tomato on her cheek. Noa was overjoyed to see Aunt Sarah, even if it meant her mom was still distant, still the moon.

"Noa-belle, you look gorgeous!" Aunt Sarah cried as if it had been many years, and not just since Isla's funeral, since they had seen each other last. Though in comparison to then, Noa probably did look gorgeous.

"I'm so glad you're here," Noa said, burying herself in Aunt Sarah's arms, trying not to feel like a traitor to her father. Aunt Sarah met Noa's eyes, understanding, the way she always did.

"Your dad called me, you know. The night she burned the soup."

Noa nodded, biting her lip. Aunt Sarah hugged her again.

Aunt Sarah didn't have kids herself, and in a funny way, Noa suspected that was why she saw Noa so clearly. Aunt Sarah saw her clean, without the blinders of a mom or dad. She loved kids, but she'd chosen to focus on her career as a high-profile class-action attorney and relished her independent life. The important thing was that Noa knew Aunt Sarah would always speak the truth to her, no matter what.

"How's my mom?"

"Says she's writing, but I doubt it," Aunt Sarah said. "Come on, don't wanna burn the moussaka." Noa followed her aunt toward the heavenly smells and basked in the details of the kitchen's newfound life: dust-free cabinet tops, folded towels on the oven bar . . . little things Noa hadn't been able to manage but had felt, so distinctly, in their lack. Even the green tomato tops, their wayward seeds on the white cutting board—their mess was comforting, evidence of life and motion. Aunt Sarah began chopping carrots. *Fresh*, Noa thought, relishing the word. *Crisp.*

Aunt Sarah continued as she chopped. "I looked in on her, she chased me out. I called Rosie to come clean and pick up your mom's prescription, not that she'll take it." Noa nodded, knowing all about that already. "When I came back, she was in her room with the door closed, I think taking a nap. Rosie said she'd spent a long time cleaning her closet, which I guess is better than nothing? At least that's what I *think* Rosie said. God knows it's been centuries since I've used Spanish."

Noa exhaled. If her mother had actually cleaned her closet, that would be a step. At the very least, actual human beings were in the house with Hannah now. And getting Rosie back meant she didn't have to do the laundry. . . .

Noa realized suddenly that she had free time, and she knew just want she wanted to do. Something had been nagging her, an almost-memory of her childhood book of myths and fairy tales buried somewhere in her closet. There was a picture in it she couldn't quite remember clearly—but she thought it showed something like the phantom light from the hallway.

"Aunt Sarah, if you don't need me . . ."

Aunt Sarah turned in surprise, dark brown hair swinging. "Go ahead, kiddo, that's what I'm here for."

• • •

NOA CARRIED THE sleeping Sasha to her old bedroom before risking turning on her closet light. Sasha sensed changes in light like a sunspot bloodhound, and Noa didn't want to wake her. She lifted Sasha carefully, turning her face-against-chest, and softly padded down the hall past Isla's door to Sasha's former room. The girls' rooms were three in a row, one-two-three, with Isla always the center between her sisters.

Noa carefully pulled back Sasha's Thomas the Tank Engine bedspread. For a girl who delighted in flowers and birds, Sasha was equally fascinated by trains and cars and things she called 'machines'—things with motors, things that went fast, things that made noise. She also had a great love for bellowing the Thomas song at the top of her lungs: "'They're two, they're four, they're six, they're eight . . .' whenever she didn't get her way or just felt beasty, which was often. Luckily Sasha hadn't yet insisted they bring the Thomas spread to Noa's room; Noa loved her own down comforter. Beneath it, with Sasha's hot hummingbird heartbeat beside her, she felt safe.

Noa returned to her room, passing Isla's ever-closed door, and flicked on the light. She was hardly ever there with the light on anymore—she left and returned in darkness. She opened the closet. Her messenger bag dropped from her shoulder.

Something was very wrong.

Usually Noa's closet was in a state of organized chaos: a collection of haphazard heaps to any outside observer, but to Noa, a landscape she controlled and understood. But now it was not that way. Now her closet was very, very neat.

Not just neat, but *Neat*. Oppressively, obsessively neat, the kind of Neat that is clearly about something else.

Noa knew in an instant this was not the handiwork of Rosalinda. She and Rosie had an unspoken agreement—if Noa could navigate it, and it wasn't in plain sight, then she could keep her mess how she wanted. No, this organization felt desperate and searching and subtextual. Noa couldn't have located her Harlow blazer without checking every drawer, and she was terrified, in an existential way, of what she might find. The room was heavy with feelings and coping and the overwhelming sense of being invaded.

Noa backed slowly out of the closet. *Mom.*

Aunt Sarah had indeed mistranslated Rosie's Spanish; Hannah had cleaned *her daughter's* closet, not her own. And then Noa understood the real reason her heart was plummeting: It wasn't her mother's presence in *this* closet—that was annoying, yes, but Noa could look and find what she needed, and in some ways, things would be easier to see. It was the implication of *where else* her mother had probably gone.

Isla's room. Isla's closet.

That black hole her teen daughter had never let her enter. The room inside the room, which had stood frozen, untouched, a shrine in Isla's death. The place of Noa's secret journals. And Noa knew—Hannah had gone through Noa's closet to get the courage to face Isla's.

Noa sprinted to Isla's room, flung open that middle door. The room itself was the same, untouched, but she flew to the closet—and fell to her knees. Everything had been wiped out. Everything. Her stories, her poems, her *words*—

Noa tore from Isla's room to the kitchen in panic. "Aunt Sarah, did mom give stuff away today? Or call the trash for a special pickup?" Normal trash wasn't for three days, but that didn't mean her mother hadn't decided she needed to erase everything *now*.

"Nope. Rosie told me to schedule an extra-large pickup though, since you haven't had a cleanup in a while—"

"Don't!"

"Noa-belle, it's just trash . . ."

"Just . . . don't! Please!" Noa turned and raced back up the stairs.

"Noa, let her rest!" Aunt Sarah called after her, but Noa didn't stop. When she got to her mother's door, she paused outside on the landing, panting, and listened.

At first she heard nothing. Then, almost too faint to hear, a tiny sob. Her heart squeezed. Noa's fingers tightened on the knob, and she forced herself to push it open, bracing herself for her mother buried under covers and dirty sheets.

It took a moment to process that Hannah wasn't in bed at all. She was in her reading chair—the hand-carved wooden rocker given to her by Christopher on their first anniversary. Her favorite chair, the one whose foot had been chewed by a stray dog they'd once let spend the night. Hannah had named the dog Cookie; Cookie had run away the next morning.

Noa's mom hadn't sat in that rocking chair since Isla. But now she sat, rocking in Cookie's chair, in clean clothes.

Reading.

Hannah was poring, teary-eyed, over one of Noa's journals. Noa's other journals were stacked neatly beneath her mother's right arm, the way she always stacked her favorite reading.

Hannah didn't greet Noa. Instead, she started to read aloud:

I have been here before, in this sandpaper place.
I have touched the walls.
With my palms facing out, I've felt the rag of the stones,
I've breathed in the glass in the air.

Noa remembered writing that poem. That poem had pushed its way up her esophagus, hot and tangy like bile. Something rough and coarse, scratched out by ragged fingernails.

Something in Hannah's posture as she held the journal, something in the timbre of her voice as she read aloud, told Noa that her mom, too, knew the Sandpaper Place—and not just because of Isla's death. Noa suddenly felt a seed hope. Was this her mother, *seeing* Noa? Touching her, learning her by the texture of her words? Her hope grew: Would they, could they peel away every skin, every pretense between them, meet raw and learn by feel?

"When?" her mom asked, fingers resting lightly on the page open before her. Tears made her eyes clear like glass.

"I'm not sure when that poem was written, exactly," Noa whispered. It didn't matter, did it? What mattered was *this* time, *this* place. This moment, that could be a new North Star between them, blowing a new galaxy past this fog of loss and coping. Spiral or Elliptical or Centaurus, or a whole new shape and dimension. . . .

Hannah's hands darted to brush back her hair. Dragonfly hands—rapid, fragile—the hands of her Mother the Writer, not Hannah the Moon.

"Noa," she said, leaning back and looking up. "I had no idea that Isla wrote."

Noa froze.

"God, I would have loved to meet her through her language. I always feared I didn't know Isla's spirit, but we were kindred, though she was far more poetic than I. . . ." A single tear rolled down Hannah's cheek, a tear of awe and pride and love—and, most painfully, most tragically, of *relief.*

Noa felt her legs stumble backward until her back hit the wall. She braced herself, every cell in her body telling her to scream, *They're mine! They're mine, not hers! Noa* was the one, *Noa* was the kindred soul, *Noa Noa Noa, who was still here!* But Noa couldn't, of course she couldn't. The relief on Hannah's face, precious but devastatingly mistaken—Noa hadn't seen peace on Hannah's face since the day that Isla died. Noa suddenly realized that her mother's most profound grief was not for the death itself, but for all the things about Isla she feared she didn't know and never could. Isla had died a temperamental teenager, a stranger to her parents. Now Hannah had a touchstone to know her unknowable daughter. Now there was a secret Isla, a *true* Isla, a girl Hannah wished, hoped, *needed* Isla to have been: writer, poet, someone not so different from her mother after all. The loss of this Isla was still a tragedy—but bearable now because it could be known and mapped, given boundaries and outlines. No longer an unfurling of all the things she'd never know to understand.

Noa couldn't take that away. No matter what it might mean, what she'd have to keep secret, or give up.

"She was secretive," Noa agreed quietly.

"A poet," Hannah repeated. She turned to look out the window, at the evening slowly glimmering outside.

As she cried, she smiled.

• • •

"SO PETER PAN, EVERYONE!" Ansley beamed from the front of Hearth Hall C the next afternoon, where the juniors had gathered to plan their float. Among them was a reluctant Noa, feeling especially put upon given what had happened with her mother the previous night. At least the setting fit her mood: Hearth Hall's auditoriums had been added to Harlow in the '80s and were dark and concrete, with small windows and bad ventilation.

"First things, first: costumes!" Ansley turned to Leticia with a happy squeal. Noa was surprised to see shy Carly Ann up front too, but guessed her overbearing mother, who ran the parents' board, was behind that.

"Well hey there, socially functional teen," Callum greeted her, sliding into the seat beside her. Even in the poor lighting, his brown curls seemed to shiver. Noa's heart jumped despite herself.

Leticia's voice saved her from having to think of a clever reply. "Girls will be mermaids and fairies!" Wolf whistles erupted, a chorus of hooting, but Noa wasn't listening. Callum was right next to her, and her skin was tingling again. She wished she'd had time to find her mythology book the previous night. Not that any of it was actually real or anything, but then, neither were ghosts. . . .

"I'm sorry about the other day," Callum whispered. "Sure you're OK?"

"I'm *fine*," Noa whispered back, a little annoyed. It took more than a slip and fall to hurt her. *Like letting my mom think my poems are Isla's.*

"You're mad at me."

Noa turned to him, irritated now. "Seriously? It has nothing to do with you."

Callum's mouth set coolly, unconvinced. She didn't explain further. If he could be inscrutable, so could she.

They sat in tense silence as Carly Ann began projecting sketches for the ridiculously gauzy and shimmery (and yet still somehow skanky) fairy costumes for the junior girls. Designed by Ansley, Noa guessed.

Callum sighed, clenching and unclenching his fingers. Noa rolled her eyes but decided to put him out of his misery. "It has to do with my mom, not you. She found my poems and . . . it didn't quite go as planned. OK?" She faced forward to avoid his gaze. "I cannot believe I'm gonna have to wear that."

"Those? I think they're OK," Callum said, with the faintest hint of teasing.

"They're supposed to be fairies!"

Callum's eyes danced, like he was laughing inside. "Looks pretty Tinkerbell to me."

"Come *on*, I know you know literature. Fairies, real fairies are tricksters, like Ariel or Puck, Shakespeare's fae."

Now Callum laughed out loud, shook his head. "*Real* fairies?"

Noa tried to look mad. "I just mean that fae are *creatures*. Earthy and . . . filthy."

Callum pressed his lips together, evidently trying hard not to keep laughing. He couldn't do it, and the words burst out of him: "Go out with me."

"What?" Noa stuttered, shocked. "I mean, no—"

"Come on. Not at school. In the world."

Noa bit her lip. Her answer had to be no. Weird things happened around him—either real or in her mind, which might even be worse. And he was strange and weirdly overprotective and impossible to read. Yes, he was attractive but also infuriating, and she had enough going on at home—

"Saturday," she said.

• • •

ON SATURDAY, NOA stood in front of the mirror in Olivia's room, straightening the black motorcycle jacket she was wearing over her favorite knit blue dress. Her blond hair was loose, and she wore a very long silver necklace with a cluster of charms at the end. She'd meant to do something more interesting with her look, since she so rarely got to wear anything other than her uniform, but that morning Sasha had thrown herself after Noa—limbs grasped tightly, hot hummingbird heart thrumming wildly—and only blessed Aunt Sarah was able to peel her from Noa's body. Their father had looked panicked at Noa's weekend departure, but Noa finally zoomed away in her cab anyway, seeing Isla's face in the window. *Get away*, Isla seemed to tell her. *Get as far away as you can.*

"Got any lip gloss?" Noa asked Olivia. Visitation regulations meant Callum couldn't come into the girls' dorm, so they'd planned to meet outside.

"As if you need it," Olivia scoffed, but opened her makeup drawer. "Mi makeup es su makeup."

"Perfect," Noa said, pulling out a very shiny wand with only a hint of rose.

"I can't wait for you to discover your love for fried food so I can see that peaches-'n-cream complexion just go poof!"

"You say the sweetest things," Noa cooed, puckering up.

Olivia took Noa's chin in her hand. "I expect an unedited report on today's proceedings. *Unedited.* I'm not Miles."

"If you're trying to live vicariously through me, it'll be a boring trip."

"Who says I need to live through you?"

Noa dropped the gloss immediately. "Excuse you! Is there a boy?"

Olivia actually blushed. "Jeremy Robsen."

Noa's mouth fell open in surprise. "Jeremy? Robsen?"

"He asked me to the Alumni Ball!"

"What did you say?" Noa demanded.

Olivia shrugged. "I said I'd think it over, but I'm gonna say 'No.'"

"Why, Livi?" Noa asked, crushed.

"Because it's *Jeremy Robsen*, I don't have the patience to handle that for a night. Not to mention," Olivia continued, "there's absolutely no way on God's green earth I could do that to Miles. He may not love me like he loves you, but he can't lose both of us to boyfriends in the same week."

"Callum's *not* my boyfriend."

"Not *yet*."

"You don't get it—"

An urgent knock sent Olivia bounding to the door.

"How did you get up here?"

Noa looked up: Callum was in the foyer, partially supporting himself with one hand on the frame. For once he wasn't his golden, shimmery self—he looked somehow dimmer, exhausted, his hair tangled. And he was frowning.

Olivia eyed him suspiciously. "The outside doors are locked until visitation and there are like, forty Monitor Nazis roaming—"

"They were unlocked, and I didn't run into anyone," Callum replied curtly. "I need to talk to Noa."

Olivia looked affronted but retreated to her bedroom, sending Noa a look as she walked by.

"I can't take you out today," Callum said shortly, not entering.

"Great," Noa said, irritated. "Because it was so easy for me to get here for you to blow me off."

"You're not understanding," Callum said more forcefully. "I'm not blowing you off, I'm . . ." Exasperated, he ran his hand through his curls. Noa could see why they were tangled.

"And?" she prompted.

"I'm not good for you!" Callum cried. "Remember in the hall when I hurt you?"

"This *again*? Nothing happened!"

"And we need to stop now, before something does. You've been through too much already. The other day you were so upset—"

"What, about my mom? God, ego-boy, that had nothing to do with you."

"You don't get it and I can't explain it right—"

Noa watched panic cross his face, and she almost felt sympathy. Almost.

"Fine," she said, cool. "You're too scared to start something, can't make up your mind? At least own it, Callum. Don't make up reasons—"

"I'm not—"

"I wasn't finished!"

Callum shut his mouth, surprised.

"And don't you dare put this on me. Fragile little Noa? You think you can hurt me?" Noa laughed bitterly. "Do you *know* what I've survived? You're Band-Aid level, Callum, at most." In some distant part of her brain, she saw other girls peek out of their rooms, knew this scene would spread like wildfire. She softened her voice to an angry whisper: "Or feel bad about this." She yanked a folded paper from her pocket and thrust it at him. "I brought this for you. Wrote it for you, actually. I've never done that before."

He hesitated, then took the poem.

Noa stepped backward into Olivia's room. "If you want to read it, come in and read it."

Callum came in quietly, sat on Olivia's futon, then read the words she knew by heart:

Cool is seeping, lightning sleeping,
dry-bone spindle, cactus eye;
nothing burns—until he turns, and sees
the tree that climbs the sky.

"My tree," he murmured.

"No, what you showed me."

Callum closed his eyes. When he opened them again, his face looked far away. "I'm sorry, Noa. I've been through . . . some things, too. Not Band-Aid things either."

"You've got issues," she said succinctly.

Callum smiled sadly. His eyes went back to the poem, sheepish. "Can I still take you out?"

"No," Noa said. His eyes creased in disappointment. "*But*," she added, pausing to let him squirm. "I'll take *you* out. Get ready for Noa-in-Charge."

From Olivia's bedroom came a muffled laugh, and a little whoop.

• • •

"QUITE THE FAIRY-TALE chariot," Callum teased Noa as the city bus jolted over a pothole. They were standing, holding onto handles, trying not to fall.

"Well *someone* didn't give me a ton of notice to meticulously plan this little affair," Noa reminded him. "And aren't you the one who thinks I'm crazy for believing in fairy tales? Oh, this is us." She hopped down the stairs at the stop, Callum following quickly behind her. Immediately they were surrounded by salt air, the sound of gulls.

"Wait, is this . . . Are we on Cannery Row?" Callum asked. He turned to take in the coastline, dotted with built-in-the-ocean hotels and one-time canning factories, now restaurants and shops. A long, winding pedestrian path hugged the ocean—embroidered with kelp beds, sequins of otters and seals—from piers to bluffs.

"I know it seems lame and touristy—" Noa began.

"Are you kidding? I love Steinbeck. He always wrote about this place. You too?" Callum's eyes were bright.

"Actually no," she laughed. "He was Isla's favorite author though . . ." she trailed off. She'd said it again, *Isla*.

"So what are we doing here, Noa-in-Charge?"

"Right now, *walking*," Noa teased. They were at the mouth of the coastline path. Callum let her lead the way. "You showed me your outside place. This is mine. I used to come here with my mom and Isla," she swallowed again. "When we were kids. *And* it's easy to get here from Harlow on short notice." She eyed Callum pointedly as a bicycle zoomed past.

"You came here before Harlow?"

"Long before, when we lived in San Fran. We didn't actually move to Salinas until Isla decided to go to Harlow. I was convinced she'd see the ocean from her window and swim with otters. I was a little . . . otter-obsessed, I won't lie. Kind of like Sasha now with trains. I guess obsession's genetic."

Callum smiled. "I like when you talk about her. You kind of . . . light up."

"I know I'm biased but she's so . . . *Sasha*," Noa said. "I look at her sometimes and I feel like I did with Isla. Like, how can this vibrant little being possibly share my boring blood?" Callum looked uncomfortable and Noa blushed. "Sorry, I hate self-deprecation, too."

"You were saying? About visiting here?"

Noa nodded, grateful to steer past the awkward moment. "I used to drag my mom and Isla to the aquarium. Isla thought otters were boring so she stopped coming—and then it was just me and my mom. And then the trips became as much about that as anything. The two of us. Our little rituals. Like we always ordered room-service omelets and tossed the potatoes over the ocean for gulls. They'd swoop in!" Noa moved her arm like the diving birds, circling Callum. Callum laughed as she twirled. She hadn't thought about these memories in a long time. He was surprisingly easy to talk to. Noa suddenly realized *that* was why he felt so unsettling—like Isla's ghost, he felt *kindred*, someone to confide in. Noa was so used to hiding, tiptoeing over and around land mines and memories. . . .

Noa continued: "We'd take this walk along the water, and I'd try to spot the otters out in the kelp. If there were more sun today, I could show you."

"Here's the sun now." Callum pointed up. Noa looked— suddenly the sun *was* peeking through where there hadn't been a glimmer before.

"I don't mind if it stays gray. It's actually what I remember. The overcast—and my mom, smiling." Noa shivered, looked away.

"Can I make one suggestion? Why walk"—Callum pointed to a two-person surrey bicycle zooming past—"when we can ride?"

• • •

"THIS IS WAY harder than it looks," Noa panted as she and Callum pedaled their red-and-white striped surrey up the small coastline hills. "They probably gave us the super-strongman version because of you!"

"We're doing OK," Callum protested. "Look, now we can coast." Noa leaned back as the surrey started to glide. She peeked sideways: Callum's hair was wind-tousled, his cheeks pink. Since the surrey required them both to steer, their hands were only inches from each other. If he slid his fingers over, would she see the light spiral again? Or had it simply been a trick of her mind before, trying to show her he was worth a chance?

Callum lifted his hand—but only to run it back through his hair.

"You look right like this," he told her.

Noa smiled. "Taking a load off?"

"Near the ocean."

"Yeah. Without it, I think I fade."

Callum lazily kept the surrey on track. "I feel the same way about being outside. I'm glad Harlow has such extensive grounds, or boarding would've been hard."

"Commuting is not what it's cracked up to be, believe me." Noa instantly regretted souring the moment, but Callum was attentive.

"Is it very hard, leaving and coming back?"

"It's like . . . being nowhere."

Something in his face told her he understood.

Callum steered off into one of the scenic overlooks. "Break?

My idea was very good on paper . . ." They both started laughing.

"Ironmen, we're not," Noa agreed.

He looked out at the water. "Now I'm going to spot me some otters."

"It's harder than you think," Noa warned. "My mom finally bought binoculars to keep up."

"Are you challenging me, Ms. Sullivan? Questioning my otter-spotting aptitude?" Callum searched the horizon and then pointed triumphantly. "There!"

Noa leaned over. "Seal."

"No, I think it's an—"

"It's a seal."

Callum furrowed his brow and redoubled his effort. "There!"

"Rock."

"Well, what about—"

"Next to it? Bird."

"Maybe all the otters are sleeping?"

"They sleep wrapped in kelp. You can still see them. Look . . . see there?" She pointed to a small kelp bed.

Callum squinted—then smiled. "Not fair."

"My magic power: otter-spot!"

Suddenly, Callum's eyes were locked on hers, the space between them shrinking. Noa felt her heart flutter—and panicked. She turned to the ocean.

"All we've done is talk about me. What about you?"

Callum's face tightened. "What do you want to know?"

"I don't know. Any brothers and sisters?"

Callum frowned. "A brother and a sister. Both younger."

"Will they come to Harlow, too?"

"No, they won't come to Harlow." Callum answered, pausing. "My little brother Judah, he's kind of a troublemaker. Hangs with the wrong crowd, always getting in trouble with our father. He played a prank that went wrong. I took the blame for him, that's why Harlow. 'Shipped off to boarding school,' I guess."

"You took the blame? Why?"

"Judah . . . isn't like me." Callum's eyes were sad but his voice was hard. "He's not ready yet to be on his own. He wouldn't have fared well here. But I can take care of myself."

"What was the prank?"

Callum's face creased.

"You don't have to tell me."

"It doesn't matter. But someone got hurt, and a lot of damage was done." He took a deep breath, looked out over the water. When he turned back to her, a teasing smile was on his lips.

"I have an idea how we can really spot some otters. Maybe level the playing field a bit."

Noa eyed him. "Your last idea was this surrey. I tremble to ask."

He paused dramatically. "*Kayak*."

• • •

NOA AND CALLUM paddled through the choppy water, dodging spray, Noa seated in front. As Callum had predicted, his eyes were just as sharp as hers in the ocean, but Noa didn't mind—she *was* Sea Girl now, on the waves, in the kelp, surrounded by salt and the vibrant alive.

"These two are my favorite," Callum said, as they tried to balance over waves near a mother with a pup. "Or no, wait, Old Muchacho with the sea anemone."

Noa laughed. "I wish I could take pictures for my mom . . ."
Hannah, Moon Mother, palely poring over 'Isla's' poems . . . Noa's
stomach tightened.

"Don't make any sudden movements, Noa," Callum said seriously behind her.

Noa didn't turn her head. "Are we being held up by a monk seal?"

"Not quite," Callum said carefully. Noa turned, ever so
slowly: An otter was swimming a foot from their kayak.

"Where did he come from?"

"I'm not sure, but he's fond of us."

"Fond of you, maybe," Noa whispered, as the otter zeroed in
on Callum like a magnet. He climbed up the kayak with furry
paws, slipped and slid across.

"Is this happening?" Noa cried, the kayak rocking up and
down and side to side. Callum grinned as they tried to counter the otter's new weight and the tides. The otter stood between
them for a moment, then bowled toward Callum.

"No, no!" But it was too late, the otter tipped the kayak up
and sideways, dumping Noa into the swirling bay. She came up
sputtering and laughing, grabbing the side of the boat to fight the
currents. Callum was panicked.

"Are you OK—"

"Are you kidding?" She grinned.

"Let's swim this in. If you try to climb in where you can't
stand, we'll capsize." He quickly stood and leapt smoothly into
the water. Luckily the rough water calmed, just as he dove in.

Luckily.

The kayak instructor frantically waved, and Noa laughed
bubbles into the water. She turned her stroke to breathe and saw

him, the double—Callum, standing at the point, watching her swim. Except Callum was right beside her. She pulled up, looked again.

Callum stopped, too. "You OK?"

"I thought—I could have sworn . . . *you* were on the point just now," she said, treading water.

Callum looked. "I don't see anyone."

"I swear—the profile was just the same! And I don't know how else to describe it—he *felt* like you." The point was empty now. She looked questioningly at Callum, back at the point. Had she imagined it?

Before she could say anything else, Callum laughed uneasily, cutting her off: "Race you to shore!"

• • •

"OTTERS AND KIDS love you, huh," Noa observed later, as they wrapped their bay-soaked selves in ridiculously expensive souvenir towels on Fisherman's Wharf.

"Kids?"

"My sister's class piled on you like kittens."

"I guess I didn't notice." Callum ruffled the Monterey, USA towel through his dripping hair. "Are you warm enough? I bought a blanket, too." They sat on a bench overlooking the marina, and he wrapped the large souvenir blanket around Noa's shoulders, rubbing it rapidly up and down. Noa's heart pounded—they were touching through the blanket. She didn't see spiraling light, but her blood rushed all the same.

Callum let his hands still but didn't take them from the blanket. His eyes, amber in the evening, met hers. "Better?" he murmured. She nodded, not trusting herself to speak. *This* was the moment, and she wouldn't turn away—

But he did. He jumped up, busied himself with the trays they'd carried over. His cheeks were red as he handed her one and kept one for himself: Each held an assortment of small cups.

"So how do we do this, then?" he asked, indicating the trays.

Noa screwed up her face in the semblance of profound thought, covering her disappointment. "This is very serious business, Mr. Forsythe. These cups represent the chowders of every clam-chowder-in-a-bread-bowl vendor on this pier, *all* of whom claim to serve the best-tasting chowder in Monterey. It is our duty—"

"Our *sacred* duty."

"Our sacred duty, to decide the victor. Begin!"

They clinked Styrofoam cups and took their first sips. The samples were hot and thick and gooey—perfect for people soaked from the bay.

"Number four's a contender," Callum said seriously, mid-slurp.

"Oooh, not number two," Noa cringed.

"Three is meh."

"I'm not impressed by four at all, Forsythe. You're clearly not a connoisseur."

"Oh yikes, definitely not two!" Callum spluttered.

"I told you! I know chowder!"

They finally came to agree on number one. Callum sat back, sighing in happy satiation.

"Tapped out? Before the dessert round?" Noa teased.

Callum looked up, confused. "I didn't get dessert."

Noa produced a cellophane bag from under her towel. "But I did. Saltwater taffy. The one thing Isla used to absolutely love."

Isla's name slipped out easily now. "She invented a game where she'd give me a piece, and I'd have to guess the flavor from the taste. There's a list in the bag that tells you, and I am absolutely horrible at guessing. Or she totally cheated, which would not be surprising."

"I am *all for* a game that you are horrible at, Ms. Otter-Spot," Callum said, taking the bag. He unwrapped a candy, and she closed her eyes and opened her mouth, trying not to blush. He popped it in. Then she did the same for him.

"Banana," Callum said instantly.

"Wait, how did you do that so quickly?" Noa demanded.

"I have excellent taste buds, no matter what *some* people might say about my chowder judgment."

Noa sucked on her taffy, determined.

"Um . . . cotton candy?"

Callum laughed. "You *are* terrible! Mandarin orange. What kind of a guess is 'cotton candy'? That's just sugar. They all taste like sugar!"

"I know, they all taste the same to me." Noa lamented. "Pick me another."

Callum did, and as he popped it in her mouth an involuntary shiver went through her.

Callum's face clouded instantly. "You're freezing—"

"I'm fine, I swear."

"We should go. It's late—"

"I'm *fine*—"

"Your lips. Are blue."

Noa bit her bottom lip. *He's looking at my mouth.* They definitely couldn't leave now. "You can go, but I'm staying."

Callum looked torn. "Then . . . at least let me try this trick Judah taught me. For warming up after . . . sneaking into our neighbors' pool."

"Judah who's responsible for pulling some prank and sending you to me? Definitely," Noa grinned. Callum walked around the bench and put his hands on the blanket on her shoulders again, this time standing behind her.

"Close your eyes."

She hesitated.

"Come on, Noa."

She sighed and did as he asked.

"Now," he continued, hands pressing against her arms, "think of something really warm—a furnace, a fire, lying in the sun . . ." His voice trailed off as she pictured those things, and amazingly, she *did* feel warmer, all the way out to her fingers and toes.

She spun. "How'd you do that?"

Callum dropped his hands and came back around to sit. "You did it. The power of the mind."

"*Callum.*"

"Keep that blanket on."

Noa wasn't going to let it go, but then she realized he was holding her hand through the blanket. The world around them brightened as the last embers of sun hit waves, turning the water orange and green then blue to gray.

"Isla called this 'magic hour,'" Noa said softly. "Do you miss Judah and your sister?"

Callum's hand tensed, but then his body seemed to sigh. "My sister died in a fire. It was the accident caused by Judah's prank. Fireworks."

Noa was thankful to be sitting down, and in the dark. Callum slipped his hand from hers, ran it through his hair.

"I didn't want to tell you, with what you've. . . . You're already the girl with the dead sister."

"Callum, no, I'm glad you did. I just, I hope I didn't—I'd hate to think I forced you."

"That's the real reason I go to little kids' class. Lily was around their age. I go . . . when I miss her."

Noa wanted to hug Callum, tell him she understood. She wanted to thank him for trusting her. But she didn't. It would've been wrong—about her, not about him.

So she returned the gift instead.

"Isla died because of me," she said, proud her voice was steady. She had never said it, not out loud. No one had said it; it had never been given words. Callum was still, but she knew his every cell was listening. "It was last Christmas break," Noa continued. "We always go to Maine, rent the same vacation cottage. It gets really snowy and Christmassy. The weekend before Christmas, our parents had some dinner scheduled. But it sounded boring and Isla wanted to stay and make mac and cheese and got into a big fight with my mom about it. She stormed out, and finally my parents had to leave, telling me to stay and wait for her. We lived together at Harlow; it wasn't a big deal for us to be left alone.

"I found her in her favorite tree after our parents drove off. I'd been upset all break because I didn't get tapped by the Beautiful Little Fools, even though Isla was a member. I told Isla that it wasn't fair my life wasn't as exciting as hers. I was never invited to sneak out to Harlow parties, I never had a million boyfriends. I was worried about stupid things.

"Isla told me if I wanted to be like her, I had to start then and there. There was supposedly some altar in the woods used by Druids or witches or something equally ridiculous, and Isla wanted to find it. Right then, that night, while our parents were away. I was scared, but I went with her. But when we got to the 'altar,' we found an abandoned old cabin instead. It was the creepiest place, Callum, like it was rotten from the inside out. We went in, and the floor collapsed.

"I got buried in rubble, trapped, and was really lucky I didn't break every bone in my body. Isla was able to brush herself off and get right up with a smile. She used the last of her cellphone battery to call an ambulance and fire truck, and when they came, she refused to let them treat her until the firemen had freed me. 'That's my sister, I won't leave her.' She wouldn't let anyone touch her because it would take a hand away from my rescue, and screamed if they tried.

"It took a couple of hours, but finally they freed me, and took us to the hospital. By some weird miracle, I ended up with only scratches and bad bruises. Isla collapsed in the foyer to the emergency room. She'd been bleeding internally the entire time—her whole abdomen was rigid with blood—because she'd waited for them to help me first. The doctors rushed her to surgery but it was too late. She never came out. She was there, and then she was dead. And then she was gone."

They were both quiet for a moment. Noa was grateful Callum didn't say, *It wasn't your fault.* This was her truth, and he understood that.

"Sometimes I think I see her," she added softly, surprising herself. "Her ghost or her face. I know it's my imagination . . ."

"Just because you can't explain it, it doesn't mean it doesn't exist," Callum replied, just as soft. "It's you, isn't it. The 'nomad girl' from your 'Lost Girls' poem? I'd assumed you were writing about Isla: 'firelight and fox's kill, blood and sweat and scratch.' But it's you, fighting."

"It's both of us, actually. Well, all three of us: Isla and Sasha and me. We're almost like . . . girl-beasts."

Callum reached over and took Noa's hand through the blanket again. Noa felt warmth rush again through her body from the place they almost-touched. They sat quietly, and it started to rain. Noa lifted her face to the sky and closed her eyes, letting the cool drops kiss her skin.

It was like a baptism, like everything made new.

• • •

"SURE YOU DON'T want to borrow dry clothes from Olivia?" Callum asked as they stood by the waiting cab in front of Harlow.

"Your mind-over-matter mojo is still keeping me toasty." It wasn't exactly true; Noa was shivering. Callum started rubbing her arms through the blanket again, clearly unconvinced.

Her eyes locked on his. This was their last chance. After all they'd confided, neither of them should feel scared. Callum looked into her eyes intently. But instead of leaning in to kiss her, he raised his hand, very slowly and deliberately, and placed it skin-to-skin against her cheek.

Fire bloomed through her veins, his fingers white-hot stars. She didn't see sparks but *felt* them, electric novas of connection. She closed her eyes, savoring the touch, but when she opened them again, his face was strained, pained even, jaw set tight. She searched his eyes, but he hastily dropped his hand and stepped back from her.

"Thank you for today," he said, somehow out of breath, turning his face down.

"Callum?" she asked, confused.

"It's late."

Uncertainly, Noa slid into the cab and closed the door.

Callum seemed to fight with himself on the curb. At the last moment, he stepped quickly to the window and pressed his palm against the glass. She pressed her own against the other side—and then the cab drove away.

• • •

WHEN NOA TIPTOED into her room that evening, Sasha was splayed across their bed horizontally, limbs outstretched toward every corner. Noa laughed soundlessly; fitting she'd share her bed tonight with a starfish.

Noa pulled on a pair of her dad's old pajamas—her favorites, so soft from thousands of washes—and carefully grabbed the journal from under her bed. Sasha unconsciously reoriented herself around Noa as she slipped under the covers, clasping her with small, strong fingers, laying the flats of her feet on Noa's thighs. Sasha always did that, maximized their points of touch.

It suddenly hit Noa how awful it would be to lose a sister at Sasha's age, like Callum had. A different kind of awful from losing someone like Isla, who was a person fully formed.

Noa opened her journal and began to write. The poem was for him.

Mermaid Hearts

We're swift in currents.
Down spiny sprays of kelp we dive,
Run hands through leaves to hunt
for snails and sapphires.

In rain we sing
high siren calls
you can only hear beneath the surface.
Aboveground it sounds like keening,
or silence.

Skin is not suited for the tides, and
Anemones collect our wave-shorn scales.
Your hair twists with mine in pulpy tangles
around the clam shells
of our mermaid-hearts.

• • •

"WHAT KIND OF intense things?" Olivia demanded. "Shaving cream," she added, sticking one hand out of the shower curtain.

Noa put the canister in her friend's palm. She was sitting in the girls' bathroom on Olivia's hall during an unexpectedly free first period Monday morning. Precalc had been canceled, and Olivia had decided to use the hour to shave her legs. She'd insisted Noa come because she wanted to hear details about Noa's Saturday with Callum—and because shaving one's legs in the Harlow showers was a lot easier with someone to hand you what you needed when you needed it, so you didn't have to put things down on the gross communal floor.

"I told you, I can't say," Noa said again, smiling at Olivia's persistence. "Man, this reminds me of the perks of commuting. My shower at home has a bench, thank you very much."

"Oh, be quiet about your bench," Olivia said. "And stop trying to distract me! Guys know when they tell a girl something, they are *also* telling that girl's best friend. It's the unwritten law. Otherwise, how will you properly dissect it into infinitesimal bits that cease to have any meaning entirely?"

"Unwritten or not, I'm playing it safe. The important part is he trusted me."

"I'm not sure why you're surprised. Razor."

"I don't know, sometimes it seems like he's fighting with himself about me," Noa said, carefully placing the razor in Olivia's hand and taking back the shaving cream.

"It *was* a little schizo how he tried to cancel on you the day of. I mean, you had to plan that whole date yourself on the fly. But to be fair"—she poked her head thoughtfully through the curtain for a moment—"you were reluctant yourself to give him a chance. Luckily wiser matchmaking minds intervened." When Noa didn't reply, Olivia ripped back the curtain.

"Spill."

"He didn't kiss me." Noa's cheeks burned. "There was a moment in the surrey, but I turned away. But after that, I made sure not to turn away . . . but nothing happened."

Olivia closed the curtain, turned on the shower, washing away the shaving cream.

"Towel." Olivia emerged a moment later, wrapped and

thoughtful. "You probably scared him when you turned away." She took the lotion from Noa and rubbed her legs.

"You think?"

"Totally. If he's sharing unnamed 'intense' things with you, he trusts you. Just be the awesome you he clearly likes and it will happen."

"It's just, I feel like we have this connection. The first time he touched me I swear I saw . . . something, like a spark." Noa bit her lip.

Olivia rolled her eyes. "Your Spidey sense brain does love a metaphor. Voila! Feel!"

Noa sighed but touched Olivia's leg. "Smooth as silk."

Olivia feigned disgust. "Is that a racist comment?"

• • •

AS THE DAY passed and Noa didn't see Callum, she began to worry he was avoiding her.

"Cheer up," Miles greeted her before the extra-help salon, flashing his golden-retriever grin and flipping her a Now and Later. With a flourish, he unveiled two take-out coffees.

"Elixir!" Noa cried in delight.

"Eh, I know a guy," Miles said proudly. It was super strong and black, just how she liked. She took a grateful, savoring sip.

"Don't worry, extra-help actually goes faster than class since there's no way to hide. I'm a pro, remember." He twirled his favorite Swiss Army knife.

Noa took another heavenly sip. "The leadership board has *got* to legalize off-campus coffee runs. Maybe I'll tell Carly Ann."

"She's off the board."

Noa looked up in surprise. "I just saw her at the float meeting."

Miles shook his head. "I forgot how lame you are as a commuter."

"That's me, Out-of-Loop Girl. Spill."

"Apparently she got all depressed, dropped all her activities. A dorm Nazi has to get her out of bed."

Noa's mouth opened in shock. Carly Ann had never been a wide-eyed optimist, but . . . "She seemed excited at the float meeting."

"I guess it all happened just after that. I don't know." He shrugged. "Brain chemicals gone haywire."

Noa thought of her mother's pale cheeks and untouched plates. "Poor Carly Ann."

"But hey, she hasn't left school yet, so that's something. Not like Annabelle," Miles said, dropping another bomb.

Noa nearly choked. "Annabelle left?"

Miles shrugged again. "Avery went to buy a burner cell and found her gone, and when he asked around, she'd been absent for days. He finally reported it, and no one has any idea where she went. They're saying she finally ran away with that townie she'd been hooking up with, but she left all that contraband behind in her room. Didn't take *anything*—"

"Just two so far?" Dr. Chandler interrupted them. "Ah-hah. Still waiting on Callum Forsythe."

Miles immediately tensed. Noa tried not to stare obsessively down the hall.

When Callum appeared moments later and saw Noa, he smiled instantly. Relief poured over her. They all sat in the front row, Noa between the boys.

Callum slipped Noa a salt water taffy. "Might help time pass."

Miles scoffed. "We have coffee."

Callum's face cooled. Miles took a sip of his coffee and spluttered.

"What happened?" Noa asked, handing him a napkin.

"It's ice cold!"

Callum said nothing, but was clearly laughing inside.

"OK, guys," Dr. Chandler said. "Let's start with a little free debate. Think big ideas. Was the Civil War a story of tragedy, or heroism?"

"Well, that's easy," Miles said immediately. "Heroism. It ended slavery."

"It wasn't just about slavery," Noa pointed out. "There were other causes, too."

Miles looked like she'd slapped him. "He said big picture. As a legacy, abolishing slavery is heroic. Seems pretty obvious."

"And yet, I asked you to debate. Hmm," Dr. Chandler said, delighted.

"Abolition wasn't the only legacy, nor in fact, the explicit aim of the war at the time," Callum said. Miles glared at him, but Dr. Chandler was pleased.

"Go on."

"I would agree with Miles that, on the whole, the legacy of abolition is heroic. But it was a *civil* war. A civil war isn't just any war." Callum paused. "It's a war within a family, a nation, sons against sons. It can be justified later with ideals, but in the moment, in the battle—it's the most treacherous violence there is. Family violence. Necessary maybe, but also . . . tragic."

"*Precisely*," beamed Dr. Chandler. Noa felt a wash of sadness, remembering again what Callum had told her about his family, and their tragedy.

"Events are more than dates and places," Dr. Chandler was continuing. "They have real costs and losses, happen to real people. Even the most just, moral war is still a war, and as Mr. Forsythe points out, a particularly devastating one in this case. Macro and micro. OK, Mr. Kessler?"

Miles mumbled something unintelligible.

Dr. Chandler nodded. "OK, moving on . . ."

Noa swallowed hard. Something told her that no matter how much candy or coffee she had, this hour was going to pass very, very slowly.

• • •

NOA TRIED TO catch Miles afterward, but he waved her off, puffed on his inhaler. "Lacrosse," he said unconvincingly as he sped away.

"Should we walk?" Callum asked softly. She turned to him, and for the first time—she'd always been too dazzled by his eyes before—she noticed the tiniest diagonal scar near his left eyelid.

She lifted her hand to touch it. "What's this—"

He recoiled instantly. When he saw her reaction, he tried to explain. "I'm just . . . really sensitive about that scar."

Noa frowned. Another roadblock. Another wall. She'd thought they were past that.

Ms. Jaycee's voice rang down the hall, and Noa heard the patter of Sasha's running feet. She turned just in time to catch Sasha as she leapt into Noa's arms.

"Home!" Sasha demanded loudly.

"Thanks for watching her," Noa said apologetically to the clearly exhausted counselor. She turned to Callum, wanting to press him about his scar, but he was staring so wistfully at Sasha she couldn't help but let him off the hook.

Sasha threw her arms around Noa, grabbed Noa's hair. "*Home.*" It was time to go.

• • •

NOA WAS SHOCKED when they arrived home to see Hannah beaming in the doorway, arms open wide. "Sasha!"

Sasha hesitated, pulling Noa's hand the way she sometimes did with strangers. Then Hannah seemed to come into focus, and she launched herself at her mother.

"Noa you have to come toast!" Her mom smiled, catching Sasha. "I'm starting a new book!"

The weight of the day suddenly disappeared. "Where will you go?" Noa asked excitedly, immediately seeing her mother against a cornucopia of backdrops: snow-capped peaks, smooth arid deserts, markets filled with spices . . .

"Not a travel book," Hannah said. "A collection of photos of 'Sandpaper Places,' based on your sister's poems. Come on!" She went inside, leaving Noa, stunned, to follow.

"Isn't this great?" Aunt Sarah called from the kitchen. "Noa, have some champys!"

"I'm gonna . . . change first," Noa called back, not wanting Aunt Sarah to see her face.

Sasha squirmed from Hannah's arms and hurled herself after Noa, grabbed Noa's fingers, and squeezed. As Noa gently squeezed back, feeling sick, she made herself a promise:

Never again would she make a present of her silence.

• • •

NOA BARELY SLEPT that night. Her mother's happiness, that old excitement, the ease of her waiting smile for Sasha—these things were water after the longest drought. But for Noa, it was like drinking the ocean, each salty swallow somehow taking, instead of giving.

It wasn't regret. The lie was important—Hannah's tentative rebirth, beyond all else, proved that. It just hurt to swallow it silently. She'd meant the vow she'd made when Sasha had squeezed her fingers—never again. For no one else would she bend like this, be invisible like this, keep quiet like this.

No one.

So when Noa went to Callum's tree the next morning, knowing he would be there, she was resolved, at least in this, to use her voice.

"Callum," Noa began, before he could say anything. "I'm sorry if I made you uncomfortable yesterday, about your scar."

"I overreacted," Callum said softly.

Noa took a step closer to him. She felt him tense.

"Am I crazy, Callum? Sometimes I think I must be losing my mind."

His face was on high alert as she moved closer, his pupils wide and black.

"Am I . . . imagining this? This connection?" she asked, closer still, close enough to hear him breathing.

"You're not imagining it," Callum finally whispered, and she swore she heard his heartbeat. He didn't move closer, but he didn't move away.

She tilted her face upward, locked her eyes on his.

"Then *show me*."

At first, it was just her, kissing him; but then he kissed her back. The tension in his body vanished, replaced by growing urgency; his hands swept to her hair, his fingers lost in its tangles; and his lips, softer and smoother than she even had imagined, met hers with building strength. His lips gave and shaped around her lips, but were also strong, guiding hers where to go. It was a whirlwind, a kaleidoscope madly spinning; she had the sense of seeing his face everywhere—in the leaves of the tree, in the air, in her hands . . . and heat, so much heat, like the spiral was inside her, in every space and cell—

With an enormous crack, a huge tree branch suddenly plummeted between them, making them jump apart. Noa heard herself cry out at their sudden separation; pain shot through her body unlike any she'd ever felt. When Callum's arms, hands, lips, left her, it was like her spine was ripped out backward.

Noa staggered, couldn't seem to find his eyes across the distance.

All Noa knew was she had kissed Callum, and in that kiss, the yoke of her world—of the world entire—changed.

PART II: CALLUM

THE KISS CHANGED EVERYTHING.

Callum could see, feel, hear it all: the spine of the tree, its ridges and grooves, the tiny hairs on the backside of its leaves. The wind's trembled pulse, the moist texture of the air—he was everywhere and everything, hummed with every heartbeat. As Noa's mouth met his, he multiplied and came apart, so that he was not only in her arms, but in the trees, on the wind, in every single atom.

It had taken the branch breaking, literally splitting them in two, to make Callum regain his wits enough to pull away. He would have kissed her until she was just a shell. On and on until she had no Light left.

He wouldn't have stopped, couldn't have—and he knew it.

Callum stumbled back, the branch stark and bare between them. Noa's cheeks were pink, her gray eyes bright, still in the moment of her own Light. She looked at him, and her eyes looked like shining silver. Callum wanted to kiss her again, her eyelids, her lips—

But he couldn't. He couldn't touch her—not ever again.

"Callum?" Noa asked, and he heard the first, tiniest hint of doubt creep into her voice. She was sensing now that something had changed. "It's OK, the tree missed me. I'm fine."

He wanted to tear his hair, to scream: *You're not fine! Because of me! I've taken Light!* But he couldn't explain; how would she understand? Even Noa, with her poet's imagination, could not possibly envision a creature as deadly as he:

Fae.

Callum looked like Noa, talked like her, but he was not like her at all—and even less what the stories, those 'fairy tales,' told. He was *creature*, the Banished son of a terrible man, an exile to this world where his magic drained to nothing—unless he stole mortals' Light. *Light*: the essence of their future happiness, their potential joy. He sucked it out and stole it, in order to feel alive.

Callum had tried to stay away from Noa, willed himself not to bleed her Light—and at times, he'd been able to control it. He'd been able to starve his special gifts, to live without Light in a muted, pale existence. Be a husk, a shell, rather than hurt her. And once, once, he'd touched her face, skin to skin, and hadn't taken Light—though the effort had exhausted him. He'd felt her spirit at his fingertips, longed to leap out to meet and drink it. . . .

But the kiss was different. When Noa kissed Callum and her heart opened up, her Light just flowed through him. There was no way to put up a barrier, no way to stop the flood from her open soul to his. And now he saw the world refreshed, the way it had been when he'd first come through the Portal: with all the depth and complexity that only Fae could know.

Flush with Noa's Light, Callum could now manipulate the elements. Draw a rainbow, grow a mighty oak, call forth rain. Small things that wouldn't tax him now, as they had in Monterey when he could barely calm the waters, clear the sky, warm her hands. As Blue Fae, manipulating elements was Callum's gift. Noa's lips had reawakened what it felt like in Aurora, home, where Light never diminished and Fae magic didn't fade. Fae didn't harm the innocent there. Every moment lived and pulsed on its own.

Even as Callum's body relished the sensations, his mind reeled with regret and pain. He was vibrant now because of Noa, because of what she no longer had. His eyes found her face, dazed from kissing, unaware. She didn't know that her future now was bleaker, that the strange alchemy of energy shaping what would come now held less joy. He'd siphoned it into his own vitality. And, worst of all, part of him wanted, hungered, *needed* to do it again.

Callum stumbled backward, held up his hands, tried to force more air between them.

"Noa, no—" he stuttered.

Confusion swept across her face. She'd start to feel it now, the withdrawal, the loss of what he'd taken. Callum tried to ignore his ache to hold her, to tell her all the things in her he loved. Because it wasn't just her Light; *she* herself intoxicated, the strange alchemy of *Noa*: poet, girl-beast, weaving beauty out of pain. That was Light itself, all on its own.

Callum had known he shouldn't reveal things about himself to her, but he'd needed to see Lily and Judah through her artist soul, her artist eyes. Was it any wonder that Noa's Light then, in particular, undid him? It made Callum forget he'd been forced out of Aurora or ever lived without his gifts. But with this kiss, all hope was gone: If he stayed with her now, he'd take it all; she'd become a husk of pain and tears, unable to feel happy, unable to live fully.

"Noa, no—I don't want—" Callum said, struggling to keep his voice from breaking. At least he'd made the branch fall to stop himself. He didn't remember consciously deciding; it must have been some internal reflex, some last flicker of his true desire to protect her.

He had to honor that desire now.

"Don't follow me," Callum said harshly, turning. He prayed she'd be too stunned to follow, knew he'd take her in his arms if she did. He yanked his hands through his curls, the curls that reminded him so much of Judah, and wished his pain could somehow give Noa back her Light. He wished the pain would give him strength to leave forever, and not simply the ability, in this moment, to walk away.

· · ·

STUNNED, NOA WATCHED Callum walk away. She had felt the axis of the world shift when they kissed, and she still felt the ecstasy. Clearly he did not. She fought the urge to run after him.

Instead, she stood frozen, listening to the air with her fingertips, tasting its chill. She had kissed Callum. Callum had left.

She couldn't move.

So she did what she had done after learning about Isla, when her mind couldn't function: She visualized her body as a machine, gave it simple, precise commands. *Step forward. Walk. Open door. Go to class. Keep your face unreadable.*

Survive.

· · ·

AT LEAST I DIDN'T LOOK BACK. It was all Callum could think as he sat in history, looking out the window, ignoring Dr. Chandler's assistant, Pierre, who was filling in. Had he looked back, her face would have haunted him. The way his mother's face, Lorelei's face, haunted him still, from the moment he had told her Lily was dead and he, Callum, was responsible.

Callum closed his eyes on that old pain. *For their own good,* he reminded himself. *For the benefit of those I love.* He'd lied to protect Judah and his family both, from what they could not endure. Now he would lie to protect Noa. It was his gift, wasn't it, as Blue Fae? To manipulate the elements in ways that others couldn't see; to understand secret energies, hidden bonds, what shapes would last. To keep things whole, even if he had to break himself.

Pierre's voice drifted in: ". . . infamous betrayal at Ebenezer Creek. Union soldiers literally burned their bridge behind them . . ." Callum closed his eyes, focused his Fae ears instead on the hum of a fly, rubbing its legs together. He should have known not to come to history. The Civil War reminded him too much of Aurora, Judah, their father . . .

Callum tracked the fly to the window, focused on each tiny hair on its black body—then his vision snapped outside. Behind the fly, through the window, beneath the tree where he'd kissed Noa, he could swear he saw himself standing and looking back. He shook his head to clear his too-clear vision, made so acute by Noa's Light—

"Mr. Forsythe!" Callum turned frontward to the titters of the class. He heard the scrape of Jeremy Robsen's teeth as he whispered to Leticia, the fall of dandruff from Pierre's scalp to the floor. When Pierre raised his eyebrows, Callum heard each brow-hair bend. "Sherman's March?"

Callum looked quickly to the tree: No figure stood there now. His eyes zoomed in, searched each branch, each leaf, each cell of chlorophyll—nothing. He must have been thinking about Judah, while the class discussed betrayal. Callum was as alone as ever since his Banishment through the Portal. The only Fae bad enough to be sent.

Except, Callum realized, *I'm not.*

He got up suddenly. With Noa's Light flowing through him, he was gone before Pierre's breath even passed his lips.

• • •

"KELLS," CALLUM CALLED, hammering on the decrepit shack of Harlow's groundskeeper, 'Mr. Green.' Or as he had been called in Aurora, Kells. There was no answering call, no rustle, but Callum watched the atoms shift as Kells breathed in and out. "I see you, Kells."

Kells exhaled painfully and began the long process of straightening his gnarled limbs. Callum could hear the wheeze in his lungs, the creak in his spine, as he dragged himself toward the door. Instead of opening it, Kells slid a wooden bar across inside.

"*Light*." He glared at Callum through the rotting slats. "The Blue Son's started draining?"

"Kells, I need your help," Callum tried to master his impatience. The shack was splintery and weak beneath his palms.

"Leave."

"Kells—"

"Just part the atoms in that door, Blue Son. *Force* your way in. It's in your blood."

"You could frighten me away," Callum challenged. "Use your gift."

Kells laughed bitterly. "You know as well as I that my Green gift has long since starved."

"I had assumed, but Noa said the students are afraid of you—" Callum's throat constricted on her name. "I thought you must still be shifting their emotions." Green Fae manipulated emotions the way Blue Fae manipulated the elements, and both needed Light to make their gifts work.

Kells finally opened the door, revealing his crumpled, filthy body. "Thanks to your father, I'm scary enough as I am."

Callum looked away. "You were spared. We both were. Our sentences could have been death."

"This is worse than death."

"She tried to save you," Callum protested feebly. He didn't name his mother, Lorelei, because the name would be too much, the hole too deep. The three syllables would remind him of her hair, black hair, so black it was almost blue . . .

"She was too tenderhearted, like most Green Fae. Bending emotion makes us feel things too strongly. Or did. Lorelei thought she was saving me by pleading for my exile. But your father *knew*. Darius knew . . . *Clear Fae*," Kells spat.

"You plotted with the rebellion—"

"Pretext, as you know," Kells snapped. "But I did learn. Otec Darius made me Gatekeeper here, and by his command I cannot help you nor any exile. I will not risk his wrath again."

"Kells, please—you're the only one I can ask. There is a girl,

Noa—" Callum struggled to find the words. "Sometimes I can control myself. At first we touched by accident when she stumbled—I didn't mean to take her Light. She saw the flare, and I denied it. I learned afterward how to restrain it, even touched her face without taking any, but—" Callum swallowed. "Then we kissed—"

"And now you radiate before me." Kells smirked.

"Teach me to live like you. No Light at all. Teach me to suppress it—"

Kells smiled bitterly. "Light follows blood and love and life, Blue Son. I am the Gatekeeper, I have none of those things. I stay here, watch the Portal, live separate and alone. That's my sentence. But you *navigate* this world, you live among them! You may suppress one touch, but your heart, your hunger, will always give you away."

"So there's no way? I'm destined to leech her Light?"

"I cannot help—"

"You hate my father for Banishing you, so defy him—"

"Not I." Kells' eyes blazed. "There are depths to Banishment you could never fathom. I will not jeopardize one punishment for another. Leave, Blue Son, before I send you to the In-Between."

Kells turned, and his gnarled back swam before Callum's eyes. Rage erupted deep within Callum, and he held the atoms of the shack a razor's breath from explosion. He remembered how it felt to use his gift to go to war—

He forced himself to calm. He was not the Blue Son, not anymore.

"Beware loving a woman you cannot touch," Kells added quietly, sadly, back still turned.

Kells couldn't help.

Callum was alone.

• • •

SOMEWHERE IN THIS terrible day, Noa's body-machine stopped obeying. Simple commands failed to keep Callum's rejection at bay. Had she pushed too hard? Had she kissed him wrong? Had—

She shook her head. She was an actress, playing Normal Happy Girl. In this scene, Normal Girl picks up Little Sister and takes her to the shuttle.

"Sasha my love, ready to go home?" Noa asked, bright smile plastered on. Sasha cocked her head, narrowed her eyes, and dropped her fist of pipe cleaners. She charged at Noa, pressed herself into Noa's leg, as if trying to fuse with her sister's skin.

"Sasha!" Noa snapped, half-dragging her from the room. Sasha's eyes flashed, twin red spots blooming on her cheeks.

"Sasha-monster!" Olivia's voice coming down the hall completely changed Sasha's mood. Sasha loved Olivia, especially her hidden tattoos. She liked to trace them, as if to feel the secrets.

"Livi!" she squealed.

Olivia chuckled, pulled a ringlet. "Glad you got your priorities straight."

"Noa's *sad*," Sasha confided.

Noa rolled her eyes, but Olivia didn't buy it.

"Home stuff?"

"No—"

Olivia nodded shrewdly. "Callum."

Noa sighed, knowing she now couldn't leave until she shared.

She quickly whisper-summarized the kiss as Sasha re-strangled her leg.

"You're sure it was . . . good?" Olivia asked carefully.

"I'm not sure of anything!" Noa cried.

Olivia hugged Noa. "Probably just a misunderstanding. We'll figure it out." Noa prepared to drag Sasha away, but in another of her drastic shifts, Sasha trotted amiably out the door.

As Noa left, Miles caught up with Olivia, huge lacrosse bag on his back.

"That Callum asshat did something, didn't he," Miles demanded as they watched Noa disappear.

"Oh stop it," Olivia snapped, but her face said it all. "She's smiled more since he arrived than she has in three months. As her *friend* you need to get on board."

"Well, maybe as her *friend*, O-liv-i-a—" Miles retorted, but cut off as Ms. Jaycee walked by chattering brightly to a gray-faced Carly Ann.

"See?" Olivia whispered, "You want Noa to look like that again? Stop demonizing Callum." She flicked his ear affectionately and continued toward the girls' dorms.

Miles rubbed his ear, frowning.

• • •

CALLUM WATCHED FROM a distance as Sasha leapt into the shuttle, Noa sliding in behind. Noa's hair, so many different blonds, was the last thing to disappear, like a star winking out. Callum shivered: Judah's hair had disappeared that way when Callum was Banished across the Portal, his copper curls the last thing Callum saw.

Callum's heart began to thunder, his temples to sweat, and suddenly he felt convinced that if he didn't keep his eyes on Noa, she, too, would disappear forever.

Noa's Light inside him strong, Callum closed his eyes and splayed his fingers, speaking to the molecules of gravel at his feet like a conductor shaping music. When he opened his eyes, the gleaming motorcycle materialized before him from the tiny stones.

Callum allowed himself a little smile. Being Blue felt good.

• • •

CALLUM HID UNDER the neighbors' trees while Noa reemerged, a beacon, in front of her home. Noa waited, bent back into the shuttle to call Sasha out. After a moment of no response, she straightened and walked away, leaving Sasha inside. Callum smiled. How quickly, how adeptly Noa's mind had adapted to her sister's—they were kindred creatures, sisters, always coevolving. Sure enough, Sasha immediately launched herself after Noa, beating her inside. Noa waved to the driver, hitched her bag, and followed Sasha to the house.

Noa hesitated at the door, and Callum tensed, but then he heard the deadbolt shut.

Callum willed himself to go back to Harlow. Noa hadn't disappeared; it wasn't like Judah and Lorelei and Darius. She was safe, and he should *go*.

But Callum didn't go. He crept into the yard, to the large oak that spanned the broad side of the house, and laid his hands upon it, creating tiny footholds. When he climbed past the first spray of branches, he lifted himself into their canopy of leaves, then tried to glimpse Noa's family through the glass-eyed windows of the house.

· · ·

NOA CLOSED THE door on the shiver, the feeling of being watched. There was no one in the yard.

Inside the house, the air was sticky from steaming pasta, boiling tomatoes.

"Noa," Aunt Sarah whispered excitedly, trotting out from the kitchen. "I need to show you something."

Noa tiptoed after Aunt Sarah upstairs to the sisters' bedrooms in their row. To Noa's shock, she stopped at the middle room, Isla's, and quietly turned the handle: *Look*.

Noa peered around her aunt—her dad was there, *inside Isla's room*, boxing up Isla's things. Not just boxing them, but *touching* them: examining them, remembering, holding them in his hands. There was tenderness in the bend of his finger as he brushed dust from a DVD, delicacy in the pull of tape from a photo. Isla's possessions—touched—were now transforming: from relics to a daughter's warm and messy *stuff*. And her father was tucking them, nesting them together in a box that would be their home. The way they had longed to be packed up, Noa thought, in this atmosphere, with this touch.

Noa's mom was kneeling on the floor, photos spread around like petals. Some were Hannah's own, professional glossies from her adventures, but some were Isla's—amateur snaps of teenaged life, frames crowded with faces and bunny ears and jokes. Noa suspected Hannah was working on some kind of amalgamation for her "Sandpaper Places" book, blending the two worlds together.

As Noa watched, her mother lifted the photo of Noa and Isla, their first day as Harlow roommates, and made it the center of the flower. Her dad knelt beside her mom to add another into the array. Together, they paused to take in the rainbow of images, moments coming full circle around them. His hand—unconsciously, like a reflex—went to rest, lightly, on the small of her mother's back.

That small touch—the naturalness of it, the inevitability of it, the relief in it—undid Noa. Her eyes filled with tears, and she understood why Aunt Sarah had been so quietly pleased. Something fragile was happening, something easily frightened and worthy of protection.

Just as Noa thought this, Noa's door slammed open and Sasha emerged, red-faced and wild-haired. She took one look at Noa and Aunt Sarah, at their careful, timid posture, and scented the need for chaos. She tore past them into the room, hurled herself across the spray of photos right between their parents. Boxes crashed to the floor, treasures spilled on the ground.

"Boom!" Sasha shrieked.

"Sasha! GET OUT!" Noa yelled, slamming her hand against the wall. Everyone—even Sasha—froze. Noa stumbled back, palm throbbing. She turned and fled, not wanting to see her parents' faces.

Aunt Sarah followed her to the kitchen.

"You OK?"

Noa started crying, quietly at first and then so much. She'd grown so used to showing nothing; it all spilled out at once.

Aunt Sarah stroked her hair. "You're allowed to lose your temper once in a while."

Noa wiped her nose on her sleeve, looked up at Aunt Sarah with a quiet desperation.

"Do you . . . ever wish you . . . got married?"

Aunt Sarah laughed at the seeming non sequitur. She paused, leaned forward on her elbows. "You know, it's funny. Usually not. I like my life."

". . . but?"

Her smile became a little sad. "But when I see things like your mom and dad, packing up the pictures of the daughter they've lost—I think, there's something there I don't want to miss."

Noa felt tears tingle, swallowed hard.

Aunt Sarah squeezed Noa's hand. "Whoever he is, Noabelle, he'd be lucky to have you."

• • •

AFTER NOA AND her aunt disappeared from the upstairs room, Callum watched Noa's father quietly calm Sasha. A dizzying wave of homesickness washed over Callum. He waited for it to pass; when it didn't, he did the only thing he could do. Something he hadn't let himself do before because he hadn't wanted to be weak. But now, when he was about to give up Noa . . .

Callum picked several leaves and cupped them in his hands. He spoke to them with his fingertips, told their dew to pool— then shaped the dew into a one-way window to Aurora. It wasn't a Portal—he couldn't travel through it, and no one could detect it from the other side—it was just a way to glimpse.

Callum sweated with the effort—this kind of magic drained Light quickly. He whispered, "My mother," and then there was Lorelei, long black hair whipping in the wind, so black it was almost blue, and her eyes piercing, searching—searching for what? He could not see. The last time he had seen those eyes, they'd been brave and still, watching her Blue Son Banished from her world. Watching silently, not allowed to show tears. Unimaginable, for Green Fae.

"Darius," Callum whispered, and the twists of Lorelei's hair became the hard lines of his father's face, tense and angry, conferring with a general. The war continued then, though which side was winning Callum couldn't tell; his father always looked that way. But there had been pain, even regret, in Darius's eyes the day he'd cast Callum out. Callum swore he'd seen it.

Callum closed his eyes, fatigue washing over him. He whispered the last name, the last face he had to see, the one, he knew, he ached for most.

"Judah." He waited to see his brother's smirk, those wild curls . . . but nothing materialized. Callum slumped back against the branches, exhausted, let the leaves and dew fall from his hands. *Good*, he told himself savagely. The sooner he used up Noa's Light, the sooner he'd rot into an empty shell as he deserved.

Noa entered her room at that moment, as if his thinking her name had conjured her. He watched as she crawled into bed beside Sasha, reached underneath the mattress, pulled out her journal, and began to write.

Callum knew instinctively this was her most natural state. In the same way he felt forces among atoms—attractions and repulsions, tensions and covalences—he sensed Noa's complete integration into herself, and he longed to be inside that circle. He wanted to be a part of her, interwoven with her, next to her and within her the way her Light was now in him. He made the tree branch move him closer.

Suddenly Noa looked up, right out the window into the night. Her eyes fixed on Callum, on his hands magicking the branch.

Callum froze. Did she really see him? She shouldn't be able to in the dark; the light was inside, not outside; she didn't have the sight of Fae. But she was staring right at him, unblinking, and the moment stretched for days.

Her expression didn't change. And then, she simply looked down, started writing again.

Callum immediately leapt to the ground and sprinted from her house, re-formed his motorcycle and leapt aboard.

She hadn't seen him, couldn't have . . .

• • •

NOA KEPT HER eyes down, her hand moving across the page. The words wrote themselves, over and over, but they were not a poem:

What did I see? What did I see? What did I see?

• • •

THE NEXT MORNING, Noa waylaid Callum after class, determined to find a way to make him talk to her again. The abruptness of his silence, the strangeness of their break—it had actually made her *see* things. She needed words, real words, not figments and illusions. Words, she knew, would heal them.

"Callum, wait—"

"Noa, if I wasn't clear, I'm not interested in a relationship with you," Callum said harshly.

Noa stuttered. "I—I wanted to give you—" She swallowed, couldn't look him in the eye. "Look, I wrote something a while back, I need you to read it. After that . . . fine. But you need to hear me—"

"Noa, *stop*—"

"No!" Noa blinked hard, bit her lip. "I feel like I'm losing my mind, seeing things that aren't—just take this." Shaking, she held out the folded poem. "I wrote it the day we went to Monterey."

"No," Callum's voice was strained.

Noa felt like the ground was sinking. "You said you'd always read—"

"*I don't want it,*" he said more forcefully. Other students began to turn; they became navy blurs as tears sprang to Noa's eyes. She blinked them back—and he was gone.

"Noa, are you OK?" It was Ansley, materializing from the blur. Noa blinked rapidly again, sure she was seeing a mirage: Ansley's hair had lost its luster; bags puffed beneath her dulled-out eyes.

"Are *you* OK?"

Ansley smiled wanly. "Just exhausted. Alumni Week, college stuff . . . what's that?"

Noa realized she still had "Mermaid Hearts" clutched in her hand. Anger began to bloom slowly inside her. "Something I need to change."

Without explaining, Noa turned to the lockers, uncapped a pen with her teeth, and rewrote the poem, determined to shove it through every window in the Boys' Annex if she had to in order to make Callum see it. She needed to be heard. She needed closure.

When Noa finished, her anger had cooled, but not her resolution.

She refused to live her life seeing Callum-shaped hallucinations.

• • •

CALLUM HAD NO intention of going to that afternoon's history extra-help salon with Noa and Miles, but Ms. Jaycee ambushed him in the hallway to tell him it had been moved to lunchtime to accommodate Dr. Chandler's assistant, Pierre. And Ms. Jaycee insisted on walking him there to make sure lunch had been delivered.

Noa winced when Callum walked in. Miles took a huge bite of bagel-and-schmear, staring Callum down. He turned to Noa, pointing out the coffee.

Callum sat silently.

"Whoa, Noa stop!"

Callum spun to see Miles grab Noa's cup and hurl it into the trash. Noa was frozen, hand still holding the small bottle of cleaning fluid she had poured into the coffee—the fluid, definitely toxic, used for cleaning ghosted dry-erase ink.

"I must've spaced for a second, someone must have left this near the milk . . ." Noa murmured, dazed.

Miles took the bottle of cleaning fluid and put it in the farthest corner of the room.

Noa began to make a new coffee, more carefully. "It's weird because I usually—"

". . . drink it black," Miles finished, glaring again at Callum. Noa looked at Callum, then looked away.

"I'm just distracted," she mumbled.

Callum studied his hands, cringing inside, as Noa reached for the bagels and the cutting board. He hadn't done magic to cause her mistake, but it seemed he'd caused it anyway.

"The lox is ridiculously good," Miles encouraged her, mouth full, from the desks he'd picked for them across the room.

Noa giggled at his muffled words, and Callum reflexively turned to watch her laugh. That was how he saw her pull the sharp knife deep across her palm.

"Noa!" Callum cried, leaping up. In an instant, he was beside her, his hands cupped around her hand, his mind straining with concentration. His fingers did it rapidly, like lightning: told the skin to knit together, made the atoms blend and move. He healed her, touched her, but took no Light, even as desire for it hammered at him from all sides. It was the hardest thing he'd ever tried, so much harder than touching her face. He pushed every ounce of magic outward, to her wound, and blocked her Light from getting in—

And all in the space of an instant, in the time it took Miles to run to her side.

"It's OK, it wasn't bad," Callum panted, stumbling as Miles reached her. He was completely drained, eviscerated; he wasn't sure he could even stand. He'd left a shallow, superficial cut on Noa's hand; there was a smear of her blood across his palms.

"I was sure you'd cut your hand off!" Miles exclaimed. Noa swayed, bewildered.

"She should sit down, she's woozy." Callum wheezed, bracing back against the wall.

"I got it, Forsythe," Miles snapped, already guiding Noa to a seat.

"Miles," Noa protested. "It was an accident—"

"*Callum's* going to go tell Ms. Jaycee we need to reschedule," Miles said pointedly over his shoulder. For once Callum agreed with Miles: He needed to get out of there.

"Wait," Noa said weakly. She turned to Miles. "In my pocket.

Give it to him." Then, to Callum: "Read it . . . please."

Miles stalked over and thrust the square of paper at him. Callum looked at Noa, cradling her hand, and did not dare to give it back.

• • •

CALLUM STOPPED IN the first shadowed doorway in the hall, knowing there was no way to stop himself from reading her words. The first poem, "Mermaid Hearts," was crossed out, and beneath it, rewritten differently:

Your Mermaid Heart

We're stalled in currents. In irons.
We once dove down sprays of kelp
for snails and sapphires.
Now we're cross-ways to the wind.

Scales are not skin.
They shear in waves and words
—or No Words—
Your hair, like sea pulp, knotted tight
Around the clam shell
of your mermaid heart.

Callum read it once, twice, three times, each word a glimpse into the mind he loved, the mind he was trying so hard to shut away. The words hummed across his back, across his shoulders, spread out and stung his hands and toes, insisting on their connection.

And he *knew*.

His plan would not work. To see her but not be with her. To know her but be cold. His plan to do right, be right, choose right.

Because he had already chosen, long ago. And informed or not, he was sure she'd chosen too.

• • •

"KELLS!" CALLUM DIDN'T wait for 'Mr. Green' to answer, simply dissolved his door.

Kells rose from where he'd been crumpled in a chair. "I cannot help—"

"You're Green, you above all should fight for—"

"Love? Because it's served me so well?"

A whip of anger snapped through Callum. He slammed Kells against the wall, pinned his chest with wide, spread hands—and suddenly, Callum was choking on the broken shards of being he touched inside. His vision blacked; he shuddered back, wrenching his hands free.

Kells smiled. "I told you I had no Light, Blue Son. You just felt what's left when you live *without*. But wasn't that your plan now? What you want to learn from me?"

Callum gasped, still fighting for air.

Kells shook his head. "The world will suffocate your love anyway, believe me. This is the mercy your daddy gave us both." Kells' lip curled. "Drain her dry. Might as well. We both know you've got it in you."

Callum's darkness, which he'd tried to leave behind in Aurora, awakened and uncurled in the snarls of his intestines, rising up and filling out to his very fingertips. His shadow-self, like they'd never been apart—

Shadow-Callum flung Kells against the wall like a ragdoll. He held up his hand—the hand that could heal and hurt in equal measure—and moved his left pinkie the tiniest hair. Kells screamed as his skin ripped itself apart beneath his ears, his eyes, his nose. Shadow-Callum smiled: It all came back so easily, like muscle memory.

Somewhere in Callum's better consciousness, beneath the shadow, a little voice cried out for mercy. But it was small, and faint.

"Your father's son . . ." Kells wheezed.

Callum hesitated, just for a moment. "He's *Clear* Fae. I'm nothing like him." He slammed Kells back again, set his arms and legs on fire. "I know you can help me."

"I can't—I . . . told . . . you—" Kells cried, strangled. Callum bent his other pinkie and the bones in Kells' shoulder splintered.

"That's *not* what you told me. You said *'Not I.'* You said, *'There are depths to Banishment you could never fathom.'* What does that mean?"

"I can't—" Kells gurgled.

"You know how I served my father's armies! I will *make* you tell!"

"There may be a way!" Kells finally cried, words tumbling together. "There is a way, I have heard tell. A legend of great sacrifice. But that's all I know, I swear, you must ask the others—"

Callum released Kells calmly, made his hands quell the fire, mend the bones, made his shadow recede. Kells gasped, shocked at the sudden relief, but Callum knew enough to recognize the sound of truth.

"What others?" he asked. "I was the first with the crime great enough. After you."

Kells' eyes were wary, but his lip still curled when he answered. "You may not know what you think you know."

. . .

MILES TUCKED SASHA and the recovering Noa into the waiting Harlow shuttle, then tapped the roof twice. They pulled away just as Olivia ran out from the hallway. "I heard Noa got hurt, what happened?"

Miles looked tired. "Callum Forsythe, what else? I told you, he's *not* good for her."

Olivia eyed him appraisingly.

"OK, Miles. Talk."

. . .

INSIDE THE SHUTTLE, Sasha burrowed her head into Noa's shoulder, then took Noa's palm in her two small hands and carefully examined the faint red mark. She licked one tiny index finger, ran it all along the line.

"Pretty," she whispered, tracing the scratch. "So pretty."

Noa remembered Callum's hands on the scratch, just like this. She looked out the window, pensive. "So pretty," she echoed.

. . .

CALLUM WAITED UNTIL midnight. Still early for his destination, but he didn't know what he'd find. Kells hadn't known much.

Wearing a dark jacket, Callum took a cab; he couldn't waste what little was left of Noa's Light on a disguise or a bike. Not with what he had in mind. The driver dropped him with a doubtful look in the rearview mirror, then the cab sped away, leaving Callum in front of what looked like a derelict canning warehouse. In daytime, it probably seemed like just another abandoned factory, but at night, it became a pulsing underground club, known for depravity and discretion. Every sense Callum had warned him away.

He went in.

The club was dug underneath the factory. The enormous bouncer took a bored look at Callum's face and waved him through, toward the hidden stairway. As Callum descended, the air grew thick and blurry, easy to feel and hard to see. The floor opened into a dark, rich cave-like basement, where phantoms of men and women—gorgeous, seeming-nude, and strangely menacing—wove through the shadows of dark-clothed patrons. Not simple pleasure dancers, Callum assumed, but promises of something else . . .

Especially *them*.

The boy and girl were in their late teens, laced tight in leather, holding hands. Callum's eyes snapped to the girl immediately, and all of a sudden he *wanted* her. For a moment, he could think of nothing but her long auburn hair, how much he wanted to caress it, what he would give to feel it in his hands . . . when a small voice inside him whispered: *Noa.*

Callum shook himself as from a daze. This auburn-haired girl was Green Fae: manipulating his emotions, playing up his lust. One of the *others* he was looking for.

Callum crossed the room to meet the Pixie, passing a half ring of dark banquettes. She watched him come, face composed to be alluring; she did not know he'd sensed her gift. The boy beside her, however—clearly her twin, equally beautiful but in harder, masculine lines—watched Callum with suspicion.

"Hello, there," the Pixie purred.

"Don't bother, Pearl, he knows what we are," the boy interrupted. His hard eyes raked Callum's face. "And he should go, for what he wants is far more dangerous than we are willing to provide."

Callum frowned. "Ah, Red Fae. Reading my thoughts as she reads my emotions."

"Go," the Red boy repeated, teeth slightly bared.

Callum smiled, equally fierce. "You won't help the son of Otec Darius?"

The boy's eyes flashed, and his sister Pearl gasped. Callum suddenly started wondering if this was a good idea after all, perhaps he *should* go—

"Stop it," Callum warned the boy. "My brother Judah was Red Fae; I know what thought manipulation feels like. I'm not leaving until you help me."

"How do you know I won't just kill you?"

"Because I am the *Blue Son*," Callum said quietly. He didn't need the boy's Red gift to know he understood what that meant. It was clear by the expression on his fiercely handsome face.

Pearl pulled her twin's hand, whispered urgently. The boy slowly nodded, his expression changing.

"My sister points out that having you in our debt may prove useful. And if you die . . . nothing's lost."

Deal, Callum thought, not bothering to speak out loud. He was careful not to think of Noa, though; the boy didn't need to know Callum's reason. The boy tilted his head toward the back bowels of the club, green eyes gleaming. "We'll need a private room."

Callum followed the hand-clasped twins into the darkness, fear beating fast through his veins. It made sense, to be afraid; but he told himself that it was Pearl's gift, and refused to let it stop him.

• • •

ACROSS THE CLUB, Miles and Olivia scrunched down in a banquette, wide-eyed as Callum followed the bondage twins to a private room.

"Believe me now?" Miles whispered. "He's some S&M psycho!" Olivia shifted uneasily in her skanky I'm-twenty-one-I-swear disguise, but didn't contradict him.

Then a scream shattered the air—so loud and sharp it sounded rabid—and unmistakably, twistedly Callum's voice. His scream went on and on, blazed and shook and exploded in a strangled cry of pain.

Miles turned to Olivia, face smug. "S&M psycho. Told ya."

A moment later, the auburn-haired girl sauntered back in from the private room, seemed almost to wink their way.

• • •

NOA DIDN'T WRITE that evening. Instead, she sat, Sasha sleeping heavy and horizontal across her legs, and traced the red line on her palm. It was so small. The slice had been deep, but the moment Callum had cupped his hands around hers, she hadn't felt pain. Only warmth. The way she'd felt on the marina, when Callum had "talked her mind" out of feeling cold—a kind of inward spark . .

. she'd seen a spark, too, the first time they touched. And *felt* it in the ocean, when the sea suddenly calmed, the sun suddenly shone. Then under his tree, the tree that climbed the sky, when her heart had thundered as their faces moved close . . .

Noa couldn't stop remembering, *feeling* and remembering, as if her heart knew something her mind couldn't name.

Her eyes wandered to the window, where she'd once 'seen' Callum perched. Her heart jumped as not he, but Isla's ghost looked back, more real and vivid than she'd ever seemed before. Noa's breath caught; she didn't dare move—it *was* Isla: gray eyes twinkling, blond hair long, Harlow uniform purposefully askew. The most Isla thing of all was her expression—that sly smile that said *I know a secret.*

Isla's lip curled, her eyes flared: *You know it, too.*

"Callum," Noa murmured. The only other person who set her tingling like this. Ghost-Isla smiled. *Go now,* she seemed to say, *in this time between awake and asleep, when anything is possible.*

Noa's mind flew. How many times had Isla sneaked from this house, and how well did Noa know her tricks? Noa could be back before morning.

Noa went to the window, Ghost-Isla's window, and started to climb out, but Isla's eyes flashed urgently.

Noa understood. "Wait for me." Swift as the wind, Noa flew down to the kitchen, took what she needed, tucked it into her sweatshirt pocket, and hurried back up the stairs. While Sasha snored throatily, Noa climbed out after her other sister, into the oak's tangled, grasping hands.

• • •

THE CAB DRIVER dropped her at Harlow. "You kids sure sneak out a lot. You're my second fare here tonight. Poor kid could barely stand up, and that's saying a lot with how tall he was."

"Tall?" Noa asked instantly. "With . . . bronzeish curls?"

"Sorta brown? He made it in OK, I watched—" Noa pushed her money at the driver. Callum didn't seem the type to party. Something was very wrong.

Noa wasn't surprised that she got inside the Boys' Annex easily—that the window was open, the hallway unmonitored. Things like visitation regulations seemed part of a very different, distant world. And Noa knew, of course, which room was Callum's: It was the one Ghost-Isla led her to.

Noa knocked, every cell buzzing.

Nothing.

Noa raised and knocked again, harder. Ghost-Isla nodded approvingly.

"Callum," Noa whispered, low but clear.

She heard nothing . . . then the weakest, feeblest cry: "*Noa*."

"Open the door!" Noa whispered in panic. "Callum!"

It took decades for his footsteps to reach the door. When he opened it, she gasped: Callum was there, but not in any way she recognized. Beyond exhausted, beyond ill, skin not pale but *leeched*. He braced himself, eyes dim and muddy, and when he breathed, his throat crinkled in like crepe paper.

"Callum—"

He strained from her touch. "It's the middle of the night," he murmured.

Ghost-Isla raised an eyebrow. Noa took a deep breath and pushed her way inside.

"Noa—"

"I'm not leaving, Callum, not unless—" She looked at Isla, to make her brave, then shut her eyes. "Not unless you tell me the truth about yourself."

When she dared look again, *Callum* looked like the ghost. He stumbled back clumsily to the black futon. "Noa," he pleaded, a cornered animal.

Noa knelt in front of him, raised her healed palm. "I know you can . . . do things. Special things—"

"Your imagination, Noa . . ." he protested weakly.

Isla glared at Noa: *Do it.* Noa swallowed, reached into her sweatshirt pocket, grabbed the smooth handle of the kitchen knife. She held the blade to her arm.

"Noa!" Callum wheezed in panic, as if unable to reach out. "Noa, stop!"

But Noa didn't stop, she pressed in the blade, drawing a bright red groove. It wasn't deep, but it bled. She winced, used her scratched palm to apply pressure, and held both out to him.

"It's OK. Heal me."

He crumpled away. "I *can't* . . ."

"You *can.* I know you healed me before." She thrust her arm at him again, slash exposed, "Just trust me!"

"*Noa.*" A wail, a moan.

Noa began to tremble; Isla eyed her. Shaking, Noa poised the knife tip against her heart.

"Noa! You cannot be serious!"

"You'll heal me," she repeated steadily.

"Stop! Stop!"

"*Make* me stop! You can't, can you, without using your ability! That's why you never touch me!"

"Noa, please, you're not insane—"

Noa's eyes flashed. "I just followed the ghost of my dead sister across the city *in the middle of the night*, and she is telling me, *commanding* me, to drive this knife through my heart, and *I will do it*!" Belief thundered through her, seared out any fear. She pushed the knife, felt it pierce her skin—

"Noa!" Callum cried, tearing his curls, imploding. *"I don't have the Light to heal you!"* Noa dropped the knife; it clattered to the floor, harmless, as she leapt to him—

"Don't touch me!" he cried, lurching back. Noa stopped, held up her hands, slowly knelt before him again. Met his panic with clear, sure eyes.

"You can heal."

He struggled, fought himself, then his body sagged. "I can heal . . . with Light."

"And the other things?" Noa pressed, knowing if she didn't ask him now, she never would. "The spark, Monterey, my hand . . ." She mustered her courage: *"What are you?"*

Slowly, he raised his chin and met her eyes. Defiant. Proud.

"I am Fae."

"*Fae* . . ." Noa echoed, uncertain. "You mean . . . fairies and pixies?"

"Fairies and pixies, demons and beasts," he replied, harsh. Then, softening: "Or snails and sapphires." They locked eyes for a moment. "Earthy, and lethal."

"I think I said earthy and filthy," Noa said, with a tiny, teasing smile.

Surprise softened Callum's face. "How can you hear this and . . . accept it?"

"The air moves . . . differently . . . around you. I get a shiver. Not bad, just . . . *other*."

Callum looked down in disbelief.

Noa struggled to explain. "I know I should be shocked, but it's strange—it's like I've felt this in you, from the beginning. And for some reason, it doesn't feel . . ."

"Nuts?"

Noa smiled. "It feels kind of like when I'm writing a poem, and I'm searching for just the right word. Suddenly I hear it, and it makes everything, I don't know, *whole*."

Callum looked stunned.

She bit her lip. "Do all . . . Fae . . . have abilities? I'm sorry, I'm just so curious . . ."

Callum watched her carefully, hesitating. "I have some . . . 'abilities,' yes. I'm Blue Fae, which means I can manipulate physical things. Calm the waters, heal your skin, warm you on the dock. I talk . . . my hands talk . . . to the atoms." He held up his hands, his long, graceful fingers, and suddenly Noa could imagine them, weaving intricate patterns in molecular pushes and pulls.

"But not all Fae talk to atoms," she pressed.

"Not all," he relaxed a little, as if relieved by her curiosity, her acceptance. "Some have different gifts. Green Fae manipulate emotions; they talk to feelings the way I talk to the elements. They can make you feel a certain way, and they themselves feel everything more vibrantly." He began to pick up speed, smiling a little now: "And Red Fae, they manipulate the mind. They read thoughts, and some can *place* thoughts and make you think what they want. My brother, Judah, he's Red. He's very tricky with that." Callum's face turned boyish for a moment. "I can't believe I'm telling you—"

Noa grinned. "So if Judah's Red and you're Blue, that means brothers can be different . . . '*Colors*'?" She searched for the appropriate terminology, the right words. "What? I'm trying to be Fae-P.C."

Callum actually chuckled. "Yes, Colorline is not . . . genetic, to use a mortal term. Judah and I are both Color Fae, but not the same."

Heartened, Noa pressed: "So why can't you heal me like before?"

Callum exhaled slowly, smile fading. His eyes went to her arm. "Our gifts run on Light. Or something we call Light. Your books might name it 'fairy dust,' I guess. It's Fae essence, what powers our gifts and makes us feel everything with all our senses—dimension and texture constantly evolving. I can't describe it in mortal terms." Despite his pallor, his eyes shone. "In Aurora, our home? We make Light like breathing . . ."

"But this isn't your realm," Noa realized.

He shook his head sadly. "This place, the mortal realm . . . it's a punishment. A place for the Banished."

"Banished? I don't understand—"

"Our Light runs out here. Our gifts and special senses drain it from us, and our bodies don't make more. We . . . fade. We hollow out."

Noa didn't want to accept it. "But you can find more Light, learn some new way to make more—"

"Make, no. That's why it is a place of punishment."

"*Find* then—somewhere—"

Callum's eyes darkened. "We can harvest it. From humans."

Noa gasped, recoiled, unable not to. "But how can we have Light? We don't have magic gifts . . ."

Callum's face became gentle, sorrowful. "Light *is* your gift. It's your potential for happiness. Your Light creates all the future moments of hope and love and joy waiting to meet you in your life. You burst with Light."

Noa tried to let her mind bend, to see the stitches weave together like words within a poem—and her heart slowly fell. "So if you take our Light from us . . ."

"We take your happiness. Moments, joys, that you will never have."

"But how—" she broke off, unable to even voice the question.

Callum slumped, body seeming to collapse. "Touch and intent. We steal your Light through touch"—he raised a hand—"and intent." He put his other hand to his temple.

When Noa still looked confused, he elaborated. "Our bodies naturally crave Light and will take it from mortals if we touch, skin to skin. We can try to master our bodies, to fight the instinct and overcome it, but it's very, very difficult. To touch someone without taking Light . . . it's torture. And if it's a certain kind of touch, with someone who makes us . . . unguarded . . ." His voice became a whisper. "Like when someone opens her heart, willingly . . ." His eyes fell to the floor, hands helpless in his lap.

"When you touched me in the hall, I saw a flash of light," Noa said slowly.

"That was just the opening of the connection," he said quickly. "I didn't mean to, I stopped myself immediately—"

"But you were so worried after that, when I was upset about my mom. You thought . . . it was because you'd taken Light?"

Callum nodded miserably.

"But when you touched my face after Monterey, there was no flash. You looked so serious—"

"I was concentrating on *not* taking Light from you. I had to be around you, but I couldn't bear to hurt you. So I tested myself. It was difficult, but possible in that guarded moment of concentration. I was stupid to think it meant that I was strong enough to . . ."

"When a mortal opens her heart willingly, you can't resist," Noa said softly.

He nodded. "The Light flows as a gift, when offered in that way."

"When we kissed," Noa murmured. Shame poured from him, but oddly, Noa felt relief. "Then you felt it, too, the power of that kiss? The way . . ." she paused, embarrassed. "The way the world shattered and rebuilt around us?"

Callum grimaced. "I felt it all. Your heart, my heart, the world how you said—shattering, rebuilding . . . I couldn't stop it, Noa! Worse I didn't *want* to stop—"

"But it felt so amazing!"

"In the moment, the transfer is euphoric. The experience of that potential happiness, all at once, as it leaves you—"

"That's not all it was, Callum!" Noa cried, surprised at her own vehemence. "It was us, too, you and me. That was euphoric on its own!"

"But it was also me, stealing moments I can't give back—"

"So you pushed me away, acted cold," she accused.

"To protect you! From what I wanted."

"Which was?"

"You! Your Light! Both at once!"

"But I don't *feel* any different," she insisted.

Callum yanked the curls at his neck. "I didn't drain you. By some miracle I was able to pull myself away—"

"The branch? That was you?"

"I don't know! I don't remember making it break. Maybe somehow I did it subconsciously, or it was fate or luck or happy little elves! It doesn't matter. The damage was done."

"But you *didn't* drain me," Noa reminded him gently. "I'm sure I have plenty of happiness left. I can tell you, firsthand, that you're responsible for creating a lot of my joy."

"Stealing *any* Light from you is too much! And don't say you didn't feel different. Are you telling me you weren't depressed or upset afterward?"

"Because you blew me off!"

"What else could I do?"

"You don't have to protect me, Callum." She held his gaze.

He watched her, silently, for a long moment. Then slowly, hesitating, he said, "I . . . had something made tonight. I don't know if it will work, but . . . if you are willing to try . . ." He tried to get to his feet, stumbled back into the futon. "Can you hand me my coat?"

Noa got up and retrieved his coat. He pulled a thin silver bracelet from the coat pocket: It looked delicate, handworked, with a tiny treasure-chest charm. He held it in his palm, studying it with desperation. "It should be ready . . . should be . . ." Suddenly, the tiny charm began to glow, the faintest, grayest blue. Callum closed his eyes and nodded, exhaling in pain or relief, or maybe both together.

"It's early for jewelry, I know," he said after a moment, turning to her with a ghost of a smile. "I was going to tell you it was a special heirloom, but now . . ." He held up the little chain. "I am told this will protect you from me, from my Fae blood. A talisman."

"You'll be able to touch me, and not take my Light?"

Callum nodded seriously. "But I also won't be able to use my gifts on you. Like healing."

"So heal me first." Noa held out her arm.

"I can't right now. This bracelet . . . was not easily made. Few are willing, and the price is high."

"You traded your Light," Noa said. "It's why you look so . . ." He managed to raise an eyebrow, and Noa blushed. "I didn't mean it like that. But you did, didn't you?"

"Something like that." He smiled sadly. "I only wish I had known sooner. But it's not a kind of magic many know or share. Here, you do it—just in case."

She took the delicate chain, light as a whisper. The small silver chest was so intricate it looked like it could even be opened, though for now it was locked tight. She brushed it gently where it dangled, faintly glowing blue, then managed to clasp the bracelet on—and gasped. The silver danced against her skin like reflections caught in ocean waves, picking up iridescences she hadn't known were there.

Noa turned to Callum, suddenly nervous—and not in the least because he was Fae.

"So . . . you can touch me now?" Heat spiraled through her veins, her cheeks.

"Yes." The current ran bright in his eyes, too.

The room fell quiet. Noa's breath became shallow as Callum slowly lifted his hand across the space between them. Gently, he laid his fingers, soft and smooth, to her cheek, skin against skin. Noa closed her eyes, lost herself in that single touch.

"You see, I'm feeling the world reshape again," she murmured. "But you're not taking any Light."

"No," he agreed. "This time, it's just us."

Noa opened her eyes as he ran his fingers softly down the line of her jaw, brushed them back into her hair. She put her hand on his, pressed it down against her neck, her collarbone. His other hand, strong and sure, touched the small of her back, pulled her in, two planets creating a new gravity, becoming a system of their own. Noa felt her eyes close, felt Callum's lips find hers, and everything else was gone.

• • •

"HOW OLD ARE you?" Noa asked, as Callum twirled her yellow hair around his fingertips. They'd been lost in touch and kiss for who knows how many moments—many more, Noa was sure, than Callum had ever taken with her Light. Now they lay on the futon, looking at the ceiling as if looking at the stars of a whole new world.

"How old am I?" Callum repeated, fingertips brushing her neck as they picked out a new strand. She heard the little smile on his lips, already learning his secret language. "Really eighteen. There's no crazy time warp across worlds."

Noa bit her lip, knowing the next question wouldn't be as amusing. "You said you were Banished," she began slowly. "Will you . . . say why?"

His fingers paused in her hair, but only for a moment. "You already know that part."

"I do?"

"When I told you about my family, how I took the blame for my brother, and my father sent me away."

"So by 'shipped off to boarding school,' you meant, 'Banished to this Light-sucking world'?"

Callum shifted, let her hair fall, and raked his fingers back through his own. "I may have shifted a few . . . details."

"Will you tell me?"

He said nothing for what seemed like a long time, and Noa was sure the answer was no. But then his fingers went back to twirling her hair. "At home, in Aurora, there's a terrible civil war. I have to start there, with the bigger story, in order to really explain my own."

"OK."

Callum paused again, shorter this time. "I already told you about the Color Fae. Blue Fae like me manipulate the physical, Green Fae the emotional, and Red Fae the psychological. But there's another Colorline of Fae—Clear Fae." His voice shifted slightly when he said "Clear Fae," making Noa shiver. "Clear Fae have no gifts," he added carefully, and then the words began to flow out fast.

"For many years before I was born, Aurora was ruled by Gwydion, a Red Fae whose reign was called a golden age of peace. Gwydion was the first leader to calm the great warring Fae families. Although the official story touted Gwydion's wisdom and leadership, most wondered if his great peace wasn't also due to magic. Many suspected he's grown his Red gift—to manipulate the mind—to levels no other Fae had reached, and was compelling everyone to live in peace."

"Like brainwashing?"

"Exactly. No typical Red Fae could do it, but since our gifts are made of Light, which is an energy that's alive, our gifts can . . . evolve. If you work at it. As our Ruler, Gwydion had access to our Sacred Scrolls and our spiritual leader, the Ancient Mystic, which no other Fae had. With their help, who knows how skilled he could have become?

"Suspicions intensified as Gwydion aged, and his concentration faltered. Tensions rose again amongst the great Fae families, and when he died, they battled again for power. Magical violence exploded, the people were divided, and no frontrunner emerged to become the new Ruler.

"Then Darius entered the fray. A Clear Fae.

"Before this, Aurora had never had a Clear Fae ruler because unlike Color Fae, Clears had no gifts. They were treated as inferior, even harassed and abused. But Darius had his own kind of magic—his charisma. He could win people's trust. And since Darius could not manipulate feelings, thoughts, or elements, he alone could be their authentic *choice.* So Darius the powerless rose to power, elected by our Ancient Rites, and the people loved him so much they named him *Otec*—Father, the one who guides.

"But once he was in power, Otec Darius grew uneasy, his very strength the source of growing fear: He felt too weak, his Color Fae rivals too strong. At the same time, he fell in love with a Green Pixie, Lorelei, who lived and loved vibrantly and showed him love in that way, too. Other Color Fae admired her, and Darius feared losing her to them and their gifts, and gradually distrusted her. She bore him sons, Blue first, and then a Red—but this only made things worse. Even his helpless sons had gifts, while he did not.

"Every Ruler has the right to enter our Sacred Temple and read the Scrolls which hold our true, unvarnished history. The Mystic who keeps them is the oldest Fae, whose power is so immense, it can 'save the Realm, or end it,' the saying goes, 'or even both at once.' For that reason, the Ruler can ask the Mystic for a single favor, and only in great crisis. For Darius, his personal fears meant Aurora *was* in crisis, even as the realm flourished. Its Ruler needed *strength*.

"Darius went to the Mystic with one intention: to get protection from Color Fae magic. Then he read the Scroll of Gwydion, and everything changed.

"It was true: Gwydion had grown his gift and brainwashed everyone into the great peace. But that was not all Gwydion had done with his magic. He'd also performed a blanket memory wipe on the Realm, to hide a world-altering truth: Clear Fae were not powerless at all, and never had been."

Noa gasped.

Callum was grim. "Gwydion had used his favor with the Mystic to sing the Clear Fae power to sleep. Then he used his gift to make all forget the power had ever existed. Unlike keeping the peace, which required Gwydion's constant, continual mind control and faded with his age, this was a single memory wipe, discrete and absolute. It would not lift, even with his death. Gwydion wrote that he'd wanted the Mystic to obliterate the Clear gift entirely, but because Fae magic requires balance, it couldn't simply be destroyed. He used his favor to have the Mystic suppress it instead, and so she did—the Clear power still there, but latent and forgotten, and so lost.

"But now Darius knew. He and his Clear Fae brethren were not inferior and never had been. In fact, they were *more* powerful than any Color Fae. Because Clear Fae"—Callum took a deep breath—"are *Channelers*."

Noa shivered; the word felt icy, sleek and dark.

"The Clear gift is not like the Color Fae gifts. It does not exist intrinsically of itself. Clear Fae can't manipulate the physical or emotional or psychological by themselves, but they can *Channel* any of those gifts from the rest of us, the Color Fae. They can co-opt us, run our Light through themselves and for their purposes, and use us as they will."

"Like prisms," Noa murmured, heart starting to pound. "But how?"

"Touch and intent," Callum whispered, for the second chilling time that night. "But when Clear Fae Channel us, there's no feeling of euphoria, not even in the moment. The touch burns and paralyzes while they force our gift, and all we can do is watch. It's like being a living corpse . . ."

Noa suddenly saw Isla, swallowed by swinging operating room doors, while she herself was frozen to her bed.

"Needless to say, Channeling is extremely dangerous. That's why Gwydion hid it. But to Darius, he had maimed an entire Colorline.

"So Darius commanded the Mystic to reawaken the Clear gift and returned, flush with power, to reveal Gwydion's perfidy to the realm. He declared a new Age of Enlightenment: a new, bold Fae world—but it was too much, too fast. Chaos erupted: many Clear Fae, so long abused, rose up and Channeled at will. The Colors found themselves as unfamiliar victims. For the first time, allegiances of family and tribe gave way to factions pure in Colorline: Fae began to trust only those they knew as themselves.

Darius called it 'growing pains,' said this was a movement about basic Fae rights.

"So Darius refused to regulate the Clear gift in any form. *Use and Let Use*, he proclaimed, mandating *Fae power without bias*. He built an elite Guard to enforce the edict, made of Clears and Colors in his control. Most brutal were the Hunters, special Clear Fae who lived to carry out Darius's every command.

"Each new Colorline alliance resisted and was broken, unable to match the array of gifts wielded by the Guard. Darius declared this as evidence that the Clear Fae were *meant* to rise above. He'd become the opposite of what he'd been before: now the most powerful Ruler the Realm had ever seen, but hated, feared, and reviled by his people.

"And still, the Resistance didn't die, not entirely. Scattered survivors from the broken Colorline alliances learned they needed to band together. Slowly and surely, they grew in strength. When I was a boy, they barely existed, but when I was Banished last year, they were waging a full-blown civil war."

"But Darius loved a Green, his sons were Color Fae—" Noa began. Callum's eyes creased, and Noa realized what he hadn't told her. "Darius . . . he's your father, isn't he? One Blue, one Red. You and Judah."

Callum nodded. "And years later, Lily, but . . ."

Noa already knew. Lily had died.

Callum pressed on. "He was loving when I was small. Fascinated by my gift, delighted by what I could do. He spent hours watching me transfigure—a drop of water from air, a toy shifted to new shape . . . but sometimes I would see something else in his eyes too, something small at first, and afraid. But soon it grew, spreading through his whole body, almost blanching out his skin."

"Your father, the moon," Noa whispered.

Callum nodded slowly. "A sliver of himself, more dark than light."

"You remember seeing that so young?"

"Fae memory is perfect from birth. I remember it exactly, every shadow. By the time Judah came, Darius was already different. Wary. I remember the first time Darius visited Judah in the nursery. He turned to ask our mother Lorelei for the small top I had loved, but before he could speak, Judah thrust the top it upward. Judah, Red Fae, had read my father's mind already. Darius never came close to Judah after that."

"But Judah was just a baby," Noa murmured.

"But Red, in the time when Darius distrusted Color Fae the most. The time when he grew so afraid, right before he went into the Temple and discovered the truth."

"Did he treat you differently too in that time?"

"Not me. I think maybe because he'd loved me from a time *before*, from a different place inside himself. Somewhere his fear walled off so Judah couldn't get inside. But I had already taken root. And because he loved me, I wanted to make him proud.

"But Judah grew up angry, defiant. He pulled prank after prank with his hooligan friends. And because Darius hated Judah's Red gift most of all, Judah used it as a weapon, repeating Darius's thoughts aloud.

"Our mother tried to love Judah more to make up for the deficit. She made him her special favorite, loved him harder when he misbehaved. She used her Green ability to amplify her kindness. But even though she loved him more than she loved me, Judah always looked at what he lacked."

"But if Judah was Red, couldn't he just . . . brainwash Darius to love him?" Noa asked.

Callum sighed. "Not Judah. The Red Fae gift, in its purest sense, is of telepathy, the ability to *read* thoughts. The gift can be expanded and extended—Gwydion of course did that when he mastered *planting* thoughts. But that takes practice and discipline—neither of which Judah had. The thing is, to be effective, a planted thought has to *feel* to the target like their own, with the shape and texture of their own thinking. Judah doesn't have the observation, perception, or . . . the *empathy* that requires. I could always sense his fingerprint, feel the intrusion. He could never have fooled Darius.

"But Judah found other ways to use his gift against our father. At dinner once, Judah read Darius's silent suspicion, that our mother was spending too much time with his Green adviser, Kells. Judah repeated it out loud, and Darius exploded. I'm not sure what he would have done to Judah, had he not been distracted by greater rage at Lorelei."

"He thought she was having an affair?" Noa asked in disbelief.

"She wasn't. But Kells was the only Green companion she had left, and I think she confided in him because he felt things the special way she did. That was crime enough."

"What happened?" Noa breathed.

Callum's face looked hollow. "She made a big mistake. She tried to use her gift to soothe him. Darius felt the influence immediately, saw it as a terrible betrayal. As punishment, he Banished Kells across the Portal to this realm. He used a pretext, said Kells had betrayed his counsel, and would've executed him, but Lorelei pleaded for his life."

"Was Judah so defiant because he disapproved of your father's policies?"

Callum laughed harshly. "Judah only cares about Judah. But we were both so sheltered anyway, we never questioned politics. For a long time we never even saw Channeling performed. I didn't understand it all until much later. Judah never cared.

"But Judah did care when he turned thirteen and my mother learned she would have Lily. Judah awaited the baby with a smug and terrible pessimism, certain history would repeat, and Darius would shun the Color Fae baby."

"He didn't hope for that . . ."

Callum smiled sadly. "I think he did. Because then, my father's anger wouldn't have been Judah's fault, you see? If Darius hated the baby, too, it would mean *Darius* was the problem, not Judah."

Noa had a sinking feeling. "But Darius didn't shun Lily."

Callum sighed. "Lily . . . was Clear Fae."

"Of course," Noa whispered.

"As Clear Fae, Lily found that secret place inside our father, that tiny garden where love grew. From the moment she was born, she was everything."

"Poor Judah," Noa murmured. "Poor Lily!"

Callum smiled warmly. "Not poor Lily. We *all* fell in love with her, Judah too. A little imp, so moody and mischievous, so quick and dark and bold. More like a creature than a person, and I mean that in the best, most earthy, most clever and strange way. I was her special favorite. Only I could calm that temper with my dancing transfigurations.

"Poor Judah!" And Callum laughed! "He said Lily was always thinking of me. Her thoughts weren't words yet but he could see her thinking of my face. He didn't really care though, Lily loved him far too savagely for that." Callum glowed when he talked about Lily. Noa glowed too, but then remembered—in the way she remembered about Isla, every morning.

"Your sister is dead." The words slipped out, an involuntary whisper; she longed to unsay them, even as she knew—oh, how she knew—that it wouldn't help at all.

Callum's energy left him. "When Lily was three, I turned eighteen and Judah sixteen, and our father expected us to enlist in his ever-growing armies. I immediately joined his Blue ranks. Healers"—he swallowed hard—"torturers too. But Judah refused. Finally Darius had him dragged to the secret Training Center, in front of the entire, jeering Guard, and gave Judah one last chance. To my shock, Judah still refused, even dared to turn his back on our father. Everyone was silent. Judah must've known what Darius was thinking, but he didn't flinch as Darius slammed his hand to Judah's chest, and Channeled."

Noa gasped.

"Judah didn't scream. It was as if he was paralyzed *past* sound. Darius was teaching him a lesson he intended to *hurt*. When Darius finally released him, Judah staggered and fled to the maze of tunnels beneath the city. There he met up with Hilo, a Green street Pixie even wilder than he was. She was his closest friend, and demanded retaliation, stoking his anger. He finally agreed to her plan to infiltrate the hidden Training Center and deface it. Judah had been wary of revealing its location, even to Hilo, but now . . ."

"She seduced him?"

Callum looked down. "Seduction . . . is a tricky thing."

"Yes, but people have to own their decisions."

Callum searched her face, like he was considering saying something more. But then he dropped his eyes again and continued. "They met up that night, but with Hilo's older brother Crispin and his friends, which Hilo hadn't mentioned . . ."

"On purpose, or—"

"Crispin took charge," Callum pressed on, cutting her off. "He didn't care at all about Judah—they were part of the underground Resistance; they'd been hunting the Training Center for months. They set the building ablaze and ran. Judah fled, believing the compound was empty." Callum took a shaky breath, slipped his hand from hers.

"But it wasn't. Lily had been a nightmare that day, and I'd been called to soothe her. I wanted to take her someplace quiet, with things I could enchant."

"No," Noa breathed.

"The fire was ravenous." Callum's voice was even, determined. Still he did not look her way. "In a blink, huge burning ceiling beams separated us. I tried to get to her, but . . ." His voice shook violently. Noa tried to touch him, but he pulled away. "When I finally got to her, I brought her outside, but I couldn't heal her—"

"Why?"

"I didn't know at first, but then I realized—it was Faefyre. A kind of demonic, magical fire. Very few know how to summon it, and its damage can't be healed by magic."

"Callum—"

"I scooped her up, and she weighed nothing. Everyone had come outside, no one knew we'd been there. . . . I saw Judah in the back, saw the moment he saw us and realized, the way he crumpled. My mother turned to look where he was looking. Her face—" Callum pulled his hair, as if punishing himself. "She was surprised at first to see us. That moment of surprise before she understood—I had to turn away.

"That's when I saw Darius running toward us. He grabbed me, I felt the sear of being Channeled as he tried desperately to heal Lily with my gift—but the pain was nothing, *nothing* compared to holding that still, small bundle, seeing Judah crumple, my mother's innocent surprise. My father's hand was curled, so gently, in Lily's hair—"

Callum broke off, almost panting. When he'd regained his breath, he added, somewhat coldly, "I didn't know about myself until later. When my mother, unable anymore to look at Lily, looked at me. I saw them as she saw them, reflected in her eyes. The scars."

Callum gently brought Noa's hand to the small scar beside his eye, the one he hadn't let her touch before so long ago. He turned, lifting his shirt. His back was spiderwebbed by scars, like lattice, delicately wrought. Noa touched them lightly—cold as ice.

He turned back. "While my parents stayed with Lily's body, I went to Judah. He'd been unable to come closer to see what he thought he'd done. Lily was the one being who had loved him without judgment . . .

"I could see it on his face; he thought it was all his fault. I knew he was going to confess if I didn't get him out of there, so I pulled him into the Tunnels. All I could think was that Darius

122

would sentence him to death, and in one terrible day, my mother would lose two children instead of one.

"I couldn't let it happen, so I ordered Judah to wait for me at home before he acted. Then *I* went to my father and confessed. Said I'd joined the rebels, revealed the Training Center, though I hadn't known the Faefyre would happen that night or I'd never have endangered Lily.

"My father nearly ripped his hair from his scalp, he was so furious. It was so unlike him, such a Judah gesture; in that moment, they were strange echoes of each other. I didn't see Darius again until full court, when he sentenced me to death. My mother pleaded for my life, and he relented to Banishment—as I had known, for me, he would. Not for Judah. But for me.

"I was imprisoned until exile, and strangely, I remember very little of those last hours. But I do remember Judah exploding into the cell, seething mad. He hurled me against the bars, held me with strength he'd never shown, beat me until I was sure he would kill me. *How dare you?* he demanded. *How dare you save me?* I remember the way his voice broke when he spat out 'save.' He swore to come forward, tell the truth, undo what I'd done.

"I flung his anger back on him, pushed him down and wouldn't let him rise. I told him I hadn't sacrificed for him; I'd done it all for *her*. For Lorelei. She couldn't lose Judah after Lily. She could lose me, but never him. Judah's penance would have to be his silence. To stay and live and let our mother love him."

"Callum . . ." Noa murmured.

Callum looked at her with that searching, desperate look again. "I thought that without me, they might heal each other, don't you see? Judah would be the good son. Darius would love him. My mother would find peace. . . . But I remember her face as I stepped across the Portal. Mourning me even though I lived . . . looking at me like a living ghost . . ."

"She didn't try to follow you?" Noa asked softly, thinking of her own mother, how if Isla had only been sent through a Portal, nothing could have stopped her.

"She couldn't. The Portal, like all Fae magic, is built around balance. To send magic through, you must send magic back. There is a Gatekeeper on this side, a prisoner himself serving a terrible sentence—and when a Fae is Banished through, Darius summons back a piece of the Gatekeeper's soul to right the balance. Magic for magic. Only Darius can do this, and it's part of the Gatekeeper's punishment to have his soul at Darius's command."

"So if your mother wanted to come, she couldn't balance the Portal, because Darius would not call the Gatekeeper's soul to balance her leaving."

"Right."

"At least that means no one can sneak through either."

Callum frowned. "Someone could sneak in without righting the balance, without sending some kind of magic back, but *his* soul would be tethered to the Portal. The Portal would wrap its tentacles, invisibly, around it, pulling back with greater and greater force until it ripped the soul from his chest and consumed him from the inside out. That will eventually happen to the Gatekeeper too, once his soul can no longer fracture. He can't even physically leave the Portal now that his soul is so strongly tethered there. But his is a long torment—someone sneaking through would be swallowed much more quickly unless they found some way to right the balance."

"Swallowed . . ."

Callum kept speaking, a child unable to stop telling a ghost story: "It digests you in what we call the In-Between, the space *between* worlds . . ."

"What happens there?" Noa breathed.

Callum shuddered, couldn't answer.

"There's something else," she realized. She took his hand, waiting.

He forced himself to continue, "The punishment for telling a mortal who we are . . . the Gatekeeper lets the Portal consume you."

"*What!* How could you risk that, Callum!" Angry tears strangled her. "Erase my memory, find a way—"

"*Never.* It was right to tell you." She couldn't see, everything was blurred, she opened her mouth to argue and Callum met it with his kiss, deep and sure. When he finally pulled away, they were millimeters apart; her hands were in his hair, her tears had stopped, but not the terrible, thundering fear . . .

"This is right," Callum repeated, eyes fixed on hers. He touched her bracelet, the talisman, eyes like steel. "Remember this Noa, never doubt it: I regret nothing."

• • •

CALLUM RODE HOME with Noa in the cab, sky lightening around them. She tucked her hair behind her ear, and light caught the silver, dancing. Callum marveled: so deceptively fragile for what it did, for what it had taken.

Noa . . . was worth it. Kells would never know.

Noa watched him, amused by something.

"What?"

"It's just—" She blushed. "You look so *tired*." Now Callum blushed. "No, I kind of *like* it. There's a quietness to you now. More than when you shine."

"I'll shine again," Callum said. "I'll recover to a balance."

"You're going to steal—"

"No. The talisman ritual wasn't quite as simple as an exchange for Light. I need to recover my . . . basic strength. Like catching up on sleep." He fought the urge to tell her more, to tell her all, but his wiser self held steady.

Noa gasped. "I just thought of something, Callum! You haven't—I mean, other than me, when you didn't mean to . . . you haven't been stealing . . . from other people?"

Callum tried not to show his hurt. "When I crossed, I took Light once, not knowing what I was doing. But when I realized how the process worked, I stopped. Until . . ."

"Me."

"Yeah. But I'd rather live a dull, mortal life than hurt anyone now."

"Dull and mortal?" Noa teased. "I wasn't accusing you. I was just wondering—you know my friend Carly Ann? How she's been so depressed? And I saw Ansley Montgomery the other day and usually she shines, a little like you. But she looked . . . faded. Like she'd lost—"

"Fair question. But depression is human, too. I certainly never took Light from Carly Ann or Ansley. Although it's very . . . Noa . . . to worry about them."

"Well, to be fair, not so much Ansley," Noa said with a crooked grin.

Callum laughed. "You don't fool me."

Noa leaned forward to the driver. "Can you possibly turn off the lights?"

The cabbie chuckled. "Sneak back in with boyfriend, yes?"

Callum glanced quickly at Noa. She was smiling. "Yes. I'm gonna walk my girlfriend inside."

Callum and Noa got out silently. Callum tried not groan as his muscles protested. They ran quickly to Isla's tree, with its secret hidden steps. Noa started climbing but turned back.

"I saw you, didn't I? In this tree. Moving it toward my window."

Callum flushed. "I had to see you—"

Noa reached out a hand. "It's OK. I felt the same way."

"I wish I had known about these secret steps though," he murmured.

Noa smiled. "Isla knew what was what."

• • •

CALLUM WATCHED NOA rearrange herself around the snoring wagon wheel of Sasha, and how Sasha shifted to shape around her, too. Callum leaned down to kiss Noa.

"Tomorrow," she murmured, a promise.

"You won't think it was a dream?"

She smiled tiredly, sadly, eyes already closing. "My dreams aren't like this."

Callum rose to go, but suddenly her hand was on his again.

"Callum?" she whispered, and he heard the tremble in her voice. He bent his face to hers. She bit her bottom lip but the whisper slipped through anyway, smoke between her lips: "Can you . . . if it . . . I mean, if it hadn't been Faefyre . . ." She swallowed. "Could you heal . . . the dead?"

Callum fought the urge to scoop her up, crush her against his chest. How he longed to tell her yes. What he would sacrifice to make it so.

"No," he said instead. "Never the dead. What's lost . . . is lost."

Noa nodded, and her gray eyes filled with tears—not of surprise, but inevitability.

She squeezed his hand. "Tomorrow."

"Tomorrow."

• • •

"I'M NOT TAKING no for an answer." Olivia was standing over Noa's commuter locker the next day, one hand on the aluminum door, prepared to corral her best friend. "We need to download."

Noa looked sleepily at Olivia, decided she didn't have the energy to fight. Yawned.

"Sasha still sleeping in your bed? You need to get some *z*'s on your own, girl. As my mother says, yawns let the devil in!"

"Your mother also says an A- is an F and cutting class is a mortal sin."

"True. But today I'm risking hellfire and cutting art so we can hit the D-Hall."

Olivia pulled Noa bodily down the hall and into Harlow's cafeteria, where she made a beeline for an open table in the corner and flung her bag onto a seat before two jazz-banders could claim it. Then she dragged Noa to the sautée-to-order pasta station. When they returned with their plates and sat down, Noa gratefully breathed in the pasta. She was hungry, and tired.

"We need to talk about Callum," Olivia said immediately, just as Noa's mouth closed on her first forkful. "Dude is *not* who you think he is."

Noa almost choked. She gulped water, gasping.

"I'm OK," she assured Olivia. "Wrong pipe."

"Yes, please don't die. That would suck." Then without missing a beat: "But seriously, about Callum. Miles—"

"*Miles?* Miles isn't exactly unbiased."

"You're telling me you know everything about Callum? He's exactly as he seems?"

"Like you, with your half-dozen hidden tattoos? And weren't you Team Callum five seconds ago? 'Give him a chance, he looks at you like Isla?'"

"That was before he was an asshat after you kissed—"

"That was a misunderstanding. We talked, we're good now. Better than good, actually." Noa couldn't help but blush.

"When the hell did you talk? Yesterday you were all upset about the kiss thing, then you left and he went—" She bit her lip.

"Olivia Lee! *'He went?'* Have you been spying?"

Words exploded from Olivia in an embarrassed torrent: "Miles-thought-Callum-was-acting-like-a-jerk-and-evil-and-wanted-to-follow-him-and-I-told-him-it-was-wrong-but-I-knew-he'd-do-it-anyway-so-I-went-too-to-make-sure-he-didn't-like-punch-him-out-or-something-so-we-followed-Callum-when-he-left-campus-yesterday."

"Olivia!"

Olivia scrunched up her face. "I know, I know," she sighed. "The thing is, I hate to say this, but Miles was right. Callum went to the sketchiest, most heinous underground club you could imagine—I'm talking under-a-bridge, don't-go-in-the-shadows, strange-syringes-thrust-into-your-leg kind of place."

Something fluttered unpleasantly in Noa's stomach. "You probably misunderstood. From the outside, a ton of places look like that here."

"I went *in* with Miles, Noa. It was a sex club. A fetish, bondage, private-rooms *sex club.*"

"There's got to be more to this story. Callum wouldn't be into that."

"Well he made a beeline for a whip-clad twosome and disappeared pretty quick to a private room."

Noa pushed back from the table. "OK, enough. I understand why, seeing that, you might get . . . concerned. But you have to trust me. Callum and I trust each other now—"

"Noa—"

Noa took Olivia's hand, tried to send her calming energy the way a Green Fae might. "O, I am so grateful you want to protect me. And I believe you saw what you think you saw. But as my best friend, you have to trust me. I understand if you don't want to trust him. But trust *me.* Callum is OK. You don't have to worry."

"How—"

"Don't be like Miles."

Olivia closed her mouth, wrestling with herself. Finally she nodded. "OK. If you really think he's not dangerous."

Noa pushed out thoughts of Light-sucking touches and In-Between hell dimensions. "He's not."

• • •

CALLUM MET NOA in the hall outside the cafeteria, just after she'd parted from Olivia. She was relieved to see that he already looked a little stronger than the previous night.

"I was looking for you—"

"Olivia cornered me—"

They laughed, and Callum took her hands. Noa nodded to him to speak first.

"I went to Sasha's class to find you. I was going to leave, but they wanted a story, and Ms. Finlee looked so tired . . ."

Noa laughed. "What'd you tell?"

"A fairy tale."

"Callum!"

He laughed. "I read *The Hungry Caterpillar*. I think I was a poor replacement though."

"Olivia dragged me to lunch."

Callum sensed her tension. "What happened?"

A hallway of students was watching them. "Let's meet at your tree later. I don't want—" Noa hadn't even said 'Miles' when Miles suddenly appeared and pulled Noa roughly away, shoving himself between her and Callum.

"Stay away from her, you *perv*," Miles warned him. To Noa's shock, she saw the glint of his silver Swiss Army knife in his hand.

"Callum, I'll see you later," Noa said quickly, and though Callum's jaw clenched, he walked away, turning to look back over his shoulder.

Noa pulled Miles to the side of the hallway. "Put that *away*," she hissed, shoving his hand, and the knife, toward his pocket. She had never seen Miles violent before.

"He's creepy, Noa! You have no idea. It was self-defense and defense of others."

"What I don't understand, Miles, is how *you* stalkerazzi'd *him* last night, and yet *he's* creepy."

Miles looked surprised, then embarrassed, then angry again. "He went—"

"Olivia already staged a little intervention at lunch and told me everything. She's not worried anymore. *She* trusts me."

"Yesterday you were almost in tears. You almost killed yourself, *twice*, in extra-help! I'm protecting you—"

"It's complicated, I can't explain, but I swear you don't need to worry. Just trust me. Please."

"Not if you're going to trust him."

Noa stopped herself, took a breath, tried to be calm. "This has been a really hard year, Miles. I need you, you know that, and Olivia. But I also need *him*. So let's make peace, OK?"

Miles didn't answer, but he seemed to cool down. Noa gave him a hug he half-returned.

But as Noa left, Miles' face darkened again, resolved to get proof. Even if he had to go back to that club alone.

• • •

AT THE END of the day, Noa closed her locker and headed for Callum's tree when Ansley, recovered to her usual golden self, waved brightly to her from across the hall.

"See you at float building tomorrow!" Ansley trilled, as she bent to listen to Leticia, who was whispering and sending Noa some serious side-eye. Noa sighed inwardly, not looking forward to float building at all. Or to questioning Callum about Olivia's intel.

As planned, Callum was waiting for her under his tree, but his smile faltered as soon as he saw her face. "What's wrong?"

Noa chose her words carefully, picking at the bark of his tree: "At lunch Olivia . . . said some things about you."

"You know I'm not human," he laughed. "What else could there be?"

Noa sighed. "OK, *please* don't hold this against her or Miles—"

"*Miles?*"

"They were looking out for me, because you, well, were blowing me off."

Callum pressed his lips together but let her continue.

"They followed you yesterday to some underground sex club. Apparently for some freaky S&M?" She cringed.

Callum laughed again, this time in relief. "I thought you were going to tell me something horrible!"

Noa was bewildered. "So you *were* at a sex club?"

Callum held up his hands, laughing harder. "No—well, yes, technically I was at a sex club, but not for the wares. Not the kinky wares anyway. They *followed* me, really?"

"Callum! Don't digress! What were you doing there?"

Callum reached over to touch Noa's bracelet. "It was the only place I could obtain this. Two Fae work there—twins—who knew how to make it."

"They're . . . strippers?"

Callum's amusement faded. "Unfortunately, it's a steady supply of Light: desperate mortals, craving touch and momentary euphoria, who are *expected* to leave more depressed."

Noa shut her eyes. "So these Fae are powerful then, juiced up on Light."

Callum nodded. "That's partly why they could make the talisman. They're exceptionally powerful."

Noa looked away.

Callum squeezed her hand. "I don't regret using them, Noa, because it made *this* possible." He lifted her hand to his lips, kissed it softly.

Noa tingled at his kiss but knew it wasn't that simple. It wasn't just them anymore, sharing a night and a confidence. Now they were carrying their bond into the world; there were repercussions, complications—not just for Callum, but for her. Secrets she would have to keep. Lies she would need to tell.

"At least I'm not an S&M fetishist, right?" Callum joked.

Noa smiled, but her stomach twisted even as Callum kissed her hair. "I have to get Sasha."

Callum hesitated. "I—I don't want to freak her out yet. About us together."

Noa felt a wave of disappointment but nodded. "Then I'll see you at float building?"

"I'm there," Callum assured her. "I'm not going anywhere."

• • •

CALLUM WAITED UNTIL Noa was safely inside before he turned to face Kells, who he'd known had been watching.

"Got what you wanted, then?" The Gatekeeper leaned heavily on the wheelbarrow of fertilizer he'd been lugging.

Callum eyed him coolly. "I found the others. They made a talisman."

Kells' tired eyes lit with interest; he swept them down Callum and up, as if taking his measure anew.

"Your brother, yes, but *you* . . ." he trailed off, almost . . . impressed.

"Thank you for your *help*," Callum said pointedly.

Kells hunched back immediately. "I *didn't* help." His gnarled hand flew protectively to his heart, and he glared at Callum—then smirked, oh so subtly.

Callum narrowed his eyes. "What?"

Kells pressed his lips together, but the smile only got broader. *"Tell me, Gatekeeper."*

"I don't get involved," Kells replied easily. He began to limp back toward his shed, hauling his barrow. "You can touch her, Blue Son," he said, without turning, "but you can never tell her who you are. In the end, will it be worth it?"

Callum watched him go, tried to calm the fear that stirred within him.

• • •

NOA DEPOSITED THE sleeping Sasha on their bed that evening, smiling at how, without waking, she stretched and curled like a bud opening and closing. Filling the bedroom with spring.

Noa went upstairs looking for Aunt Sarah but found her mother instead—in Hannah's own room, not Isla's, where she'd been practically living as she worked on *Sandpaper Places*.

Inside, Hannah was in her bathrobe. In the dark.

Noa's heart fell: Moon-Mother, shadowing once more.

"Mom?" She went to her mother's side, knelt beside the writing desk where Hannah was sitting. "Mom, are you OK?"

"Isla's poems," her mother whispered.

"You—you don't like them anymore?"

"No, I love them. But they're so . . . so much I never saw, the loneliness she felt . . . I never saw her, Noa. I tried, but I didn't see, and she didn't *feel* seen—" Hannah broke off, biting her bottom lip, the way Noa often did. Noa wanted to hug her mother tight enough that the pain would go away, wanted to tell her something that would fix it. But confessing now would only make Hannah feel more blind.

Then Noa remembered the poem she'd written, some unknown hour, she'd thought for Callum's mother Lorelei, who was unable to find her son. But now she knew: It was her mother's poem, too.

Noa ran to her room, tore out the journal's page, folded it into a triangle, point over point, the way Isla always had.

She gave it to her mother. "It was in Isla's things."

Hannah took the folded paper carefully, with a care that reminded Noa of Callum. She watched her mother read it:

Traveler-Woman

We're travelers, you and I,
though our maps are not the same:
yours span mountains, ridges and peaks you can feel;
Mine run flat like the plains.

(But traveler-woman, you and I pulse with the self-same gift
We breathe the same sky, drink the same wind, move endlessly
in search)

Today on the horizon I glimpsed you strong and tall:
You towered sheer above me—a beacon for the birds.

And did you feel me underfoot? Slipping dark and deep?
My coverlet of silty silk? My hair of milky weed?

We hunt apart, as vagabonds, and though we never meet—
You're my sun,
and I'm your root,
and between us
    orchids grow.

Hannah started crying. Noa lurched for her.

"Mom—" but Hannah wasn't listening, still crying, reading, mouthing words. Noa backed away quietly and bumped into her father, who'd been peering in from the hall. He caught her gently.

"I'm sorry, Dad, I didn't see you," Noa whispered.

"It's all right." Christopher led her into the hall, his touch tentative, an origami father crane. He pointed shyly to a grocery bag. "Blintzes?"

Noa smiled slowly, just as shy. She and her father hadn't made blintzes together for years. Not since she and Isla had been small.

Back then, blintzes had been her mother's favorite, but the cooking was the point of it: the many-stepped and careful recipe that became ritual between sisters and father, marked by secret touchstones only they could know. How Isla, for example, always bought a new box of matzo meal, forgetting they still had some left over. They'd use the new box, then add it, laughing, to the cluster of almost-full boxes multiplying in the freezer. And how even if they were wearing unimportant clothes—dirty soccer uniforms, smocks from art—they'd don green aprons from LARRY'S DELI, which no one remembered visiting.

Noa's job was to make the pancake batter, Isla's to sweeten the cheese, all the while their dad heated crepe pans and boiled noodles (for noodle pie made later). And while he did that, he'd hum show tunes they'd compete to name—except he hummed terribly and sometimes threw in nonsense tunes to try to trick them, insisting the melody was lost in translation. Sometimes Hannah would appear on the landing, frantic, thinking she'd heard her two girls scream—but they were merely squeals of outrage at Dad's obvious efforts to cheat.

For a time, Noa pleaded with her father every weekend to make blintzes, to fill the kitchen again with flour and laughter and "Old Man River" out of tune. Her fingers itched to separate eggs and fold the pancakes, blond hair like Isla's, in ponytails. And for a time, they did make them, every weekend. Then all of a sudden, Isla preferred her weekends on the phone; the cleanup became burdensome; Christopher's work stretched into later hours. Hannah wanted to limit cholesterol; the crepe pan began to heat unevenly. Little shifts and big shifts: the ritual was practiced and then it wasn't, as if it had always been that way.

But now here was Christopher, Dad but different: not Dad from Then, but not Now either. Christopher, trying to be New. They didn't have Isla, and Noa knew there'd be no show tune on his lips. His eyes were older, sadder—but scared and hopeful, too.

They went to the kitchen quietly. Noa pulled out the bowls—the large plastic yellow, a burned bubble on its bottom, in which

Isla mixed the cheese; the green one with the lip, where Noa beat the batter. The crepe pans—two for efficiency—blowing off their dust, rinsing them beneath the kitchen faucet. Her father was unloading ingredients—eggs, butter, milk, a brandnew box of matzo meal. He held the last an extra moment, then stood it beside the rest.

They cooked in quiet, spoke instead through body language. A dance of moments with steps they remembered, with dips and glides to fill Isla's part: Noa made the filling, Christopher manned both pans at once. Noa Now, just like Noa Then, watched his careful fingers turn the crepes. His hands, both Then and Now, moved just the same; everything else, only, had changed.

Then Christopher's hands gave her the plate of crepes, and Noa turned to fill them on the island. This had been Isla's very special talent. Noa closed her eyes, then like a prayer, slipped the spoon into the sweet-cheese filling, dolloping its coolness on the center of the first crepe. She took the edges of the crepe—so thin—and folded them back in fragile origami . . . and the last side tore, leaking white to the plate below.

Noa bit her bottom lip, fought a terrible urge to cry.

"It's kind of you." Suddenly, Noa's father was beside her, those careful hands helping hers to fold the next without splitting the crepe. His warm, sure fingers guided hers. They weren't so much bigger now, and almost just as slender. They moved together: filling, folding, flipping—another unbroken blintz.

"It's been kind of you," her father said again, his whisper gentle, like his fingers. Two more unbroken blintzes, their hands moving more quickly now.

"What I mean to say is I think it meant a lot to her, that poem today."

Noa's cheeks grew warm; her finger pierced the crepe. Another one ruined. But her father simply lifted it and put it aside, laying out the next, beginning again.

"It's been kind to let her think those poems were Isla's. It's helped her."

Noa's heart caught, her fingers tensed—but her fingers were in his fingers, and he kept them moving among the crepes. Though she stuttered, together nothing tore. Noa had no words; her mouth was dry; she knew only fill, fold, flip . . . and then somehow, she was doing that—fill, fold, flip—all on her own, making no mistakes. Her father stood beside her, still focused down, but she didn't need his hands. And then the last pancake was filled, the last blintz folded. She stood, her fingers quiet, looking at the plates before them.

"Beautiful," he whispered.

"Back in the pan, to seal them off," Noa said softly, the way he'd used to say. But he didn't move to take the plates. He stayed beside her, looking at the little yellow envelopes.

"Isla's were better," she said.

He squeezed her shoulders. "These are tougher than they look."

• • •

THE ACTUAL EATING of the blintzes passed in a blur. Aunt Sarah had three more than anyone else, warning Noa they'd have to start substituting some healthier ingredients. Sasha also enjoyed them—having been born after the blintz-making period, this was her first encounter—but enjoyed deconstructing them even more, then licking their mush from her sticky fingers. Even her mother seemed lighter, teasing Sasha about an imminent bath. Sasha basked in Hannah's attention, like sunlight after a long, long rain.

Then Noa, dreading it, broached float-building the next evening. Given how difficult it had been for Noa to leave the previous Saturday to go to Monterey with Callum, she was prepared for the same anxious resistance from her parents. Especially since the word 'float' would conjure Isla.

To Noa's surprise, however, her father spoke up immediately. "Sounds like fun."

Hannah swiveled toward him, uncertain. Christopher swallowed, neatly dabbed at his mouth with his napkin. He laid his fork beside his plate, then looked at Noa. His gray eyes met hers, and he blinked twice, so naturally anyone would swear it unintentional.

• • •

THE JUNIORS MET in Harlow's largest art studio. Ms. Jaycee checked them in, gave a little squeal that she couldn't *wait* to see what they came up with, and twirled out the way that she'd come. Jeremy Robsen watched her go, then verified she was out of eye and earshot.

"We're good!"

To Noa's horror, almost everyone in the workshop gave a little whoop and began gathering their things. Ansley and Leticia giggled and ran to a large closet to change into more glamorous clothes while Jeremy and a group of four or five guys pulled Natty Lights from their bags and chugged.

"You got this, right, Noa?" Leticia called as the entire group headed out. Her pearly smile shimmered fiercely with her newly plum-hued lips. Noa was dumbstruck. Olivia and Miles arrived, confused, and Jeremy ran immediately to Olivia, pulling her away.

"Come out with us, we're sneaking to town—"

To Noa's shock, Olivia actually looked torn. So much for not being interested.

"Seriously, O?" Miles said, rather rudely. "We came to help Noa." Olivia blushed—actually blushed—and waved Jeremy away, clearly failing to suppress a grin. Interesting.

As the group pranced out, Noa heard Leticia assuring Ansley, "They'll take care of it. Noa can call her *boyfriend . . .*"

"No one offered me a beer," Miles grumbled when they were gone, flicking his Swiss Army knife. He bent to pick up the blueprints. "We're supposed to build *this*?"

Olivia looked slowly around. "At least the foundation is here, and the costumes." She unzipped a garment bag and shrieked in delighted horror. *"Gross!"* She pulled out a mass of gauzy, glittery, sequin-y madness. She extracted one very skimpy outfit: "Skanky, too."

"I approve!" Miles called, smiling for the first time since their fight. More lusty than his golden-retriever grin, but Noa would take it.

Olivia lifted another costume with no midriff and no straps. "This blue fairy's gonna have a real support issue."

"Blue what?" Callum asked. Noa smiled huge at his voice, running to take his hands. "Sorry I'm late," he said. "Uh, those are the fae costumes?"

"Very accurate depiction, I think," Noa responded, deadpan. "That blue one especially."

Callum narrowed his eyes in mock-offense, and she grinned, squeezing his hand.

Miles glared.

"OK, I need to stop looking at these before I go blind," Olivia said finally.

"We should probably start," Noa agreed. "If we have to build Neverland by ourselves, time is not on our side."

"Neither is the company," Miles muttered.

Noa shot a concerned look at Olivia; Olivia shook her head lightly: *Leave him be.* Noa wished, for the millionth time, that she could explain the strip club to Miles, but of course she couldn't. Callum's hand tensed in hers; she squeezed it again.

The flatbed had the beginnings of Neverland but was generally a mess: a papier-mâché-peaked sea jutted up from one side, a soaring pile of uncut mountains towered unsteadily on another, and random accessories of jungles and fairies and pirate ships were piled everywhere, clustered and cluttered. The whole fiasco was topped with tools and scattered painting supplies, some of them clearly spilled.

"At least they left it organized." Olivia paused while handing Callum a hammer as if reconsidering the wisdom of her choice, but then shrugged. "Keep your hands to yourself, Forsythe."

Callum smiled a little, and Olivia winked.

Miles turned to the Neverland Sea and began angrily affixing mosaiclike tiles to the rising peaks. Noa slipped her hand from Callum's apologetically—why stoke the fire? Callum looked disappointed, but nodded.

"*Peter Pan* is so creepy," Olivia observed. "Who the hell wants to be a kid forever? Imagine never being free of your parents!" The look of horror on Olivia's face as she said this surpassed even her earlier reaction to the costumes. Noa laughed.

"There's another way to look at it," Callum replied, ignoring when Miles sighed under his breath. "*Peter Pan* isn't about the dependence of childhood, but the boundlessness of it. No limits to your imagination, no reason you can't leap up and fly . . ." He sounded so wistful, Noa thought he must be remembering Aurora, what it was like living flush with Light. The way he couldn't live here.

"And the simplicity," Callum added. "When 'bad' is clearly marked by pirate eye patches—"

"And poison can be cured by happy thoughts," Miles finished sarcastically.

Noa saw Callum's cheeks flush, and she touched his arm gently.

"I'm surprised you like this fairy tale, Forsythe," Miles continued, slamming the sea tiles into place.

"And why is that?" Callum asked tensely.

"I dunno. Isn't *Beauty and the Beast* more your style?"

"Callum, let it go," Noa whispered.

"You know *Beauty and the Beast*," Miles continued, his voice growing louder, "where the innocent maiden falls for the hideous, lying, *perverted*—"

Fire suddenly erupted in front of them, behind them, all around them at once. The float bed, the spilled paint, the piles of garment bags and materials waiting to be cut—everything ignited into giant, licking flames. In a blink it was the biggest fire Noa had ever seen: huge, everywhere, everything.

Olivia screeched; Miles and Callum forgot each other, twisting madly in the enormous rage of flames. Noa clutched Callum's arm as a ball of fire shot right at her head, like it wanted to devour her; its spray of sparks burned her face and lit her ponytail, which Callum quickly suffocated. Then the fire seemed to roar, and the entire room choked so thick with heat and smoke no one could see or touch anything.

Noa heard a terrible thump from Miles' direction. Her heart lurched, she dropped Callum's arm and sprang toward Miles, but the truck bed had become a burning pyre she couldn't scale.

"Miles, I heard him fall!" she called at Callum. He nodded immediately, used his height to leap onto the float's scalding frame.

"He's conscious, just passed out!" Callum shouted across. "Wheezing, though!"

"His asthma!" Noa cried, her fear multiplying.

From the other end of the float, Olivia screamed in an unholy register, followed by a sickening crunch. Noa whipped around, couldn't even see her friend.

"Olivia! Olivia, if you can hear me, I'm going to get to you!"

"Noa, no!" Callum yelled from behind her in the flames. "Get out! The exit's the other way! I'll carry Miles!"

"I can't leave Olivia!" Noa cried back, trying fruitlessly to fight forward. Balls of fire kept forming from somewhere, zooming at her head and spraying her with burning sparks when she ducked. She made enough headway to shield her eyes momentarily and see Olivia unconscious on the ground, a huge gash across her forehead, seeping blood.

"She's hurt!" Noa yelled. "She's hurt badly!"

"Noa, get *out*!" Callum screamed wildly.

"Go around and heal her!" Noa pleaded, knowing only she and Callum were conscious now. "Use your gift, Callum! Heal her now!" Tears stung her eyes but turned instantly to smoke. She could barely make out Callum coming from behind Olivia on the other side. He seemed to mouth something, but Noa couldn't hear him; her vision was blacking out as between them, the float combusted into a giant wall of flame.

Noa waited, listened, prayed, but still didn't hear Olivia's voice. But she finally heard *his*:

"I don't have the Light!" He was calling it, over and over.

"Take mine!" Noa cried immediately. She forced herself forward a few more steps, reached as far as she could go. "Reach across and take it!"

"Noa, no!"

"Do it!" she commanded.

Callum pushed his way toward her, screaming out in pain—from the flames or her command, she wasn't sure. As he got close enough to reach to touch her, one of the Neverland mountains fell between them, flushing them back in a sea of red.

"Callum, please! Don't let her die!" Noa shrieked, hot spray in her eyes. She heard him scream as he reached his hand into the fiery debris, stretching his fingers as far as they would go—and finally, finally they touched.

Nothing happened.

"What's wrong?" Noa cried. They were touching; Olivia was dying; and nothing was happening!

"Noa, the talisman!"

Noa grabbed at her wrist, fumbled with the chain—but it was hot, too hot, she couldn't get it with one hand. While she tried, the rest of the mountain range collapsed, and Callum wailed as he lurched his burning arm free.

"Callum!" Noa cried, knowing now it was impossible. She couldn't get the bracelet off, he couldn't get to her, Olivia was hurt, Miles left behind . . . Noa alone could reach the exit and she couldn't move, think, breathe. She fell to the floor, coughing, retching—and saw across to Callum's crouching shape. He was kneeling by the lump that had been Olivia, a bright white light flying between them.

"Light . . ." she murmured, not understanding. Then she saw: It was Miles, unconscious Miles. Callum had brought Miles: his body, too, was heaped there. Callum was drawing Light from *him*. Olivia lay at his other side, gash still gushing, face ice white and pale.

"*Thank you*," Noa tried to yell.

"Please, Noa, get out!" Callum called. But if she left, how would the three of them get out? Even Callum couldn't carry both, if he could even reach the door.

"Come with me!" Noa cried, forcing her voice to work though she could no longer see him. She didn't hear an answer, the fire roared, and she felt her heart implode. "Callum!" Tears blinded her, she tried to get to the exit, bring back help, but now it was too late. The explosion had blocked her in.

"Help!" she screamed blindly. "Someone help us!"

Her brain turned fuzzy, oxygen almost gone entirely. Her knees gave way, her eyes fluttered closed, the room turned soft . . . she thought how warm it was, how nice it would be to lie with Callum under this sun and fall asleep, so blissfully asleep. There he was, leaning over her, with his halo crown of curls . . .

"GET UP!"

Noa blinked, unable to understand. The face, the curls, the voice—they were like Callum's, so like his, but they weren't his at all. Hands—unfamiliar, but somehow familiar, too—grasped her roughly by the shoulders, hoisted her up and carried her forcefully through the flames. Her mouth and nose were filled with ash, but she could smell and taste him, too—Callum's smell and taste, but sharper: spicy, bitter, bright. He thunked her down in the cool, clean hallway, whipped around, and ran back into the flames.

"Get them—Callum and Miles and Olivia!" Noa croaked even thought it didn't make sense, because he was Callum, Callum had saved her, but it wasn't Callum, too. He glared at her, affronted at being given orders; she shrank against the wall. He raked her face with his eyes, seemed annoyed, then sprinted back inside.

He reemerged a few minutes later—the longest minutes of Noa's life—carrying Miles over his shoulder like a sack of potatoes. Behind him, coughing and retching, came Callum, *her* Callum, covered in ash, with Olivia protectively in tow. Callum laid Olivia down with utmost care, and Noa saw, with horrible vividness, that Olivia's wound was not healed at all.

"Her head—" she choked.

"I tried, I couldn't . . ." Callum huddled over Olivia, trying to press her wound.

"You can! I saw you, you took Light from Miles—"

"Noa," Callum grabbed her by the arms, tried to make her understand. "I can't heal Faefyre."

Noa snapped back hard against the wall. "Faefyre? But who . . . what other Fae . . ."

Callum's sorrow turned to rage. He turned toward her savior, the boy who'd pulled her and Miles free—the one who was Callum but also wasn't. The boy was leaning against the wall, scowling, even bored. Not Callum, but a different version of him, like some strange approximation.

Callum named him, just as Noa knew: "*Judah.*"

• • •

THERE WAS NO time for explanations. Callum yanked Judah's arm, made him help bring Olivia and Miles outside. Judah rolled his eyes, but did it.

In the cool night air, Callum lowered Olivia carefully to the grass, then went to Miles, whom Judah had dumped beside her. When Callum was satisfied Miles would be OK, he went to Noa, held her gently. "No burns, we're lucky. Any longer, there'd be scars."

"You weren't even in there that long," Judah scoffed from Noa's left. Noa tried to get her eyes to focus. His voice was like Callum's, but rougher, harsher. Without Callum's gentleness.

"So you haven't changed at all," Callum said icily.

"I just saved your little concubine!"

"Saved us or set us ablaze with one of your stupid pranks?"

Judah's face turned red. "I didn't start that Fyre."

"I've heard that line before, Judah. Or don't you remember the *other* Fyre you swore you didn't set? Somehow this time I'm less inclined to believe you."

Judah took a menacing step toward Callum. "Watch it, brother."

Callum didn't flinch. The air between them seemed to crackle, sharpening Noa's waking senses. She looked between them, profiles squared in anger: like her and Isla, they were almost-echoes, impressionist-twins, but one was an imposter. When you looked closely you saw the difference: Judah was slighter than Callum, darker: his curls a burnished, blackish copper. He wasn't as tall, but his features were finer, more delicate, as if drawn by tiny, precise strokes.

Sirens split the air.

"Later," Callum growled at Judah, eyeing the approaching fire trucks.

"Yes, I will wipe their minds when they get here!" Judah said suddenly, insulted.

Callum narrowed his eyes, and Judah sighed, exasperated: "I'm better at it now. I had a lot of time *alone* to practice."

Callum clenched his jaw.

"Of course I have the Light!" Judah snapped. "I don't know why you'd even wonder. Look at all the mortals here, it's not like there's a shortage."

"You're reading Callum's mind, aren't you," Noa said, trying not to show her fear.

Judah shot a scathing glare at Callum. "How much does she know, Callum? Not to mention—" Judah grabbed Noa's wrist harshly, flung it down. "A *talisman* against our blood? Are you insane, or just deranged?"

"Let's not discuss whose choices are more suspect," Callum said evenly, aloud.

But Noa wasn't listening. "A talisman against your *blood* . . ." she said slowly. "You can't hear me. My thoughts. Because a talisman that protects me from Callum protects me from you."

Judah scowled, raked his eyes across her face again, trying—and failing—to get into her head.

"That's why you looked so upset in the hall," Noa told him.

"I was upset because my brother the *martyr* always makes things worse—"

"Enough!" Callum snapped. "We have to get through this right now before we can deal with . . . everything else. Judah, make the firemen think it was a false alarm. But only after they've sent Olivia and Miles to the hospital for treatment." He turned to Noa. "Fae magic can't undo their wounds, but mortal medicine will help. I got a bandage on Olivia. Miles seems steady; they'll be OK."

Judah sighed sarcastically. Callum ignored it.

"While they're unconscious, Judah can still talk to their sleeping minds. He'll make them think there was some small accident but no fire."

"Why?" Judah whined. "Such a waste of Light. They're just mortals, and they're already out of it. Let's drain 'em and be done." Noa's mouth opened in horror, relieved Judah couldn't read her thoughts. The more he spoke, the more he scared her.

"They'll be fine if they get help," Callum said firmly. "And we have to protect our secrets, do we not?"

Judah looked pointedly at Noa. "I don't know, do we?"

"Callum, don't let him hurt them." Noa dared a quick look at Judah, who glared.

"He won't," Callum assured her.

Noa edged closer to Callum. "What about the Fyre? Who will put it out if he . . . mind-controls the firemen away?"

"Faefyre burns itself out once the target is out of range,"

Judah said impatiently, as if she were supremely slow. "I'm sure it's out already."

"Who was the target?"

Callum glared at Judah. "We'd have to ask the firebug."

"I told you I didn't do it. But fine, don't believe me. What else has changed."

For the first time, Noa saw in Judah what Callum had named Fae: beast, creature.

Lethal.

"The fire trucks are here," Noa pointed out quietly.

Callum snapped to action. "Judah, go. Noa, I'm going to go finish the float, so no one knows anything went awry. I'll use my ability, since I have the Light from Miles anyway."

"But you can't fix things damaged by Faefyre," Noa said in confusion.

"I can't *heal* it. Living Beings. Magic. But inanimate stuff I can fix."

Judah snickered. "The Mighty Callum's mighty power—to build a high-school float."

"Let's just get this done, *little* brother. And then you're going to tell me why you came here and why you did this. And so help me, it better not be because you were bored."

Judah stuck out his chin, but Noa thought he looked a little stung.

Callum turned to her. "Noa, coming?"

She bit her bottom lip.

Judah smirked. "She prefers me. Smart girl."

Noa put a hand on Callum's arm. "I just don't trust him to make sure Olivia and Miles . . ." she trailed off, feeling Judah's eyes on her neck.

Callum understood anyway, smiled coldly at Judah: "Smart girl indeed."

. . .

"DON'T TAKE THEIR LIGHT!"

Judah had already glamoured the firemen and EMTs; all that was left were her friends.

"I *should*," Judah grumbled. "Why don't you be useful and keep an eye out."

Noa turned reluctantly turned to watch the EMTs, who, thanks to Judah, were happily oblivious. When she turned back, Judah's hands were on the unconscious Miles' forearms. Instantly, Noa ran and ripped him off.

"I said *don't*!" she hissed, gray eyes flaring. He looked surprised, especially at her nails, dug into his arm. She let go immediately, stepped back.

Judah's mouth twisted up in amusement, a little like Callum's small, sly smile, except Judah's gleamed in his eyes.

He rubbed his hand over the fingernail welts. "When they're unconscious I have to touch them to compel them. As I'm sure *Callum* has told you, we can touch people without taking Light. It takes touch *and*—"

"Intent, I know." Embarrassment flushed Noa's cheeks, and she scolded herself: who cared what Judah thought of her? "Callum *also* said that sometimes you can't stop the transfer, when your heart . . . is open." She cringed, especially when Judah grinned.

"So *that's* why the talisman. Couldn't keep it in his pants, eh? Priceless. Well, not *priceless*, in the literal sense." He smirked at the talisman, lost for a moment in some delicious thought. "Now if you're done interrupting me, I'll finish and we can get out of here." He held up his hand in a mocking vow: "No Light, I swear on Callum's earnest virtue." He looked at Miles. "Besides, this one's already been drained tonight."

Noa's stomach dropped—that had partly been her fault.

Judah took Olivia's hands next. "That cut's ugly," he observed. "And . . . done. *Finally.*" Judah motioned for the EMTs, turned to Noa, and rolled his eyes at her worried face. "She's *fine*. Concussion, a few stitches. Get a grip."

For the first time, anger overcame Noa's fear. Judah hopped down, and she counted to ten before following, wanting distance between them.

Before Noa got to ten, Olivia stirred. Noa whirled to her, clutched her hand. "Livi? You OK?"

Olivia bleared at her groggily. "I think I . . . slipped on that paste I spilled, and then . . . I don't know . . ."

Noa wiped a tear and nodded. "You brought Miles down with you, hit your head. But you're gonna be fine, promise."

"Ooh, I feel some lovely painkillers," Olivia said, eyes rolling in pleasure.

"I made sure they gave you the good stuff. In the name of your future doctorly awesomeness."

"Good work." She smiled, lopsided, eyes closing.

"See you when you're better, O," Noa whispered, stroking Olivia's black hair.

But then Olivia woke suddenly, eyes alert, and gripped Noa's hand. "I had a dream Callum carried me. I don't know how but you're right . . . he's good." Her eyes fluttered shut again, and the

EMT took over. Noa jumped down from the truck.

"You kids need to be more careful," the EMT warned.

As Noa walked toward Judah, waiting cross-armed in the dark, she agreed:

"*Very* careful."

• • •

"YOU LIVE IN this hovel?" Judah snorted inside Callum's Annex dorm room, where they'd met up again. Callum said the float now looked convincingly student made. It probably wouldn't win, but it wouldn't raise eyebrows either.

Callum clenched his jaw. "It's a dorm room. If I want to pass as a mortal—"

"God, why? They're eventually gonna notice their Light is fading anyway, even if they don't have the name for it, and you'll have to move on."

"He doesn't steal Light," Noa said, putting a protective hand in Callum's. "He knows stealing happiness isn't right."

Judah laughed. "So what, you plan to crust up like Kells? Live like a troll and rot away?"

"It's not right," Callum repeated steadily.

Noa turned to Callum. "Wait, Kells, your mother's friend? Is he here, too?"

Judah threw up his hands. "A miracle! Something Callum *hasn't* told you."

Callum's hand tensed in hers. She pulled him over to the futon—their futon, where they'd shared his story—while Judah plopped onto the desk chair, twirling lazily back and forth.

"Kells is the Gatekeeper," Callum told her quietly.

Noa froze. The Gatekeeper, who could send Callum to the In-Between.

"Crusty old guy, you've probably seen him around," Judah said brightly. "So ugly he's hard to miss."

Noa turned quickly to Callum. "What does he mean, 'around'?"

"Didn't you know? The Portal's here! On this very campus!" Judah crowed.

"You didn't say he was here, Callum! What if *he* set the Fyre?"

"Not possible," Callum assured her quickly. "The Gatekeeper is locked into a small radius around the Portal. He couldn't have made it to the workroom. It had to be a Fae in range," Callum glared at Judah. "And Kells doesn't have the Light—hasn't in a long time. Besides, he wouldn't need to set a Fyre to punish me, he'd just . . ."

"Send you to the In-Between," Noa whispered.

"And *that's* just a walk in the park," Judah drawled.

Callum whirled on him. "And just how, pray tell, did you happen to cross the Portal, Judah? Could it be that you took the chance I gave you, the chance I paid for with my *freedom*, and Lily paid for with her *life*, and screwed it up? Got Banished anyway?"

"I guess you know everything about me."

"I hoped, I *prayed* you would change, but you're the same." Callum shook with anger. "You were supposed to take *care* of Lorelei, Judah. That was our deal." He wiped at his eyes but wasn't crying.

Judah looked away. "I wasn't Banished."

"What?"

"I. Wasn't. *Banished.*" He turned back to Callum, face hard. "I chose to come through voluntarily, to find *you.*"

Callum looked stunned. Then suspicious. "Liar. No one can choose to come through. Magic for magic."

"Not true. No one can choose to *stay* without righting the balance. But anyone can come." Judah sighed. "No one wants to, except me apparently, thinking my ungrateful big brother might not want to live in hell alone."

Callum sat back, shaken. "How . . . long do you have?"

Judah shifted his eyes. "As long as I want. I've found a way to . . . manage . . . the balance problem. Until I find someone magical to send back for good."

Noa shivered, and Callum tensed. "What do you mean, *manage?*"

Judah rolled his neck and sighed. He narrowed his eyes at Noa, but she stayed put. Annoyed, he finally flipped his left hand, revealing a strange spiral scar, black inside his wrist.

"The Mark of the Portal's tether," he said. "As time passes, it grows larger, stronger, pulling me back toward the In-Between. When I right the balance with someone magical, the Mark should disappear, leaving me free here like you."

"And the temporary solution?" Callum demanded.

"Someone magical is ideal," Judah said lazily. "But I've discovered someone *non*-magical works for a while, too. You just have keep feeding one in every so often, to buy another chunk of time."

Callum processed "feeding one in" much more quickly than Noa did, leaping to his feet.

"Judah! Do you even know where they go?"

"Eh, Kells thinks the In-Between, since they're not a balanced exchange."

"Kells *knows*?"

"Of course he does, he's the Gatekeeper. He sees what goes through the Portal," Judah said, exasperated.

"Wait—he's sending innocent people to the In-Between?" Noa panicked.

"I don't *know* they're in the In-Between. Kells is a liar. He could probably get them back," Judah said.

Callum tore at his hair. "You're sending innocent mortals into the Portal!"

"Yes. *Mortals*," Judah said simply, twirling.

Callum fell back to the futon, stunned. "You sound . . . like Darius."

Now Judah leapt up, eyes flaring. "I'm *nothing* like Darius."

"'Just Color Fae, just mortals, here to use as we wish.'"

"Darius *Banished* you, his own son. I sacrificed everything to *find* you! And now *I'm* the villain?"

"How long have you been here, Judah?" Callum demanded.

Judah squirmed. For the first time, Noa could see he was the younger brother.

"Tell me!" Callum shouted, making Noa jump.

"A while," Judah finally answered.

Callum clenched his fists, mind going lightning fast. "You didn't make yourself known."

"I wanted to watch you first, make sure this realm hadn't twisted you." He said it off-handedly, but it sounded like a lie.

"You've been testing me. Toying with us. Didn't care when it put Noa in danger."

"Fine, I started the Fyre, OK? Happy? That what you want to hear?"

Callum held his gaze. "That's not what I *mean*."

Judah watched Callum's face. Noa looked from one to the other.

"Use your words, I can't hear thoughts!" Noa reminded them.

"Tell her," Callum ordered. "I know I'm right."

Judah sighed, but somehow, his bluster wasn't convincing. "It was a laugh, Callum. She would never have gotten hurt."

"You don't know that."

"Hello? What are you talking about?" Noa asked more urgently. "This obviously concerns me. I have a right to know."

"You shouldn't," Judah muttered.

Callum glared at him.

"I pulled some pranks, all right?" Judah finally admitted, throwing up his hands. Noa's heart started pounding. "When you kissed, I was in the tree, and I dropped a branch to spoil the moment. Big deal. Noa should thank me for that, actually. From what it looked like, you were gonna drain her dry." Judah raised a smug eyebrow at Callum, but Callum didn't flinch.

There was more.

Judah sighed. "There was an incident, with some cleaning fluid and some coffee . . ." he said, letting his eyes wander to the wall. A little smirk pulled at his mouth.

"How?" Noa asked, taking Callum's hand.

"I suggested it to your mind, of course. That you needed milk, that the cleaner was milk . . . Of course, that was before your little *trinket*." He motioned dismissively at Noa's bracelet.

Noa breathed out, hard. He'd messed inside her *mind*.

"She could have been hurt," Callum hissed.

"You all were there! Just a little chaos, Callum. Come on, we used to do worse in school."

"Not to people without powers, who we couldn't explain it to. And we're older now!"

"And the knife?" Noa asked. "When I almost cut myself? Your idea of a joke?"

"Hey, don't go blaming that on me. That was one hundred percent *you* being distracted. My guess, because Callum gave you the cold shoulder. The knife would have been a decent trick, but I couldn't be sure Callum would risk healing you, and I didn't actually want you to get hurt. As *I said*"—Judah threw a pointed look at Callum—"pranks are only fun when they're harmless. I do learn."

Noa turned to Callum. "You know, when I kissed you, I thought I saw you, somehow, in the tree. Like you'd fragmented. . . . At the time, it felt like you were everywhere."

"Just little ol' me. Version 2.0," Judah piped up. "Sorry to burst that bubble."

Noa's mind reached back across her different memories, which now felt vulnerable, unmoored. "Monterey," she said. "You followed us to Monterey."

Judah looked surprised, then defiant, as if this, for some reason, was something he wanted to deny.

"I may have."

"I saw you on the dock. When we were in the kayak," Noa said. "But you didn't play any tricks on us there."

"No," Judah said reluctantly. "There, I just watched."

Noa thought she saw a twinge of sadness, but she couldn't be sure. He looked down, and she saw how long his lashes were, rich and thick like mink. Like a small girl's, protective of his eyes.

"And you say you've come here for me." Callum scoffed.

"The pranks were only some fun. I'd never hurt you . . . or her."

"My name is Noa," she said firmly.

"Fine. Noa." On Judah's lips, her name sounded strange. Different than she was used to hearing it.

"You're going back to Aurora," Callum told him. "You can't stay here."

"We're brothers, we should be together! I came so we could live here, together."

"And what? Steal people's Light to fuel our new lives? This is *their* world, Judah."

"Then I'll glamour them after if you're so tenderhearted. They can't be bothered by what they don't remember."

"And the Portal? You'll just keep feeding it innocent people?"

Judah huffed in exasperation. "I came for *you*. I can't go back. Darius—" His voice wavered. He raked his hands through his curls—the same gesture Noa knew so well from Callum. "It's only a few people, Callum! A teacher, a girl who *wanted* to escape . . ."

"Dr. Chandler?" Noa cried, tears springing to her eyes. "That's why he suddenly disappeared? And Annabelle! She didn't just run off for some guy, leaving her precious stash of contraband behind—" Noa wiped desperately at her eyes, humiliated and angry.

Callum whirled on Judah. "See her face? That's harm! When are you going to stop hurting people with your selfishness?"

"Who else?" Noa demanded.

"I dunno. Strangers."

"And Light!" Noa pressed. "Who've you drained? Carly Ann, right, my friend? She finally got on the leadership committee and now she can't get out of bed!" Callum tried to steady Noa, but she flung his arm away. Judah's face didn't flicker, but he seemed to move his body back.

"I don't take so much at once anymore. I learned from that girl. That—"

"*Carly Ann*." Noa wiped violently at her cheek. "And Ansley, you took Light from her. She recovered sooner, but that doesn't make it better."

"It's our nature! Even your precious Callum. He drained your friend *this night*."

To save Olivia, to heal her," Callum protested, too quickly.

"Which you couldn't do," Judah snorted. "And even so, would *that* justify stealing his happiness? Who decides? And can you *swear* it was only that? Don't forget, brother, I've been watching you. I've seen how that boy baits you, I've read your body language *and* your thoughts." He leaned in closer. "And when I glamoured him tonight, I felt how deeply you drained him. You took more than healing would've needed."

Callum almost growled—but didn't deny it.

Noa leapt away from him. "You drained Miles?"

"No, but . . . it's hard, Noa! To take a small amount! And the adrenaline—" At the look of loathing in Noa's eyes, Callum put his head into his hands. "You were screaming at me to heal Olivia. To take *your* Light!"

"*My* Light, Callum! Mine!"

"I did it for you—"

"Stop doing things other people never asked for," Judah snapped.

Callum spun on Judah. "You're poison. You poison everything, just like in Aurora!"

162

"Stop!" Noa shouted, unable to bear anymore from anyone. "He's your brother. He came for you."

"This isn't one of your poems, Noa. He's not some tragic hero to redeem. He's *broken*."

"You're the broken one," Judah shot back. "Making that stupid talis—"

"*Don't*," Callum warned, ablaze.

Judah looked just as fiery—but didn't say another word.

"I have to get out of here," Noa murmured. Callum tried to grasp her, but she wrenched away with strength she hadn't known she had. "*Don't* touch me." He was hurt, but she couldn't stop seeing Miles' gray, unconscious face.

Callum was right: This wasn't a poem, with a couplet at the end to shift everything into place.

Noa stepped back from him, from them—and walked out the door.

• • •

"GET OUT, JUDAH." Callum said quietly, staring at the place Noa had been.

"Sure you want your wicked, wicked brother running free? What if I accidentally throw some innocent through the Portal?"

"You're right," Callum said. "You stay. I'll go."

He walked out the door, slamming it behind him.

• • •

CALLUM DIDN'T WASTE time; he went straight to Kells' shack, angry and full of Miles' Light. He turned the door to water, splashed through, grabbed Kells by the arm and hurled him against the wall.

"How dare you not tell me about Judah." Callum slammed Kells hard against the wall again. The atoms in the Gatekeeper's body hummed at his fingertips.

Kells grinned through his pain. "I believe it now, Blue Son. I didn't before, but now I do. Tell me, can you feel the difference?"

Callum slammed Kells again then let him drop into a heap.

"Why didn't you tell me about Judah?"

Kells coughed blood. "Do I owe some debt to you? The son of my jailer, who comes to torture me?"

"Judah came through that Portal long before I approached you," Callum said, breathing hard.

"I cannot interfere—"

"You kept it from me out of *spite*."

Kells' mouth curled. "Did the Red Son mention, too, all the little friends of that girl he's been feeding the Portal?"

Callum growled, flung Kells against the opposite wall, then grabbed him by the gnarled shoulders and began to pull his atoms apart.

Kells cried out in triumphant agony: "Your father's son! At last!"

Callum staggered backward, released him. "You're not even worth it."

Kells watched him go, smiling through his pain.

• • •

SNEAKING IN THAT morning, Noa found Aunt Sarah scrambling eggs and dancing to her iPod in a way that meant she was A) listening to embarrassing '90s grunge rock and B) under the mistaken impression she was alone. Noa tapped her, and Aunt

Sarah squealed, leaping a foot in the air. Noa giggled. It was a relief after the horrors of the night before.

"NOA," Aunt Sarah shouted, music still on. Noa laughed again and pulled out Aunt Sarah's ear buds. "Noa-belle, why are you back?" her Aunt said, at a more appropriate volume. "Weren't you sleeping at Olivia's after the float-building?"

"Just wanted to come home."

"Isla-style after-hours, eh?"

Noa's eyes widened. "You knew about that?"

"She had this place wired when she was eight. Your parents may be oblivious, but it takes one to know one." Aunt Sarah held up the pan. "You are in luck because I made way too much scrambled goodness, in case the Sasha-monster rose and roared." She spooned a generous helping onto a plate and patted the stool next to her at the island. Noa smiled—it had been a while since she'd eaten Sunday breakfast up there.

Noa picked up a fork, then looked around.

"Hot sauce?" she asked.

Aunt Sarah dropped her mouth in mock-offense. "Don't you even want to taste it before you smother it in Sriracha?"

Noa shook her head. "You can't do naked eggs, Aunt Sarah." She grabbed the hot sauce from behind Aunt Sarah's head.

Aunt Sarah grinned. "Naked eggs?"

Noa groaned, and Aunt Sarah swatted her. "Don't make me feel old!" She leaned in conspiratorially. "I was just going to *say*, I kind of assumed that spending the night at *Olivia's* may have been code for someone else . . . like the mystery boy that keeps you up daydreaming with your light on all night?"

Noa blushed.

Aunt Sarah looked smug. "Takes one to know one. So what? You have a falling out?"

Noa sighed and leaned on her elbows. This was the kind of conversation she'd always imagined having with Isla one day. Never her mother—but Isla definitely.

Aunt Sarah, she decided, might be an OK substitute.

"I guess, hypothetically speaking, you understand," Noa began.

"Of course."

"What if you found out someone . . . what if you thought someone was this one way, but then you saw them be . . . different."

"To you?"

"No, but to family. Angry, and almost . . . cruel. But the other person totally deserved it and is *really* screwed up—"

Aunt Sarah laughed. "Well, people are at their worst with family."

"But . . . they're people they love . . ."

"It's a testament, Noa, to *how much* they love. It's hard to be completely honest with anyone else—even yourself. You can only risk it when there's trust."

Noa nodded slowly.

"Think of Sasha—how purely she rants and rages. She must feel so safe here to do that, she knows she'll never lose our love. She is her true, authentic self at all times—even when she's a terror. And she's right—because we never love her any less. Sometimes, we love her more."

"Are you sure you don't have kids?" Noa teased. Aunt Sarah smiled, and Noa suddenly noticed that her hair looked darker than usual. Aunt Sarah always took great care with her hair. "Hey, when did you dye—"

"EGGS!!!!!!" Sasha's banshee cry ended their conversation.

She bowled into the room like a super-powered tumbleweed, leapt up on Noa's lap, made a full-palm grab for Noa's eggs.

"Oh, Sasha my love," Noa said, snatching the plate lightning-quick. "That will singe your taste buds."

"Share mine, Sash," Aunt Sarah said. "Come sit on my lap."

Sasha looked at Aunt Sarah's eggs, then at Aunt Sarah, then cuddled her face into Noa's hair, giggling. "*My* Noa."

"Aren't you hungry, Sash?"

"No eggs. *Noa.*" Sasha wrapped her hands around Noa's neck, craned to cover her cheek with kisses.

"Don't I get a kiss? Or a hug?" Aunt Sarah asked, holding out her arms.

"*My* Noa! *My* Noa! *My* Noa!" Sasha shrieked, burying her head further into Noa's hair.

Aunt Sarah looked a little sad, but held up her hands, then deftly cleared Noa's spicy plate.

"I guess I shouldn't be surprised," Aunt Sarah said from the sink. "'Noa' was her first word."

Noa spit the hair out of her mouth that Sasha had just put there. "Are you sure it wasn't 'No'?"

"I was there."

"Good morning." Hannah entered the kitchen foyer in her special weekend bathrobe. Noa smiled in surprise.

"I came home early, Mom."

"Great, honey." Hannah's tone said she hadn't remembered Noa was gone. "Sasha," she continued, "want to see my pictures?"

Sasha studied Hannah carefully, then tentatively climbed from Noa's lap (their brief love affair forgotten) and went over, lifting her arms to be picked up.

"Too big for that now, Sash. But I'll hold your hand," Hannah told her. Sasha obediently took her mother's hand and followed her out of the room, socked kitten feet padding quietly along.

"She hasn't even shown me yet," Noa murmured to Aunt Sarah, turning. "Hey, I thought you hate Sriracha?" Aunt Sarah was dipping her bagel in hot sauce.

"Delicious," Aunt Sarah said, swallowing with a grin. Then her face creased up. "Or . . . yeah. Ew." She rinsed her mouth avidly. When she could talk, she said, "Did I ever tell about my fetish for rodeo clowns? They really—"

"Aunt Sarah!"

Aunt Sarah shrugged, took out some scissors, and started haphazardly cutting her newly-dark hair. The hair she'd worked so hard to grow long . . .

The smile fell from Noa's face. She leapt to her feet and snatched the scissors away, looking around. The Sriracha-covered bagel, the rodeo clowns, the scissors. . . . Finally, in a dark corner of the hallway, she saw him: Judah, with a gleeful smile on his face. He wiggled his fingers in a little wave. Noa slammed the scissors down on the island.

"Aunt Sarah, I think you want to go hang out in your room for a while," Noa said pointedly. In the corner, Judah pouted, but a moment later, Aunt Sarah left the kitchen.

Once Aunt Sarah was gone, Judah took a few steps into the kitchen, but Noa stormed past him.

"Not here," she hissed, and pulled him after her to her room. "What are you doing here?" she demanded once inside with the door closed, trying for a forceful whisper.

"I followed you home and had a little fun with your aunt.

You should *really* lock that window," Judah said with rising volume. Noa slapped her hand over his smirking mouth.

He blinked, and she took back her hand, only then comprehending what she'd done. "I'm sorry." She swallowed, asked more calmly: "What are you doing here?"

He grinned. "You're afraid of me."

"Not with my bracelet." Even she could hear her nerves.

"I can't read your mind, but I see fear, right there." He raised his hand to her eye, and she shrank back. Hurt flashed across his features.

"Maybe the fear is because you stalked me and tormented my aunt," Noa said.

"What is with you and Callum? Have you lost all joy?"

Noa frowned. "Due to recent events, I would say yes."

"Right. I heard you in there. It's all my fault that Callum's acting *mean*. But not to worry, because it just means he loves me extra-much!" Judah rolled his eyes. "You don't actually believe that crap."

Noa bit her bottom lip, tried not to look away. His eyes were smaller than Callum's but more demanding. It was hard to meet their stare.

"My brother hates me, Noa," Judah continued. "It's hate, not love. Because I sent him here. Because it's my fault. Because he's good, and I'm bad." Judah suddenly closed her in, backing her up against the wall. "You *should* be afraid of me, Noa," he breathed. "I can't hurt you, but there are others here simply *full* of Light."

Noa shoved him away as hard as she could. "Don't touch my family."

"You think I won't?" he hissed.

"Noa Noa Noa!" Sasha suddenly flung open the door and ran

in, sliding right between them. Noa's heart seized as Sasha froze and looked at Judah.

Her little sister, Sasha her love, was in Judah's reach. Noa dreaded the monstrous hunger she would surely see on Judah's face. For who had more Light than Sasha?

But when Noa dared look at him, he, too, was frozen, face somehow tender. Sasha unfroze first and walked to him. He stood quite still; she pulled his arm to lower his face to hers. When he did, she examined him with her fingertips, and he smiled at her—a smile that made him gentle, almost shy.

Then Sasha grinned mischief, as if recognizing a fellow troublemaker.

"Sasha," Judah said softly. "You remind me of my sister. I miss her very much."

"I want Noa eggs," Sasha replied just as softly, and Judah laughed. A true laugh, not a scoff, and different than Callum's—higher-toned but sadder. Sasha clapped her hands, then pushed her fingers into his curls.

"Springy," she said.

He nodded. "Very."

"Sasha?" Hannah called, approaching from the hall.

Noa grabbed Sasha's hand and pointed Judah to the closet. Before he closed the door, he caught Sasha's eye and laid a finger to his lips. Sasha nodded seriously as Judah shut the door between them.

"There you are," Hannah said brightly, coming in. "I found some oatmeal!"

Noa watched Sasha, never more nervous in her life. Sasha ran to Hannah, squealing "Yummy in the tummy!" and followed her to the kitchen.

When they were gone, Noa slowly opened the closet, stepping back quickly.

She waited, then finally asked, "Well, what was that?"

Judah shrugged. "I forgot what it was like with small children. She's older than my sister was, but still, the thought patterns are so different."

"Different how?"

"Kids think in images. Colors. Quickness. No deceptions, no lies to themselves and traps and tangles—" He smiled, a little sadly. "For someone who reads minds, it's a relief."

"I guess I never thought what that might . . . be like." She bit her lip. "I lost a sister, too. Isla. She was older."

"Well, boo-hoo for us both then."

Noa's heart sank a little. "Why did you come here? Not here to my house. To this world."

"I told you. Callum. So he wouldn't be alone. Siblings shouldn't . . . leave each other alone."

Noa didn't know if she believed him; his body language tightened up like armor.

"So why start the Faefyre? It wasn't like the other pranks. Forget me, *he* could've been hurt—"

"I *didn't* start that Fyre," Judah snapped, making her flinch.

"You already admitted—"

"I said that because Callum believes it anyway," Judah said icily.

"Judah, come on. Who else could it have been? Callum says he and Kells are the only ones Banished, and clearly, nobody sane would *want* to come . . ." she trailed off, glancing at his angry, pulsing Mark.

Judah slapped his hand over it. "I don't know who did it and I don't care if you believe me." A knock made them both jump. Noa looked at him. He backed into the closet with a grimace, leaving the door ajar.

"Yes?" Noa called.

Hannah peeked back in. "I'd love to show you my photos too, you know. With Isla's poems."

Noa forced a smile. "Maybe in a bit? I may need to . . . help finish the float."

Hannah's face fell.

"But later, definitely," Noa added more enthusiastically.

"You'll be really surprised," Hannah said proudly, closing the door. Noa shut her eyes, relieved.

Judah came out, eyes narrowed. "Aren't *you* the poet? Callum said something about 'this isn't one of your poems'?" Noa pressed her lips together and said nothing. "Isla's the dead one, right?" he added bluntly.

When Noa didn't respond, Judah shook his head in disgust. "I know what you're doing. You wrote those poems, and you're letting your mom think *she* did. The dead one. You're giving your mom what she thinks is a piece of your sister back. *Saving* her, by sacrificing yourself." Judah grabbed Noa by the shoulders. "It's not *heroic*, Noa—it's a lie. And believe me, I *know* lies. Isla didn't ask you to maim yourself for her. She wouldn't *want* it. Don't make her into you for your own martyrdom. It's *sick*."

Noa shook him off, trembling. "We're going back to Harlow, and on the way, don't you dare say one more word to me."

• • •

172

THEY RODE IN silence. Noa told herself not to care. Judah's words were only meant to hurt. Callum was right: He was irredeemable. Broken.

When the cab arrived at Harlow, Noa silently paid, slid out, and slammed the door. She didn't care when the cabbie grunted, didn't wait for Judah. He caught up to her on the path to the Annex, but she refused to look at him, kept her eyes steadfast ahead—

—which was why she was so shocked when he flung a hand across her mouth and leapt with her behind some bushes.

"*Mrph!*"

Judah eyed her sharply. The look on his face made her forget her anger and seize with fear. He stared at her, silently asking if she understood—there was danger, they needed to be quiet. She nodded, eyes wide, and he slowly removed his hand. Carefully, he guided her within the bush to look through the branches. When she did, she gasped.

Callum was being backed against the wall of the Annex by the tallest, broadest man Noa had ever seen. Callum's height but twice as wide, and every inch was muscle. His hair pierced jet black to his shoulders; he advanced on Callum like a rabid dog. Noa clutched Judah's arm, wished he could hear the questions she was too afraid to voice. She pulled on him—should they run to Callum's rescue?—but Judah held her back, grip tight. She started crying hot, confused, desperate tears, silent and unrelenting.

Seeing this, Judah loosened his grip, moved his hands to her shoulders. His touch was softer—more comforting than punishing. She bit her lip, more terrified than ever by his kindness.

By the Annex, Callum ran out of places to retreat. With horrible strength, the larger man slapped his palm to Callum's chest, and Callum's head snapped back in a voiceless scream. A blinding light flashed at the place where they connected, and then they both vanished.

Noa fell back into the bush, trembling.

"What was that?"

"That," Judah said, jaw tight, "was Clear Fae. A Hunter." His eyes had never looked so dark. "And he just caught his prey."

PART III: JUDAH

"LET'S GO AFTER HIM!" Noa tried to scramble up, but Judah tightened his hold, pushed her back down. She was all heroic impulse and no thought, just like Callum. She'd get them both killed.

"Go where? The Hunter Channeled Callum's gift. They've obviously changed form and spirited far away from here." Her fingers tried to pry him off; he squeezed harder. She yelped angrily, and he smiled. Most girls would whine.

Judah locked his eyes on her furious gray ones, tried again to will his thoughts into her mind. It would be so much easier if she just did what he wanted—but again, she didn't soften. Judah glared at her bracelet. Its links shivered, as if feeling his hatred.

"I mean it," Noa said, twisting violently. "I'll scream!"

With a sigh, Judah released her. "Scream your lungs out. Maybe someone who can stand you will come running." He got up, brushed the dirt from his pants.

"Aren't you going to . . . come with me?" she asked in disbelief.

Judah snorted. "They turned into wind, or dust, or tiny mites. They're GONE."

"Then we have to find them—"

"That was a *Hunter*. Clear Fae. I told you."

"I don't know what that means!" Noa cried, throwing up her hands.

"It *means* he's gone and I'd better *get* gone, or he'll get me, too. Got it?"

Noa's mouth opened in shock. Judah told himself to ignore her. He didn't owe Callum anything. Especially not suicide.

"It's *Callum*." Her voice trembled. "You can't abandon him—"

"Abandon *him?*" Judah fought the urge to hit something. "Look, I don't know what Callum told you about Hunters, but they're hand-picked mercenaries of my father. They *don't stop*—and if you get in their way, they hunt you, too. Light doesn't replenish here; he could Channel me to nothing."

"What if he Channels Callum to nothing!"

A bright voice trilled across the grass, interrupting them: "Noa!" It was that golden girl, the pretty one. In mortal terms, anyway.

"You're visiting your brother," Noa whispered urgently, turning to the girl, voice becoming forced and overbright: "Just coming back now, Ansley?"

Judah could've blown it up, would have—but for some reason he didn't. He looked at Noa sidelong, curious. She seemed to care what Ansley thought.

Ansley's thoughts rang loud and clear. *How does she find these strange, cute guys? Wait, I know him, he seems familiar—*

No, he's a stranger, Judah thought at her immediately,

supplanting her thoughts with his. He'd already suppressed her memory after taking her Light, but his skills were shaky, no matter what he'd said before. *A hot stranger,* he couldn't help adding, smirking as her expression reflected the new thought. It was always easier when you planted the truth.

Ansley turned again to Noa. *She's actually kind of pretty, up close . . .* Judah slid his gaze. He'd already noticed Noa's compelling gray eyes, but actually, her skin *was* kinda dewy, and her hair, its different yellows . . . He snorted. That was the danger of reading other people's thoughts. You could forget and think they were your own.

". . . handling the float," Ansley was saying. *Too bad she's not like Isla, could've tapped her for the Fools.* ". . . and who's this?"

"Callum's brother, visiting," Noa answered quickly.

Mmmm, those Forsythe boys . . . Ansley smiled at Judah, flirting. "Wanna come with to see the float?"

"Now?" Noa's face practically screamed.

"Yes, now." Ansley laughed. "To explain what we all 'built'?" *At least Isla knew how to cover her tracks.* "Hey, was Jeremy helpful?"

"Jeremy?"

"Robsen? He wandered back to the workshop right after we left? He has this . . . thing . . . for your friend." *God knows why.* Ansley winked at Judah. "Maybe they're waking up together." Judah almost rolled his eyes at her crude attempt to sparkle. Ansley was no Pixie.

Noa seemed bewildered.

This was the perfect time for Judah to cut and run . . . but did Noa have to look so shell-shocked? It was so like Callum to have inspired such insipid devotion. In females of any species, apparently. Judah supposed he should stay a little longer, just to make sure Noa didn't implode.

When they reached the workshop, Ansley squealed. Noa's eyes widened too: not a single smudge of smoke. Judah felt a little stab of pride—then realized she'd probably already forgotten *his* role in the night's cleanup.

"You gorgeous girl!" Ansley exclaimed, thinking, *We could win!*

Judah didn't get it. The float itself seemed unremarkable: a wood-framed island, purple mountains, a pointy-tiled sea. Everything static and unmoving, unlike Aurora. . . . Judah clamped his mind shut, but his arm and chest spasmed anyway, as they always did when he slipped and thought of home.

Ansley and her crew were looking at the costumes now. Frothy, sequined crap, some long black hair . . . Judah bit his cheek hard—*a wig, a stupid mermaid wig*—but the spasm flared anyway, even though he knew it wasn't Lorelei's hair. His mother's hair was finer, blacker, so black it was nearly blue—and in Aurora, where he'd never go again.

"You've *outdone* yourselves!"

Judah winced and spun to see what creature could possibly be so shrill and saw Ms. Jaycee, in her twee pink-and-white striped 'weekend' polo dress. He watched her zero in on Noa.

"Noa, honey, are you *OK*?"

"I'm fine," Noa answered unconvincingly.

"I'm so *happy* you joined in!"

Judah bristled; the creature's saccharine words said one thing, her thoughts something quite else: *In Truth, This Girl Needs Help.* Judah shut out her mind, unable to endure it.

Ms. Jaycee leaned in, as if to be discreet, but didn't lower her voice at all. "As much as I hate to go back on my word, I really think you should start talking to me, just a few times a week, after school."

Noa sputtered, horrified. "But you said . . . and I have Sasha . . ."

"But that's the best part! Sasha will come too!" Judah wanted to rip the creature's pointy polished nails from Noa's arm. "You *both* need someone to trust. We'll start tomorrow, OK? Great work, kiddos!" Ms. Jaycee released Noa and bounced from the room before Noa could protest.

Another, stronger spasm shot through Judah; he grit his teeth and went to Noa. "I see you have harpies in this dimension, too."

Noa looked like she might cry. "We call them 'school counselors.'" She shook herself. "It's not important. *Callum* is."

The strongest yank of all seared up Judah's arm and chest. He stumbled backward, gasping.

"Are you OK?" Noa cried, reaching out.

"Fine," Judah said harshly, turning away. He looked inside his wrist—the Mark of the Portal was darkening and growing; he should've realized his time was running out. The Portal, not homesickness, had been pulling at him, while he'd been wasting time with Noa.

"I'm leaving," he said curtly.

She grabbed his arm. He shook her off. "What about Callum?"

"I told you no!"

"I'm not letting you leave—"

"Fine! Later! Your house!" The pain was excruciating now.

"Judah—"

"*Later.*" Then he annoyed himself by adding, "Don't do anything stupid."

. . .

JUDAH STUMBLED OUTSIDE, spasms hitting faster, finally violently yanking him east. He'd let himself get distracted—the Fyre, Callum, this mortal, *Noa*, he should've just abandoned. Until that Portal was balanced and he was free, he could not let that happen again. Not for anyone.

Judah fell as another spasm wrenched him east, his vision blurring. He actually might not make it, he realized, if he didn't feed *someone* in and soon—then he saw the figure walking—not walking, *bouncing*—and even in his pain he smirked. If only there were time to savor it.

Judah waited for a pause between spasms, then summoned his Light to sprint like lightning to Ms. Jaycee's side. He spun her, clamped her arms, stared into those patronizing eyes: *You're not afraid. You won't protest.* He steered her quickly east, not even pausing to take her Light. Though she deserved it.

The pain pulled and wrenched, becoming almost unbearable, but at least it jerked them in the right direction, finally crashing them into Kells' door with Judah's bones ripping at the joints.

"Kells!" Judah screamed, spine shuddering, wrist white-hot. "KELLS!"

A moment later—decades to Judah—Kells shuffled to the door. "Left it late, Red Son."

Judah shoved him aside, stumbling toward the Portal and pulling glassy-eyed Ms. Jaycee after him.

Kells laughed lightly. "No time for niceties?"

Beneath its tarp, the Portal hissed and steamed green gas, then roared and yanked Judah off his feet; he crashed to the ground, writhing in pain, sliding backward. "Help me, Kells!" He cried, grabbing the leg of Kells' cluttered table to resist the pull.

"Oh, I cannot interfere," Kells said apologetically, eyes alight.

Judah moaned in frustration as much as agony. He gripped the table leg, but the whole table, even piled high with heavy tools, began to slide back too. Judah closed his eyes, screaming and straining, and reached out to Ms. Jaycee's mind: *Uncover the tarp, and just . . . step . . .* he broke off, screeching as another spasm seized him. He heard a monstrous sucking howl behind him; the vortex had opened up inside its frame and devoured Kells' tarp. The table slid; Judah mustered all his concentration: *Jump in, jump in now!*

Ms. Jaycee walked serenely to the sucking gateway as easily as walking to a mirror, her hair whipping in the building wind. Peaceful, unafraid, she smiled bright—and leapt into the Portal's maw.

Once Ms. Jaycee crossed the Portal, Judah's pain evaporated, and the table stilled. A dull, red circle of light beamed outward from the Portal, a solitary ripple through the air; and then was gone. The vortex closed, the Portal sighed, and Judah slumped over on the floor, panting.

"Well that was exciting," Kells observed.

Judah got up slowly. The spasms were gone, and his Mark had faded; only a dull sensation of being tethered remained.

He'd bought himself a few more days.

"I won't get careless again."

From what I recall, careless is your thing, Kells thought at him.

Judah ignored him. Until he found another magical person to balance the Portal once and for all, he needed to limit interaction with Kells. Thanks to *Callum*, he was now complicit in Noa's knowledge, and he sure as hell didn't want to risk being swallowed by the In-Between.

Judah pushed his way out past Kells. Would there ever be a time, Judah wondered, when he wouldn't have to run?

• • •

WITH CALLUM KIDNAPPED, and Judah off doing God-knew-what, God-knew-where, Noa couldn't bear pretending to be Normal Noa when she got home. She went straight to her room, greeting no one—and found Sasha, arms wrapped defiantly around Noa's bedpost, with Aunt Sarah standing behind her in sweaty frustration.

"You're *back*," Aunt Sarah said in obvious relief. "We're having a bit of a moment."

Noa tried to push Fae thoughts away, focus on this newest problem. "What's the matter, my love?"

Sasha simply glared Aunt Sarah's way.

"We've been reading and grocery shopping and doing all sorts of nice things," Aunt Sarah explained. "But now Sasha wants to do a puzzle outside, and I have to start dinner."

"I'll take her," Noa said immediately, realizing that going outside was actually exactly what she wanted. She did not want to wait for Judah inside this house.

Sasha shrieked, raced to Noa's closet and ran her hands over the different colored puzzle boxes. Aunt Sarah mouthed *thank you* and left. Noa closed her eyes. *Hang on, Judah will come, together we'll think of a plan.*

"Otters!" Sasha decided, pulling the largest box from the bottom of the stack: an ocean scene above and below the water line, kelp forests lined by fish and topped with otters. Noa wished she hadn't picked that one. If Noa let her eyes unfocus, she and Callum were there too: the otter climbing in their boat, tipping them, with Judah on the dock—

"Noa!" Sasha yanked her. Noa knew better than to request a different puzzle; she'd just have to focus on the pieces, not the pattern. Colors and evolving shapes, to occupy time and hands while she waited for Judah.

Time Callum may not have.

"We need the mat, and our big coats," Noa reminded her sister. Sasha bounced flat to the floor, scrunched forward and eased the rolled-up blue foam mat from beneath their bed. The magic mat that took puzzles, Sasha's favorite inside activity, to do outside, her favorite place. She hated being zipped up in rules and walls.

It was very cold in Salinas once the sun went down, so they sat on the lawn in parkas, and Sasha carefully unrolled the mat.

"Edges first," Sasha ordered, dumping the tiny pieces, as if Noa hadn't taught Sasha this very method. Whatever else may be happening, Noa could find some relief in this sorting stage, her favorite part, when every so often, Sasha would thrust up her arm and shriek, "Corner!" with her most special smile. If Noa found a corner, she always slipped it back in for Sasha to find.

They assembled the frame quickly and began to work, quietly searching, trying, failing, linking. Sasha insisted on doing the otters—of course—while Noa found solace in the kelp that blurred easily to abstract patterns. The silence was soothing: girl-beast Sasha always worked intently, barely shifting, except when Noa turned on the lights and heater, and she reshaped to the change in air.

But Noa couldn't focus. *Callum* . . . Judah was sure taking his sweet time.

"Here! It fit! It fit!" Sasha was impatiently trying to force two pieces together. Noa looked: Sasha was right, the two pieces looked like they should couple—their patterns and shapes seemed congruent, but they refused to truly interlock.

"Fit!" Sasha said again, fist curled in indignation. She looked up in appeal to Noa and froze, staring into Isla's tree. *Callum's tree.* Sasha dropped the pieces, eyes glinting, lips rolling up: a tigress, scenting something.

Noa turned: Judah emerged into the halo of the porch light, as if shaped by shadows stretching out their fingers.

Sasha pounced to him, and Noa thought she might even hug him, but then she stopped a foot away. Slowly she reached out and took his hand, examining it in hers, the way she sometimes held lost trinkets—a broken top, linked paperclips, an old tin ring—things only she knew were precious.

Finally, Sasha pulled him forward. "Come."

Judah's eyes met Noa's, and she flinched. His eyes, his firm-set mouth, those darker, coarser curls: Callum's but not Callum's—

Please tell me you have a plan.

Judah's face tensed as he sensed her desperation, even if he couldn't hear her thought. She turned, afraid to see his disgust. She didn't care what he thought of her, as long as he saved Callum.

Sasha pulled Judah to the grass. "Me, otters. You, waves."

Noa put her hand over Sasha's. "No Sash, my friend Judah and I need to talk—"

Blood rushed to Sasha's cheeks.

"We can help," Judah said pointedly.

Noa's mouth opened. "We really *can't*. Sasha, you must be hungry."

Sasha was preparing to explode, but at the mention of food, nodded. Noa blessed the world for small miracles.

"Well, it's a good thing your dinner's ready. Who's this Noa-belle?" Aunt Sarah had just come onto the porch, her dark hair sleek in the dim light. Noa froze in panic as Aunt Sarah wiggled her eyebrows. "Is this, perhaps, that *friend?*"

Judah coughed, choking.

Noa flushed, unsure which was more embarrassing—having Judah mistaken for her boyfriend, or how obviously ridiculous he found that notion.

"I didn't know you were inviting him over," Aunt Sarah said.

"I'm sorry, I—"

"I surprised her. Couldn't stay away," Judah interrupted, eyes gleaming mischief. Aunt Sarah studied him, amused.

"Well, let's . . . *not* tell your parents. I'm not sure they're ready." Noa's aunt hadn't moved her eyes from Judah. She looked almost . . . longing. Noa looked at him, tried to see what she was seeing. But she only saw the boy he wasn't. Aunt Sarah finally turned back to Noa. "Just stay out here to chat with . . ."

"Callum," Noa said immediately.

Judah clenched his jaw. "That's me, Callum."

Aunt Sarah's eyes seemed to laugh. "You two have fun. I'll bring you out some stir-fry."

"Thanks—and sorry!" Noa called after her. She turned to Judah and was surprised to see him looking back. He looked away immediately.

There wasn't time for this.

"Judah—"

"*Shh*," he hissed. Aunt Sarah had reemerged with steaming plates.

"Smells delicious," Judah said. "Thank you."

"Polite." Aunt Sarah nodded approvingly.

Once Aunt Sarah was gone, Noa flung her plate down. But Judah was wolfing his.

"How can you eat right now?"

Judah shrugged, mouth full: "Need food to live. You don't?" He slurped up a long, clear noodle. "Your Realm does food good." He smiled, basking in her frustration. "Eat," he commanded. When she glared, he rolled his eyes and took another huge bite. "Eat, then talk."

Noa sighed and picked up her stir-fry—which really did smell good—and did as Judah required.

• • •

JUDAH COULD'VE LAUGHED at how Noa devoured her stir-fry. She obviously hadn't known how hungry she was. Just like Callum, swept up in big dramatic events and forgetting normal things.

Judah felt a little twinge, wished she would eat slower. When she finished, he'd have to tell her no, he wouldn't go after Callum. It was self-preservation, not selfishness . . . so why did he dread saying it?

"How do we save him?" she said, even before she'd finished her last swallow.

"Not by doing puzzles."

Hurt flushed Noa's cheeks, immediate and vibrant. "You know I would've gone right away! *You* convinced me we need a plan—"

"I never said *I'd* make a plan. In fact I specifically said I wouldn't."

"You have to! You owe him—"

"I don't owe him anything."

"But you—I can't—" Noa choked on angry tears. He knew it was humiliating to her but told himself he didn't care. "I bet the Hunter only took Callum because *you* sneaked through the Portal!" she retaliated.

Judah's eyes flared. "Oh, really? Because I can think of something else, something worse—*telling a mortal what we are.*"

Noa gasped in horror. "Then we have to go to the Gatekeeper, explain—"

"Then we're worse than dead in less than an instant."

"I can't have done this . . . he can't be gone because of me . . ." She was crumbling right in front of him; it became too much. He grabbed her shoulders.

"Listen to me. *Listen.* It's not your fault. I promise. Kells couldn't recruit a Hunter; he's an outcast, just like us. And even if he could, he wouldn't need one. He would just feed Callum to the In-Between. There's nothing worse than that."

"But you just said—"

Judah looked away. "I lied, OK? I do that." He let her go. Trembling, she wiped her eyes and for a fleeting instant, he wished he were Green.

Noa was still shaking, then all of a sudden, she stilled, staring across the darkened, empty yard. "She's here . . ." she murmured gratefully, a silent tear sliding down her cheek.

"Who?" Judah asked, scanning the empty yard.

"*Isla.*" Noa's face looked oddly hollow, the way Lorelei's had looked when Lily had died and Callum had gone and Judah was all that was left.

"You mean a ghost?"

Noa focused slowly on Judah. "You don't believe in ghosts?"

He frowned. "Oh I know there are ghosts."

Noa looked back across the darkness, then closed her eyes. "She's gone," she murmured. Then her eyes snapped open, cavernous and wild: "*But she's never gone.*"

"Fine!" Judah burst. "I'll help! But then my debt is settled, hear me?" He eyed her hard, needing her to understand. "My debt to him—I owe him nothing after this!"

Noa's whole body sagged in relief. Her hand went to her wrist, her silver bracelet.

"What?" Judah demanded.

Color slowly warmed her cheeks. "Callum," she murmured, then looked at him. "And you."

Noa went inside to pretend to go to bed, but before she closed the door, she smiled into the darkness, to Judah who was waiting, Judah who was there.

• • •

NOA WAITED FOR Sasha to fall asleep with her bracelet pressed against her heart, the tiny chest charm almost thrumming. Finally, she heard a tapping at Isla's window, Callum's window. She looked: Callum—*No, Noa, not Callum. Judah.*

Noa opened the window; Judah poured inside with night-time air. Noa looked meaningfully toward Sasha, lightly touched Judah's hand. He snatched it back—and Sasha stirred.

Noa leapt to cover Sasha's mouth—but Judah blocked her, slipping between them to sit on the bed by Sasha's side. Sasha blinked at him, stretching up, then burrowed in against his chest. Noa watched intently: this was different than Sasha purring into Callum—Sasha and Judah together were somehow more dynamic, ions counterbalancing their charge.

"She won't tell," Judah said, then rolled his eyes. "I can read her mind, remember? She knows I'm a secret."

"She's *three*."

"Fine, I'll modify her memory," he huffed. "But I had a sister once myself, you know."

Noa bit her lip. "All right. I . . . trust you." Noa leaned, kissed Sasha. "Back soon, my love. Don't tell."

Judah sighed. "She *won't*. Let's go."

• • •

ONCE OUTSIDE, HIDDEN in dark, Noa turned expectantly. "So?"

"So what?"

"What's the plan!"

"Well, it's not to run out into the night and yell, 'Here Hunter, Hunter.'"

"It's been *three hours*. Who knows what that monster's doing—"

"Exactly," Judah snapped. He checked himself. "Look. The two things we know about Hunters are they live to please Darius, and as Clear Fae they need to Channel to use powers. Darius is in

Aurora, thankfully, so we can set aside *that* nightmare. Better—but still most likely suicidal—to try to stop the Hunter *here*."

"We saw him use powers. He and Callum disappeared."

"He was Channeling Callum. But I guarantee he wasn't hunting before that without juice."

"So he . . . recruited . . . someone?"

Judah frowned. "Recruited, enslaved. But the problem is who?"

"Callum said he and Kells were the only exiles. That's why he thought you started the Faefyre."

"They *are*. Or so we've been told. And as *you* put it, no one besides me is moronic enough to sneak across."

"I . . . didn't mean it that way. And I don't think I said 'moronic.'"

"Whatever. It actually helps us. Narrows down the possibilities for who the Hunter is Channeling. If we can track the helper—"

"We find him," Noa finished. "Olivia and Miles!" she exclaimed suddenly. "They followed Callum once to this club, this weird sex club, secret bondage stuff—" Judah snickered. Noa ignored him. "Callum told me that's where he made my bracelet."

Judah sobered instantly, snapped his fingers. "Your *talisman*. That takes serious magic to make. Obviously Color Fae."

Noa almost gloated. "The kind of magic a Hunter would want?"

"Are you *smirking*?"

Noa bit her smile. "It's just . . . for a guy who said he didn't want to help, you seem pretty excited."

Judah looked away. "So where is this place?"

"I . . . don't know."

"But you said Olivia and Miles do."

"Yes!"

Judah nodded. "Then we find out."

• • •

THE NEXT MORNING, Noa found Olivia in the Harlow hallway first thing and cornered her against the commuter lockers. "Olivia, I—" she cut off, seeing the bandage on her best friend's forehead. "Um, how are you feeling?"

"Digging the street cred. Way tougher than a tattoo."

Noa tried to smile, but remembered how serious the injury had really been. Now she was involving Olivia in Fae business *again*.

There was no other way.

"O, remember when you and Miles—"

"B-T-Dubs, about Miles?" Olivia interrupted. "They obviously did not give him the happy pills they gave me."

Noa's guilt deepened. "O, I need—"

Ansley walked up with Leticia in tow, interrupting them. "So you and Jeremy?"

Olivia blushed madly. "What do you mean?"

"Hasn't he been helping you . . . *recover*?"

"I haven't seen him since you guys left—" Anxiety crept over Olivia's bandaged face.

Noa, too, had a terrible sinking feeling. An Annabelle/Dr. Chandler/through-the-Portal kind of sinking feeling. "He still hasn't surfaced?"

"Bet you a hundy he passed out on the grounds," Leticia laughed to Ansley. Noa could barely look at Olivia. Leticia turned to Noa. "Where's Callum?" she purred, smug.

"Um—"

"Sick," Judah supplied, suddenly appearing beside them in Callum's uniform. The sleeves were too long, the shirt too broad, but he wore it tussled, like it was meant to be that way.

Leticia took him in approvingly. "I could show you some fun, if he's tapped out."

Judah leaned in. "I bet you could."

"Precalc, Teesh," Ansley reminded her.

"I'll walk you," Judah volunteered, taking Leticia's arm and sending Noa a meaningful look telling Noa to talk to Olivia. Noa understood, but found she was slightly annoyed anyway. She turned to Olivia, who was now anxiously chewing her lip.

"Um, Livi?"

"I should look for Jeremy. He wouldn't just disappear."

"Maybe you should wait a little. Leticia's right, he's probably sleeping it off." Noa hated herself, but if she was right, then Jeremy was on the list of people she would need to figure out how to save—after saving Callum . . .

Callum.

"You know that . . . sex club you followed Callum to? I need to know where it is."

"What?" Olivia replied in disbelief.

"Olivia, *please.* I can't explain, I just need to know—"

A lacrosse stick slammed against the wall, cutting Noa off. Behind it thundered Miles, buzz-headed Coach Stogner on his heels.

"Kessler! Get on that bus or that is *it!*"

Miles, dark as a thundercloud, spun and threw up his hands. "Fine! I *quit!*"

"Ho-ly," Olivia murmured as he stormed by, looking nothing like the gentle boy they knew, not even glancing in their direction. "Is Miles on 'roids?"

Noa closed her eyes. The world was spinning too fast.

"We'll deal with him . . . later," she managed. *And everyone else, I swear.* "Tell me where to find this club."

• • •

"I'VE BEEN LOOKING everywhere for you," Noa hissed when Judah sauntered back into the hallway, where Noa had been waiting after getting Olivia's intel. Judah's dark hair glinted glossily; his golden skin glistened. A moment later, Leticia came inside through the same door. She smiled impishly at Judah, then lightly wandered away.

Noa spun on Judah. "You *stole* her *Light*."

"Believe me, she doesn't think highly of you."

"Judah—"

"You really think we can save Callum if I don't have Light?"

"I—" Noa cut off, hating herself.

Judah smiled, smug. "At least I wiped her memory. Callum couldn't do that."

"Callum does a lot you can't. And . . ." She lowered her voice. "Did you throw Jeremy Robsen into the Portal? The night of the Fyre?"

"Sorry, teenage boys aren't my style."

"So he's just missing."

Judah scowled. "Look, can we do one missing person at a time? But you're right about one thing. I can't heal like Callum." He paused, softening awkwardly. "You should say . . . good-bye

. . . to Sasha. Just in case." He looked away. "The rest of your family covered?"

Noa bit her lip. "I told Aunt Sarah I'm spending the night at Olivia's."

Judah nodded, didn't meet her eyes. "Sasha, before we go. Just in case."

• • •

FROM A DISTANCE, Judah watched Sasha speak excitedly to Noa in the hall outside her class, thrusting up a Band-Aid on her finger to show her older sister. Even though they didn't look alike, Judah could tell that they were sisters: the stubbornness in the jaw, the quickness of the hands—Noa had a lot of Sasha's fire, and Sasha had Noa's focus in her blaze. Judah had heard siblings could be like that, growing toward each other. He and Callum, of course, had climbed apart, but maybe Lily would have grown his way—or helped him grow toward hers.

Noa's face was rapt. *You are heard*, her body said, *you are important, and loved.* Finally, quickly, Noa kissed Sasha's Band-Aid; Sasha jumped back in horrified delight. Noa hugged her, then Sasha squirmed free to run back into the class.

Judah knew Noa hadn't said it was good-bye. She'd done it as he would have done it, if he'd had the chance: with just an ordinary moment. Unremarkable moments were the ones you missed most—the ones you didn't realize were precious at the time, and so later could not remember.

The moments you lost, when you lost a sister.

• • •

"STAY HERE," JUDAH told Noa as they approached the exterior of the menacing club.

"No way. I'm coming too," Noa said, more bravely than she felt. The abandoned-factory facade reminded Noa uncomfortably of the derelict cabin she'd found with Isla. Except that here, the shadows not only oozed but thrummed with bass.

"We don't know what kind of Fae are in there, and they could figure out that you know about us. It's pointless to save Callum just to be swallowed by the In-Between," Judah said.

Noa frowned. "Whoever they are, they helped Callum and made the talisman, so they're probably on our side."

Judah scowled. "They're not in this Realm on *vacation*, Noa. Stay. And if you're smart, take off that stupid bracelet so I can hear you if you need me."

Noa's hand flew to the bracelet. "It protects me—"

"Only against *me*! I'm not the one you need to fear!" He flipped up the collar on his blazer—Callum's blazer—and stalked to the door, pounding it with his fists. Once he disappeared inside, Noa stood in the alley, breathing in urine and trash. The talisman thrummed.

Screw this.

She went inside.

• • •

"YOUR FANBOY'S BACK," Fabian drawled to Pearl, scanning the evening's crowd. "A consecutive-day record." The twins were perched in their usual spot—at the back of the club, past the half ring of dark banquettes.

Pearl tossed her silky auburn hair, ignoring him.

Fabian flared. "I don't know why you fixate on a *child*."

"Because I need a break from balding, old, and lecherous."

"Fine. One more time. But that's *it*. Breaking his wits completely leaves a trail."

Pearl's eyes gleamed. As much as Fabian taunted, he liked to make her happy. Then hawklike, he tensed.

"What?" she asked.

"Red Fae." Fabian scanned the shadows. "I hear him, and he hears me."

"Who?"

"I think he is a Son . . ." Fabian lowered his voice as Judah emerged from the dark. ". . . of *Darius*." The name sizzled off his lips. Pearl took her brother's hand.

"Son of Darius," Fabian greeted Judah icily. "Your brood have a nasty habit of being Banished. First the Blue Son; now the Red?"

"You know me, but I don't know you," Judah replied evenly, searching Fabian's mind but finding nothing, like looking into filing cabinets with empty drawers.

"Rooting around, Red Son? I know a few more tricks than you."

"Just trying to recall *your* Banishment."

"Oh, it was so long ago," Fabian said easily. "And this realm is so depressing. I'm sure I hardly recall myself."

Judah tried again, but Fabian wasn't lying; he didn't seem to have a memory of his crime. Judah looked at Pearl.

"She has a worse memory than I do." Fabian smiled.

"Fabian and Pearl," Judah said, reading their names at least, from her. Pearl was thinking the names—and just the names—over and over. Judah tried to break past that—but then relaxed, losing his sense of urgency.

"Stop that, Pixie," he snapped immediately. "Green gifts don't work on me."

Pearl scoffed but didn't test him. Her eyes wandered to the shadowy corner to his right, and a hungry smile poured itself across her mouth.

Fabian rolled his eyes. "Go, play with your little trinket. I'll deal with this." Pearl's eyes lit as she slipped away. Judah didn't even turn to watch her go.

Fabian studied him. "It's a rare man who can resist watching my sister leave."

"I'm immune," Judah repeated, keeping his mind blank. Fabian looked impressed.

"Maybe you should join us here. Manna everywhere." His gaze swept hungrily across the craven patrons.

"You feed off their pain," Judah scoffed.

"*Your* gift seems active. Got that Light from somewhere."

"Not like this."

"They come to *us*."

"And your sister's gift plays no role in that?"

Fabian narrowed his eyes. "I'd heard the Red Son was not so . . . insipid . . . as his brother. You disappoint."

Judah clenched his jaw. "I know what you did to him."

"Oh, perchance we've met a time or two . . ." Fabian drawled.

"Callum's been taken. By a Hunter." Judah watched Fabian blanch. He listened carefully for any hint of foreknowledge—all he heard in Fabian's mind was panic.

"This is *your* fault," Fabian hissed, suddenly advancing on Judah, face as red as his hair. "Your family is a *blight*. Your father Banishes us, your mongrel brother brings Hunters—fleas, following the mutt to hell—" He launched himself onto Judah's shoulders, pinned him to the floor. "You know why else I like this club? It's a good place to *experiment*. I've grown my gift like you can't imagine." He dug his nails into Judah's struggling shoulders, drawing streams of blood, slapped his other hand across Judah's face. "I've been Banished here for *years*, Red Son. I can melt your mind . . ."

In an instant, Judah's world went black—then all he could see, feel, hear was Lorelei, crying for her son. *"Don't leave me! Don't leave me, no!"* Her long black hair—so black it was almost blue—became the ocean, became a void, until there was nothing but her scream and its echo, reverberating and reverberating and reverberating. The keen filled everything, every cell, until Judah thought he would explode into his mother's pain—

Then, as from across a long, long hallway, came Fabian's voice, taunting him, building and gaining strength: "He demanded we make a talisman! Oh, I helped him, yes I did, and I loved *every. single. second.* And you know what the best part was?" Judah heard a cry, and this time he knew it wasn't Lorelei's—it was his own, from his own mouth. He knew he'd broken, was crying like a child; he couldn't stop, only listen—

"The best part, *Judah*, was that he didn't even *need* one. It's the oldest magic there is—*true love*. When you love a mortal truly, and earn her love in return, your gift no longer works. You're blocked, as natural as breathing." Fabian was so close Judah felt his spit, even as he could only see Lorelei in pain. "Of course you two brats wouldn't *know*. The great sons of *Darius*, study the most basic, primal lore?" Fabian snorted, and heat seared through Judah's skull, blowing his mind outward—

Then the smack of something cold and hard, and Judah realized he could control his arms, his eyes. He was still on the floor, shoulders bleeding, but above him, Pearl had Fabian by the arms.

"You'll expose us! It's *enough*."

Finally Fabian stopped struggling, glowered down at Judah's panting, prostrate form. "You're lucky she's here."

Judah tried to stand but couldn't, his entire body still trembling. He tried to glare at Fabian but could barely speak, Lorelei's scream still echoing in his ears, her face ghosting in his eyes. . . . He crumpled back to the floor.

Pearl took Fabian's hand. "He's nothing. Leave him."

As they walked away, Pearl asked, "What did he want anyway?"

Fabian allowed himself a tiny smile. "Seems there's a Hunter in our midst."

• • •

JUDAH FINALLY MANAGED to pull himself under an abandoned banquette, trying to shut out the scream, her face. He'd never experienced Red torment like this—not an image of his mother, but her, *exactly*: Lorelei, alive and screaming, forever in that moment . . .

"Judah? Judah!" Noa was suddenly over him, trying to stop his shudder. Her hands were on his shoulders, red with his blood.

He wrenched himself from her. "Don't touch me! Get away!"

"Judah—" Her eyes were terrified.

He forced himself to his feet. *"You shouldn't be here."*

He stumbled angrily to the stairs, not stopping to look back.

• • •

NOA HURRIED OUT after Judah into the night. "I'm sorry, I just wanted to—I needed to make sure you'd be OK—Judah, what happened?" She tried not to show how scared she was. He'd never looked so . . . wrong.

"They don't know where Callum is," Judah said shortly.

"But will they help? They helped him make the talisman—"

"They're not his friends, Noa! How naive can you be? They're exiles, *bad Fae*!"

Noa tried to steady her voice. "What was their crime?"

"Who cares? I read their minds, and they don't know where he is. The boy was shocked to hear about the Hunter. Terrified." He scoffed. Noa refrained from mentioning that he, Judah, had had the very same reaction.

"Stop it!" Judah whirled on her. "Stop simpering!"

"I wasn't—"

"Didn't you see what happened in there? He almost *melted my mind*, and for nothing! He knew nothing!"

"So we find another way—"

"Are you so blind? This is *Callum's* fault. Seeking out these kinds of Fae?" His anger overflowed, seeped out his pores. It scared her.

"So what do we do?"

Judah glared ferociously . . . then slumped.

"I have no idea."

• • •

"TELL ME WHERE IT IS, Blue Son," The Hunter, Thorn, warned, as he sharpened his favorite mortal invention—the screwdriver—into a razor point. "Actually, don't. I'd prefer you hold out longer."

Callum eyed the lethal tool. Thorn had intrinsic talent for

torture, no magical gift needed. He'd lost count of the hours he'd been chained in this suffocating, windowless room, of the instruments that had cut him, bled him, stabbed him . . . There was nothing here: just walls, his chair, and pain.

Callum wished his consciousness would abandon him, that his mind would break and go away, but it was just the opposite— he stayed painfully, unbearably present, for every detail of every device. The humans, Thorn purred, just so *industrious*. They had to be, with no powers of their own . . .

Callum screamed as Thorn stabbed the screwdriver through his thigh.

"Tell me where it is."

Callum was glad he had no idea what Thorn was after—had he known, he wasn't sure he could hold out. He closed his eyes and tried to think of Noa, of her hair with those different shades of gold, gray eyes like the sea—

A scream tore from Callum's mouth despite himself as a twin screwdriver drove through his other thigh. A quiet knock sounded at the door of what Callum now thought of as his tomb.

"Enter!" boomed Thorn, without turning. Callum didn't bother either. It was always them.

"Someone came to look for him," Fabian reported quietly. Callum looked up, wincing with the effort. Fabian was tense, not smug as usual. Pearl was twirling her hair anxiously. "It was his brother."

Callum didn't dare breathe.

"What did you tell him?" Thorn asked, unconcerned.

"Nothing," Pearl said immediately.

"Your thoughts?"

"He's unskilled," Fabian said. "It was simple to block him, even for Pearl. Just as they always said."

Anger boiled in Callum, even if it was the truth.

Thorn turned to consider Callum, heaving and bleeding under his chains.

"Could it be? Are you *not* so brave? Do you truly . . . not know?" He mused a moment. "If the brother is here . . . I suppose it's possible . . . I've captured the wrong son."

"No—" Callum protested.

"Silence or I kill you and then him."

Callum shut his mouth, in no position to argue.

"Shall we retrieve the Red one?" Fabian asked.

"*Color Fae*," Thorn spat. "No elegance. Why waste energy when we know he'll come to us? He wants his brother, does he not?"

"You don't need us then?" Fabian asked through gritted teeth.

"On the contrary. In the meantime . . ." Thorn eyed Callum hungrily.

"But, sir," Fabian insisted, "if the Blue one doesn't know where it is, won't breaking into his mind with my gift . . . be a waste?"

Thorn laughed loudly, yanked a screwdriver from Callum's thigh and hurled it into the wall, where it stuck an inch from Fabian's face. "Have *imagination*! He has secrets, boy. *Many secrets . . .*"

"Oooh," Pearl shivered in delight. "He's afraid, I feel him quickening—"

"The virtuous have the most to hide," Thorn gleamed. "I promised you information for your allegiance, did I not? Don't you want a little more?"

Thorn held out his hand, and Fabian obediently stepped into reach, bracing himself. Thorn's palm hit Fabian's chest, and

Fabian arched back in a soundless scream and burst of Light. Callum wailed as Thorn crashed into his mind.

"MORE LIGHT! WE NEED MORE LIGHT!" Thorn yelled as the Channeling wavered, then broke, leaving Fabian on the floor. "Why are you so low? Get a human in here!"

"Who?" Pearl asked shakily, looking at Fabian's slumped form.

"I don't care! Your pet! Hurry up!"

Pearl tripped over herself and ran out, returning a moment later pulling a schoolboy behind her who was simpering in her Green thrall.

Callum looked through blurry eyes at the newest human battery. It had to be his fading vision, surely . . . The boy stared happily at Pearl, as Fabian reach out toward him—then Thorn touched Fabian, Fabian touched Miles, and for Callum, everything exploded.

• • •

THE SCHOOL FELT eerie and cold when Judah and Noa returned.

"I'll go to Olivia's so we can show up at breakfast together. Are you—"

"I'm fine," he snapped, "I'll go to Callum's."

"But—"

"I'll think of something and find you tomorrow. I'm *fine,* but I'll need to recover my energy to baseline overnight since Fabian—" he broke off, clenched his teeth. "I can't heal like Callum, but all Fae recover somewhat with time."

Noa nodded. "Callum told me that, after he got the talis—"

But Judah didn't wait to hear her finish, already walking away into the night.

She wanted to follow him, but went the other way instead, toward Olivia's.

Behind her, when she could no longer see him, Judah stopped and watched her go.

• • •

OLIVIA WAS SLEEPING when Noa let herself in, using the key always hidden above the doorframe. She lifted the edge of Olivia's sheet and slipped in beside her, sure she would never fall asleep, but before she knew it, Olivia was singing in her ear: "Wake it up, little No-ser!"

Noa groaned, fuzzy-brained, and reached for the crumpled mound of yesterday's (and last night's) clothes. She pulled them on, reeking of smoke, and scraped up a messy ponytail.

"You have lost your touch," Olivia scolded, chucking a Ziploc of stolen D-Hall cereal at Noa's head. "Chow to go. I'm swinging by the office to see if Jeremy's still absent."

Noa's stomach sank. Judah had promised he hadn't fed Jeremy to the Portal, but she couldn't shake her uneasiness.

"I hope he didn't pull a Carly Ann and just go home altogether," Olivia said.

"Carly Ann left?" Noa replied, stunned, sadness for her friend overwhelming her.

"Guess it got too hard. You know how it is."

Noa looked down; she did. But she also knew Carly Ann was mostly Judah's fault. *Another thing we'll make right*, Noa promised herself. *We'll find a way.*

"Get some coffee," Olivia called as she left. "And, girl, when did you start snoring?"

As the door shut, Noa became overwhelmed by everything—
Dr. Chandler, Annabelle, now maybe Jeremy—Noa had to find
a way to save them—poor Carly Ann, and Miles, who needed a
friend-tervention STAT. But to do it all she needed *Callum*, who
was out there, suffering . . . and Judah—was he OK?

The one thing she would not do was wait.

Noa went immediately to the Annex to find Judah, arriving
just as Miles happened to be stalking out. His face was dark, hair
and clothes messy. Not careful-messy—everything-sucks-and-I-
don't-give-a-rat's-ass messy.

Noa sped up to meet him. "Miles!"

He barreled past her, hitting her shoulder; in the jolt, his
pocket knife clattered to the ground. She bent to retrieve it, then
held it out, calling after him, "Wait!"

Miles stopped but didn't turn around. Instead, he slowly,
deliberately put in earbuds, then continued walking away. Noa
stood frozen, watching his back recede, his knife smooth upon
her outstretched palm. Finally she closed her fingers around it
and tucked it carefully into her pocket.

• • •

JUDAH WASN'T IN Callum's room. She finally found him lurk-
ing outside Sasha's classroom.

"I was just checking on her. I didn't want to intrude," Judah
said defensively. "I know she's not my sister."

"It's OK. But are you . . . OK?"

Judah took her elbow, pulled her into the grounds so they
could talk. They ended up by Callum's tree.

"You look tired," Judah observed.

"Gee, thanks," Noa rolled her eyes, then caught herself. "Great, now you've got me doing that."

They stood, suddenly awkward for some reason. Noa blushed, looked down. "Are you—"

"RED SON."

They both whirled, shocked by the booming voice. Beyond Callum's tree, they saw the Hunter's face—or something that *looked* like it, but strangely magnified, like a projection from a nightmare.

Judah shoved Noa, hard, into a thorn bush, as the phantom head flew toward him, whipping his hair with furious wind. "YOU KNOW WHY I HAVE COME."

"I know you've stolen my brother!" Judah yelled back at the phantasm, straining against the rushing air. The head was three times as wide as Judah was, the mouth alone big enough to consume him, had it been made of flesh and teeth.

"SPEAK *YOU* OF STEALING?"

"You've kidnapped a son of Darius! You're good as dead!"

"WHO DO YOU THINK SENT ME, BOY? HE WANTS *THE RING.* I SHOULD HAVE KNOWN *YOU* WERE THE THIEF." The ghoul-Hunter's massive eyes were dark, his stubble huge like floating knives.

Noa huddled deeper into the bush, which also shook fiercely in the wind. The branches whipped and cracked, thorny teeth snagging her hair and skin; she could barely hear, the roar of wind and ghoul deafening and distorting. Noa didn't care what was being said; she just wanted Judah to run, run *now*, not stand there so angry and defiant—

"I don't know what you are talking about!" Judah yelled into the phantom.

The phantom simply smiled, lips stretching to reveal boulders of teeth: "BRING ME THE RING OR THE BLUE SON DIES." The wind began to swirl, howling into a tornado—and the phantom vanished in a vortex, hurling Judah backward.

In the sudden stillness, Noa scrambled to him, steadied herself against him as he steadied against her. For a moment, they held each other up.

"He was projecting astrally." Judah winced. "It's an extension of the Red gift. . . . I never learned it."

"It wasn't really . . . a giant head?"

"You can project whatever image you want. I was clearly the target; he didn't see you."

Gradually, Noa's pulse calmed, her mind clearing from its panic. She grabbed Judah's arm, suddenly angry. "You stole a ring?"

Judah's face contorted, pulling away. "You automatically assume I'm the bad guy?"

"You said you came here for Callum!"

"I did!"

"No you didn't! You stole some ring and ran away!"

"That's not how it happened! That's not—" Judah cut off. "What does it matter? You've made up your mind. I'm bad, he's good, and that's it." He turned on his heel.

She wrenched him back. "Oh no you don't. You don't get to walk away. You don't get to come into this world, *lie* about why you came, get your brother *kidnapped*, and leave *me* to pick up the pieces!" Her time of babying him, of tiptoeing around his feelings, was long, long over.

"I didn't lie."

"You did."

"I didn't!"

"You did!"

"I DIDN'T!"

"Then what about the ring!"

"IT WAS MY RING!"

Noa's eyes widened. She stumbled, bit her fist not to scream. She hadn't really wanted to believe—*Breathe.*

It took every single fiber of her being to restrain herself enough to ask.

"What does that mean?"

Judah was defiant: "It means, it was more mine than his."

"More yours than the Hunter's?"

"*Darius's,*" Judah hissed.

"So . . . you just stole it?"

"Semantics!"

Noa was livid. "So coming through the Portal wasn't some big heroic gesture at all. It was just you, running from another of your idiotic pranks."

"I came for Callum! But I also took the ring, because it was more mine than his!"

Noa scoffed. "Darius doesn't seem to think so. He sent a Hunter after it."

"He has no right! It was my mother's and he—" Judah's pain was so profound that Noa's own anger faltered. He pushed it away as fast as lightning, but she had seen it all the same.

"Judah," she said, more calmly. "Maybe it's a misunder-standing—"

"It's no mistake," Judah retorted. "I'll tell you, since you obvi-ously won't trust me. After Lily died and Callum *left* . . . everything went to hell. Darius decided to punish all Color Fae, including my mother and me. He cast us out, married some Clear Pixie and adopted her Clear son. He *humiliated* Lorelei, took everything she had from her, even her Lover's Ring!"

"I don't understand—"

"It's not like a crown. Not a piece of state. It's a simple band, a tradition of the poorest Fae—plain, tin, but woven with one strand of hair from every child. My father took even that from her, to give to his Clear *whore*. . . . I was all she had left!" Judah spat. "Her heart was *broken*. We had to live in the Tunnels, eat rats, and she wept, oh she wept for that ring . . . Lily, Callum, it was the last she had of them—"

"It had your hair too," Noa reminded him quietly.

Judah looked away, as if that detail was irrelevant. "I heard Darius was planning a public coronation, where he'd give *Fayora* the crown and ring. To punish my mom for 'enchanting him against his will.' So I *stole it*. I stole it, and gave it back to her."

Noa hoped he couldn't see how her heart was breaking for him. "What did she say?"

A strange look passed quickly over Judah's features. "I gave it to her when I told her I was leaving to find Callum. She . . . was proud of me. But . . ." His voice began to shake. "But she pressed it into my palm, curled my fingers around it." He mimed the actions, every muscle remembering. "Told me . . . to keep it, as my link to her, so I could remember how proud she was—" He broke off, brushed his eyes, turned away.

When Judah spoke again, his voice was hard. "So I won't give it to Darius. He can't have it—not there, and not here either."

"Why—why didn't you just tell us?" Noa asked softly.

Judah scoffed. "Callum?"

"Me, then."

"You were just a mortal." He looked down. "I won't give up the ring, but we don't need it. The Hunter was Channeling the boy from the club, Fabian, to astrally project to me."

"But you searched Fabian's mind—"

"Fabian's more . . . skilled . . . than I am. He must have blocked me at the club. But I've felt him in my head before. I know the Hunter was Channeling him."

"Noaaaaaa . . ."

Judah and Noa turned to see Sasha running toward them, Ms. Finlee following. Sasha looked so forlorn Noa almost laughed despite everything.

"Oh, Sash," Noa said comfortingly, hurrying to meet her. "What's the matter?"

Sasha pushed her little fist into her stomach.

"Stomach ache," Ms. Finlee supplied. "She may have eaten something off the floor. I was taking her to the office but—"

"She found me," Noa nodded. "She does that."

"School policy is to send her home. I tried calling—"

Noa turned to glance at Judah, still at Callum's tree, as Sasha twined her arms around Noa's neck. "We'll take her home."

• • •

"'HAVE A CARROT,' said the mother bunny . . ."

". . . *And she did*," Sasha whispered, finishing *The Runaway Bunny* with the special line she and Noa had added. Noa and Judah tucked her into Noa's bed, and Sasha eyed him carefully.

"*My* Noa."

Noa had to bite her lip to keep from laughing. It took Judah a minute to realize he was being dismissed. Sasha pointed him to the closet. He shrugged and went, but Noa caught his smile.

Sasha curled around Noa, snuggling in with the warm dots of her toes.

"Noa?" she whispered slowly. "My tummy . . . OK."

Noa breathed out carefully. "That's OK Sash. That's why home is here."

"You stay now?"

Noa bit her lip. "I'm not sure, Sash. I may have to spend a few more nights at school."

"Then home?"

"Yes," Noa said.

"Promise?"

"I promise." Though Noa couldn't see Judah, she could feel him, listening to her lie.

"OK," Sasha said bravely.

Noa waited to be sure her voice wouldn't tremble. "Sash, have I ever told you about Isla's parachute?"

"Uh-uh."

"Maybe you weren't big enough before."

"I'm big now!" Sasha insisted, and Noa nodded, smiling.

"I agree, so now I'll tell you. When I was little, not much bigger than you, I was getting ready to go to Harlow with Isla. But I wasn't as brave as you. I was afraid of wearing the uniform, and being so far away all of the time without Mom and Dad."

"You sleep. With Isla," Sasha said seriously.

"Yes, I slept there, just like Isla. And I knew she'd be there too, but I was still scared. I told Isla, what if I need you, but can't find you? Or what if I need you, but you're not there?"

"Yeah," Sasha murmured.

"Isla told me I'd have to use the parachute. She locked her door, and reached under her bed . . ." Noa reached down and brought up her hands as if they carried a heavy weight. "And she brought out the most beautiful parachute I'd ever seen. Do you see it?"

Sasha examined the empty air above Noa's palms, eyes wide.

"It was hand-woven by fairy-gypsies, fae-gypsies, Isla said. See how it's every color under the sun? And here"—Noa pointed— "here's a treasure map to Neverland, and here," she pointed again, "the tracks of wildebeests and bears."

"Here," Sasha said, pointing to a new spot, "*Runaway Bunny* carrots."

Noa smiled. "Yes, and here, the patterns of Daddy's stars."

Sasha ran her hands over and over the imaginary cloth.

"It's fine like silk, and bright like gold, and light as a feather of air," Noa told her, "and when you're scared, or you feel lost or falling, it will float you home."

"Yeah?"

"Yeah," Noa said. "It will hug you if you're lonely, it will warm you if you're cold. It will rescue you and lift you up and help you fly. And it has every map you'll ever need, to guide you out, and guide you home."

"Isla's," Sasha whispered, tracing patterns on Noa's hands.

"It was Isla's, and then it was mine, and now, I'm giving it to you. And even though it has every single path and map—"

"All," Sasha echoed.

"It folds and folds, into the tiniest triangle that can fit in any pocket, or even down your sock."

Sasha's hand went instinctively to her foot.

"It will always be there, always," Noa told her. "Just remember, it's a secret."

"Magic," Sasha nodded.

Noa smiled and crinkled up her nose. "Yeah."

"Like Judah."

Noa caught her breath. "What do you mean, Sash?"

Sasha didn't say. She just kept running her hands over and over the parachute.

"Tuck me?"

Noa tucked the parachute around Sasha, who was asleep by the time she'd finished.

"Magic . . ." Sasha murmured. Whether Sasha was awake or dreaming, Noa never knew.

• • •

"I WISH I could have seen the parachute. It was too dark by the time I was freed from my chamber," Judah said when they were outside the house again.

"Don't make fun of me."

Judah looked confused. "I wasn't. I wish I could've seen it."

"Judah," Noa said incredulously, "it's imaginary."

Judah looked stunned at her stupidity. "That doesn't mean it isn't real." Before Noa could reply, Judah was on to other things. "I think we should talk to Kells, before we go back to the club."

"What? *You* said that's way too dangerous!"

"We need help, Noa! The Hunter has Callum *and* the twins—that's Blue, Red, and Green powers!"

"But you—"

"I'm—I'm no match for them, don't you see? Fabian tricked then tracked me. And his sister . . . not to mention *Callum's* gift. I don't get this. It was *your* idea. You said Callum was worth the risk!"

Noa stopped. Wasn't she willing to risk anything, everything, for Callum?

Even . . . Judah?

"Listen," Judah pressed, "Kells hates me and Callum, but, Noa, —*he may hate the Hunter more.* The Hunter's Clear Fae, sent *directly* by Darius. In a sense, he's Darius's *true* child, much more than me or Callum, who after all, Darius Banished. So the enemy of Kells' enemy . . ."

"But Callum said he can't leave the Portal anyway—"

"Information, Noa. He *knows* who's tethered to the Portal, and when they'll have to feed it. He knows, for example, that in about twenty-four hours, I will have to send another person through unless I right the balance. He knows I last sent back . . ." Judah swallowed hard. "Your teacher—"

"Who? *When?*"

Judah shifted. "After the Fyre, the Portal was pulling me, and she was making you unhappy—"

"*Who?*"

"That counselor," Judah mumbled, looking away.

Noa held her head in her hands, unable and unwilling to absorb this too.

"Judah—" She broke off, afraid to continue.

"My only point," Judah said, "is that the Hunter's a Portal jumper too. He wasn't Banished, he was sent on a temporary mission. *He has to feed the gateway, too.*"

Noa felt sick. "Oh my God, *Jeremy*. It was the Hunter . . . and God knows who else—"

"Noa, we can *use* it," Judah said. "Kells will know when the Hunter's time is running out, when he'll be sucked back and vulnerable. It may be our only chance."

Noa tried to feel hopeful, to reach down deep and find some kind of resilience, but it felt like the night the soup pot burned: everything charred black.

"Kells also loved my mother once," Judah added quietly, something catching in his throat. "So maybe for love of her, if not hate of him . . .

"Noa, we have to try."

• • •

JUDAH HAD TRIED to cover just how afraid he was to approach Kells. Noa at least had agreed to stay out of sight this time—it was one thing to hope Kells might divulge information, quite another to expect him to ignore a mortal's knowledge. It was tricky: Kells might be able to maneuver *around* the Gatekeeper restrictions, but not openly defy them.

"I want to be able to see," Noa told Judah as they approached the shack. Judah tried not to look at the creases by her eyes. They were moons-old, deeper than any pain caused by him and Callum. If the worst should happen—and most likely it would—at least that this would not be the thing that broke her.

Somehow, that made him think of Lorelei.

Judah led Noa quietly to a nook outside the shack between the bushes. He motioned for her to crouch and look through the boards, where the slats didn't quite come together—when suddenly, the entire shack shook, as if in an earthquake. Judah froze; Noa yanked him down beside her.

The nook was small, cramped, their bodies pressed tightly together as they looked together through the crack.

"Kells!"

They were too late; the Hunter was inside, already back to feed the Portal. All they could do was watch.

"Kells!" Thorn boomed again, and the gnarled Gatekeeper shuffled out. Beside Thorn, Kells looked even more deformed, sickly in the green light spraying from the Portal behind him. Even Kells' ramshackle furniture and cluttered tools, tinted green, looked mutant and alive.

"Where's the offering, Thorn?" The Portal pulsed hungrily, hissing and spitting in its frame, belching out green gas.

"Oh, I've no offering this time," Thorn grinned.

Judah's pulse quickened. Something wasn't right.

Kells sensed it too, uneasy: "You have what you came for then? The ring?"

"Not yet."

"If you've brought no mortal—"

"Nasty business, being tethered," Thorn interrupted lazily. "So *inconvenient* and messy, finding all those humans to stretch my time. Much better to right the balance good and *final*, don't you think?"

"You'd have to stay here. And you'd need a true exchange,

magic for magic—" Kells broke off, realizing too late. "No! You can't!" But Thorn was already upon him, snatching and whipping him back and forth so hard they heard every bone inside Kells break. But Kells didn't die; Thorn was careful not to kill him. Judah felt a piercing pain on his forearm and looked down to see Noa clutching him, nails dug in, as she watched in horror.

"*Magic for magic*," Thorn roared, and hurled the Gatekeeper through his own Portal, into the jaws of the In-Between.

The Portal shook, then the entire shack began to quake. Sparks blurred and built within the green, swirling into a blinding golden spiral: a fireflower, unfurling petals of molten gold.

Noa gasped, Judah too. It was unlike any beauty he'd ever seen. Nothing like when he fed the Portal mortals and it belched out sickly green—this was a golden supernova, the gateway balanced, magic for magic across the worlds.

Thorn cried out in ecstasy as his tether and Mark vanished. The light subsided, and he reached upward, feeling every particle of sky.

"*Freedom.*"

Judah fell backward. Kells was lost, Thorn stronger than ever. But none of that even mattered: What mattered was getting Noa far from here, and fast.

He grabbed her fingers—still digging their half-moons— wrenched her up and away. She didn't protest, sped up beside him, knew instinctively to flee.

• • •

EVEN BEFORE CALLUM'S door latched, Noa was frantically upon Judah with questions.

"What just happened? Did he kill him?"

"Kells isn't dead—he needed to be sacrificed alive to right Thorn's balance—"

"Then Thorn's free," she interrupted. "And you—"

"I still have time. A day, maybe a day and a half. See my Mark? Not angry yet."

Noa couldn't look. "At least we don't have to worry about Kells finding out about me now."

Judah rubbed his neck.

Noa's heart sank. "This is worse, isn't it."

"There's a reason for the Gatekeeper. The Portal is inherently unstable because it was opened by dark magic—Fae blood, sacrifice. Kells was a way to guide the sacrifice, keep it contained . . . but now . . ."

Noa saw the sweat of fear at Judah's temples. "Judah, what does that *mean*?"

"I don't know. The Portal needs constant feeding. It used to slowly feed off Kells so he could exert some control over its . . . needs."

"Which means?"

Judah threw up his hands. "It's on its own, who knows! But I'm guessing it's a pretty crappy time to be tethered to it!"

"Judah, we'll find a way—"

"And Thorn did it to *stay* in a world without Light? It makes no sense—" Judah paced so hard the floor could've given way.

"We have to trade the ring!" Noa cried. "We have to get Callum *now*!"

He whirled on her. "Are *you* insane? We're not setting foot near Thorn." Noa opened her mouth but Judah cut her off. "Actually, I don't care what *you* do, but I'm getting far away from the Portal. I'll mind control people and send them back with my blood."

Noa grabbed him. "What about Callum?"

"Callum's lost."

"He's not! The ring!"

"Darius doesn't get that!"

"Why are you being so selfish?" Noa cried, shoving him backward. "Callum would do it for you! He was *Banished* for you!"

"SO WHAT?"

"So what? So *what*? He's your brother!" Noa yelled. "No, I take that back. You can't be brothers, you can't, because you are nothing, *nothing like him*!" Furious tears welled in her eyes.

"I never *said* I was like him—"

"You're right," Noa snapped. "You're just . . ." She searched for the word that would be her weapon: "*broken.*"

She watched it detonate.

"Broken," Judah hissed slowly. "*I'm* broken. Callum's good and I'm bad. He's the hero and I'm the villain. He's *whole,* and I'm *broken*?" Judah slowly advanced on her—and

her anger fragmented into a million shards of fear. His face looked bestial, inhuman, white canines glinting. She grasped the talisman; the chest throbbed inside her palm.

Judah laughed—horrible, bitter. "*You don't even know what that is.*"

Noa's back foot smashed into Callum's bed; she fell backward, landed on the mattress with a jolt, clutching her trembling wrist to her heart. Judah didn't seem to register that she'd fallen, or maybe didn't care. He made every sentence count.

"A *talisman* is the most shameful, most *evil* of the dark magic.

Perfect Callum let that Red Fae viper carve off a piece of his *soul.* Chip it off! Not a metaphorical piece, a *hard, physical* piece, a concrete chunk of essence. Chiseled, bloodied—" Judah's face distorted, words hot and toxic. "It's a violence that can never be undone, leaves a void in his deepest center—"

Noa shivered even as the charm now seemed to scald her skin.

"And do you know, Noa," Judah pressed, "what happens when you leave a space in someone's soul? *Things* rush in to fill it up. Dark things. Bad things. Dirty, perverted things. Nature hates a vacuum. Maimed souls are fertile ground. Now, I may be 'broken,' but I am nothing so broken, so terrible as *that.*"

Noa choked, fell off the bed onto the floor. Judah faltered, finally shocked back to himself. He stumbled back, torn between hate and hurt, and something else.

"Callum's broken," he insisted, voice now trembling terribly. "And *you're* the one who broke him."

The tiny charm seethed and pulsed; Noa felt the ceiling falling and the floor pushing up, as if she the world was compacting her. She'd felt this way only once before, in the hospital with Isla—Noa frozen to her bed, watching Isla disappear through swinging operating room doors, her bed pushing up, roof crushing down; organs smashed and heart rolled out thin like crepe paper, just as friable and cheap. Noa had promised herself never to feel that way again. She'd swapped her marrow for diamond granite, had never passed through hospital doors again—

She would not go back to that place.

"Judah," Noa said firmly, getting up. "Callum made this talisman to protect me. I didn't know what it entailed; I would not have asked him for that, which you well know." Judah stuck out his chin. "He didn't make it for you, Judah, but he would have. To protect you. Just like when he came here."

Judah exhaled forcefully through his nose, fighting his hardest.

Noa continued, clear and even: "I know your mom gave you that ring because she was proud of you. But she was proud of your *sacrifice*, Judah. *That's* what she was commemorating. She would want you to save your brother. She would forgive you for not being able to save both."

Judah was shaking now. "He didn't break his soul for you," he finally managed to reply. "Because he'd already broken it for me. When he took my Banishment, when Lily . . . it broke him. It broke us all."

Noa wanted to go to him, touch him—but didn't.

He shuddered. "We'll trade it."

Noa exhaled in relief. "Where is it?"

He flushed with shame. "Your house. I hid it there, the night I followed you home."

• • •

THEY LEFT CALLUM'S room in silence. Noa wasn't sure how she felt about what Judah had done. Hiding the ring at her house had endangered her family, but Judah hadn't known her then, and *that* Judah felt like someone else entirely. He'd changed since then, or she had—or maybe they'd changed each other.

Miles passed them in the hall, shoving past Noa's shoulder again. Judah whirled, growling, but Noa beat him to it. She'd been wrung around enough today.

"Miles!" She caught the tail of his shirt.

"What?" he demanded.

His face took her aback. "Nothing, you—you kind of ran into me."

"I'm late for lacrosse."

"I saw you quit," she reminded him, "and you're dressed up." Miles was wearing what Harlow guys called their 'lady-killers'—a trendy polo and tailored jeans. Miles simply snorted and walked away.

"I have your pocket knife!" Noa called after him lamely, but he didn't stop.

Judah looked at her. She shook her head. "One boy at a time."

• • •

SASHA WAS STILL napping when they slipped back in through Isla's window. Noa fought a sudden urge to nestle next to her, pull down the covers.

"Over here." Judah was at Noa's white, curved dresser. He reached for one of the small boxes on top—gifts Hannah had brought home from her adventures—and selected the gray oval, low and flat like a pebble, from Shanghai. The one Hannah had said held sounds from a busy farmers' market.

Inside was shiny, brightest red—and it was empty.

"Gone," he whispered, stunned. "Stolen . . ."

"Are you sure you hid it there?"

Judah's buried his face in his hands. "I thought it would be safe—"

"Wait," Noa interrupted. As if on cue, Sasha snored. "There's your thief." She smiled. "She's a magpie, Judah. She collects lost things."

Noa paused to make sure the coast was clear, then led Judah to Isla's room.

Isla's closet was no longer Noa's hiding place, but it was still Sasha's. In the far corner, Noa reached to feel for peeling paper. She pulled out the square cigar box from Cuba, camouflaged by Sasha's faded scraps.

Noa sat back with the box on her knees, Judah waiting beside her. She stopped, offered it to him instead.

He carefully opened Sasha's nest of treasures: lone earring backs, a broken pin, a buffalo nickel that once was Isla's. And in back, on top of a scrap of handkerchief, around a fountain pen without ink, was the ring. Bent and tarnished, not looking precious at all.

But the tender way he lifted it . . . a piece of his mom, and home.

Judah closed his hand tightly around it for a moment, took a deep breath, then opened his palm.

Noa saw a glimmer. "Judah, did you see that?"

"See what?"

"The ring . . . there, it just did it again."

Judah polished the ring on his shirt, held it to his eye. Sure enough, the inside was emitting, every so often, a few translucent sparks.

Judah looked bewildered. "It's never done that before. Maybe it's Fae alloy reacting to this realm." He pulled the scrap of handkerchief from Sasha's box, wrapped the ring carefully, and put it into his pocket.

"Sorry we have to trade it, Judah," Noa murmured.

Judah swallowed. "I'll—I'll meet you outside." He got up shakily. She waited a moment before following, to give him privacy.

"Noa, did you see this?" he called from Isla's room.

"What?" She came out of the closet, joined Judah at Isla's desk, where Hannah had left a mock-up of her book.

"She's almost finished . . ." Noa murmured, touching the oversized pages, their glossy letters and bright photos. She lifted the top page, gasped: her "Sandpaper Places" poem now spoke from the haunting Monterey coast, fog stretching its thumbs into wilds of the waves. *Adrift*, Noa thought, touching froth that could have been clouds or currents, *though I never used that word.*

Noa turned the page—Traveler-Woman," her mother's poem, and Lorelei's, was dancing in a wild almost-garden: a reckless plain of succulents open to the sky. Survivor-blooms everywhere, so many shapes and colors—stars and planets, carousels—with climbing buds and rings of leaves. Where had her mother found this place, what realm and what terrain? It could only exist *between*: two worlds, beings, souls. A common place where orchids grew, for traveler women to take their meat.

Noa stumbled backward. Her north star shifted; the axis of her earth moved. Her mother the moon wasn't waning but waxing: every day more silver, more reflective, more bright. A sailor's guide, a light over the sea. There was still much, so very much, her mother didn't see and couldn't know, but Noa understood now so clearly, there was much she did.

"Noa," Judah said, turning to a page she'd missed: blank, or almost blank—the page of the dedication.

"*For Noa*," Judah read, "*who shines the light.*"

Noa backed away from the table, tears filling her eyes. When she reached the wall, she closed her eyes, let her body slide down.

She felt him sit beside her, felt his hand almost touching hers.

"We need to go," Noa said finally, though in truth, she wanted to stay inside this moment, inside this still and special place, with Judah.

But Noa rose, then went back to Isla's desk, her mother's mock-up. She held three fingers to her lips then touched the pages, one-by-one. *I. Love. You.* Their secret code from when she was small. She'd forgotten it until this moment. She never would again.

Judah was watching, and Noa somehow knew she didn't need to explain. She touched the talisman, knew he couldn't read her mind, but she was sure, so sure, he'd known exactly what she'd been thinking.

• • •

AS JUDAH CLIMBED down the tree, Noa quickly grabbed her journal, wrote the poem she kept hearing. At the window, she hesitated and went back, ripped out the page, folded it up and put in her pocket with Miles' knife. She'd suddenly realized she didn't want to leave that poem behind.

Sasha snored, turning over.

"I'll be back," Noa promised softly, picking up a stray puzzle piece, adding it to her pocket. *To put away later*, she told herself. *Not because I want something to remember her by.*

She turned the words over side-to-side as she climbed out, as if they really were the truth.

• • •

"YOUR LITTLE BROTHER will come soon," Thorn said, examining Callum's bleeding face. He sat back, bored, picked his nails with a knife. "The good son and the bad son," he mused, "the hero and the punk."

Callum pressed his lips together against any cry of pain. He wouldn't give Thorn that satisfaction. Even if it meant dying, mute, in this windowless tomb of a room.

"Not that I would trade my birthright," Thorn continued, "but if I had to be mongrel Color Fae, I do see the fun in Red. That Fabian does nice work." He leaned in, "Who'd have guessed your delicious secrets?"

Callum tried to swallow the fire in his throat, look defiant—but like red-hot steel, Fabian had scorched his way through Callum's mind, razed his memories inside out. Callum had tried to hide things, but in the end it was too hard—

"Why, Thorn?" Callum gasped, forcing his mind away from its last corner, the very last place he still protected. *Her.* "Why have you done this?"

"I am Hunter! Otec Darius enlisted me."

"Not why you came," Callum wheezed. "Why you murdered Kells to stay. Why not complete your mission, get your glory?"

"I assure you Kells lives, though I'm guessing he wishes he didn't," Thorn laughed. "Who knows where the Portal sent its hated keeper. And I assure you, I'll get the ring."

"But now you're here," Callum pressed, trying not to wince. "A prison . . ."

Thorn hurled his knife into the wall, nicking Callum's ear.

"Wrong, Blue Son. That's what Otec Darius *tells* us, what he wishes us to think. But I have *seen* . . ." He strode to the wall, yanked the knife free, held it close to Callum's eyes. "I was going to do it, get the trinket and go back—but now . . ." he spread his arms, as if the dark, small room contained a universe. "I will *become* Darius."

"You balanced the Portal . . . to try to rule this realm?"

"*Try?* Look around. Mortals are powerless!"

Callum did his best to look dismissive. "Judah won't give you the ring. He's selfish."

Thorn smiled. "He's tender like a child. I don't need that Green bitch to tell me that, or your secret thoughts."

The door to the chamber slammed open. Callum winced at the sudden brightness, unable to cover his eyes. When it closed again, he sighed in relief. He was a darkness-dweller now.

"The Red Son sent me a mind message, or attempted to," Fabian said immediately.

"Ready to trade?"

Fabian nodded curtly, Thorn laughed, and Pearl licked her lips.

• • •

"I'M REALLY STARTING to hate this place," Noa shivered in front of the club. The derelict warehouse seemed even more menacing, if that were possible.

"*Stay outside*," Judah commanded. He hadn't wanted her there at all but had known she would insist. Probably thought he'd cut and run if she didn't watch him.

"I'm *going* in. I'm not leaving Callum alone—or you."

"Right," Judah mumbled. She looked confused, but it wasn't worth an argument. "Look, this is a clean trade. The ring for Callum. Get in, get out."

"And capture one of the twins," Noa added, surprising him. "For you . . . to throw through the Portal? So you can . . . stay."

She blushed a little. "You don't agree? I thought . . . I mean, then you'd be free, you wouldn't have to . . ." She looked away. "Maybe it's a stupid idea."

"No," Judah said quickly. "I just didn't know you . . . wanted me to stay."

Awkwardness again. It was happening more and more.

Noa bit her lip. "It's not up to me . . . but if you stay, I don't think you should . . . you know, hurt people . . ."

Judah scoffed, angry at himself. "I don't know why you even think I *want* to stay here. So let's just get my brother, all right?" He stalked toward the entrance.

"Wait!"

Judah spun. "If you insist on being stupid and coming in, we can't enter together."

"But—"

"But what, Noa?"

"What if . . . something happens?" She cringed.

He narrowed his eyes. "If you're really scared, take off that talisman so I can hear your mind if you need me."

Noa stepped back, clutched the tiny silver chain.

Judah shook his head. "That's what I thought. Nothing's changed." He began to leave, then paused. "Just . . . stay safe."

• • •

NOA WAITED IN the alley, the chest charm warm against her palm. Now that she knew what it held, Callum's soul, she had to protect it, the way it protected her.

After a sufficient break, Noa slipped below, hiding in the heavy curtains lining the walls where she had hidden the last time.

She tried to calm herself: Soon she would have Callum back, not just a piece but *him*, tall and strong, his arms around her, everything just as it was . . .

"Isla," Noa breathed, as her sister's ghost materialized beside her. Isla was scowling in frustration.

Tell me, Noa implored helplessly. *Tell me what I'm supposed to do.*

• • •

JUDAH FOUND FABIAN immediately. He was waiting in his favorite perching spot in back, beyond the half ring of banquettes. Judah didn't see or feel Pearl anywhere.

"You hardly require a tag team," Fabian laughed, plucking the thought from Judah's head. "Besides, Thorn wants a clean exchange. The ring for your worthless brother. No muss, no fight."

"You expect me to take you at your word? Or him? He threw Kells into his own Portal."

"Yes," Fabian drawled. "Must be dreadful to be tethered now. Probably makes you wish you'd been properly Banished, like us." His gaze was cold.

"I'm fine."

"We'll see. My sister's with a client I'll need to wipe soon, so let's keep this moving. Hand it over."

"My brother first."

Judah tensed for Fabian, ready.

The ring. Now. The command hit Judah from every neuron. He tried to put up walls, push the compulsion out. It felt like pushing back a tidal wave with a paper shield. The pressure finally subsided, a glint in Fabian's eye.

"Interesting."

Judah smirked despite himself. He wasn't completely unskilled. He could resist, sometimes, he just had to *want* to. He might actually save Callum if he kept his wits about him, kept the ring safely hidden in his—

"Your secret pocket, oh so banal!" Fabian crowed.

Furious, Judah shook his head to clear it, snarled. "I'll make you regret that."

"I'd *love* to see you try."

• • •

ISLA'S STARE BORED into Noa: *Nothing goes back to how it was, it never will, it never does.* It ran over and over in Noa's mind, like Isla had set it on a loop. She shook her head, closed her eyes, but Isla was there too, inside her lids: *Nothing goes back to how it was, it never will, it never does.*

Noa opened her eyes, angry. Isla nodded, pleased, and moved toward the center of the salon. She paused, waiting. Noa followed.

Nothing goes back to how it was, it never will, it never does.

Isla led her to the half ring of banquettes, where before she'd found Judah, suffering. They were close, too close, to where Judah and Fabian were facing off. Noa's gasped: Fabian looked absolutely lethal.

But where was the girl, the twin? Was Pearl hiding, to take Judah by surprise?

Noa followed Isla's ghostly gaze to Pearl, just behind the last banquette in the shadows with a man, only two velvet booths from Noa. Noa almost gagged: Pearl was draining the man with relish, back arched, her long red locks twisting in demented ecstasy. She seemed almost to levitate, her body turning—and Noa nearly screamed.

It was *Miles*, in his silly lady-killer duds, being leeched of all his Light! Losing everything that made him good and kind—all that made him Miles!

Noa instantly leapt over the back of her banquette, raced to wrench Miles from Pearl's grip. Miles cried out in pain or surprise, relief or death itself, then he crumpled through Noa's arms, sliding unconscious to the marble floor.

Noa fell to her knees, grabbed him, shook him. "Wake up! Miles, *please*—"

Talons dug into Noa's shoulder, flung her across the floor into the wall. Miles' body toppled awkwardly, mouth hanging slightly open. Noa scrabbled toward him, needing to close his mouth—it looked wrong, the mouth of a stuffed animal, a thing—but the talons whipped her back again. Noa slid so fast the cold marble seared her skin.

"He's mine, schoolgirl," Pearl hissed. She glowered over Noa, ferocious in her beauty—white skin too smooth, green eyes too sharp, red hair thick and choking—her beauty toxic, fed by Miles' Light—

Noa reached for Miles again; Pearl slammed her back. "I said he's mine!"

Fear and panic exploded inside Noa. She forgot how to breathe, to think, existed only in terror—

Green Fae. The voice was small, from a distant corner of Noa's mind, the place that was still Noa. *The terror isn't real*, it said, across the panic—*the terror isn't real!*

Noa tried desperately to listen, but the emotions were too strong, overwhelming any reason. She fell backward, writhing, as

231

Pearl changed course like a hurricane and descended over Miles.

Just as Noa felt her bones would break in fear, Isla showed her face again. Noa locked her eyes on the ones so like her own, and Isla held her fast, moored her to a *real* emotion. A *real* pain, a real memory which couldn't be usurped. Noa felt the difference, and it freed her. Isla looked meaningfully at Noa's pocket: Noa reached in, felt the smoothness of Miles' knife. Before Pearl even realized Noa was free, Noa sprang forward like a human cannon-ball, knocking Pearl from Miles. She and Pearl slid together into the back of a banquette, and Noa leapt to pin her, Miles' knife open at her throat.

Pearl's eyes flashed. *"Who are you?"*

"His best friend," Noa whispered fiercely, leaning in. But even as she said it, her adrenaline was fading, brain catching up to where she was and whom she'd pinned. The panic swelled again. She should have stayed in the galley! Should have done what she was told!

"Stop!" Noa cried, forcing Pearl's gift out. She thought of Isla's loss, and Isla's love, pressed the knife and drew crimson drops of blood.

Pearl gasped in shock, looked from blood to knife to hand— and then the bracelet, on Noa's wrist.

Pearl's eyes met Noa's, glinting—and she exploded, twisted, pinned *Noa* back, knife now biting Noa's throat.

"*You're* the reason," Pearl crowed. "And my plaything's your friend, how apropos." She glanced toward Miles, still a heap. "He met me that night too, you know. The night the Blue Son begged us to maim him. Since then, well, he's been quite my little fanboy . . . though I confess, he hasn't really had a choice."

Rage mingled with Noa's terror. Pearl didn't notice, or didn't care. "Have you come with the brother then, that pitiful Red Son? That *is* delicious. And you knew what I was doing before, you felt my gift. One of them told you about us, the little fool. Too bad Kells is gone—"

Noa struggled fruitlessly as Pearl turned the knife so its point was piercing Noa's throat. She leaned in so close, Noa thought absurdly that Pearl might kiss her.

But Pearl just smiled her horribly beautiful smile, raised a brow as if to say *get ready*, and screamed a scream that shattered Noa everywhere.

• • •

"YOUR BOSS SAID a clean exchange," Judah stalled, stepping backward as Fabian sized him up to take the ring by force. "Do as you're told and get my brother."

"I'm no one's lapdog," Fabian snapped. "And you irritate me, so I'm gonna have a little fun."

"I'll block you out—"

"Maybe me, maybe for a little. But Pearl and I together?" Fabian smiled. "Do you know what Mindworms are, Red Son? Pearl and I have learned to hatch them inside mortals; they're born by blending gifts, like Red and Green." He was taunting Judah, relishing each word. "A Mindworm lives on its own, inside the mind of the victim, chewing true thoughts and feelings and hatching new ones of its own. A Mindworm, for example, keeps Pearl's fanboy hungering for her, even when they're apart; and at the same time, it wipes his knowledge of what he's doing, and what's been done. And that's just in *mortals*."

Judah focused not on Fabian's words, but on every step of his advance. He had to keep him talking, think of a strategy, fast. "I resisted you once today—"

"A ploy, so you'd reveal the ring. I grow tired of talk."

Fabian roared, and Judah's mind exploded. A jumble of images strobed across his eyelids—Callum and Darius, Lorelei's hair, Lily, cold and dead—

Judah wailed, stumbled back, tried to press his hands over his pocket. But his hands kept going, took out the ring—

Lily cold and dead cold and dead—

"No," Judah yelled, pushing the cloud of Fabian's gift away, heaving its sludge from Lily's face. He closed his fist on the ring, braced himself on his knees, panting.

"Interesting." Fabian cocked his head. "Did you know, Pearl's gift intensifies through touch?" Like lighting, he was on Judah, hands slapped to his bent shoulders. *"And so does ours."*

Judah didn't even feel the hands, lost every sense that mattered. Except to hear Fabian, taunting: "Green Fae tap the limbic system, but *we* siphon neural pathways. That's what I'm doing now, little Judah. I'm burning through the circuits of your brain!"

Images slammed Judah from all sides, even more relentless than before: Darius's rage, Channeling his son; Callum's face, hearing Judah's confession; Lorelei's tears, her naked finger; *Lily cold and dead, cold and dead, cold and dead—*

Fabian broke the connection, panting. Judah was on his knees, immediately searched his hands.

"I have it," panted Fabian, amusement gone. "You cost me quite a bit of Light."

Judah could barely breathe, eyes blurry on the ring now in Fabian's hand. His mother's ring with Lily's hair . . .

"This stupid, useless ring," Fabian sneered, slumped and breathing hard. "Darius takes it to shame your mother; you steal it to spite him; now Thorn wants it as some kind of stupid symbol of his power, like the crown that makes him emperor. And it's *nothing*. Worthless!"

"Not . . . worthless . . ." Judah wheezed, still unable to stand upright.

"You're right. It *could've* saved your brother's life. But now it won't." Trembling with fatigue, Fabian slipped the ring loosely over his pinky, the only finger it would fit.

Judah burned. "*Take that off—*"

"What? *This?*" Fabian shoved his hand into Judah's face, knowing Judah was too weak to snatch it back. As he held it there, the small sparks Noa had noticed began to multiply and swarm, pouring out all around the band. Fabian drew his hand back toward his face as all his fatigue lifted.

"Of course . . ." he murmured, awestruck. "Of course he'd never tell . . ." Judah watched, panicked, as Fabian began to glow. "It makes *Light,* in this realm . . . *This ring makes Light!*"

Judah knew instantly it was true. Fabian shone.

"With that ring, here—" Judah breathed.

"*You'd be a god,*" Fabian finished. "Thorn knew . . . or discovered . . . that's why he balanced the Portal, how he plans to rule—"

That's when Pearl's inhuman, banshee screech cut across the club.

"*Pearl!*"

It was Judah's only chance—without dexterity or agility, he

used brute force of weight, bowling into Fabian. Startled, Fabian fell back, the ring flying off his pinky. They heard it tinkle to the ground, roll into the shadows.

Fabian screamed, lunged at Judah, slammed his hands to Judah's temples. Supercharged by his brief moment with the ring, he unleashed himself on Judah's mind.

Judah couldn't even scream before everything was eviscerated.

• • •

PEARL'S SCREECH COULD shatter glass, but Noa barely heard it, because with the screech, conjured *by* the screech, Faefyre spewed from Pearl's mouth. Pearl's back arched, and a column of flame barreled toward the ceiling, writhing and uncoiling into a deadly flaming serpent.

"Faefyre is the Green's best secret," Pearl bragged, as the serpent twisted and grew wings, "I doubt even your *lovers* know." The serpent's pistol eyes locked on Noa, and it swelled toward her small, cowering figure—and dove. She collapsed on top of Miles, trying to shield him, as all around her, air caught fire.

"Faefyre comes from passions," Pearl crowed, voice seeming disembodied in the smoke. "Rage and lust and envy, and above all, *hate*." She screamed again, and another serpent of Fyre shot out and bloomed, circling above Noa.

"You set the fire at Harlow," Noa wheezed, seeing nothing, choking smoke.

"That was Thorn, Channeling me. *Clear Fae leech*," she spit. "But this Fyre, can you tell? It's sharper, *hotter*, because now I know you *personally*. It's born from what I'm feeling in this moment—loathing for your *irritating* face!"

Noa felt the difference—heat so thick it clogged her, flames coating her in scalding gel. The new serpent circled; the first swarmed to it to dive again—

Noa shut her eyes tight, huddled harder on top of Miles. She could do nothing, run nowhere—

"Judah!" she screamed. *"JUDAH!"*

"He can't hear you, child," Pearl laughed. "Fabian's destroyed his mind by now."

Noa's body began to convulse, her lungs spewing smoke. It seemed the serpents wanted to suffocate, then scald; soon, she knew, she'd just be flaming skin.

"Judah," she whimpered voicelessly, clutching at her throat. She yelped as her talisman, now white-hot, seared into her neck. She looked at it, bewildered—then immediately began to fumble with the clasp. It burned; she could barely see; but finally, finally, the bracelet fell.

JUDAH! She screamed inside her mind, reaching out to his. *JUDAH!* Her vision blurred then blacked.

I . . . need . . . you . . .

• • •

JUDAH WAS DROWNING in an echo chamber of Lorelei's tears and Callum's screams. His feet sank into a wamp of Lily's putrefied remains: kidneys, eyeballs, heart. There was no sound but Darius's curses; no smell but Faefyre he had caused; no time but now, evermore and everlasting, the slow-motion death of his own mind.

Then, as from a long, dark corridor, a different sound, a distant hum. He couldn't hear the words precisely, and as he strained, the rest slapped him down. Lily's bowels, rotting in his fingers . . .

"*Udy.*"

Judah whipped around. Lily's liver slipped under his fingers; he vomited—Callum's heart, self-mutilated, thrust up and out his mouth.

"*Udy.*"

Judah coughed and spluttered, got to his feet, Darius's Channeling hand searing on his chest—

"*Udy, listen.*"

And there: beside, below, where she hadn't been before, he saw her:

The one he loved.

The girl whose gaze held no judgment, crossing space and time. The face he saw when he awakened, before he slept. The girl he'd been determined to throw away, dismiss—and had come to love, to *need*, instead.

Lily.

"Udy," Lily said, the name only she had called him. "Listen."

Judah looked at her, alive and whole, and fell trembling to his knees. "Lily," he breathed, touching her curls, her hand, her cheek.

"*Listen,*" Lily repeated. He knew he should do it, listen, but why, why do anything but be with Lily, look at Lily, when he had found her here again—

"Udy, *listen.*" Lily shut her eyes. Obediently, because he never could refuse her anything, Judah shut his too. He opened his ears and listened, because Lily had told him he must.

Then, from another long, dark hallway, from behind a door to someplace far away, he heard another echo. Faint, hard to decipher. He didn't want to try.

"*Judah . . . I need you . . .*"

Judah's eyes snapped open. Lily nodded. *Noa.*

"I have to go," he said, immediately moving toward Noa's voice. He paused, turned back.

"I'm sorry, Lily."

Lily cocked her head, the way she often used to do. "Listen, Udy." She smiled.

Judah turned toward Noa, knowing if he looked back, Lily would be gone.

• • •

JUDAH WAS SUDDENLY back in his aching, sweating body, choking on smoke, unable to move his limbs. He blinked through ash: Fabian was pinning him, looking strangely dazed, and the club around them was on fire. Judah pressed him back, and Fabian sputtered to attention. Fabian, too, it seemed had been paralyzed by the force of his torture. Registering Judah, Fabian instantly grabbed him and tried to break back into his mind.

But Judah saw Lily, heard Lily, chose to listen only to her. It was simple now, even easy, to block out Fabian's gift. He could *see* it—a tar-like, viscous fog—and he easily pushed it back. He became the wind, directing it, blowing it back into Fabian's own mind. Fabian resisted, but Judah broke through, forcing the dark amoeba to latch itself on Fabian.

Instantly, Fabian's brain opened itself for Judah, memories strobing and flashing in Judah's inner eye. The boldest, repeating most—and thus the most painful, Judah knew—looked like the twins' Banishment—no, some kind of ritual, with burning flames. There was Darius, chanting, and blood fed to the fire,

239

and—somehow—Lorelei? She was terrified. Fabian and Pearl were children, screaming, thrashing—and beside Lorelei, two more young faces, eyes open wide. Two boys: one tall, one slight, both dark. Brothers—

Judah gasped, losing the connection, letting Fabian slip free. He fell off-balance, bewildered. That was his face, and Callum's—they were the boys, witnessing that terrible exile. But Judah didn't remember it, or them; surely he would have remembered—

Fabian fell instantly to the ground, searching through the ash. Judah snapped to the present. The club was on fire; Fabian was after the ring—

But with that ring, he and Callum could live here forever, with their gifts, never hurting anyone!

He had to get it first.

Judah lunged, hitting Fabian just as his fingers unearthed the ring. Fabian fell forward, losing it; it bounced and landed inches from a patch of spreading flames. Judah fell on top of him. They struggled, evenly matched and evenly exhausted—then Judah thought of Lily. He roared, pressed Fabian back, slapped his hands to Fabian's chest—

Get me the ring, he compelled, with every ounce of strength he had; *then go immediately to the Portal and jump through.* Judah wiped blood from his bleeding arm against Fabian's temple, to ensure the Portal would reset *his* balance and no one else's.

Judah . . .

Noa's feeble cry broke Judah's concentration, so much fainter than before. Noa, who'd cried to him and set him free, the girl he'd risen up to save.

Below him, Fabian gleamed as he heard Judah's thoughts. "You can't do both," he whispered. "Me and the ring—freedom— or that girl?" *Quick, quick*, he added, grinning, *if it burns in Fae- fyre, the magic dies . . .*

Judah, Noa pleaded, faint, from where he couldn't see. *Miles . . . here too . . .*

She had instants, not even moments. Judah glared at Fabian, his tormentor, who knew all his secrets; and the ring, its bound- less freedom, he and Callum forever without Darius . . .

There was no comparison.

Judah flung Fabian, away, sprinted toward the homing bea- con of Noa's mind. Behind him Fabian wailed, and Judah knew the ring had burned, was gone.

Judah flew to the heart of the Faefyre, not even feeling the searing flames. Noa was clearly its target, huddled over a lump of smoking rags—*Miles*, probably dead. Either way, he'd have to save them both.

This Fyre was beyond any Judah had seen, and Judah knew it wouldn't stop until its target was maimed or killed. He couldn't count on it to burn out if he took Noa far enough away; some- how, he'd have to shift its target.

Without hesitating to consider the risks or the enormity of skill it would demand, Judah reached out to the Fyre's mind— and with a scorching, searing pulse, connected. Its consciousness was scalding, ravenous, too volatile to safely hold inside—but he held it, screaming—and saw the Fyre's red-hot thought was Noa, huddling over the black shape of Miles' lifeless body.

Judah writhed, still screaming, and visualized a large, dark cloud—a fog of intentions—and cloaked it around the blaze's mind. As it seeped in, combusting, the images of Noa and Miles vanished, and the Fyre saw two new faces: Fabian and Pearl.

Slowly, painfully, as if drawing from Judah's own muscles, tissue, sinews, the flames curled back from Noa, stretched and shifted their desire. But Pearl and Fabian, it seemed, had fled; the flames could not be sated. They roared and built and coalesced into a single, massive dragon. Judah screamed with the agony of it, for its wings were his wings, bursting forth inside him too— and then the dragon roared, spewing fire onto itself, and combusted in a giant vortex of thick black smoke, blowing all three of them into the wall.

Slowly, so slowly, the smoke began to dissipate—

And everything was still.

• • •

EVENTUALLY, JUDAH PEELED his body off the wall. Noa was already on the ground, dragging herself toward the flattened lump of Miles.

Be OK, please be OK . . .

Noa's wrist was naked; Judah saw her bracelet loose against the wall. She hadn't seen it; it would be so easy to make it disappear—

He picked it up.

Miles, you have to be OK . . .

"Noa," Judah said. She turned; he offered her the bracelet. Relief washed over her.

Noa stuck out her wrist, and he clasped it clumsily, fingers brushing her skin. She looked at him with that searching look again—but the bracelet was fastened. He couldn't hear her thought.

Miles moaned. Noa flew to his side, saw his eyelids flutter. She watched him wake and recognize her face—and then watched hatred cloud his eyes.

"What have you done now," Miles whispered, just before his eyes rolled up and he passed out again.

Judah found himself somehow at her side, reaching to still her trembling shoulders.

"It's a Mindworm. Fabian told me they had done it . . . to Pearl's 'boy.'"

"Pearl said . . . since he followed Callum here, for me . . ."

"It's not your fault, Noa," Judah said fiercely, gripping tighter. "The Mindworm kept him coming back. They hatched it in him by blending their gifts; it contorts his thoughts and feelings even when they're gone."

Noa seized in panic. "It's still in him, alive?

"I—I'll try to reverse it—"

"Can you? You can barely stand—"

"He's . . ." he closed his eyes, unable to watch hers. "Still suffering—"

He heard her gasp, and decided not to force her to make this choice.

Judah let Noa go, bent over Miles and closed his eyes. He called on Lily, one last time. Her rosy cheeks and dark, sweet curls materialized within his mind, and Judah could feel the dampness of her hand in his. He touched Miles' temples, and dove inside.

He saw the Worm immediately—dark and spiny like a centipede, and growing every second. Judah took a deep breath and stretched his mind's hands tightly around it. It roiled and writhed, scales like sharp serrated knives—Judah cried out and pulled its ends apart, ripped it in half, tore skin from skin—but from the bloody, ragged edges, new Worms grew: two now, instead of one. Judah fell on Miles, gasping, felt Noa coming up behind.

"Stay back!" he cried, not breaking focus. He needed Lily—and there she was. Tumbleweed-tornado Lily hurled herself on one Worm. She pinned it, and Judah's mind-hands grabbed the other. Lily's eyes met Judah's, and he knew what he had to do.

Screaming, Judah forced the Worms out of Miles and into *him*, his own mind. They had millions of spiky suckers on their endless feet. Judah made his mind volcanic gas and blew the suckers upward, breaking their seal, then screamed both Worms out his mouth.

The Mindworms uncoiled serpentine in the air—then crusted up like salted snails, and imploded.

"Did it work?" Noa cried, when Judah slumped over, panting.

"You didn't see them die?"

"See? There was nothing—Judah—*Judah!*"

But Judah fell, his entire body seizing violently. Then his body froze, eyes unseeing, mouth wide open, and toppled to the floor. Noa fell on him; he was breathing, but barely—

"Noa?" Miles asked groggily behind her. Noa turned, and for a moment, somehow felt joy.

"Miles! *My* Miles!" She crushed him with a clumsy, sloppy hug, making him laugh and groan.

"Whoa, Noa . . . easy chica." He sat up gingerly, looked around the burned-out Club. It was eerily empty, except for them.

They had to get out of there, fast.

Miles was bewildered. "Did you follow us? Me and Olivia? We were following . . . Callum . . ." He blushed sheepishly. "I know you like him, Noa, but I was worried—wait, where's Olivia? And where did Callum go?"

Noa tried not to show her panic. "That was a while ago, Miles. Can you remember anything since then?"

"Since then? What? Are you mad at me? Don't be mad at Olivia, I made her—"

"Bygones, Miles," Noa replied, trying not to cry. "You don't remember this place at all?"

"No . . . but," he coughed, "were we in a fire?"

Noa didn't know how to answer him. "Miles, how do you feel? Do you think you can walk?"

Miles shrugged his limbs, testing them. "I think so. I'm mostly smoky . . . and confused."

"OK, because I need your help. We have to get Judah out of here, he's hurt—"

"Who's Judah?"

"Callum's little brother. You've met him, you just . . . don't remember. It's OK." She bit her lip, hoped that was true. It seemed like when Judah had killed the Mindworm, it had also erased any memories since Miles had been infected—starting with Miles' first contact with Pearl the night he'd followed Callum. Noa's Miles was back, but there had been a price.

He's better off this way, Noa told herself. *It spares him pain.* But Noa knew, better than anyone, that painful memories were sometimes important. *It's different for him*, she told herself. *It was enchantment, not real life.* She looked at her bracelet, tried not to think: *But for me, enchantment is real life.*

"Thank you," Miles was saying into his cell phone.

"Who was that? Did you call the police?"

Miles looked at her strangely. "No, a cab. Thank God for away games and contraband cells." He waved his secret prepaid prize, apparently not remembering he'd also quit lacrosse.

Miles helped Noa brace Judah against the wall. Her body ached and trembled, craving oxygen, clean air.

"Let me, Noa. You're like Olive Oyl, all wiggly arms." Miles hoisted Judah up, scoop-hold style. "Do *not* tell anyone I carried him like this."

Miles awkwardly followed Noa to the fire exit. As they hobbled out, her bracelet jumped.

"I won't give up, Callum," she murmured, back to the shadows. "So you don't, either."

• • •

IN THE CAB, to Noa's dismay, Miles' recovery continued to unravel, with Judah slumped unconscious in front. At first, Miles had continued talking to Noa, asking questions, piecing together what happened; but then his eyes had suddenly flickered closed in sleep. Noa had thought he was kidding, but when he'd awakened a second later, he was bewildered again, unsure where he was and how he got there. He remembered nothing again, since the night he'd followed Callum.

By the third time this happened, Noa told him only very brief information, leaving out all mention of the club. *Simpler*, she reasoned. *Safer*.

And she didn't have to keep reliving it.

"Miles, Miles," she nudged him gently, waking him for the sixth time when they arrived.

"Noa? Are . . . we in a cab?"

"Yeah, we just got back to school. You fell asleep." She ignored the cabbie's rearview stare. "Help me carry in my friend. He—had too much to drink."

"I'll say. Hey, he kinda looks like Callum."

"His little brother. Help me take him to Callum's room."

"Sneak you into the Annex at this hour?" Miles teased. "You owe me big." Noa turned so he wouldn't see her distress.

In silence, they carried Judah to Callum's room. A dorm monitor was making tea, but was so bleary Noa managed to slip behind a vending machine until the coast was clear.

Callum's door, however, was locked. Noa reached into Judah's pocket, blushing, felt around. The key was black and sooty. Her throat constricted.

"He put that through some crazy dryer?" Miles asked.

Noa didn't answer, just opened the door, helped haul Judah to Callum's futon.

"Hopefully he'll sleep it . . . off . . ." Miles began to slur, eyes flickering. She caught him as he was about to fall, shook him until his eyes became alert.

He looked around, saw he was in Noa's arms.

"Is this a dream?" he asked nervously. "You don't live here—"

"Um . . . yes, this is a dream," Noa told him impulsively. It was easier than the truth. Miles took her hand; she let him, to keep him calm.

Miles obviously couldn't be left alone, but neither could Judah . . .

"And now in this dream," Noa improvised, "we're going to take a little walk."

"OK," he said happily, entwining his fingers with hers.

Noa carefully led him out of the Annex to the Girls' residence quad and Olivia's room.

Miles' eyes widened eagerly. "What kind of dream *is* this?"

Even in her worry, Noa smiled. He was definitely *her* Miles again.

Noa knocked softly, and as soon as Olivia opened the door, pushed inside. She got Miles to Olivia's bed just as he collapsed with a loud snore.

"What the—Noa? Wait, Miles?" Olivia blearily groped for the light switch.

"Miles, um, isn't feeling well."

Olivia squinted at Noa. "Did you guys go out partying? Is this a *Hangover* situation?"

Noa shook her head, squirming. Judah was still in Callum's room, alone and unconscious. "Sort of. I can't really explain, but . . . he probably won't remember stuff. I need you to watch him, OK?"

Olivia became alert. "What happened? What's going on?"

Noa bit her lip. "Please, Olivia, please. Just—don't ask. Trust me. You said you could do that before. Please."

Olivia's eyes narrowed. "Does this have to do with Callum?"

Noa didn't want to lie, so she said nothing.

Olivia sighed. "OK, fine. But he's gonna be OK right?"

"Better than he's been," Noa hedged, hating herself.

Olivia raised an eyebrow. "OK. You want to stay, too?"

"I can't—and I'm so sorry but I can't . . ."

"Can't explain. Right."

Noa couldn't meet her best friend's eyes. She turned to the door. "Thank you, Olivia," she said quietly, unable to look back

. . . which is why she didn't see the ash-black, bent tin circlet fall from Miles' pocket to Olivia's floor.

• • •

JUDAH WAS STILL unconscious, in the same place on the futon: sprawled awkwardly, left arm outstretched. Noa immediately repositioned him more naturally, and as she did, her hand brushed his bare collarbone, her face a breath away.

She blushed, backed up.

Not sure what else to do, she sat on the ground, her back against the futon frame. Her whole body sagged.

Miles was hurt, very hurt; Judah unconscious (maybe forever); she'd abandoned her family and almost burned to death. Not to mention, she'd pushed Olivia's trust and loyalty probably beyond its limit, *and* they hadn't found Callum, let alone managed to save him.

Noa gripped the talisman in her hand, but it felt cold and still. Was Callum even alive? Could Miles recover? Would Judah wake up? They were all gone, everyone was gone like Isla, and Noa tried and tried, yet always failed to bring them back. They bled where nobody could see, were kidnapped where nobody could follow. One moment they were there and saving you, the next they were gone.

"No!" Noa cried, shoving her palms against the rising floor. "I don't allow it!" A wail, a war cry, a scream: "I forbid it!"

Noa launched herself up, grabbed Judah's shoulders, shook hard: "I forbid you to leave!"

When he didn't respond, she raged. She flung him down and clawed at the silent, icy talisman. "Is this what you hate? That he gave me this? I didn't know what it was!" The clasp was too small for her anger; finally she ripped the links apart. She hurled the broken chain into the corner, heard it hit the wall with a satisfying clash. "It's gone! Come back! You have to come back!"

Judah didn't wake.

Noa's anger dissolved, and so did she. She crumpled beside him, reached for his hand, thought of the first time Callum had taken hers.

"Light," she murmured. Judah would heal if she gave him Light! *I can't heal like Callum*, Judah had said once, and it was true he wasn't Blue. But all Fae could recover if they had Light.

When Judah had collapsed in the club, Noa had known, had *felt*, that it wasn't so much physical as *spiritual*, and wasn't that what Light was all about?

She roughly wiped her cheeks and knelt toward Judah. She lifted her hands, not sure quite how to do it—then snatched his hand, clasping it tightly in both of hers.

Nothing.

"No!" she cried, furious. She looked at Judah's chest—he breathed, he was in there somewhere. She wracked her brain for everything Callum had ever said about taking Light. It wasn't just about touch, but touch *and intention*. Judah had to *want* to take her Light. But he was unconscious; how could he want anything?

But—Noa remembered, *the kiss*. Callum hadn't wanted it, but couldn't help the transfer. Noa's heart pounded at the memory, body seizing up in ache . . . she'd been so open, they both had, and the Light had flowed between . . .

Noa took a deep breath. She enfolded Judah's hand again,

now gently. She closed her eyes, relaxed, tried to make herself be *open*. She even tried a meditation Hannah had taught her in happier times: *Breathe in, I am a light, Breathe out, I am a peaceful soul.*

Nothing.

Noa grit her teeth, held his hand tightly. She had to find a way inside him.

It came to her instinctively. *Sasha.* Sasha was their connection. Judah had loved Lily the way Noa loved Sasha. Sasha reminded him of Lily, but it was more than that—Judah and Noa had lost sisters, yet Sasha led them both back to the light. Judah was *different* with Sasha. Vulnerable, hopeful.

Open.

Noa reached into her pocket, pulled out the stray puzzle piece from home. She pressed it between her palm and Judah's, a beacon, and with all her heart, she thought: *Share my Light—*

Their hands began to glow.

It was different than it had been when she kissed Callum. This time, she could feel the warmth pool in her chest and then sublimate outward, a million golden stars. The world spun again, as with Callum, but this time *she* was at the center, the heart, and the movement came from her. She looked at Judah's face as through a golden haze, and as her elation rose, so did the color in his cheeks.

Judah's eyes flickered, and he sat up with a startled gasp. His face was more peaceful than Noa had ever seen it; it made her even warmer to be causing him such joy. He turned to her and saw their hands—

—and immediately he ripped himself away. He shuddered,

seized, forced his broken body back into the futon, as far from her as he could go.

Noa fell slightly forward, golden haze disappearing. She was dizzy, braced herself against the futon's frame. When she looked up again, he looked horrified.

"Where's the bracelet?" he cried, beside himself. "Put it back on! Put it back on now!"

Noa was shocked, bewildered. "Judah—"

"Put it on! Put it on *now*!"

It was a plea unlike any he had ever made, desperate and . . . afraid. Noa looked toward the bracelet; he still didn't see it; so she got to her feet and tumbled toward it. She fumbled with the broken link, got it to rehook.

She looked at him, confused.

He was pale. "Why . . . why did you let me do that?" he demanded.

Noa smiled, she couldn't help it—his deep-set frown, those tense, knit brows: Judah was back!

"I had to," Noa said, swaying a little on her feet. "You collapsed after you helped Miles, you needed Light—" Judah eyed her warily, cradled the hand she'd touched. "Are you really upset?" Noa asked, incredulous. "You wouldn't wake up! I had no choice! What, you can save me from Faefyre and Miles from a Mindworm, but I can't save you?"

Judah tensed, a cornered animal. "No, no, it was . . . kind . . . of you—"

She glared at him, offended and, truthfully, hurt.

"It's just," he paused, looked down. "I swore to myself, I'd never . . . not from you, not like Callum."

Noa sighed, sat on the futon carefully apart from him. "You didn't do it. I did. And I'm glad I did. Now you'll be OK."

"You have no idea what you may have lost—"

"Well, I know it wasn't you."

Judah looked at her, almost the way he sometimes looked with Sasha. But then he noticed her face, her clothes. "Wait, are you OK? The Fyre . . . did I get to it in time? And Miles? What about Miles?"

"You saved us," Noa told him. "Though it nearly killed you."

Judah tried to stand and moaned.

She leapt up. "You're still injured?"

Judah sat back, shook his head. "Not physically. You were right, I just went too far below baseline Light. I'll recover. In time."

"I'll give you more—"

"No!" Judah yelled, lurching away. He tried to calm himself. "I just need time."

"OK," Noa said reluctantly.

He relaxed, and his face began to droop.

"Sleep, Judah, gather your strength," she whispered.

A ghost of a smile played on Judah's lips. "No good to you weak, huh . . ." And then he was asleep.

Noa was exhausted, too, but sure she'd never fall sleep, probably would never sleep again. But as Judah's even breathing reached her ears, her eyelids shut, she leaned back beside him, and the world blurred itself away.

• • •

NEITHER SLEPT DEEPLY. Judah kept shifting, groaning softly, and Noa could feel them both just below the surface, as if watching through a veil. She was conscious but unconscious, restless, and woke barely an hour later.

She looked at Judah. He was awake now, too, but still. Staring at the ceiling.

"Judah?" she whispered. He didn't move a muscle. She wondered if he'd sensed her wake, as she had him.

"Miles," he said, focus sharp on the ceiling. "It worked?"

Noa literally did not know what to say.

He turned to her, and she felt a shock: He looked . . . afraid.

"He's better. Much better," she said quickly, sitting up. "He seems like Miles, and he doesn't remember the twins or what they took . . ."

"That will hit him later," Judah replied grimly.

"But you reversed it, the Mindworm—"

"I got rid of it, but I couldn't reverse what had been done. I don't think there's a way to give back Light . . . maybe one of the soothsayers in Aurora, *maybe*, but not someone like me." He sighed. "At least he won't have to remember the twins."

Judah sensed her tension, sat up too.

"What. Else."

Noa bit her lip. "It's . . . it's not just the twins. He . . . can't remember anything since meeting Pearl. And"—she swallowed hard—"he can't seem to make new memories either. He . . . falls asleep . . . and sort of . . . resets. . . ."

Judah raked his hands through his hair. "I was so stupid, to think I could help . . ." he muttered angrily. "I always, always hurt them—"

Noa grabbed his hands. "Don't say that! Don't *do* that! He'll get *better*," she said, so forcefully it even surprised her. "And even if he never remembers another thing, I'd rather have him be *my* Miles than that awful thing they made him."

Judah clenched his jaw, flung himself back down, again staring at the ceiling.

You saved us, Noa added in her mind, somehow knowing he wouldn't want her to say it. But it was truth, so she thought it to him with all her heart, even as the talisman meant he wouldn't hear.

In silence, Noa lay back down next to him. He was examining his hands now, turning them over and back, with those careful, precise eyes—and she finally noticed, gasping.

"Your *hands*." They were red and welted, laced with new and angry scars. "Callum will heal you—"

"Faefyre," Judah reminded her, voice oddly light. She reached to touch them, and to her surprise, he let her. She traced the patterns: ice.

"They don't hurt at all," he said, almost in wonder, turning his palms over and over. He spoke slowly, patiently, carefully picking words like wildflowers. "Lily . . . I was always afraid she'd suffered . . . but these burns don't hurt . . ."

What a strange kind of miracle, Noa realized, for Judah to have been hurt in such a way to ease a greater, older pain. Few things could alter the story you remembered; those things were precious, even when they were scars.

"Judah, Pearl set the Fyre. And the one at Harlow."

"You mean my 'stupid prank'?"

Noa bit her lip. "We should have never thought you did it. And I haven't, for a while."

"Because of Thorn." Judah snorted.

"No, because I . . . I try to listen." She flushed.

Judah looked at her with that small, fragile look again. She looked down, and he turned back to the ceiling. "You do listen."

He suddenly sat up again. "Wait, she set both Fyres?"

"She was bragging about it being the secret Green gift."

Judah froze, face darkening. "Of course," he muttered, "rage, jealousy, hate . . ." He seemed to remember Noa. "She probably thought you'd be too dead to tell."

Judah got up, wincing, clearly agitated.

"Judah!"

"I'm fine."

"I'll give you Light—"

"No!"

"Then damn it, sit back!"

Judah sighed, but obeyed. She sat down, too. "That explains, at least, why I was able to get to you before it consumed you," he said.

Noa looked at her own limbs, realizing for the first time she had no scars. "What do you mean?"

"The Fyre came from Pearl's emotions—she hated you, so it went after you, but I guess in some perverse way she also didn't want Miles to die. In the Fyre's mind, I saw his figure, too, but he was black while you were red. I thought it was because Miles was dead, but I think now it was because her feelings for him protected him. She probably didn't even realize she'd done that, probably never had admitted to herself that she cared. But she did, so while you were on top of Miles, the Fyre was trying to figure out how to finish you off without hurting him—so you lasted longer."

Noa studied him hard. "That's not what you were upset about just now. Tell me."

"Tell you what?"

"*Judah.*"

Judah scowled, but gave in. "I assume Callum told you

about the Fyre in the Training Center. Where Lily . . . and he took the blame?"

Noa nodded.

"What did he say? About the Fyre?" His eyes were like a laser.

She cleared her throat. "Darius Channeled you, you and your friends decided to get revenge, it got out of control with Faefyre . . ."

Judah smiled bitterly. "That's the gist of it. The way Callum likes to tell it, anyway. Did he mention Hilo?"

"The girl? I mean, the Pixie? With the brother?"

"Crispin."

Noa nodded reluctantly. "He said Crispin set the Fyre, and Hilo kind of . . . tricked you." She winced, prepared for anger.

It didn't come.

"I loved her," Judah said simply. Noa sat absolutely still, almost forgetting to breathe. "From the time we were small. She was my touchstone. My hope. Callum never mentions that part."

"No," Noa said slowly, "he left that out."

"Maybe he didn't understand it. I'd told him that I loved her, but I'm not sure he knew what that meant then." He looked at Noa, almost sad. "Maybe he does now."

Blood surged to her cheeks. He looked away.

"Hilo was my first friend, way before any pranks. She was a slum-rat I met in the Tunnels, where we both went to escape and hide. It didn't take long for me to love her, to fall in love with her. She . . ."

Judah trailed off, then started over: "It's true, Darius humiliated me that day. But I would have let it go. I always did. Hilo's father was a monster too, but he left different marks. I was the only one who knew her secret. And she knew mine." He swallowed. "We did pull pranks, but just harmless things to let off steam. Callum always thought she was the ringleader, but most of the time she reined *me* in. So many times, she stopped me from becoming what I might have been. She told me I didn't have to be what Darius imagined, that his story didn't have to be my story. And it wasn't, not with her. With her, I was . . . better. Worthy."

Judah looked down. "After Darius Channeled me, I was . . . bewildered. I met Hilo in the Tunnels, thinking she'd do what she always did: pull me from the darkness. Remind me how to rise. But this time, she was different. Maybe it hit too close to home. A physical assault. She demanded we hit back. She planned the prank to deface the Center, and I agreed. Our pranks were always harmless. Declarations only. I trusted that she wanted me to feel strong.

"But that night, Crispin showed up. He was a Red Fae bully, a burlap sack who grunted and tormented in equal measure. Maybe he learned it from their father, I don't know, but Hilo and I had always avoided him. That night she swore he'd followed without her knowing.

"Once we got to the Center, the Fyre was raging before I realized what had happened. It was only later in the Tunnels, when Hilo came to me in tears—her brother had set this Fyre, her brother had killed my sister. She hadn't known. Could I ever, ever forgive her?"

"I don't understand, Judah—"

Judah glared at Noa, tears in his eyes. "Hilo's brother was

Red, Noa. *Red.* The only Green there that night, the only one who could have set that Fyre and sent it after Lily, was *her.*"

"Judah—"

"Do you know?" Judah continued fiercely, shaking. "Until this day, I *thought* . . . somehow . . . I was afraid *I* might have set that Fyre!" He heaved for breath. "My lack of skills, my hate for Darius—some invocation I didn't know that I was making—I prayed it was Crispin, but I feared, I feared that it was *me*—"

"Judah, no—"

"And she let me, Noa! She *let* me think it! She knew how convinced I was that I was bad. She knew and she *used* it and she *lied!* I trusted her, Noa, I *loved* her . . ." He buried his face in his hands, shaking, and Noa couldn't bear it. She didn't care how he might hate it, how it might make him think she pitied him—she put her arms around him and held him. And for a moment, he let her.

"I didn't see her after that," Judah said finally, pulling free. Noa scooted backward, but he reached out to stop her. "It was . . . too hard to see her. But I still . . . even though I learned to live without her . . ."

"You still loved her," Noa murmured.

He nodded. "A part of me. Until this moment . . ."

They sat close, so close, in silence. Noa wanted to tell him something, but didn't know the words herself.

Suddenly he cringed into her, his body spasming harshly.

"Judah!"

He winced and groaned, but the spasm passed. They both reached to turn his wrist at the same time: the Mark of the Portal was pulsing, growing black.

"It's not too bad yet, I'm just weak." He pulled away from her, curled his hands into tight fists, but not before letting his eyes linger—so briefly—on his ring finger.

"Your mother's ring . . ." Noa murmured.

"Gone," he said. "Burned up in the Faefyre."

"Judah . . . I'm sorry . . . I know how much it meant to you. But your mom gave it to you because she was proud of your *courage*. Coming here for Callum. The rest . . ." Noa shrugged, tried to peer into his face. "That was just tin."

"Not exactly, as it turns out."

"What do you mean?"

"Remember when we found it, it seemed to make those golden flecks? That was Light. That ring makes—made—Light here."

"But—" Noa shook her head. "Wait. Wouldn't that mean that you, that Callum, could live here, fully, never hurt anyone? We have to go back! Find it in the ash—"

"Faefyre, Noa," he reminded her gently. "The magic's dead."

Noa shook her head again, not willing to let go. "I don't understand—you had that ring the whole time you were watching Callum. You never noticed it made Light?"

"It wasn't making Light then, I'm sure of it. Somehow it got . . . I don't know, activated, between then and now. When Fabian slid it on . . ."

"That ring was freedom, Judah, for you and Callum," Noa realized.

"It . . . could have been."

"And it just . . . fell into the Fyre?"

Judah's body contorted again, more violently this time.

"You said you still had time!"

"The Portal—without the Gatekeeper—it's erratic—" Judah said through clenched teeth.

"What can we do?" Noa asked, jumping up.

The spasm finally passed. "Nothing," he panted.

"There has to be something!" she cried. "We'll get someone, send someone through—"

"Who, Noa?" Judah interrupted sharply. "Have someone in mind?"

"I—" Noa faltered. "No, no of course . . ." Shame burned her cheeks.

"The Portal's unstable now anyway, Noa. Who knows how it would react to a mortal? I don't think it was ever really designed to accept them."

Noa's mind went into overdrive. Judah's tie to the Portal was the last thing they needed now.

"Wait—what happened to the idea to use the twins?"

He shrugged. "I failed."

Noa studied him carefully.

"Leave it alone, Noa."

She was right. He was hiding something. "What happened to the ring, Judah."

"I heard something, OK?" he finally snapped. "I had them both—Fabian for the Portal, the ring in my sight, and I heard something else and I had to make a choice!"

"What possible choice—"

"You, Noa! I heard *you*! You called to me to save you, and there wasn't time for both."

"No . . ." She lost her breath. "No, you shouldn't have—"

"I don't regret it."

She was trembling. He lifted her face to meet her eyes. "Lily told me to listen for you."

"You see . . . Lily? Her ghost?"

"Never before meeting you," Judah whispered. "But I hope to now, and for the rest of my days." His face was close, so close, the space between them shrinking—

"Callum," Noa said suddenly, lurching back, away from the vanishing distance between them. "We need to save Callum!" She wiped roughly at her eyes. Her chest was pounding, her breath shallow and painful. Her brain was stuck, skipping, the volume breaking all her speakers: *Callum! Callum! What did I almost do?*

"—going to rest," Judah muttered, curling away from her into the futon. His back moved like it was broken, with wasted hinges, rusting joints, all twisted far too tight.

What almost happened? What almost happened? What did I almost do?

Her thoughts reverberated, bounced around the walls of Callum's room. She forced herself to look at Callum's jacket on the wall, to notice Callum's books—his volume of Emily Dickinson, which reminded Noa of the first time she'd seen him in class—*A certain slant of light* . . . the moonlight, now on Judah—*Callum!* Noa interrupted herself. *Callum Callum Callum!*

Noa couldn't stay there, in that room, *Callum's* room where Judah lay; she needed air. She flew toward the door, realized she was sweating, tore off her blazer and left it on the floor. It smelled of smoke anyway, horrible smoke, thick with memories that hurt. Maybe by the time she took it back, it would smell of Callum's sheets and Callum's clothes, not everything that happened since, everything she'd almost done—

As Noa crossed the threshold, Judah moaned in fitful sleep. She turned back; unconscious, his face was pale and strained, its weariness exposed. She bit her cheek but went back in. He'd hate her for it, but she did it all the same: knelt, placed her hands lightly on his back, thought again of Sasha. Her Light flowed to him—for some reason more sluggishly than before—probably from her own exhaustion.

Judah sighed a little but didn't wake—and when she finished, his face seemed peaceful. Noa lowered her eyes as she got up.

"For saving my life," she murmured.

Keeping her face away, Noa left, this time not stopping until she was outside, cold air stinging her cheeks. She sucked the coolness in, wanting the taste of anything, anything besides the acid tang of rising guilt.

• • •

NOA. CALLUM DRIFTED in and out of consciousness, her gray eyes blurring. Sometimes when he saw her, Callum couldn't tell: Was he awake? Asleep?

Mostly Callum knew she was only in his mind, but how could that be, when her face was what stirred his lungs to breathe, his heart to beat?

When her face kept him alive?

Pain stabbed through Callum's ribs. Alive, but dying. His muscles squeezed, contracted, then spasmed out against his chains. But this wasn't the pain that Noa helped. Noa helped the outside pain, the pain *inflicted*, by Thorn or Fabian or Channeling. Callum would think of her when that pain came, and her gray eyes anchored him to something no one else could touch.

This pain, the inside pain, came when Callum was alone. Nothing helped this pain.

Guilt.

With this pain, Noa was the victim. He'd brought this darkness to her life. Callum looked around his new prison, the tomb after the tomb within the club: Thorn had brought him here, to Kells' shack, after the Fyre. A fitting place, the home of the Portal that devoured lives. *Callum* devoured lives. Innocent lives. Noa, Judah, Lily . . .

Callum wished he could undo it all. He'd carved a talisman from his soul, but it wasn't enough. The damage had started earlier, long before they'd met. It started the day he'd seen her, chosen her.

Doomed her.

The truth from every chamber of his heart: blood out, blood in—*Noa.*

The only thing, *the only thing* Callum had now was the tiny corner he'd protected. The one secret place he hadn't let Fabian and Thorn find. Her. He'd kept her safe, at least in that. Thorn could crush him with the rest: Darius and Lorelei, Judah and the lies. Secrets no less devastating, but less original: deep, discolored grooves of scars, mapping histories of pain.

Alone, he remembered Lily's face, peering into his, not even frightened or confused; his face reflected in her pupils, desperate to be calm—*Trust me*, he'd tried to tell her in that look, when he had known, terribly, what had to happen next. *Keep your eyes on mine.* But how do you explain to a girl that small what is being asked, required, taken? Her eyes had locked on his, blinked and blinked then closed—and then her body had gone still. Then

Judah's face, not then but later, as he beat Callum with his fists. The hatred not for Callum, but himself: Judah would carry it forever, no matter who went through the Portal, no matter what story was told.

When Thorn and Fabian had found the faces, made them live and wail, Callum clung to the one thing he could hold concurrent—Noa's eyes. Gray eyes only, while the rest was taken, torn, ripped free, exposed; flung to the teeth of wild beasts, to the suck of the dying sea, to the maw of the In-Between itself—

And then, *then*, the smoke had come.

That acrid, choking, viscous smell. *Faefyre*. The smell he never would forget.

It was the third time he had smelled it, but somehow in that tomb, in that club, it was more noxious than ever before. His psyche had shut down; he'd existed in smell alone. He'd barely felt when Thorn Channeled him, chair and chains and all, to transport somewhere new: Kells' shack, pulsing green in the Portal's sickly light.

At least the smoke-pus smell was gone.

"Gutless Color Fae rodents!" Thorn slammed Kells' door behind him, rattling the uneven, slatted walls. In one hand, he held a portable electric generator of some kind, wrapped with tentacles of twisting wires. He slammed it down on Kells' wobbly kitchen table, glaring.

"They think they can outrun *me*? They'll suffer, once I have the ring." Thorn slammed his hand so hard the table cracked. "How hard could it have been, to wrest it from your idiotic brother?"

Callum tried not to look at Thorn's new toy.

Thorn grinned. "No matter. As you see, I don't need Fabian and Pearl to make you suffer. Humans are so *inventive* . . ."

Callum thought of Judah, tried to smirk.

"What's funny?"

"You're just so . . . desperate. Scurrying and raging over Darius's worthless little ring . . . crossing *worlds* to fetch his trinket for him like a dog . . ."

Thorn laughed.

Callum tried not to show how much that scared him.

"Can it be that you so underestimate your father?" Thorn asked, thumping the already broken table. "Come, boy! You haven't been Banished for that long. The Otec never cared about some *sentimental* trinket. Even *less* about that Green whore—" Callum growled, and Thorn laughed harder. "He named her whore, not I. And that ring, *that ring* . . ." Thorn suddenly leapt to Callum, shoved his chair, let it and Callum's head slam backward on the floor. He bent over, breathed each word into Callum's mouth: "*That ring makes Light.*"

Thorn slammed Callum upright again. "Blue Son! Did you hear me?"

Callum sputtered: "But, but that would mean—"

"*Power*," Thorn gleamed. "Absolute power . . ."

"*No*," Callum denied fiercely. "Darius would never want such a thing. This realm is his prison—unless . . ." Callum swallowed, already knew, had known from the beginning ". . . unless Darius has other plans for this Realm, that require Light."

"Plans like . . ." Thorn's eyes danced, feeding on Callum's anguish.

"To conquer," Callum whispered.

"What's that?" Thorn bellowed with his hand to his ear.

"To enslave this realm!" Callum yelled, words spewing from his mouth. Of course it was true, there was no other way, Darius wanted power, *needed* it, because he couldn't bear to be afraid. That ring would make him fearless—give him a world where only *he* had gifts—

"How do you know?" Callum demanded wildly. "He'd never tell the *hired help!*"

"Watch it, boy—"

"That's what he called you Hunters: hired hands—"

"I was his right hand," Thorn hissed, "which you would know, had you not been Banished like some foul stench."

Now Callum laughed. "I may not read minds, but I know that's a lie."

"Fine," Thorn said evenly. "I overheard him. I took the mission to earn favor. It's more important than you know these days." Callum shivered at Thorn's tone, knew it was the truth. "But that was before I knew . . ." Thorn lifted his hands, as if to say *behold, what miracle this place!* "Lightless, yes, but have you watched these mortals? No gifts, and yet, *imagination.* There is more pain and suffering here than in any other realm I've seen. Instruments of torture, and all their lovely lies . . . I was prepared to hate it here, to come, retrieve the ring, and leave—but Blue Son, this place . . ."

Thorn leaned in close again. "That's why Darius has so rarely used this prison—because he *knows* it's not a prison truly, but a world, waiting. . . . So now I beat him to it, for *I* will use the ring."

"That's why you balanced the Portal?"

"And why I used Kells." Thorn smiled. "Without a Gate-keeper, this Portal will eventually implode, and the realms will be severed. Permanently."

"Then you'll have a ring, but no one to Channel."

"I just need one of each. Those twin brats, and you. Seems Darius Banished the perfect number."

"Judah . . ." Callum realized.

"I imagine he'll be sucked into the Portal's supernova, or I'll kill him once I have the ring."

"Well, I know my brother, and he's miles away by now. The minute Pearl set that Faefyre? He doesn't stay and fight, even when you try to make him. *Especially* then."

Thorn cocked his head at Callum, genuinely curious. "Why do you hate him so?"

Callum flinched. "I don't."

"You forget, boy, I've seen into your mind. I know all its hidden cracks."

Not everything, not the most important thing.

Thorn smiled, as if even without Fabian, he'd heard Callum's thought. "I'll find that too, you know. That last little nugget? Yes, I've sensed it. I'm *very* curious. And curiosity for me . . . well, it tends to cause obsession." Thorn walked his fingers over to the electrode device. "So why don't we try these humans with their knickknacks? See if things really are better, how do they put it? The 'old-fashioned way.'"

• • •

NOA DIDN'T KNOW where she was walking, couldn't see much in the dark, but the motion soothed her. Right foot, left foot, right . . . When her mind began to wander, she numbered her steps. Anything to keep her thoughts predictable and painless.

Her free thoughts hurt. They leaked in around the numbers, closing in over her eyes: first just specks at the periphery, soon a blindfold. In an instant, the stone was back, the stone she felt in place of her heart.

For what else could explain it, that she had almost kissed Judah while Callum, her Callum, could be dying, awaiting rescue? It wasn't Judah's fault, she couldn't lay blame there—he was hurt, in pain, bereft. He'd sacrificed his chance for freedom—the ring, the twins—

to save Miles, to save her . . .

For Callum's sake, Noa reminded herself. He'd saved her for Callum's sake. And here she was, almost kissing his brother—

She'd been delirious, must have been, from the trauma of the Fyre and the shock of finding Miles. Or this feeling of connection was an aftereffect of giving Judah Light. Didn't Callum even say that in the moment of the transfer, it felt like ecstasy, because joy was running through you?

Noa's chest loosened, felt warmer, more like it housed a heart. That was the reason. Because in truth, she loved *Callum*—yes, she decided, loved—his soft amber eyes, the gentle way he touched her face; his sensitivity, his tenderness, his concern for others. Judah, remember, had fed innocent people to the Portal; he'd drained Light from others—from her *friends*—

without a second thought. Callum would never treat others in that way.

But, a tiny, tiny voice inside her whispered. *But*.

Noa shook her head, to shake away the whisper. She looked

up, realized at some point she walked back inside the Annex, and was standing at Miles' door. But he was at Olivia's.

Noa felt along the top of the doorframe for Miles' extra key—the same hiding place Olivia used. Noa had warned them both it wasn't smart, but neither ever listened. Miles said he didn't care if someone ganked his shrimp-ramen-smelling laptop.

Noa chuckled, then her throat tightened. Would Miles ever be that way again? Not in this vacant, forgetting way, but *her* Miles, who smiled even when he knew the truth?

Inside, everything still looked like her Miles; maybe that was why she'd come. Crusty bits of uncooked ramen, clothes crumpled on the floor. Noa wanted it to comfort her, but instead she felt a chill: This felt eerily like entering Isla's room, right after she was gone . . .

Miles isn't gone. He would be saved, and so would Callum. Judah would—she clamped her mind. Judah would do whatever. If she had Callum, did it matter?

Needing distraction, Noa knelt beside Miles' bed, pulled out the bin o' contraband he kept hidden underneath. She grinned: He'd been holding out on Olivia—he had an entire Costco box of Red Vines, which she guessed he planned to dole out strategically. She snagged one herself and chewed, looking through stuff clearly meant for teammates: fireworks and firecrackers, tricked-out squirt guns for Assassins, some slightly skanky-looking weed. And replacement pieces for a vaporizer. *I'll have to make sure he isn't toking too much these days.* She caught herself again: *If things get back to normal. When* they *do.* She took a few things, on a whim, realized she wasn't wearing her jacket, and shoved them in her pants pockets to transfer later. She leaned back and sighed, exhaustion finally setting in.

Outside the window, the faint blurriness of sometime-dawn began to smear across the night. Sharp edges smudged, the way they always did before the gold started to speckle through.

The light would come; day would break; all would be bright and full and new.

• • •

JUDAH WOKE AND lay still, staring at the ceiling. Noa was no longer in the room. He felt it.

He wasn't sure how long he'd slept—he still felt weak, although a little better than before. It was hard to tell what time could do here. In Aurora, he couldn't have healed broken bones, but he *would* have regained his energy. The effect was clearly muted here. He'd guessed as much.

But he'd lied to Noa anyway. No way he'd take more of her Light.

Judah didn't have a problem taking Light from mortals in general—that brooding mopiness was Callum's special, self-hating burden. Mortal sacrifice was necessary for Fae life in this realm. But from *Noa* . . . his stomach twisted. If he could give back the Light she'd given him, he would. He'd made himself a promise that night he'd followed her home and hidden the ring: he'd never take Noa's Light, not like Callum had.

So much for that.

She'd saved him. He could not change it. He was getting stronger, better—because of Noa.

For Callum's sake, he reminded himself.

Judah scowled. Hadn't he professed to come here to do the same? Sure, he'd been fleeing too, but he'd still come after Callum.

Judah winced as the Portal called him, though not as hard this time. Or maybe he was stronger. The pulls were so erratic now, but he should still have time before—

You could have set yourself free.

But Noa . . .

Judah shook himself. *Callum.* He'd saved Noa for Callum. Judah owed him that.

But Judah couldn't stop seeing it, that moment, their bodies drawing close. A trick of the light, momentary confusion, post-traumatic stress . . .

Except. There were other moments, silent ones, shaped by looks and words unsaid. Had those been confusion too? And the way he felt, the *hope*—she was not Hilo, she was not Green, it *had* to be real—

Another spasm, this one stronger. Judah twisted, gripped the futon frame, squeezing his eyes shut. It passed, and he sat panting. When he opened his eyes, he saw Noa's jacket crumpled on the floor.

For some reason, he didn't want to leave it there.

Gasping, Judah forced himself to his feet. Every muscle screamed, but as he moved, Noa's Light spread out inside him: his heart pumped it through his veins. It was healing him. By the time Judah reached Noa's jacket, he could walk and bend easily. He didn't have much energy, but he would live to fight again.

Judah picked up the jacket carefully and lightly shook it out, the way Lorelei had showed him. Her hair had rippled left then right, that sea of black, almost blue. Judah had felt safe then, blanketed by the smell of clothes both warm and clean.

A tiny, folded square of paper sighed from Noa's pocket to the floor. He picked it up, unfolded it. Noa's handwriting, he knew, even though he'd never seen it before.

Judah didn't hesitate or wonder if he had the right. He read.

Imposter

Forged in fire
small and dark and shaped in coal—
you,
black ash shadow
the sun can never move.

Around you, halos of blue turn red,
you
smudge, you spill,
a chrysalis of smoke
your cloak, your softest sinew.

Fire-boy, boy bleeding coal,
You were born in flame.
You sear my skin, Red dance begin
Let ashes singe my name.

Judah's hands shook; he read it again and again. His whole body trembled with it; he could not look away. *Forged in fire.* His fingers burned where they held the paper, but he couldn't let go and didn't want to.

Slowly, carefully, Judah re-folded the page along the lines her hand had creased, the grooves her fingers had pressed together. It became smaller and smaller, a tiny white square stained with smoke and ash, smaller than his hand, than hers. He tucked the poem back inside her jacket pocket. When he released it, his air went with it, and exhaustion swept over him. He moved gingerly back to the futon, laid back down. He wanted to sleep, would give anything to sleep.

But he lay in the dark, eyes open wide.

· · ·

WHEN NOA RETURNED to Callum's room, Judah was staring out the window. The night was still in its porous stage; the charcoal bleed of dawn continued. Noa decided to pretend nothing had changed.

"How do you feel?"

Judah moved subtly, just out of her reach. "Stronger, thank you," he said tonelessly.

Noa searched his face, looked away. Did it matter, as long as he was up and ready to help find Callum? "Have you figured out how we should go after Thorn and the twins?"

"The twins fled, and *we* aren't doing anything." Judah replied, with that same terrible detachment.

Noa's cheeks burned. "I have a right to help! I've *earned* it! After what we just survived—"

"You want to save Callum or not?"

"If you're upset I made you lose the ring—"

Judah cried in frustration, finally glaring at her. "*That's* why you think I'm upset?" He tried to master himself. "Noa, you could die. I can't let you—" He turned back to the window. "Callum won't survive it."

"But Judah, if the twins are really gone—"

"Thorn can still Channel Callum."

"But you have a gift too. That's one ability to one."

Judah snorted.

"And with *me,*" Noa added, "We'll outnumber him. He doesn't even know about me."

Judah clenched his jaw. "You hope."

"Judah!" Noa stopped herself, looked down. "I owe him too, OK?"

Judah exhaled slowly. "Fine."

"So let's find Thorn and Callum. They're clearly no longer at the Club."

Judah grimaced. "I know where they are."

"How?"

"The same way I know the twins aren't with him. I reopened the Astral connection Fabian made for Thorn to message me. I sent him a message back."

"When you're so weak?" Noa shrieked. "Without telling me? He could have tracked you—"

"I may not be as skilled as Fabian, but I'm not completely incompetent!"

Noa bit her reply. Her protest had been worry for him, not condescension, but it would be useless to tell him that.

"And I didn't consult you because I had decided you wouldn't be involved," he continued. "Besides"—he faced the window again—"who knew if you were coming back?"

Noa closed her eyes briefly. "What did you tell Thorn?"

"Said I had the ring."

"But we don't have it—"

"Thorn doesn't know that. Apparently the twins fled so fast

they didn't even tell him what had happened. He was pretty pissed, actually." Judah's mouth curled a little.

"Does he know what the ring does? I mean, what it really does?"

Judah shrugged. "Who knows. Hunters are so obsessive; he could just want it because Darius told him to get it. But it's possible. Either way it's gone. Telling him I had it was the only way to get him to arrange a trade."

"So where are . . . they?" For some reason, she didn't want to say Callum's name.

"We're set to meet where he first projected to me. The oak."

"Wait, he's at Harlow? Callum's—" She swallowed her guilt. "Callum's here? Outside?"

"No. We're meeting in the open, so there won't be any tricks. At least, that's what he said. But Callum's somewhere close."

Noa studied him. His eyes were glinting. "You know."

Now Judah smiled, a genuine Judah smile, with that little smirk-like twist. "Seems I picked up a thing or two when Fabian was torturing me. While I was in Thorn's mind, I took a little peek around. I only caught a glimpse, but I would know that place anywhere."

Noa jumped a little, excitement rising. "Tell me!"

"Kells' shack," Judah grinned back.

"But that's not far from Callum's tree!" Impulsively, she leapt and hugged him. He hugged her back, laughing, and then they both seemed to realize what they'd done. They both stepped back, cheeks aflame.

But Noa couldn't help it, the grin crept back.

"What?" Judah asked.

"The best part, Judah. You're meeting *near the Portal*. Once Callum is safe, we can throw Thorn through and you can—"

"Stay," Judah finished slowly.

Noa bit her lip; he truly hadn't thought of it, only about Callum. But was it really a betrayal, for her to want to save them both?

• • •

"WRONG AGAIN, BLUE Son," Thorn said smugly, as Callum gasped, struggling to make his lungs work. For the past hour, Thorn had tested all methods of non-magical, electrified torture on Callum's brain, sending shock after shock with his mortal-made device. Thorn had been particularly tickled when he'd slipped on an ominous black glove, which had remote sensors built into the fingerpads. Apparently, Mortals used it for inter-active video games, motion-capture, but Thorn had discovered it worked equally well in communicating with the snaking wired leads he'd stuck to Callum's chest and temples, connect-ing Callum to the generator. In hospitals, those kinds of leads monitored brain and heart function; in Kells' shack, they gave Thorn access to torment both.

Moments before, a ghostly shade of Judah had appeared in front of Thorn. Callum had been sure he was hallucinating, his neurons firing their dying throes. But then the apparition had spoken with Judah's voice, and Callum realized Judah was projecting Astrally. Even with his mind throbbing, Callum was impressed.

Except Judah's new skill would get him killed.

Judah, Callum had thought feebly across the unknown dis-tance: *Stay away and let me die.* It wasn't only Judah's welfare at stake—if Thorn possessed their mother's ring, this whole world was doomed.

"Your weakling brother moves just as I maneuver him," Thorn smiled. "But then, you already know how easy he is to manipulate. Who knows that better than you?" Thorn bent over Callum, looked closely at the electrodes on Callum's temples, Callum's chest. "What Clear Fae could have done with these, with just a few tweaks . . ." Thorn's eyes wandered behind Callum's chair, to the undulating Portal. Within its frame—much like a giant, standing mirror holding vortex instead of glass—it vibrated erratically. "I wonder how it will devour him, now that it has no keeper."

Callum closed his eyes, sent again the futile prayer Judah didn't know to listen for.

Stay away, and let me die.

• • •

MILES BLINKED SEVERAL times, unsure where he was. He was in bed, but the sheets were unfamiliar, and in the dark room were shadowed shapes he didn't recognize. Then with a painful kind of grinding, metal pistons seemed to shift inside his head, screeching through rust and oxidation.

"Olivia's room . . ." He sat up awkwardly and was rocked by a heavy, reverberating migraine.

"You remember," Olivia said from somewhere to his left. Miles turned slowly, gingerly. She was sitting anxiously, hair bent and messy—not from sleep, he knew, but from braiding and unbraiding, the thing she did when she was worried.

"I slept . . . here," Miles said carefully, brain still grinding.

"Do you remember last night?"

Miles closed his eyes, even though the room was dark.

"Noa?" he asked, at first unsure. "She brought me here . . . from somewhere. I don't remember. We were in a cab."

Olivia nodded. "That's the extent of what I know, too. I'm just glad you remember that. You've been . . . having trouble. All night."

"Yes . . ." His memory like molasses, slow and viscous. "Waking up."

"A lot. Waking up *a lot*. But now you seem . . . more like you."

"Because I remember last night?"

"No I mean, from before. The last few weeks . . . cutting class, quitting lacrosse—"

"What?" Miles interrupted, bewildered. "What are you talking about?" His forehead creased in confusion and he groaned.

"You . . . don't remember that?"

"I remember the cab . . . sort of . . . and you and I, following Callum—"

"That was *weeks* ago," Olivia cried.

"There's nothing after that, until last night . . ." Miles said uneasily.

"It's OK, you're OK," Olivia said quickly, to herself as well as him, though clearly not believing it. "How do you feel now?"

"I feel . . ." Miles fumbled for words. "Strange. Where's Noa? I think I remember her last night—"

"She asked me to watch you—"

"But where did she go?" For some reason, Miles felt frantic.

"I—She asked me not to ask," Olivia admitted.

"If I'm like this, Olivia, she could be worse!"

"No," Olivia assured him quickly. "She was normal."

Miles didn't know what to do; his heart was pounding.

"Something's wrong. Something's very wrong! Don't you feel it?"

"She asked me to trust her—"

"It's that Callum kid!" Miles said fervently, cursing himself for not remembering sooner.

"Come on Miles—"

"The last time I can really remember is you and me following him. Then I have a mysterious personality transformation and my memory gets wiped out? Until Noa drops me on your doorstep unable to remember anything at all? Let me guess, when we followed him, he wasn't out buying Girl Scout cookies." Olivia took a shaky breath; Miles saw on her face that he was right. "We have to find her. He could be putting her in danger!"

"Callum hasn't even been around," Olivia protested uncertainly. "He's been sick. She's been—spending time with his little brother . . ."

"Judah," Miles said immediately. "He was in the cab, too."

"Yeah, he came to visit, right after that night we worked on the float."

"With Callum. When you and I both got hurt."

Olivia paled. "An accident."

Miles looked at her hard. "How do you know?"

"Because I remember!" she said quickly. "At least . . . I feel like I remember . . ."

He pounced on her uncertainty. "It doesn't feel right, does it."

"I—I never really noticed before. But the memory feels . . . weird."

"I'm telling you, O, this all started with Callum," Miles said emphatically. "We have to find Noa."

"But you're not well—I gave my word to Noa—"

Miles leapt up, blood pumping. "Livi, she's your best friend. Break it."

• • •

JUDAH WINCED AGAIN and doubled over, gasping in the exposed grounds. They'd just left the wing with Sasha's classroom, still had ground to cover to get to Callum's tree. Noa tried to hold him steady. It was the third spasm since they'd left.

"It's OK, it's passed," Judah heaved.

"Is there any way to stop it? Or predict when it might hit you?"

Judah shook his head. "The Portal's so unstable . . . it's getting stronger, but not so strong we need to worry." He flipped his wrist: the Mark was dark, but apparently not as angry as it would get.

"You'll feed it the Hunter soon."

"Callum first. Then I'll try."

Noa breathed. Their plan was simple. Judah would distract Thorn at Callum's tree while Noa freed Callum from the shack. Thorn didn't know Judah had an accomplice, or that they knew Callum's location, and Thorn didn't have Fabian to read it in Judah's mind. So they had a chance. Once Noa had Callum, Judah would throw Thorn through the Portal, and they'd all be free.

But how will he? a small voice asked. *What if Thorn throws Judah through instead?* To free Judah, Thorn had to be fed in alive. Magical life for magical life: a dead body wouldn't work. How would they possibly overpower him?

Noa wiped her sweaty palms down the front of her jacket and paused. There was something in her left pocket, but she only ever used the right. She reached in—it was her poem, 'Imposter,' still folded exactly, if slightly singed. She put it back into the right-hand pocket, with the other things she was carrying.

Noa told herself to be strong. *I can do this.* She and Judah locked eyes, looking at each other at exactly the same time.

They were all in danger now.

• • •

MILES AND OLIVIA snooped around Callum's empty room. Miles had picked the lock with alarming facility, making Olivia wonder what exactly he was learning on those lacrosse trips.

"They were here, recently." Miles concluded. "But it's nearly dawn! Where would they go?"

Olivia was staring out the window, pointed. Two dots were disappearing around the corner of the outside grounds, barely visibly in the dim pre-dawn light.

Ever since Miles had made Olivia pay attention to her memories, an icy block of unease had slowly built inside her. Some of her memories just felt . . . wrong. The wrong shape, as if roughly filed to fit inside her head.

"You think that's them?" Miles asked her, squinting.

"Where are they going? There's nothing out there . . ."

"Still think we should leave it alone?"

Olivia's conviction was tensing like a coil, wrapped tighter and tighter around her heart: "We follow."

• • •

JUDAH SAW THORN first, black figure in front of Callum's tree, stone-still, backlit. Judah shivered in the morning cold as Thorn's black hair rustled in the wind.

Judah hoped he and Noa had separated in time. Her secrecy was key. To his relief—not that he could show it—Thorn seemed entirely fixated on his approach.

As Judah got closer, though, his fingernails bit his palms. Thorn was unarmed. His hands, gloved against the cold, were empty.

Cockiness, Judah realized, shivering. Thorn didn't expect much of him.

Judah stepped slowly across the dew-wet grass. Morning was seeping in, ray by ray.

He focused: keep Thorn distracted. Give Noa cover. He walked slowly and deliberately to the spreading oak, stopping several yards from the Hunter.

"Where's my brother?" Judah called.

"Where's my ring?" Thorn studied Judah, smiled. "I don't need to read your mind, Red Son. I bet you're stupid enough to have it on you."

"Where's my brother?" Judah repeated, willing himself not to move or blink. Noa was sneaking, with agonizing slowness, behind Thorn to the shack. *Watch him*; Judah commanded himself, *Don't watch her. It'll give her away.*

Thorn, it seemed, was in no hurry. He cocked his head. "Impressive to still be the lesser son when the other's a Banished traitor. You *do* fail well."

Judah couldn't help it; his eyes darted to Noa, only for a moment, just as she was slipping inside. Like lightning, Thorn whipped around, her back foot disappearing—

Thorn turned back, annoyed. "What's the matter? I'm not worthy of your attention?" Judah fought the urge to collapse in relief; Noa hadn't been seen. His reaction, however, incensed Thorn, who bared his teeth and growled, crouching—

The time for banter, it seemed, had passed.

• • •

NOA GASPED. THE shack had decomposed since she and Judah had watched Thorn with Kells. Her shoes slipped on the old dirt floor, now covered by some kind of creeping algae. The yeast-smelling air was choking thick, and everything was damp.

Noa breathed carefully, looked around—it was nearly impossible to see. The light was sickly green and pulsing, throbbing from the Portal in the back. When she saw it, she retched: no longer a magic mirror, the Portal looked *alive*. It seemed to *see* her there, and hiss. *This* was the thing with its tentacles in Judah.

Fighting every survival instinct she possessed, Noa looked away from the Portal to search the shack. *Find Callum.* That was her job.

As she waded through the clutter—a broken kitchen table, a rotting bureau, an old work table heaped with rusting shears and garden tools—she saw nothing, nothing at all, that indicated Callum. No sign of recent habitation, no secret cage. She searched more frantically, used her fingers where eyes failed: slime and wet, damp and stick, but no Callum anywhere.

"Callum," Noa pleaded, whisper shaking like her hands. The Portal hissed; she had no time; *Callum, please be here . . .*

• • •

THORN YELLED IN frustration as he tried again to corner the slippery Judah. Callum's tree, it seemed, had not been the wisest choice: Judah darted in front, behind, around it, keeping bulky Thorn off-balance.

"Just give me the ring," he growled. "What do you care for family loyalty?"

Judah composed his face too late.

"*You know.*"

"I don't know anything," Judah smirked, slipping again around Callum's tree.

Thorn seethed. "It's *my ring*, boy—" He lunged, predictable in his anger. Judah slipped up into the branches.

But still, Judah felt uneasy. Why wasn't Thorn trying harder? It was almost like he was . . . toying with him.

"Old man," Judah taunted uncertainly, "without gifts or the twins, you're helpless."

When Thorn chuckled—chuckled—Judah's stomach plummeted. Almost lazily, Thorn picked up a fallen branch.

"Helpless?" Thorn repeated, amused. He strangled the branch with both his hands; it shimmered, atoms shifting, and became the sharpest, curved long knife.

Judah lurched back, fell from the tree in shock. Cat-like, he flipped to his feet, but Thorn was waiting.

Thorn grinned, and raised the blade.

• • •

NOA LOOKED AGAIN and again through the shack, fear becoming panic. Her heart hammered in terrible rhythm: not here! not here! no time! no time! She'd been too long already; Judah wouldn't last; she had to give up, accept Callum was gone, was still and utterly lost—

But for some reason, she wouldn't let herself leave. Her bracelet jumped; she grasped it, gasped: Isla had appeared.

"He's here," Noa pleaded, scared. "I can feel him here, I know it—"

Isla raised a brow, unimpressed.

"He's *here*," Noa insisted.

Isla rolled her eyes.

"I know he's here, the same way I know you are!"

Isla finally nodded. *Look with your heart*, she seemed to say. *See him the way you see me.*

Noa turned back, took a shuddering breath and closed her eyes. She put her talisman against her chest. *Show me the way.*

And then, like infrared, she saw him: Callum, a burning light. Chained up to a chair in the back corner, not far from the Portal. Head slumped, body limp, shackled and numb.

Noa ran to him, eyes snapping open, but still she couldn't see him. She reached into the nothingness . . . and *felt* him. Smooth, soft skin she would have known anywhere.

Gently, at first shyly, she touched his face, his eyelids, pressed her ear against his chest. She heard his heart. He was there, her Callum: corporeal but hidden, present but invisible, alive but somehow cloaked. Breathing, beating—but he didn't react to her touch, nor wake to see her face.

"Callum!" she cried, a whisper. "I'm here, Callum, wake up!" She grasped the shoulders she could feel, imagine, but not see; she shook him as hard as she dared. She ran her hands inward up his neck, across his collarbones, up into his curls. He was wrapped in chains and lines, had things pasted to his head and chest she couldn't see to remove. She tried to tilt his face toward hers, to rest her cheek against his cheek. His cheek was warm and hers was wet; she was crying silent tears.

Finally, miraculously, when Noa couldn't bear another breath so close and yet so separate, he stirred. His head pulled up slowly, drunkenly; she felt the flicker of his blinking lashes.

Noa pulled back, cupped his invisible face.

"Callum, it's me, it's me Noa. I've come to take you home—"

"*Noa*," Callum's voice was groggy, bleary, fighting through a trance. She felt his neck go limp again, quickly scrambled to support him. He was struggling to hold on.

To the left, the Portal belched an enormous cloud of sickly steam. Noa clasped Callum's shoulders, tried to pull him from his invisible chair. Callum seemed to fight her.

Noa racked her brain, trying to understand. "Light, you must need *Light*." She fumbled with her bracelet; Callum's resisted harder. "It's OK Callum," Noa whispered frantically. "Just a little, to get you free—"

"No!" The word strangled out. Like from a vivid, bloody gash, not from a mouth at all. "No Light . . ." He strained. "I'm being . . . Channeled . . ."

Then Noa understood. Why Callum was invisible, why he didn't want her Light. The lines and pads she'd felt against him— they were some kind of electrodes. Somehow Thorn was touching Callum *remotely*, Channeling him from afar, making him turn himself invisible. If Noa gave Callum Light, it would go to *Thorn*, who was controlling Callum's gift—

Noa's heart almost stopped as she realized what that meant:

Thorn wasn't powerless right now.

And Judah didn't know.

"We have to go *now!*" Noa whisper-cried, shaking so hard she could barely use her hands. "I'll pull off the leads—"

"No!" Callum gurgled out again, more terribly than before. "He'll sense it—through the gloves—" Noa let go of the sensors just to make him stop. She bit her hand, not knowing what to do. If she left the sensors, Judah could die, but if Thorn realized, they all would . . .

"*Callum, help me,*" Noa pleaded. It didn't matter that he was cloaked now; the whole world was blurred and frantic. "Tell me what to do . . ."

. . .

"HOW?" JUDAH SAID in bewildered terror, looking at the magic-made long knife in Thorn's hand. Thorn had obviously manipulated the atoms in the tree branch, changed them to into the weapon. But that meant Thorn was Channeling Blue—

"You said Callum wasn't out here!" Judah screamed in outrage, fear momentarily forgotten. He looked frantically with absurd hope but saw no sign of his brother.

Thorn gleamed, too proud not to reveal his trick: He held up his left-hand glove, wiggled his fingers. Up close, Judah saw that it was bulkier, heavier than the right glove which held the knife.

"Marvelous inventors, mortals, all their wireless technology. Plus a few tweaks I Channeled from your brother, while we awaited you." He appreciated his left-hand a moment, then suddenly leapt at Judah, whipping the knife out and upward with his right.

Judah didn't have time to plan; he went on instinct. He ducked from Thorn and somersaulted beneath the swing. Thorn spun to follow with the unwieldy blade, and lodged it deep into Callum's tree.

"Enough!" Thorn roared, leaving the blade and disappearing, reappearing moments later to corner Judah against stuck-knife and tree. He had Judah by the throat, his right-hand fingerspan alone enough to choke him—

"*Where's my ring?*" Thorn hissed so close he spit in Judah's face.

Judah squirmed, struggled for air; Thorn lifted Judah by his neck and slammed him again against the tree. The whole trunk trembled; Judah's vision blotched and blurred—

"Then I'll just look *myself*," Thorn ripped the Channeling glove from his left-hand with his teeth, disconnecting himself from Callum, and slammed his bare palm against Judah's chest. Judah screamed without voice as the Hunter Channeled him with everything he had. He swallowed and spewed Judah's Red gift back on its maker, pick-axing horribly into his brain.

Judah's consciousness spasmed in Thorn's rabid, unskilled teeth; Judah begged himself to shield his thoughts. Thorn was looking for the ring, he wouldn't know to look for—

NO!

It was too late. Thorn whipped to the shack, incredulous—

He now knew Noa hid inside.

• • •

AS SUDDENLY AS Noa's world had dissolved into blind help-lessness, it came back together: Callum suddenly materialized, visible and awake.

"Thorn stopped Channeling me," he murmured, bewildered. "But why . . ."

"Who cares? Let's get you free!" She fumbled with his chains, vision obscured now by happy tears alone—but couldn't budge the heavy shackles. "Callum, change them!" she said. "Make them turn to dust!"

But Callum was panting, wheezing, his eyes still having trouble staying focused.

This time, Noa didn't ask permission. She tore her bracelet from her wrist and grabbed Callum's hand. *I give you Light!* she thought, with more determination than she'd ever thought anything in her life. The pathway opened obediently, easily—and immediately, Light flowed out.

It was different, so different, than when she'd given Light to Judah. Maybe because she felt, initially, so much more in control this time. Or because the danger was so close. Or maybe because Callum had been so long in captivity, because he was already semi-unconscious and so desperately in need. But in a matter of moments, he was drawing on her like a surge, a flood. He drank harder, faster, took more and more from her very center. And as he grew stronger, fed by her Light, so did his thirst—his hunger almost violent, painful, until Noa cried and shoved because any more would surely kill her. But he was instinct, animal, couldn't hear or feel her; she crashed to the floor, fumbling for her bracelet. Not until she had it linked was he finally forced to break away.

Callum seemed dazed, but once the transfer stopped, he blinked quickly into consciousness. He saw her sprawled on the floor; she watched him realize what he'd done.

"Noa! Noa! No!" He shrugged off his chains as if they were made of tissue; he knelt to her where she trembled, dizzy and unsteady. "I didn't know what I was doing—it was survival instinct, I never meant—" She felt his soft, familiar hands, now strong and sure, and knew that she forgave him. He was alive again, with her . . .

"We have to . . . get you out . . . Thorn . . ." Noa murmured thickly. Callum clutched her fiercely. The Portal hissed.

"Noa," he whimpered, burying his face in her hair. "I'm so sorry, so sorry . . ."

The haze of the immediate release was lifting, and Noa grew stronger by the moment. The yeasty mold—she smelled it now; the dirty floor, slippery brown with breeding slime. Noa wanted to show him she was fine—weary, wobbly, but *OK.* Scared but not broken.

Noa forced her muscles into motion. She made her eyes focus, pulled herself up against him, showed him, with firm fingers and strong hands, that she was Noa.

"Worth it," she told him, words cleaner now, and crisper. "I own my choice."

His eyes raced across her face.

"You have to know I'd never, not on pur—"

Suddenly, Callum was snatched up by two huge hands, one bare, one gloved. Noa watched in horror as the hands flung Callum like a rag doll across the room, into the work-table piled with its shears and blades and tools. Noa couldn't even bring her hand to her mouth before the giant hands—Thorn's, she realized—came back and snatched her by the shoulders, lifting her off the ground. Sticky, humid breath stuck to her neck; Noa knew his face was millimeters from her hair.

Thorn tossed her up and reclamped her by the arms, bound and facing out, unable to even struggle. Pinned, paralyzed, helpless, she watched Judah rush in, breathless and off-balance; and Callum try to get up, slip badly on a fallen trowels, spades, smash his head on Kells' table and crumple to the floor. Thorn pulled Noa backward, and though Noa couldn't turn to see behind her, she saw that terrible throbbing light, the horror on Judah and Callum's faces, and knew Thorn was dangling her in front of the Portal's jaws.

"No!" Judah yelled, leaping toward her. Noa was jerked violently backward in retaliation, right on the Portal's edge—she felt its hiss, its stinging steam. Judah instantly froze, sudden loss of momentum vibrating down his spine like a shivering wind-up toy.

"Ah-hah," Thorn said. "Seems the best leverage wasn't your brother, but your *girl*."

In the corner, Callum cried out in fury, pain, maybe both, hauling himself up clumsily against the work table with a terrible, awkward lack of grace. When he stood, Noa gasped; one of Callum's legs had entirely lost its shape. It looked like a flesh-colored bag of splinters, a watery sack below the knee.

"Touched a nerve, Blue Son?" Thorn drawled, eyeing not Callum's leg, but Judah and Noa.

"She's Callum's girl, not mine," Judah snarled. "She means nothing to me."

"Oh really?" Thorn jerked her back and Judah yelled.

"That's what I thought." Thorn tightened his straight-jacked stranglehold on Noa; his bulk pressed inward on her ribs. "Give me the ring, Red Son."

"I don't have it, I swear," Judah said plaintively, panic clear.

"Don't even try," Thorn snapped, spinning suddenly to

Callum, who had started to move clumsily toward Judah. His leg, Noa saw, was painfully knitting itself together, but slow, like beetles moving through molasses under the skin.

"Quit that too, or she's done!"

Callum stopped healing, though his eyes remained aflame.

"Back to you *Judah*," Thorn hissed, impatience obvious. "Give me the ring or we see what the Portal does to her without a keeper." The Portal belched and hissed as if in response. Noa couldn't see it, but shut her eyes anyway in fear.

"Truth be told, I'd been planning to throw *you*, Red Son. But I'm guessing it will be even more disgusting if we give it a *mortal*—"

"No!" Judah and Callum cried together, their arms reaching up at the same time as they kept their feet planted: contorted mirrors of each other.

"I don't have the ring! It was devoured by Faefyre!" Judah confessed desperately. Callum tore his eyes from Noa to stare at him.

"You lost it?"

"An accident, the Faefyre, we were trying to rescue *you*—"

Callum looked stunned.

"You *lost my Light*?" Thorn roared unintelligibly, whipping his throttling hands to Noa's throat. She could barely breathe, her fingers scrabbling fruitlessly at his.

"Stop!" Judah leapt at Thorn, who swiftly shifted to strangle Noa single-handedly and used his other to throw Judah back.

"Don't punish her—it's not her fault—" Callum begged, falling over his useless leg.

Judah suddenly screamed, body contorting toward the Portal.

Thorn's eyes glittered. "Maybe *Judah* should feed her in, buy himself more time."

Judah screamed again, body writhing; his wrist flailed, the portal Mark huge and black.

Noa's vision clouded as her oxygen was squeezed away. Her hands stopped moving, fell limply to her side. Her eyes dropped down, and that's when she saw it: blood like a river, gushing from Thorn's leg.

He'd been injured, she realized, in his scuffle with Judah outside, probably from some swinging blade. He didn't seem to notice, maybe hadn't even felt it in the rush of battle. Behind him, right before the Portal, were Callum's heavy chains, tangled in a lump.

Noa forced her eyes back up, toward Judah. Beside him on the floor were the garden shears from the work-table; they'd slid across the algae when Callum had been thrown. Noa knew neither brother would be able to reach her in time, let alone pull her free, but if Judah grabbed and threw the shears at Thorn, maybe Thorn would stumble backward—against his injury and over the chains—and fall *with her* into the Portal. She'd take him with her, and set Judah free.

He needs to read my mind.

How many times had Judah implored her, cajoled her, threatened her to remove her talisman? How many times had she refused, afraid to let him in? And then in Callum's room, when he'd been hurt, Judah had screamed at her to put it back on almost the moment she'd taken it off. He hadn't wanted to hear her thoughts then and hadn't wanted to take her Light. She hadn't trusted him, then he hadn't trusted her.

They had to trust each other now.

Noa concentrated on sending every drop of blood, every scintilla of energy to her limp hands. Slowly, heavily, she moved the right to unclasp the left.

"Time to say *good-bye*," Thorn told them, swinging Noa forward to get momentum—just as her bracelet skittered to the floor. The noise surprised Thorn, broke his motion, just for an instant—and in that instant, Noa glued her eyes to Judah's.

Throw the shears at his legs! He's wounded, he'll fall!

Judah locked his eyes on hers—but nothing registered on his face. Overwhelming panic swept through Noa as Thorn retightened his grip.

The shears! The shears! she thought madly. Still, Judah looked only helpless, blank.

Callum cried out, hands shoved against his leg to heal it as quickly as he could. Noa knew he'd be too late.

This is it, she realized. *They can't save me.*

Behind Noa, the Portal snapped and crackled, a giant firecracker—

Some last spark of fight-or-flight adrenaline kicked in, and Noa began to struggle. Hard.

Surprised, Thorn lost motion once again; Noa reached for the one thing she still had up her sleeve, literally, which she hadn't remembered until this very moment—a handful of Miles' fireworks and firecrackers, which she'd taken from the box of contraband in his room. She reached into her pocket, hurled the handful behind her to ignite within the Portal. A riptide of cracks and bangs and colored lights unleashed—not as frightening to Noa as the Portal, but shocking Fae-born Thorn.

He spun at the sudden noises, explosions, lights, and dropped Noa instinctively.

Noa's vision swam in the sudden flow of oxygen; she flattened to the floor and rolled away from the Portal while Thorn groped for her above her head. Noa silently thanked Sasha, who had taught her many times that the lower someone was, the harder they were to catch.

Callum and Judah had also leapt to action the instant Thorn released her. Callum's leg looked merely broken now, not shattered, and he charged Thorn with Judah at his side. But while Callum aimed for the Hunter, vengeance and rage contorting his face, Judah ran toward Noa, and like Thorn, didn't anticipate her somersaulting move. He slipped on the algae, thicker near the Portal, and tumbled down beside her.

Judah grabbed her shoulders.

"I'm OK," she assured him. "Callum, look out!"

Seeing Callum coming, Thorn had grabbed the very shears Noa had wanted Judah to see. Judah leapt up as Thorn spun, shears outstretched, to give Callum a killing blow. Callum was still injured, not agile enough to leap away—

"No!" Callum cried, as Judah leapt between his brother and the blade, taking the shears to his own side instead.

"Judah!" Callum howled in a voice Noa had never heard before, not even when she herself had been in danger. Something between a sob and a scream, all wrapped up in "*NO!*"

"It's OK . . ." Judah managed, breathing unsteadily as blood poured from his side. The shears had cut right down his side then slid on blood and algae across the floor. "I'll be . . . OK—"

"*No you won't!*" Thorn bellowed, flinging Callum aside. All bluster gone, all laughter and manipulation vanished, Thorn was now pure Hunter: single-minded and filled with hate. He slammed his hands to Judah's shoulders: "*I will finish you.*"

Noa screamed and scrambled to Callum's side as the propulsion of Thorn's hatred, Channeled through Judah's gift, created a terrible tunnel of Light encasing him and Judah. It was blinding, suffocating, horrible and beautiful—an ice-like translucent cage built of the most exquisite pain and vengeance, the most frightening kind of bond.

"Callum, do something!" Noa cried, gesturing wildly at the chrysalis of Light. Callum stumbled up, tried to approach the magic wormhole—it flung him backward, sizzling, as if he'd been electrocuted. He slammed into the wall, crumpled to the ground.

Noa ran to him.

"I can't break in; it's just too strong—" He gasped.

"We have to save him, Callum, please!"

"Wait, Noa—we can hear them—"

Inside the cage of Light, Thorn and Judah were speaking, and Noa and Callum could hear their voices, somehow carried through.

"You're wounded, you can't win," Thorn was telling Judah, as he bore into Judah's mind.

"Then . . . I'll die . . . trying . . ."

Thorn tried harder; the tunnel grew brighter; Judah screamed—

"Callum, please! Change the atoms! Make the barrier disappear!"

"I'm trying, Noa, but I can't link in—"

"Something, *something*!"

Inside the tunnel, Thorn yelled as Judah fought him from inside his mind: "You don't even know who you're trying to save! Who you're dying for!"

Noa looked at Callum, intent upon the cage.

"I *know* who Callum is!" Judah strained back.

"He is not worth your sacrifice—"

"He's worth a hundred mes! He gave his life to save me!"

"You're wrong, Red Son!" Thorn howled, voice nearly deranged. "He didn't come to save you! I've seen inside his mind, I know ALL his secrets! You think that Fyre was your fault? The Fyre that killed Lily?"

"It happened because of me!" Judah wailed.

"No! It's a lie!"

Noa couldn't turn away, strained to hear every word, didn't dare to look at Callum.

"Here's the truth!" Thorn screamed, "The tru—"

Thorn's neck suddenly exploded with blood mid-sentence. The Channeling vortex disappeared, the tunnel of Light vanished, and Thorn collapsed onto the floor in a hulking, bloody mess.

Noa blinked, trying to understand what had just happened— Thorn's head was hanging, connected to his neck by skin alone, unseeing eyes open wide, frozen in their final instant of psychotic gleam. In his neck were the garden shears, three inches deep, and across the room, arm still aloft, stood Callum.

"NO!" Judah screeched in a terrible, breaking voice. He stumbled over to his dead tormentor, collapsed on top of him, tried fruitlessly to resuscitate him. "You killed him! How could you kill him!" he screamed at Callum, words shattering with each desperate, useless pump.

"I saved you," Callum protested, hobbling to Judah on his broken leg. Judah flung him off. Callum looked stung.

But Noa understood.

"Send him through, maybe it's not too late," she said, rushing to Judah. She pushed the dead Hunter, with his wide-open eyes, into Judah's shaking arms.

Judah shook his head, moaning. "It won't work, he's dead—" Judah's words were strangled as the Portal yanked him off his feet. Noa caught him, pushed him back from the Portal with all her might.

"You have to try!" she cried, and Judah fruitlessly shoved the dead Hunter into the Portal's blinding light.

The Portal hissed and spat and crackled, and Thorn's body shot up in the air; then the Portal opened wide and swallowed him whole, roaring out a spray of billions of red sparkles.

Fireworks, Noa thought suddenly, absurdly, as one landed on her skin, smudging. She screamed: not fireworks, but sizzling, spewed-back blood.

The Portal rumbled, pulled Judah violently as if furious. Noa grabbed his hands, tried to pull him the other way, but even together, they were not strong enough—

And then, grudgingly, the gateway rippled red, and then back to sickly green.

Judah's body relaxed.

"What happened?" Callum asked anxiously. "Did it work?"

"No," Noa answered. "It didn't, did it, Judah? That wasn't anything like when we saw Thorn balance the magic with Kells. That time was a golden shine, a blinding spiral. This . . ."

". . . was something different," Judah finished grimly, flipping his hand to show the fainter, but still present, Mark. "It's similar to when I've thrown mortals through." He winced, shoved his hands into his still gushing wound. "I may have a little time, but who knows what a magical corpse buys you." He winced again. "It feels tight, the tether."

"We have to get out of here, now," Callum insisted. "We'll figure out what to do about cutting your tie later. But I don't want you—either of you—in the line of fire! That thing looks like it could erupt—"

"Did you not hear me?" Judah spat. "I can't go! I'm tethered and without Kells this thing has a mind of its own! I doubt I can leave this shack until I right the balance or die! And *you* did this to me! You killed him—"

Noa looked down, biting her lip, unshed tears burning in her eyes. Callum had saved Judah. It had been heroic . . . hadn't it?

Callum was pleading. "I didn't think of it, Judah—I just wanted to save you—I thought maybe the shears . . . non-magical . . . even if I couldn't touch the forcefield myself—" Callum reached again to Judah, who stumbled away.

"You didn't kill him to save me," Judah hissed. "You did it to *shut him up*. You heard him start to tell me *the truth* about the Fyre. Tell me, brother, what secret was worth my freedom, my *life*?"

Callum looked shocked, and Judah looked so dangerous— Noa leapt between them. She grasped Judah's shoulders, looked into his eyes.

"He saved your *life*," she told him. "You're just hurt, and scared. You need Light—" She pressed her palm to his chest, closed her eyes, bracelet was still off from when she'd dropped it while the Hunter held her.

I give you Light.

But nothing happened.

Noa calmed her mind, thought harder, thought of Sasha:
I give you Light!

Noa opened her eyes, confused, searched his face. He
recoiled from her, pushed her away.

"I don't want your Light, Noa," he said quickly, harshly. "I
told you that before!"

Noa faltered backward. She thought she saw something else
flicker across his face—something vulnerable and scared—but
then he scowled harder.

"Put on your bracelet, I—I don't want to hear your
thoughts!"

Noa felt slapped across the face. She turned, saw Callum,
holding it. Quietly, he fastened it for her around her wrist.

Noa looked at Judah: his face didn't seem to relax at all, even
with her mind now shielded. It was like nothing had changed.
His eyes raked her face; she had to look away.

Noa turned to Callum. "Heal him." *Give him the Light he
won't accept from me, the extra Light I gave to you.*

Judah grimaced, but let Callum take his arm and heal the
wound he'd taken in Callum's place. It took longer than Noa
thought. The wound was deep.

Even as Judah's skin regained color, his face stayed icy. As
soon as he could, he snapped his hand away from Callum.

"Judah—" Noa pleaded, but Callum held up a hand to
quiet her. If Judah's face was hard, then Callum's was tender, so
tender and sad Noa thought it would break her heart.

"No," Callum whispered. "He's right. I haven't told him the
truth. Thorn saw it in my mind. Judah deserves it." Callum
faced Judah heavily. "Please know, I would never sacrifice your

future to keep my secret. I truly meant to save you. That's the only thing I was thinking when I killed him."

Judah clenched his jaw, ran his hand harshly through his hair. *So like Callum*, Noa thought. *And yet so different.*

"What I am going to tell you, it isn't easy," Callum said carefully. "And had Thorn not told you, in all honesty, I don't think I ever would have. Not because you don't deserve the truth, but because I am . . . I feel . . . ashamed. Know that, even if I can't say I wish I'd acted differently."

"The Fyre that killed Lily was my fault," Judah said quietly. "Hilo set it, but I showed her where to go, gave her the chance. What about that isn't true?"

Callum leaned against the broken kitchen table. He began to massage his broken leg, but Noa noticed he didn't heal it. Maybe his heart was too heavy. Maybe he felt he didn't deserve it. Behind them, the Portal belched and heaved, building back up again. It was morning outside the window. Class was starting. It seemed like a different world.

"Hilo," Callum replied finally.

Judah tensed. "My Hilo?"

Callum looked pained. "*My* Hilo."

Noa's breath evaporated. Hilo was Judah's, had always been Judah's. The one person who was Judah's *own*. Noa remembered the night he'd told her about Hilo, the night he'd realized it was Hilo, and not Crispin, who set the Faefyre that killed Lily. His heart had broken then. Would Noa have to watch it break again?

"What do you mean, *yours*?" Judah demanded. "I met her in the Tunnels when we were small. You could never navigate the Tunnels, she's barely even *met* you."

"You met her first. But when you got a little older, I found her once in the Tunnels, by accident. I was looking for you; you'd run away. As you say, I was hopeless and got lost till Hilo found me."

"So she found you, so what."

"It was that age, Judah, when everything was changing. I could see it in her eyes, her silly schoolgirl laugh—"

"That's a *lie*!" Judah snapped. "The other Pixies may have loved you, but not Hilo. You're nothing like what she would want."

"It's not a lie," Callum said patiently. "And while I did not . . . reciprocate . . . her feelings, I realized I could use them." Callum glanced at Noa. "I . . . manipulated her."

"Why?" Noa asked uneasily.

"So she'd spy on Judah," Callum admitted. "I was tired of always worrying where you were, what trouble you were getting into, how you'd anger Darius when you got home. And Lorelei . . ." Callum swallowed hard. "She loved you best. When you'd disappear, she'd worry."

Noa had never heard that envy in Callum's voice before. It made him more familiar somehow, more like her and Judah.

"When I saw how Hilo felt about me, I realized I could use her to rein you in. Tell me what you were up to."

"You took her from me, and sent her back to me a traitor."

"If you want to call my love for you treason."

"And what were Hilo's duties, tell me. To lie to my face? Tell me I was good?" Judah's voice was even, but he was breathing fiercely.

"No," Callum said patiently. "She was to watch you, and tell me what pranks you'd planned. And . . . rein you in, where possible."

"So she was your spy, your lovesick mistress. So she loved you and didn't love me. Fine, Callum, it's nothing new. Everyone always feels that way."

"Not our mother," Callum said quietly.

"It doesn't matter anyway, I still led Hilo to the training center—"

The Portal hissed more loudly, making Noa shiver. "Judah, let's get you out of here—"

"No!" Judah snapped. "I want the truth!"

Callum frowned but pressed on: "Hilo began to get passionate about politics and Color Fae rights. I—I should have educated myself better. It was hard, because of how much I wanted to see good in Darius—"

"Politics is boring," Judah interrupted. "I used to tell her that."

"Yes, but it's important to this . . . explanation."

"*Confession*," Judah corrected.

Callum bowed his head. "Hilo joined the Resistance. She and Crispin. They showed me what Darius was really doing and I began to believe, too." He looked away, studied the wall. "We wanted to make a dramatic statement and planned to use the Training Center. Hilo promised me that you would be uninvolved and far away. But at the last minute, something changed her mind—"

"Darius Channeled me. Hilo was outraged, told me to strike back."

Callum nodded. "Yes. But we were planning before you got involved."

Noa went to Judah. "You weren't the instigator, Judah, don't you see? Your vengeance wasn't the cause."

"It wasn't even the objective," Callum agreed. "It was

political, a scheme hatched without you, planned specifically not to include you."

Judah was silent. Noa fought the urge to take his hand. She moved back, took Callum's instead. She couldn't yet process what Callum's confession meant for *her*—the way it changed his story and how she might feel about it—but she knew confessing was hard, and brave.

"Why?" Judah finally asked. "Why didn't you tell me it wasn't my fault? All this time . . . thinking my vengeance killed her . . . Lily—" His voice broke, breaking Noa's heart.

"You weren't supposed to be there," Callum pleaded. "I took the blame because it was never yours, don't you see?"

"But you let me think it was mine! Which is worse!" Judah cried. "Why? Did you think I would hate you, if I knew the truth? That I *could* hate you?"

"I—I don't know," Callum stuttered, unable to hold Judah's gaze. "Partly, I was a coward. When you were there, saying you had done it—how could I explain? How could I confess? I was ashamed!" Callum held Noa's hand harder. "And I thought—or maybe I just told myself—it was for your own good."

"How?" Judah asked incredulously. "How could it possibly be for my good?"

"Because! I needed you to stay and let me be Banished, for Lorelei. She needed you more than me! But as you were, you wouldn't have survived. You and Darius would have killed each other, or you would have run away—only *guilt* would yoke you there and make you try!"

"That wasn't your decision!" Judah yelled, and Noa looked at her hand, wondering when she'd let Callum's go.

"You're right," Callum conceded. "But I also *hoped*, Judah. I thought if I was Banished, if I was the 'Bad Son,' Darius might—"

"Love me?" Judah snorted. "You can't manipulate love. Love doesn't work like that."

Callum turned white, looked down. Judah's eyes widened. "Unless—unless . . . oh, please . . ." He swallowed hotly, panicked. "Tell me now and tell the truth, Callum: Did I even love Hilo? Or did you have her use her Green ability to bind me so I would listen? Have . . . have I ever even *been* in love?"

Callum's head was in his hands. When he looked up, he looked broken.

Judah howled unintelligibly, beyond words.

Then, when he could talk: "You manipulated everyone and everything . . . fancying yourself a soldier . . . our sister *died*, Callum. The single worst thing in my life was, and *is*, her death. *Lily's* death. And second to that *only* is the shame that I have carried, *thinking that I killed her*. When *you're the one* who killed her!" Judah lunged; Noa again jumped in between, not knowing how she felt or who was right, only that Judah could not kill Callum. Not here and not like this.

"Judah!"

"He left me there, Noa! Alone! Thinking *I* should have been the one to go . . ." But against Noa's hands, the fight went out of Judah; he crumbled into her.

Callum spoke softly behind them: "When you came to visit me in the cell, before my exile, I *wanted* you to beat me, I was glad . . . you don't know the shame . . ."

"You left me there with *Darius*," Judah whispered.

"I thought I was helping—"

"I don't believe you!" Judah leapt from Noa. "I don't believe you," he trembled to his knees. She knelt beside him, held him as his voice grew soft: "I don't believe you . . ."

"I was trying to do the best for all of us," Callum whispered.

Judah raised his head slowly, but he didn't look at his brother; he looked at Noa.

He took her hands, locked his eyes on hers.

"My brother is a liar, Noa," he told her softly. "Hilo said she saw a better me, something worth saving. She was lying, too." He took a breath. "But I have felt love, real love. And I know there *is* a better me, and I know there's someone else who sees it too."

Laughter and shouts from students outside filtered in strangely through the walls.

Judah held her hands between them. "*You*, Noa. You have no gift, no trick, no magic, but I love you. I have been in love with you for some time. I've ignored it, buried it, denied it, because I thought you deserved someone good, like Callum. I've told myself it didn't matter that you make me alive, and Light, and *good*. But I am different in your eyes—and I want to be the person you see. I love you, Noa. I was made for you. I have traveled worlds to find you."

Noa felt the pressure of his hands, his heart, felt Callum watching too.

"Judah," she said softly, slowly pulling her hands free. "Judah, no—"

"Don't tell me no!" he cried, leaping to his feet. "Don't tell me you haven't felt it! 'Being of fire!' 'Red dance begin!' I've seen your words!"

"You read 'Imposter'?" Noa's heart seemed to cleave in two inside her. Callum's hands lightly touched her shoulders. Her mermaid heart loved *Callum*; she had already decided. . . . "I care about you, Judah, but not like that—"

"You're lying too!" Judah shouted, kicking over Kells' broken table. It splintered to pieces, and behind him, the Portal flashed and burned. "I *know* you love me!"

"That's enough, Judah," Callum said firmly behind Noa. She half-turned, put a hand against his chest. This was not his fight.

"Judah, I *care*—"

Judah tore at his hair in frustration. "My gift doesn't work anymore! Don't you see? I can't take your Light, I can't hear your thoughts! It's the oldest magic, Fabian told me!" He lurched forward, grabbed her hands. "You don't *need* a talisman if you're in love and are loved back. Gifts don't work on mortals when that happens! Remember earlier, when you tried to give me Light to help my wound? I *couldn't* take your Light. You had your bracelet off for all that time and I couldn't hear your thoughts! You love me! And I love you!"

Noa's knees shook beneath her—she couldn't think, could barely breathe . . . she had removed her bracelet when Thorn was holding her, had thought her plan to Judah to grab the shears and he hadn't seemed to hear her . . . then when he'd been wounded, she'd tried to give him Light and failed, even though her bracelet was still off . . . but Callum *had* taken Light from her, too much even, only moments before. . . . What did it mean? It was too much to process, too much to handle, too much to feel—

"No, Judah," she heard herself sobbing desperately. "No Judah, it's Callum. I've been searching for him, we've been searching for each other. The talisman, he broke his soul for me! He—I love him, I love *Callum*—I'm so sorry—"

Judah was ashen, stricken. "So it really is a lie? That I'm worth loving? Hilo loved Callum more, Darius loved Callum more, even our mother, our mother wanted him—"

"That's not true, Judah, you know it's not!" Callum insisted.

"You told me yourself how proud she was when you saved her ring," Noa pleaded. "Remember? She said she'd never been more proud—"

"I *lied*!" Judah wailed, hysterical. "She cursed me! I brought her the ring, I gave it to her when Darius had left and Callum had left and only *I* had stayed, and she was *angry!* 'Little troublemaking thief, always making her life harder!' Not like *Callum*. Why wasn't *he* the one who'd stayed? So I told her I would get him, I ripped the ring off her finger and ran away through the Portal!"

"You left her?" Callum cried.

"*She left me!* Just like Hilo! And you! And Noa!" Judah's eyes grew wild. "You can deny what I know you feel, but I'm not running away this time, and I won't let you either—" Suddenly, Judah had her face in his hands, and his lips were on her lips, pressing hard and strange. She didn't know what to think, how she felt, how to breathe—only that she was shoving him away, slapping him with as much force as she could.

At that moment, when life couldn't be more fraught, more tense, when one more word would shatter worlds, a bright clear shriek rang through the air, followed by a flash of chocolate curls: "NOAAAA!"

Sasha, running into the shack like a human homing pigeon, leaping into Noa's arms.

"Sash?" Noa stuttered.

"I found you!" she laughed. "I found you!"

"You ran away from class?"

"The car!"

"Sasha, oh Sasha my love—"

"*Your love!*" The words echoed guttural and strangled, ripped from Judah's spine. His welted cheek, his broken heart, madness in his eyes—all this as the Portal sucked him violently, horrifically, inexorably back toward its jaws. There was no stopping it, his time was up, he was flying backward—he reached out, a wild beast of desperation, stretched his fingertips as far as they could go—

—and grasped Sasha, Sasha, from Noa's arms. Laughing, trusting Sasha, who let Noa go, who flew across to Judah—

—and past him, into and through the Portal in his place.

As Sasha's last curl disappeared, the Portal swelled into a brilliant golden glow—a blinding bridge of yellow, unfurling petals of golden fire. It built into a translucent spiral of white light—so beautiful, so clear—before winking out completely, swallowing itself in the quietest little pop.

"Sasha!" Noa screamed, rushing to the place where the Portal had just been, where now there was nothing but an empty frame. And Judah, standing safe and still.

"Sasha!" Noa whirled on Judah. "How could you! How could you!"

But Judah wasn't listening. He spun on Callum, raising his arm. "What—"

Noa didn't let him finish—she pounced on him, yanked back his arm, scratching, clawing, hitting. "You monster! *I have already lost a sister!*" But her fists couldn't do enough damage, her tears couldn't hold enough pain, not for the black hole swallowing everything inside her. She was in the sandpaper place, the horrible sandpaper place where Isla had died and people were lost and everything spiraled to nothing nothing nothing—

"She slipped! She slipped, I swear!" Judah tried to block her blows, grab her arms.

"I didn't choose you and you hurt her! You killed her! How could you! How could you!"

"Noa, STOP!" Judah cried, finally grabbing her forearms fast. He yanked her to attention, looked directly in her eyes. "I was dying, Noa, I could feel the Portal—I just wanted to touch her hand, remember Lily, before . . . But she slipped, Noa, I swear she slipped—"

Noa dissolved into tears, crushing her face against his chest, not knowing if she believed him or if it was simply too horrible not to. She unraveled against his shirt. Everything else was meaningless now: that Judah had said he loved her, that she had said she loved Callum. None of it mattered, all of it was far away, all that mattered now was that Sasha was gone. . . .

Only a tiny, tiny voice inside had time to wonder. She'd chosen Callum—so why was she in Judah's arms?

She yanked backward, "Callum!" stumbling at him through her tears.

But he was frozen, face white as a sheet. He didn't see her, hear her, even seem to notice her at all. His eyes were glued to where the Portal had been, where Sasha had disappeared.

"Noa," It was Judah who spoke, Judah who functioned. "Noa, look—" He lifted his wrist, the one that held the Mark— but no Mark was there.

"What—I don't—"

311

"Did you see the Light? The way the Portal vanished?" Noa tried to listen to his words, but all she could see was the hole where Sasha used to be.

"Noa, *the Portal balanced.*"

"But—but that makes no sense—you said, to balance, it had to be—"

"Magic for magic." Callum's voice, a whisper.

Noa turned slowly to Callum, still so still, like he couldn't bear to look at her. She walked in front of him, made him look her in the eyes.

"Sasha's not magic," Noa told him slowly.

Judah joined her, rubbing his naked wrist. "You still have secrets, don't you, brother. Talk."

Noa looked between them. Callum took a deep, shuddering breath. She wasn't sure if his next words were aimed at her, or Judah, or at the universe itself:

"She's magic. Sasha." Callum paused, and the whole world stopped as he spoke his next words: "She's Lily."

Noa stumbled back, tripped over the fragments of kitchen table. Judah stayed standing, frozen in shock.

"Explain."

Callum's face crinkled up, a small child caught in a terrible lie.

"*She's Lily, Judah.* She's Lily *cloaked.* I had to do it." He sagged, defeated . . . and to Noa's anger . . . *relieved.*

"I faked her death and brought her here, to *save* her. I wanted to tell you—I wished I could so many times . . . That's the real reason I planned the Fyre with Hilo. She didn't know, but that was my plan all along—use Faefyre to fake Lily's death and bring her here, away from Darius."

Noa heard the words but could not process their meaning.

Judah, however, seemed to understand "Lily's *alive*?" Hope in his voice now, even through his pain. "But . . . but why, Callum? She was *loved*—even by Darius—his Clear Fae princess—"

"Because she wasn't Clear Fae, Judah."

"She was. She Channeled my gift—"

"Yes, but she could do more. She was something *more*." For the first time, Callum looked at Noa. "She was special, beyond anything that came before." He turned back to Judah. "She could Channel like Clear Fae, but she didn't need to; she had *all* the gifts within her. Blue like me, Green like Lorelei, Red like you, and Clear like Darius—all on her own. I spent so much time playing with her, watching her; one night I felt her read my mind and knew she couldn't be Channeling because that was not my gift. She had it herself. So I spoke to her through my thoughts, and she told me back, *inside my head*, what she could do. And then, she *showed* me."

"We spoke through thoughts," Judah said, "but I always assumed she was Channeling me. I never imagined—"

"No one could have, it's never been seen. But you see, how dangerous if Darius discovered? If he raised her in his beliefs, or hurt her trying to replicate her power, or if he killed her because she was a threat? He loved her, but I don't know—could Darius love anything more than power? Could his love ever outweigh his fear?"

Judah seemed awed. "How? How did you do it?"

"I told her through my thoughts never to show what she could do. And I began to plan our escape, somewhere Darius would never follow—"

"The ring, our mother's ring," Judah interrupted. "It had Lily's hair. In this realm, Callum, *it made Light*. No one knew why, but that must be why—because of her hair, because she was—" The pieces began to fall together quickly. "When I first came with the ring through the Portal, it wasn't active, but then I hid it at Noa's house, and Sasha—Lily—stole it . . . when I recovered it, it was like it had been turned on . . . she . . . she did that . . ."

"I couldn't allow her to grow up around Darius, don't you understand?"

"You went to Hilo—"

"I pretended to be a soldier too—"

"But that was a cover."

"No one knew my true plan but me. I told Lily stories, mind to mind, for weeks leading up to the fire. She learned by heart the tale of the little princess, who had to help her knight to steal her away from the monsters. I showed her again and again how she must, when I told her, alter her own elements, her atoms, to make her body appear dead. I showed her that if a Blue Fae tried to heal her, she was to overcome it, because I knew Darius would Channel my gift for just that purpose. Then I showed her that she must cloak herself, make herself invisible, and stay close by my side while I was jailed and Banished. I showed her to take my hand, and go through with me.

"On this side, I wasn't sure how we'd manage, but then we learned: Lily still made Light here. She could do magic. So I told her a new story, mind to mind, and showed her how the little princess, safe in a new world, would go to a new family, one which could love her simply, safely . . ."

Noa's mind was catching up.

"I searched everywhere for the right family," Callum was saying. "But mere mortals, how could they understand how precious Lily was? How sensitive and difficult and wonderful and wild? And then . . . I found Noa."

Callum looked at her, remembering every detail: "Sweet, strong Noa," he said hoarsely, "who was so brave. I saw you at a grave, the link between shattered, hollow parents. You stood between them, palms upward, open. Rising like a sun.

"I followed you home. I watched you through the kitchen window. I listened to the soft push of your pen moving in the night. And what I saw, what I heard . . . you *tried*, Noa. You tried and tried and never gave up. And I knew."

Noa looked away from him, at the wall. Callum turned back to Judah:

"So I continued the story for Lily, inside our minds, and I showed her the last things the princess had to do: Forget me, forget her past. Then bind her own powers and become an ordinary, beloved girl. I showed her how to build the memory shift, so she would be inserted, as 'Sasha,' into any consciousness that encountered her. Seamlessly, as if she'd been a Sullivan from birth. Even you, Judah, seeing her, would not recognize her face; and she, seeing us, would no longer know us as her kin. Only I would remember.

"I showed her all of this, the happy ending to the story, and then I released her hand, and let her fly from me."

Callum cut off, then added softly: "I'd planned to stay away. But I couldn't. I watched from the outside, unable to forget. I never intended to meet Noa"—he swallowed—"let alone to . . . But I couldn't help it."

Callum went to her now, knelt beside her. "The way you loved Sasha. It was the warmest Light in this realm. You drew me to you. I picked you for Lily, for Sasha; I didn't know I'd need you too. Your 'mermaid heart.'" He tried to smile.

But Noa didn't hear her own words echoed back. Sasha, her Sasha, was not hers? How could that be? The love she felt, the memories she had—they were written in her bones, they flowed through her veins, they were her DNA. Sasha's hummingbird heart was Noa's heart, Sasha's starfish arms were Noa's arms. They slept wrapped around each other, breath on each other's cheeks, hair tangled in each other's hair.

And yet, suddenly, it was so clear at the same time as it wasn't: Sasha wasn't like Noa; she was like *them*, like Callum and like Judah—the curls, the face, the manner. Her strangeness and her moodiness, the magic in her laugh. She was Judah and Callum, Callum and Judah, Lily from a different world—and yet she was Sasha too, in Noa's blood, pumping through Noa's heart. Inextricable as ever, twined deep in Noa's soul.

"She's mine," Noa murmured, first softly, and then with anger. "She's mine! You cannot have her!"

"Noa—" Callum began.

"No! No! How dare you! How dare you try to take her from me!"

"I'm not! I wouldn't, I never could! Don't you see? She was yours, she was yours before I even came—"

"How dare you! She's my sister! She's *my Sasha!*"

"Noa, *stop*." This time it was Judah, Judah's hands on her shoulders, but she didn't want to feel him either. She shoved him off, white with fury.

"And you? Where's your anger now?" she demanded, whirling on him. "He lies about the Fyre, and you're ready to kill him! But he lies about your sister, tells you she's *dead*—and you have nothing to say?" Noa spun back to Callum. "All those times we talked, when I thought you were confiding in me! When you told me about Lily, about her death, I thought—I thought you *trusted* me, and it was all lies and deception!"

"Noa, please!"

"And the kids! Visiting Sasha's class, and me!"

"Noa, listen: I never thought I'd know you, and once I did, I vowed never to tell you. I knew it would make you feel like you were losing Sasha. But you're not, she's still Sasha, she's still *yours*. Yours is the life she knows! And the way you love her, it's beyond what I could have dreamed—"

"Stop it!" Noa cried, slapping him. "Stop speaking like you care about me. You made me think I had a sister! I have already lost a sister!"

"Noa, no, you aren't losing her, I promise!" Callum cried.

"Then where is she?" Noa demanded.

"I—I don't know."

"She must be in Aurora," Judah said. "To balance the Portal the way it did, she had to have been exchanged, exchanged alive. She must be back in Aurora . . ."

Noa's tears ran hot and scalding down her cheeks. She didn't bother to wipe them. "Then I have to go there."

"Noa, stop. You can't. And the Portal's gone! We'll find another way—" Callum began, but Noa had no time for reason or plans or logic. She ran past him to the frame that had once held the Portal, shook it hard.

"I have to go," Noa cried. "She's my Sasha, I have to save her—"

"But how?" Judah said, rushing to her. She whirled on him so hard he stumbled, falling back. She searched the room wildly, madly, and saw the garden shears still bloody from Thorn's neck. She ran to them, grabbed them, opened them against her skin.

"Noa, no! She isn't dead, don't take your life!" Callum cried, tripping over Judah.

But Judah understood. "Sasha's blood sealed the Portal, her special, magic blood . . ."

Noa wasn't listening; she thrust the shears deep across her chest, knowing only one thing without question:

"Her heart is my heart!"

She dropped the shears, faced the empty frame, opened her arms wide in offering. Noa's blood ran crimson-bright. The frame began to shake, to shine, as the Window built on balance spiraled out anew. A blinding spray of Light burst forth; Noa's silhouette backlit by gold—

"Noa, it's too dangerous!" Callum cried.

Judah leapt to his feet. "This is what family does, Callum. We go through the Portal for each other, no matter the cost!"

Noa didn't wait for their permission, didn't listen or explain. Arms still open, she barely felt as they each took one of her hands—and with all the force she had inside her—poet, traveler-woman, mermaid-hearted girl-beast sister to Sasha—she sprang forward, pulling them all, a fevered daisy chain, into What Came Next.

EPILOGUE

Aurora
(before)

WHEN JUDAH FINALLY stopped struggling, when they were beaten, bloody brother-mirrors, Callum let him rise. The darker, slighter boy levered himself up against the bars. This cell had somehow caged it all: Callum's lies, Judah's anger, and guilt enough for Lily's loss to drown them both. Judah bled from a gash above his eye; Callum wiped a smear from his broken nose.

"You'll be the first Banished there, since Kells," Judah said.

Callum smiled a little. "Always first."

Judah scowled.

"You stay," Callum warned him again. "For Lorelei."

Judah's jaw clenched, but he didn't argue. When he spoke, his voice trembled, like it had when they were young: "Do you go right through, or . . ." He turned, afraid.

"The Gatekeeper's supposed to make sure I don't get caught between."

"But what's it like? The In Between?"

Callum stayed tall, and still. "Lorelei once said it's the place where you find out."

"Find out?"

Callum met his little brother's eyes. "What you truly want. What you'll truly give. And if, in the end, it's enough to save your life."

ACKNOWLEDGMENTS

THIS BOOK COULD not have come to be without so many people (and fur people!). My love to everyone who helped bring this adventure into being:

Mark Pedowitz . . . guru, reader, listener, champion: you made this happen

Bill Haber . . . who never takes credit but deserves so much

Bruce Vinokour . . . my superagent, for always fighting for me, and protecting me #teamCAA

My tireless editor Annie, and all the rest of the wonderful team at Alloy (Lanie, Sara, Hayley, Katie, lightning-fast Romy who squeezed out those extra days for me) . . . For believing. And editing. And never giving up!

Andrea . . . endless lifesaver, bestower of safe & happy places, twin Kauaian Angeleno (and rescue dog mom—Hello, Enya!)

Jordan . . . for kicking around ideas those early, early mornings, while we shamelessly spoiled Molls and Ninj. I'd still be stuck at Part II without you . . .

Kauai . . . my refuge, my safe place, the home of Sasha's spirit (and my mango lady)

Da, David, Anne, Angela, Jamie . . . do I even have to say?

Janet . . . for giving me Olivia

Terrace Boys . . . Miles is the best of all of you

And, so deeply:

Jamaica . . . for teaching me how

Annette . . . for being there when I felt so small

Mikey & Michelle . . . for making me part of your MOMA, for always reading and suggesting, and for the gift of safest harbor

Olivia & Avery . . . for showing me Sasha, and crazy dancing for Aunt Birdy

Mirah . . . copyediting master!

Jeremy & Rachel . . . endless (beautiful) cheerleaders

Dad . . . for accepting my artist soul, letting me go my own way

Mom . . . for sharing your gift and your passion. We are traveler women, bound by leaves, budding words . . . our poem a succulent, always growing—and surviving.

And my Ninja. 'Nuff said.

LAUREN—OR "BIRD" AS she is often known—is a screenwriter and novelist lucky enough to call both Los Angeles and Kauai home. Bird also counts herself lucky that writing exists as a profession—how else could she share the crazy, fantastic worlds in her head? Bird studied writing at Harvard University with novelist Jamaica Kincaid, where she won several prizes including the Edward Eager Memorial Prize for fiction. She's a proud member of the Writers Guild of America. You can follow Bird on twitter (@birdaileen) and Instagram (@birdaileen) for trilogy updates.